John Hannibal Sheppard

The Life of Samuel Tucker

Commodore in the American Revolution

John Hannibal Sheppard

The Life of Samuel Tucker
Commodore in the American Revolution

ISBN/EAN: 9783337058302

Printed in Europe, USA, Canada, Australia, Japan

Cover: Foto ©Raphael Reischuk / pixelio.de

More available books at **www.hansebooks.com**

THE LIFE

OF

SAMUEL TUCKER,

COMMODORE IN THE AMERICAN REVOLUTION.

BY

JOHN H. SHEPPARD, A. M.,

LIBRARIAN OF THE NEW ENGLAND HISTORIC-GENEALOGICAL SOCIETY.

"His biography would make a conspicuous figure, even at this day, in the naval annals of the United States."

Ex-President John Adams.

BOSTON:

PRINTED BY ALFRED MUDGE AND SON,
34 School Street.
1868.

To the

HON. PELEG SPRAGUE, LL. D.,

A Scholar, Statesman, and Eloquent Advocate.

Twenty-four years Judge of the
District Court of the United States for the
District of Massachusetts,
An office which he elevated and adorned with
Incorruptible Integrity and profound Knowledge of
Admiralty Law,
Until failure of health compelled him to retire
From his laborious duties,

This Life of
COMMODORE SAMUEL TUCKER,
Written by his Encouragement, and published with his
Approbation,
Is affectionately and respectfully
Dedicated by the
Author.

January, 1868.

TABLE OF CONTENTS.

Introduction to the Life of Samuel Tucker, . . . 13

CHAPTER I.

His Parentage and Birth, 19. Childhood and Education, 21. He runs away and enlists in the Royal George, 22. At seventeen enters before the Mast in a Merchant Vessel, 24. As Second Mate saves the Ship from two Algerine Corsairs, 25. Married, 25. Takes Command of the Young Phœnix, 27. Singular Incident in London; his Imprudence, Peril, and Escape, 29. Returns Home as Passenger in a Ship of Robert Morris, Esq., which he saves from Destruction, 30. Commissioned by Washington as Commander of the Franklyn, 31. Anecdote of the Express with his Commission, 37. Leaves Beverly on his first Cruise, 39.

CHAPTER II.

State of the Country when War began, 40. Number of Troops at Cambridge, 41. Their Destitution of Military Supplies. 41. Want of a Navy, 42. General Washington orders several small Vessels to be armed and sent out, 43. Several States do the same,

44. Scarcity of Powder, and Captain Mugford's timely Prize, 45. Early Navy of Massachusetts, 46. Attack on Louisburg in 1744, 46. Flag and the National Banner, 47. Thirteen Ships ordered by Congress to be built, 48. Captain Manly's Escape, 50. Commodore Hopkins, 52. Title of Commodore, why and when given, 53. Rank of Captain assigned, 54. Why Tucker's Name is not there, 54.

CHAPTER III.

Cruise of the Franklyn, 56. Takes a Transport off Long Island, 57. Thanks of Washington, 57. Another Prize, 58. Captain Weston's Anecdote of his Sea Fight, 59. Took many Prizes, 60. Transferred to the armed Schooner Hannah, 61. Takes several Prizes, 63. Captain Martindale's Statement of his Humanity to the Conquered, 62. Numerous Captures, 63. British Losses on the Sea in 1776, 63. The American Navy, 66. His first Claim to the Title of Commodore, 64. Appointed Captain of the Frigate Boston, 67. Severe Battle, and Capture of an armed Ship, and Commodore Manly captured by the Rainbow, 68. Death of Lieutenant Magee in the Fight, 69.

CHAPTER IV.

Again appointed Captain of the Boston, 71. Takes Hon. John Adams, Envoy, and his Son, to France, and Instructions, 72. Voyage commences, 74. Three large Frigates in Pursuit of the Boston, 74. Terrible Storm; Ship struck by Lightning, 75. Tucker's Reflections, 77. Escapes the Frigates, 78. Strange Sail a War Ship, 80. Captures the Martha, 81. Sends her Home, 83. A Gun bursts, and Lieutenant Barron wounded, 84. Barron's Death and Burial, 85. The Boston enters the River Garonne, 86. Arrival at Bordeaux, 86. Numerous Visitors to the Frigate, 87. Repairs, and starts on a Cruise, 88.

CHAPTER V.

Ship of War, 89. Bay of Biscay, 90. Takes Scotch Brig John and Rebecca, 91. Eclipse of the Sun, 91. Britannia and Elizabeth, Prizes, 91. Mr. Adams's Letter, 92. Mr. Adams's Instructions, 93. Took Scotch Brig, 95. Shameful Treatment by French General, 95. Forty-seven Men taken from the Boston, 95. Crew they left, 97. Sells three Prizes, 98. At Nantes, 98. At Brest, 98. Sails in Commodore Whipple's Squadron, and in Company with French Fleet of forty Ships, 99. Saves Life of Cabin Boy, 100. A letter describing the Boston in the Storm, 101. The Squadron on the Banks of Newfoundland, 100. At Portsmouth, 100. Judge Sprague's Remarks on Tucker in his Eulogy on Adams and Jefferson, 102.

CHAPTER VI.

A Letter of John Paine, 105. Visit to his Family, 105. Agreement of Whipple, Tucker, and Simpson, to cruise, 106. Convoys and protects a Fleet of Merchant Ships, 107. Keeps off two British Frigates in Voyage from St. Eustatia, 107. Fights and captures the Pole Frigate, 110. Cruises with the Deane, 111. Commands two Frigates, with Orders from Whipple, which entitles him Commodore, 115. Letter from Jos. Reed, 114. Takes Prizes, 116. Sale of the Pole, 117. Boston Gazette enumerates Prizes, 119. Tucker's Account of several Captures, 121.

CHAPTER VII.

Attends Court Martial, 122. Petition of Whipple, Tucker, et al., for Employment, 123. Their Squadron of four on a Cruise, 125. They are sent to defend Charleston, S. C., 126. Description of Charleston Harbor, &c., 126-129. Sir Henry Clinton and Vice-Admiral Arbuthnot invest City by Land and Sea, 128. Tucker destroys the Beacon Lighthouse, 131. And Fort

Johnson, 132. Enemy passes Fort Moultrie, 137. Vessels sunk in Cooper River, 137. Whipple sends Guns and Men to man the Fortifications, 137. Advance of the Enemy, and Distress in the City, 138. End of Siege, 129. Capitulation, and Tucker's Parole, 140. His Benevolence to the Distressed, 141. Their Letter of Thanks to him, 142. The Censure of Writers unfounded, 143–145. Anecdote of Tucker's Surrender and Striking his Flag, 146.

CHAPTER VIII.

Return to Boston, 147. Exchanged with Captain Wardlow, 147. Takes Command of the Thorn, 148. Josiah Everett, an aged Marine on board, his Character, 149. Everett's Description of the Capture of the Lord Hyde, 149–151. Newspaper Accounts of same, 152. Taking of the Elizabeth, and bloody Battle, 154. Captain Weston's Narrative of the Battle, 156. Writes to Lee about his Prizes, 157. His nine Cruises and Prizes, 158. At Home, 158. Thorn a Privateer, 159. Letter of William R. Lee & Co., 160. July, 1780, makes his last Cruise, 161. Captured by Frigate Hind, 161. Carried to St. John's, at entrance of St. Lawrence, 162. Makes his Escape in an open Boat, 162. Captain Young's Letter, 163. Leaves Chebucto in his open Boat, crosses the Bay, and reaches Boston, 164. The Correspondence and Explanation, 165.

CHAPTER IX.

His House in Fleet Street, 166. Expensive Living, 167. Mrs. E. Perkins's Account of him, 167, 168. Time of Residence in Boston, 169. Imprudent Loan to a false Friend, 170. Applies in vain to Congress for his Pay, 170. Court of Inquiry on Harding, 171. Goes to Sea in Merchantman, 172. Loss of his Ship Cato, 172. Removes to Marblehead, and buys a

Grist Mill, 173. Applies for Command of a Revenue Cutter, 174. General Hamilton's Letter — "too late," 179. Buys a Farm and moves to Bristol, Maine, 181. Applies for Command of one of the new Frigates, 182. Unsuccessful; reported to be dead, 183.

CHAPTER X.

History of Bristol, 185. Alexander M'Lean, 186. Captains Popham, John Smith, et al., 187. Early Settlement at Pemaquid, 188. Grants of Land there, 188. Forts, and Wars with the Indians, 189, 190. With the French, 191. Dunbar rebuilds the Fort, 192. Description of Pemaquid, City of Jamestown, Fortress, &c., 193–196. Tucker's Manner of Life on his Farm, 196. His Family, 198, 199. Loss of his Son, Samuel, 199. His sorrowful Letter to Rev. E. Hubbard, 200.

CHAPTER XI.

Land Titles and Lawsuits, 202. Betterment Law, 203. Insurrection, 205. Murder of Paul Chadwick, 207. Militia called out, 208. The Great Trial, 209–212. Tucker's Petition to the General Court for Redress, 213. Committee by Legislature appointed, 214. The Remedial Statute, 215. Tucker's Capture of the Crown, 216–221. Refuses to take Command of the Gunboat Flotilla, 222.

CHAPTER XII.

A Selectman for Years, 224. Representative to General Court, 225. Reception in Boston, 225. Representative in Maine twice, 226. His Memorials to Congress, Correspondence, &c., 227–234. Journey to Washington in 1820, 235. His Reception at the Capitol, 236. Again petitions Congress, 238. Letter of Mr. Adams, 241. Invitation to Belfast, and Reply to Committee, 243. A Freemason, 244. Member of Agricultural Society of Maine, 245. Interesting Anecdote by Professor Johnson, 245. Interview with Major C., 247, 248. Singular Anecdote of the Widow, 249. Congress grants Pension, 251. His Death soon after, 253. His personal Appearance, 255. His Grave, 257. Conclusion, 258.

APPENDIX.

  PAGE

Copy of his Original **Log-Book**, ... 262 to 327

General Signals for **the Fleet**, ... 328

Certificate of his Baptism, **and Extracts from Family Bible**, . 335

Diversions forbidden **to Officers by Congress**, ... 336

Letter of Captain Glover, ... 338

Crew of the Boston appointing **Prize Agent**, ... 339

Memorandum of Shares of Prize **Money**, ... 340

Men taken, or who died in the Boston, **1778**, ... 341

Certificate of French **Sailors** in 1778, ... 342

Muster-Roll in the Boston to France, **1778**, ... 343

Muster-Roll in the Boston, after her Return **on a** Cruise, 344–355

Tucker's Letter to the Navy Board, and Grade of Officers, . 356

The three War-Ships named Boston, ... 358

Account Current of William R. Lee, and Invoice, . . 359, 360

Letter to **William Jennison**, ... 361

Letter from **Tucker to Dr. Brown**, ... 362

Letters **of Hon.** M. L. Hill and John Holmes, . . . 362, 363

Letters of Hon. John **Chandler and General Knox**, and Reply, ... 364, 365

Copy of Memorandum among **his Papers**, ... 365

Correspondence between General Wm. King and Tucker, . 366

Ritchie's Letter to Samuel Tucker, ... 367
List of Appleton's Notes loaned to D. C., ... 368
Song written at Bristol, Maine, ... 369–371
Anecdote of his early Cruising, ... 371
Note on Frigate Hancock, ... 371
Some Chronological Dates of early built Vessels, ... 372
Early Ships of War compared to the present Navy, ... 374

INTRODUCTION.

THERE is one kind of aristocracy, which, in almost every age and country, has been admitted and acknowledged to be popular among all classes of men, and is congenial to our notions of the largest liberty — the aristocracy of mind. It is confined to no privileged rank, limited to no condition of wealth or inheritance, dependent upon no external influence nor patronage. It is the gift of God to man. We feel its power, and willingly yield to its ascendency.

It is this which gives such a charm to biography; and whenever we find a man of intellect working out his own glory amidst and above his fellows, we are delighted, improved, and benefited; for aristocracy of mind is usually allied to excellence in some art or science, and is often connected with all that is beautiful and noble in human nature.

On this account a generous public are anxious to erect a monument to departed worth, and embalm the memory of illustrious men in some enduring record of their lives. Who would not wish to preserve the reminiscences of every patriot, warrior, and statesman who assisted in accomplishing our independence and making our country take such an exalted rank among the nations of the earth? Indeed, it may be a question if the world does not owe more of its knowledge of the Grecian and Roman republics to Plutarch's Lives, than to the writings of Herodotus, Thucydides, or Livy.

Of those heroic men who were distinguished in the American Revolution on land or sea, the far greater part have been depictured by able pens. Monuments have been erected, biographies have been written, and the elegant historian has adorned their memory with unfading wreaths. Thirty millions of a free and happy people felt their hearts burn with patriotism at the unrivalled success of the late eloquent Everett in redeeming, separating, and consecrating as a holy place of remembrance that beautiful spot on the banks of the Potomac, where the FATHER OF HIS COUNTRY lived and died.

But there is one man, of no mean rank in the day of struggle, — a pioneer of our infant navy, — who took more prizes, fought more sea fights, and gained more victories, than, with a very few exceptions, any naval hero of the age, who lies in a humble, rustic cemetery, where the place is but little known, with only a frail slab of slate to preserve his name, and whose exploits are almost forgotten amidst the splendor of our national prosperity which he helped to achieve.

"Who is Commodore Tucker?" was recently asked by a scholar, and one of the *élite* in the Athens of our country : so little is known of him by the present generation. And yet he was a very remarkable man in the war of the Revolution. "His biography," said the late President John Adams to the Honorable Benjamin W. Crowninshield, secretary of the navy, in a letter of January 18, 1816, "would make a conspicuous figure, even at this day, in the naval annals of the United States."

It is a singular fact, that either from the remote and humble retirement of his declining years, or from the inadvertence of writers in searching the early annals and documents of the Revolution, or it may be from the effulgence of so many brilliant stars in the historic zodiac, the deeds and services of Commodore Tucker have been neglected and suffered to pass unnoticed or forgotten. He is scarcely mentioned in Marshall's, Sparks's, or Irving's Life of Washington, or even in Cooper's elaborate History of the Navy of the United States of America.

By referring to the Journals of Congress, Vol. III. p. 91, the high estimation in which the services of Tucker were appreciated will be seen. For the Marine Committee reported, "That there were several very fine prize ships in the State of Massachusetts Bay, very suitable for the service of the continent, and which may be fitted out at a small expense; and Captain Daniel Waters and Captain Samuel Tucker, who were early employed by General Washington in cruising vessels, and were very successful, and strongly recommended by the general and others, are, in their opinion, proper to be appointed to the command of two of them: Whereupon,

"*Resolved*, That the Marine Committee be empowered to give directions to the agents to purchase three ships, and order them to be immediately armed and fitted out for the services of the United States, to be under the direction of the Marine Committee.

"*Resolved*, That Daniel Waters and Samuel Tucker be appointed captains in the navy of the United States, and that the command of the other ship be given to Captain Paul Jones, until better provision can be made for him."

These resolutions were passed March 15, 1777.

President John Adams, to the last of his long and honored life, always spoke in terms of admiration of the bravery and exploits of this naval commander; and no one among our eminent statesmen of that period had such an opportunity to know the man, and witness his talents and heroism, as Mr. Adams. He was conveyed as ambassador to France, in the frigate Boston, under Tucker's command, and while on that dangerous mission his departure was watched by a British seventy-four and two frigates; yet the captain, with great nautical skill, not only evaded their pursuit, but captured on the passage the British armed ship Martha.

With auspices thus favorable, sanctioned by a name so venerable and august, and encouraged by the admiration of distinguished men who knew him well, I have ventured on this SKETCH OF THE LIFE OF COMMODORE SAMUEL TUCKER. The preparation of it, commenced some years ago, has not been without much labor and difficulty of research. It is a long time since his death.

His fellow-laborers in the field of fame had nearly all preceded him to the grave. The particulars and detail, therefore, of many of his daring deeds on the ocean are lost irrecoverably, or rest on tradition. Yet there is much preserved. In the latter part of his life he wrote a memoir of his principal engagements with the enemy, and adventures at sea. This was committed to a gentleman — the late Moses Shaw, M. D., of Wiscasset, and at that time collector of the port — to prepare his life for the press; but the papers and materials were destroyed when his office was burned. The commodore, however, had fortunately retained his log-book, or journal of his voyage to France, with several letters and copies of correspondence. These valuable documents, after his decease, were deposited by his grandson Colonel Samuel Tucker Hinds, of Bristol, in the library of Harvard University, there to be preserved in the archives. By an order from Colonel Hinds and the politeness of John L. Sibley, Esq., librarian, the writer of this Sketch has had the use of them.

After the separation of Maine from Massachusetts, in 1820, Commodore Tucker was chosen a member of the legislature of that new State. The Honorable Peleg Sprague, of this city, and the late Albert Smith, Esq., formerly United States marshal, of Maine, were also members. They were well acquainted with him, and gave the writer several anecdotes of his prowess and peculiarity. Indeed, this sketch was read to Judge Sprague, and with his advice and approbation is published. By his permission it is dedicated to him. I was

2

also **personally** **acquainted** **with** **Commodore** **Tucker** when I resided **in** **Wiscasset,** **Maine.**

No pains have been spared **to obtain facts and correct** information. I visited Marblehead, **his birthplace,** twice ; went to Hamilton to **see his nephew, who resembled him** **much in appearance ; and made a journey to Bristol,** in Maine, **where his grandson Colonel Hinds** resided. Under the hospitable roof of the latter I passed **several** days, and obtained many interesting anecdotes **of this** remarkable man. With him I visited the grave **of** Commodore Tucker, in Bremen, and rode by the house where he made his last home. It was, indeed, a " Bleak House," on a cold, lonely hill. I saw several aged people who **were intimate with him, who** related **many** **incidents** **which** **occurred** **in** **his** **cruises** **on** **the** deep.

The materials **of** this Sketch have thus been **gathered** from various sources — newspapers, **particularly** in the days of the Revolution, narratives **of the aged,** annals of the time, and documents left by the **deceased.** From the scrupulous care with which facts **and** incidents have been gathered, sifted, and examined, **I have reason to** believe **that a truthful narrative has been furn**ished.

Some **years since a number of articles** touching his **life and battles with English cruisers in** the Revolution **were published in the Boston Journal,** under the signature **of " A Stranger in Boston."** They were my own, and **having been prepared with some care,** they have been **incorporated in this Sketch.**

LIFE

OF

SAMUEL TUCKER.

CHAPTER I.

Boyhood and early Education.

SAMUEL TUCKER was born in Marblehead, Massachusetts, November 1, 1747, as appears by the memorandum of births in the old family Bible, and in the records of the "First Church of Christ in Marblehead," which are in good preservation — Liber XI. beginning with 1740, — his baptism was noted under date of November 8, 1747. He was the third child of Andrew and Mary Tucker, who had eight children, viz., Andrew, Mary, Samuel, William, Nathaniel, Elizabeth and Benjamin (twins), and Sarah.

It has been said that his father, Andrew Tucker, was one of three brothers, who emigrated to America from Dundee, in Scotland, when young men. It may be true; but so many instances are referred to and repeated as a kind of ancestral axiom by those who are hunting up their descent from the early settlers in this country, that among the members of the New England Historic-Genealogical Society who are best versed and most skilful in tracing pedigrees, this tradition of "three brothers" invariably excites a smile of incredulity. It was said one of these brothers settled in South Carolina, one in Virginia, and one, Andrew, in Marblehead. Should the writer, however, be enabled to procure an accurate genealogy, it will be inserted in the Appendix; for there was an Andrew Tucker at Marblehead in 1663.

His mother's maiden name was Mary Belcher, an English lady, reputed to have been handsome, and well educated. Of a figure tall and stately, tasteful in dress, of winning manners, and fond of social life, she was often called the "Lady Mary." Her natural gayety descended to Samuel like an heirloom, and he cherished it during a long life.

His father followed the sea, and was much respected as an upright, skilful shipmaster. Before the Revolution he was in affluent circumstances, and lived in much style. The house which he built more than a hundred years ago on Rowland Hill, near the bay, is still standing, though its gable ends have been changed into a more modern fashion. On this building he laid out much cost. His rooms were decorated with rich paper-hangings, for which he sent to France; the paper was thick as cloth, and figured with vermilion and black stripes, as appears by fragments still preserved. I was surprised at the specimens of tasteful workmanship and durable material shown by the tenant, who occupies this sub-

stantial, pleasant mansion, which, in its day, was one of
the first and best structures in the country. It was here
that Samuel was born and brought up.

Of his early instruction there is no authentic account,
and few are the anecdotes of his boyhood. That his
schooling was not neglected we may be assured, for his
father wished to give him a collegiate education, and for
that purpose put him to a preparatory school. He was
well grounded in reading, writing, and arithmetic — the
elementary foundation of all knowledge acquired in
future life. He learned to write a good hand, and com-
pose with ease in a plain, business style; and in declining
years, when an ungrateful country suffered him to labor
for his support under the grinding pressure of poverty,
he evinced, by teaching navigation to young mariners,
that he had been no drone in his school-boy days.

Marblehead, the home of his childhood, is a jutting
peninsula, with rocky shores, and a narrow harbor of
a mile and a half in length, exposed to the breezes
and roar of the Atlantic, and for more than two hundred years celebrated as the nursery of American seamen. Here, from his birth, young Tucker breathed the
ocean air, and with its salubrious draughts inhaled the
spirit of adventure. Often did he see the shores and
docks lined with fleets of fishermen, and he was accustomed to gaze upon crowds gathering on the wharves and
streets, when some homeward-bound ship came in sight.
He heard the songs of the mariners, and their stirring
tales of other lands, as each crew of gallant tars set foot
on their native shore. He fed on excitement. He was

surrounded by incentives to a sea life. The very boat he whittled into shape with his jackknife, then rigged, and set afloat in some little cove near his house, was but an image of the great ship which his soul, in the visions of boyhood, thirsted one day to command on the ocean. Everything around him on this almost sea-girt rock only served to awaken his boyish breathings for future fame, and make a man of him. Even in the soft down of youth he was a daring lad in all his sports, and if fear ever came upon him, it was after the danger was over, when his imagination looked back. Indeed, what son of Marblehead ever knew fear, when the path of duty lay before him?

THE CHILD IS FATHER OF THE MAN, though often quoted from the writings of a great poet, was never more applicable than to the boyhood of Samuel Tucker. It is no wonder that his bent of mind should have been averse to the wishes of a fond father, and that he turned away from the thought of academic groves and the classic cells of a college. For such was his repugnance to the still life of literature, that his feelings became violent, and at eleven years of age he formed a desperate plan of seeking his own fortune in the perils of the deep. He ran away, and embarked in an English sloop of war, the Royal George, bound on a cruise to Louisburg, to intercept a French transport. It is said, however, that his father, instead of discarding the impetuous boy, afterwards wisely gave his consent, and apprenticed him to the commander of that ship.

This took place in the year 1759, when the immortal

Wolfe died in the arms of victory at Quebec. Thus commenced his first step in the path to eminence in nautical life ; and. as it were, by leaping almost from the cradle into a man-of-war, he. braved the hardships of a sea-boy's lot, and began to form that lion-hearted character which in after years no danger could terrify, no trial discourage.

The discipline on board of a British ship of war was severe, proverbially so. The seaman who offended an officer, or violated any order or regulation in the most trivial degree, found but too often little or no mercy. To crush all the finer feelings by terror, and to exercise force on all occasions, was for the most part the barbarous policy of naval government. The law of kindness was unknown. The old tar might become callous from long and hopeless endurance, but the young novice, often impressed into the service by a press-gang, in his homeless and hopeless state experienced sufferings that were terrible. The distribution of ardent spirits, too, as a part of his rations, increased his calamity. It led to disobedience and the lash, and by reaction the pain and disgrace induced a reckless resort to the cup to drown misery. Thus these evils aided each other ; and *rum and the cat* made the war ship a picture of pandemonium.

To such trials and discipline there is no reason to believe that young Tucker was much exposed in the Royal George. He never complained of peculiar hardships, nor of cruel, unkind treatment. Nor at any period of his life did he lament this early escapade in the choice of a profession. On board of the ship he was no idle boy. He was anxious to gain knowledge. He acquired a mastership of nautical science, and aimed to unite naval tactics with skill in navigation. That he was an apt scholar, coming years made plain; for in this situation he obtained a thorough acquaintance with British signals — a knowledge which afterwards proved of such eminent advantage to him. And he learned the art of manœuvring his ship in the face of the enemy, and managing her in the fury of a tempest. Few of our naval commanders then understood maritime tactics so perfectly as this young man at the time he was commissioned by General Washington, who seemed almost possessed of a divine gift in discovering talents and merit by intuition. How long his service lasted in the Royal George, what cruises were made, what dangers were encountered, till his education was completed, is now unknown. We must pass over six years of his life, before we hear from him again, and then we shall find him rising rapidly as a mariner; for at the age of seventeen he enlisted on board of a vessel from Salem, bound on a foreign voyage, in the capacity of second mate, his brother being first mate; and here he performed a daring exploit — one of those shadows that "coming events cast before" them. The vessel had arrived within a few hours' sail of Lisbon, when two Algerine corsairs were discovered with crowded sail in pursuit of them. The captain became frightened, and then, like all cowards, flew to the can to get courage; but he drank so much of the intoxicating draught, that young Tucker persuaded him to go below, and leave the mate to manage the ship. The corsairs came upon them rapidly. The danger was appalling. His brother, the mate, grew alarmed, and Samuel fearlessly took the helm. As it was drawing towards night, he saw there was hope, and the intrepid lad steered the schooner towards the pirates, and, it is said, "luffed under the bow of the windward corsair," and kept sailing off and on towards the two, whereby one pirate firing on his vessel, the other would be exposed. In the mean time the Algerines felt sure of their prey. But as soon as it was dark, he ordered the lights to be put out, and making all the sail he could, bore away under cover of night; and in the morning the schooner was safely moored in the port of Lisbon. At one time she was within pistol shot of the guns of the nearest corsair; yet he managed to escape their grasp. The sequel was singular. That cowardly and contemptible captain, alarmed at owing his preservation to a mere stripling, and hoping to conceal his own infamy, put Samuel on board of an English frigate then in port; but the facts soon leaking out, he was honored by the generous officers, and immediately appointed a midshipman.

How long he continued in service on board of this frigate, there are no means of knowing; probably not a long period, for, according to the usual custom of sea life, he must have been promoted and sailed as mate one or two voyages, for he was master of a merchantman when he was married, December 21, 1768, soon after he became of age. His wife, Mary, was the daughter of Samuel and Ann Gatchell, of Marblehead. Mr.

Gatchell was deacon of the Congregational church of that place — a worthy and estimable man. On his marriage, Captain Tucker took part of his house, — which was a double one, — and afterwards moved to his own father's on Rowland Hill, probably to take care of him, for he had been unfortunate, was reduced in property, and had become a victim of disease.

From a letter of Commodore Tucker to Captain Joseph Hidden, of Marblehead, dated December 23, 1817, a glimpse of the family history at the time of his marriage reaches us. He says he was at the expense and trouble of maintaining his father some time before his death, and that he took care of his mother, "who had no other to look up to for succor or aid in the least," more than thirty years after her husband's death. She died in 1808. His father, therefore, must have died about the time of the Revolution, between 1775 and 1778. He remarks in a postscript, "that his mother appointed him her guardian some time before her decease." This widowed parent always lived with him. She shared his home and his fortunes when he removed to Bristol, Maine. She lived to a great age, — ninety-one years and six months, — and now lies near him in the churchyard of Bremen, formerly part of Bristol — an evidence of maternal and filial affection ever sacred and ever honorable. She was said to have been a superior woman, of strong mind, of a cheerful temperament, and a member of the Episcopal church.

As a shipmaster, Captain Tucker was too well qualified and skilful to bemoan the want of employment. He was seldom long in port.   Among his papers there is a letter to him from Jeremiah Lee, to take command of the brig Young Phœnix, on a voyage to Bilbao, for salt. This was dated July 20, 1774. January 13, 1775, he is sent out in the same vessel to Charleston, S. C., thence to the Isle of Wight, and, under the advice of the consignee, to procure and bring home a cargo of salt. Discretionary power is given to sell the brig; and if there is a war with England, to return and seek some safe port at home; for, said the patriotic merchant, a true Marblehead man, "then I shall be in the Provincial army, as I am determined not to survive my country's liberty and privileges."

An anecdote was related to me by Captain Weston, which deserves a place in this Sketch. It occurred when Tucker was a young man, in the command of the Phœnix. On his first voyage to Bilbao, a Spanish port, once the largest in the Bay of Biscay, the vessel was approaching the coast, and by an adverse current was forced on a dangerous reef, through the carelessness of the pilot. It lay near the mouth of the harbor. The crew, alarmed at the terrific breakers, with the captain's permission took to the long-boat, except the second mate and a boy, who declared they would not leave Captain Tucker in peril, and sprung back into the vessel. As for the pilot, who was to blame, he was sent below into the cabin. There he began to pray for deliverance, while Tucker, looking down the gangway, cried out to him, " Pray for me also."

Thinking there was still some chance to save the brig,

as it was luckily flood and not ebb tide, the captain let go an anchor. When the tide had risen, so that the vessel could float, he ordered the cable to be cut, and passing over the reef, reached the harbor in safety. It was said by those who came on board, that he had made a wonderful escape, as it was a great chance that the brig had not bilged and gone to pieces, since no vessel had passed over that dangerous reef for several years. Thus, by his courage and presence of mind, he saved the property of his owners from destruction.

No more is heard of the Young Phœnix; she undoubtedly made a prosperous voyage. But Captain Tucker is next found in London. The war had broken out, and the news of the battle of Bunker Hill arrived in that city. It is said that one day he saw an inspector examining some boxes and casks of guns and ammunition, marked for " Boston," and exclaimed, " I would walk barefoot one hundred miles, if by that means these arms could only take the direction of Cambridge." On his return home in the fall, his wishes were fulfilled; he recognized these same boxes, by their familiar marks, in the camp of Washington. They had been captured by Captain John Manly, in the armed schooner Lee, from Marblehead, and were safely landed in port.

During his residence in London, he was offered his choice — a commission in the army or a command in the navy. He refused both. When he was urged one day to take one of these situations, and was promised, if he would consent, that his gracious majesty would give him an honorable and profitable office, in his haste he rashly replied, " D—— his most gracious majesty ; do you think I would fight against my native country? " The man to whom he uttered this hard-shelled patriotism was one of the enlisting officers, and immediately left him. A friend, who happened to hear the offer and reply, stepped up to him and urged him to withdraw and keep out of the way, for surely he would be arrested for speaking factiously against the king. On this hint Captain Tucker immediately left London, travelled about fifteen miles into the country, and stopped at a tavern. He soon found out that a brother kept it, and told him he was in trouble, and a fugitive. The landlord asked him, " Have you been guilty of any crime? " " No." " Have you done anything against government? " " No," said Tucker. Then he added, " I will protect you."

Soon after the landlord saw some horsemen entering the yard in great haste. He suspected they were in pursuit of his guest, and he thrust him into an adjacent closet and locked the door. The officers came in, and one of them inquired if he had seen any traveller pass that way since morning. " No; I have seen no one pass this way." The officer then gave him a description of Tucker, his face, figure, dress, and manner, saying, " He is a rebel from America, and has damned the king; and since he left London he has had time to reach this place." He then gave orders, if he came this way, to stop him. The landlord rejoined, " Certainly, if he comes this way, I'll take care of him." And he did.

Captain Tucker soon made his escape from England,

and returned home in the first vessel he could find, which happened to be a ship from Philadelphia, in which Robert Morris, Esq., was interested. This was the distinguished merchant of Philadelphia, and a zealous patriot in the Revolution, of whom Mr. Cooper, in his Naval History, remarks, " The duties of an agent of marine subsequently devolved on the ' superintendent of finances,' the celebrated Robert Morris, a gentleman who appears, throughout the war, to have had more control over the affairs of the navy than any other civilian in the country." (Vol. I. p. 86.)

He embarked on board this vessel very near the 1st of October. On the voyage a furious storm arose, and the ship, in which was a cargo of much value, was in jeopardy, and the captain and crew expected every moment she would founder. They began to despair of life, when Tucker stepped up, cheered all hands, advised them to make an effort, and, taking the helm, guided the vessel through the tempest. To his skill and knowledge the crew and ship owed their preservation.

How little does any one know upon what particular event, and sometimes trifling incident, the future destiny of his life may depend. Yet in biography such instances are not unfrequent; and it is pleasant, as far as we can, to trace the links in the chain of events, and observe how they are put together, sometimes as though by an unseen hand, and for some important agency. Such a link was the saving of this ship and her valuable cargo in Tucker's future life. It made a friend of a powerful man. Mr. Morris, the owner, thereby discovered the merit of this skilful mariner. Grateful for the rescue of his property from destruction, he introduced him to General Washington; and very soon this pioneer of the American navy was in his element, his foot on the quarter deck of command, and his eye gazing on a boundless horizon in pursuit of the enemy's cruisers.

On his return home, it is said he was appointed a lieutenant of a company, belonging to the fourteenth regiment, commanded by his friend, Captain Glover. If so, his service was of short duration; for he received a commission as captain of the Franklyn, under the hand of General Washington, bearing date January 20, 1776. It is as follows, and, it seems, he was afterwards transferred to the Hancock.

By his Excellency George Washington, Esq., commander-in-chief of the army of the United Colonies of North America.

By virtue of the power and authority to me granted by the Honorable Continental Congress, I do hereby constitute and appoint you to be captain of the armed schooner Franklyn, in the service of the United Colonies of North America; to have, hold, exercise, and enjoy the said office of captain, and to perform and execute all matters and things which to your said office doth or may of right belong and appertain, until further orders shall be given herein by the Honorable Continental Congress, myself, or any future commander-in-chief of said army. Willing and commanding all officers, sailors, and persons whatsoever, any way concerned, to be obedient and assisting to you in the execution of the commission.

Given under my hand and seal, at Cambridge, this 20th day of January, Anno Domini 1776.

G. WASHINGTON.

His Excellency's command.

STEPHEN MOYLAN.

Captain Samuel Tucker is now appointed to the command of the armed schooner Hancock, in the service of the United States of America, and is to be obeyed as such.

By order of the General.

JOSEPH WARD, *Ad. C.*

BOSTON, 3 Sept., 1776.

As the letter of " Instructions," issued at the camp in Cambridge, was one of the earliest of the kind in the Revolution, a copy is here introduced.

SIR: You, being appointed captain and commander of the armed schooner Franklyn, in the service of the United Colonies, are to pay all obedience and attention to the following instructions: —

1st. You are to proceed immediately on a cruise against such as may be found on the high seas, or elsewhere, bound inward or outward, to or from Boston, and take and seize all such vessels as are employed for the purpose of aiding and assisting the ministerial troops or navy.

2d. If you should be so successful as to take any of

the said vessels, you are immediately to send them to the nearest and safest port to this camp, under a careful prize-master, directing him to deliver said prize unto the agent by me appointed there. If no good agent should be in that port, notice is to be given to the nearest agent thereto, at the same time, account of such capture is to be transmitted to headquarters, with all particulars thereto belonging, by **express**.

3d. You are to be very diligent and particular in your search after all letters and other papers tending to discover the designs of the enemy, or any other kind, and to forward all such to me as soon as possible.

4th. Whatever prisoners you take must be treated with kindness and humanity — their private stock of money and apparel to be given them, after being duly searched; and when they arrive at any port they are to be delivered up to the agent, if any there; if not, to the committee of safety of such port.

5th. For your encouragement and that of the other officers and men to diligence and activity, over and above the pay, which will be the same as in the army of the United Colonies, you shall be entitled to one third part of every vessel and cargo, after condemnation in the Court of Admiralty, which shall be by you taken: if the prize is an armed vessel in the ministerial service that makes no *resistance*, as an inducement for you, your officers and men, to act with spirit and courage, one half of said vessel and cargo will be allotted to you; which parts are to be divided in the following proportions, viz.: captain, six shares; first lieutenant, four shares; ship-master, three shares; steward, two shares: mate, one and a half shares; gunner, one and a half shares; gunner's mate, one and a half shares; privates, one share each.

6th. As **Captain Manly is appointed commodore of** the **four schooners now fitted out, he will fix upon** proper **signals by which you may know each other, and** you are to **obey him as** such in all **cases; and should it so** happen that a prize is taken in sight of other vessels **fitted** out at the Continental, provincial, or private expense, **the** rules which take place among private ships of war are to be observed in the distribution of the prize money.

7th. You are to be extremely careful and frugal of your ammunition and **other stores, by no means to** waste **any of it in salutes, or any other purpose, but what is absolutely necessary.**

8th. **As** you, your officers, **marines, and sailors, are** now engaged in the service **of the United Colonies,** you are in every respect subject to **the rules and regula**tions formed by Congress for the government **of the** army raised for the defence of American **liberty — a book** of which **you** will receive herewith; **at the end** thereof you and your **officers** must **subscribe** your **names.**

9th. **As it is very apparent that the ill success** which **attends the major part of** these armed vessels, since **their being first fitted out, was owing to the officers who com**manded **not being industrious and active in the execution** of their **duty, you will take notice that a fondness to be** on shore, **or keeping unnecessarily in port, indolence, and inactivity, will meet with every discouragement. All** officers found guilty of such crimes, or in any shape neglecting to do all in their power for their and the public good, shall be dismissed the service with infamy and be rendered incapable of any honorable station in the army or navy.

Signed by order of his Excellency, General Washington.

STEPHEN MAYLAN, *C. G. M.*

CAMBRIDGE, 20th January, 1776.

GEORGE WASHINGTON was appointed commander of the Continental army June 15, and arrived at the camp in Cambridge July 3, 1775. He found a large force of brave and resolute men, poorly equipped, and in need of firearms, powder, and artillery. To meet these emergencies he procured several vessels, manned and armed them, and issued commissions to capture the enemy's ships and transports, which were hovering over the coasts, and thus obtain supplies for his troops. The first armed vessel sent to sea, after hostilities were commenced with Great Britain, it is generally conceded by writers of our naval history, was the schooner Lee, of which John Manly was commissioned as captain. She sailed from Marblehead in the latter part of November, 1775, and soon captured the British brig Nancy, probably furnished with military stores for the troops in Boston ; for Captain Manly found in her an abundance of ammunition, muskets, and cannon, and they all reached Cambridge most opportunely. It is very likely this was the same, marked for Boston, which Tucker saw in

London, and afterwards at the headquarters in Cambridge, as related on page 28. On the 8th of December, Captain Manly took three more store ships, and brought them safe into port. Other vessels of war were sent out that fall by General Washington; but they were of little avail, and less fortunate than those under the command of the intrepid Manly. If we may judge from a clause in the "Instructions" to Captain Tucker, "the ill success" which attended the major part of them was "owing to the neglect or indolence of the officers" who commanded them. These Instructions evince at the same time the confidence reposed in Tucker, and were highly complimentary to his character.

And here it is worthy of remark that this document bears the image and superscription of Washington's mind; his style was peculiar; it emanated from a clear head and an unerring judgment. No military chieftain, nor ruler, nor statesman ever wrote in a diction more dignified or appropriate, nor with more felicity or conciseness of expression. His language was always transparent; you could see through the very thoughts of his mind. All the orders, messages, and correspondence of this extraordinary man are full of beauty and simplicity, easy to be understood, and free from all diplomatic ambiguity. This peculiarity is noticed here, because within a recent period an attempt of the most ungenerous kind has been made in the Life of Alexander Hamilton, ascribing to him that style and diction which were Washington's, and his alone. His writings differ as much from those of Hamilton as Cæsar's

Commentaries do from the orations of Cicero. Hamilton might sometimes have suggested thoughts to Washington, but they were only raw materials for a wisdom which surpassed that of all men to work upon. Hamilton was a great and powerful writer, and his noble feelings would have scorned to adorn his reputation with the plumage which belongs to another.

In these **Instructions to Captain Tucker,** though strict discipline and vigorous action are required of each naval officer, and any neglect of duty is denounced with inflexible severity, yet humanity to the captive beams forth even to the sparing of his little *peculium* — his stock of money, and his apparel, when the hand of the victor is upon him.

An express with the commission was hurried off to Marblehead — at that time a seaport, with clusters of small stores and humble dwellings dotting the shore, though now a flourishing town, with about eight thousand inhabitants. At his paternal home, near the sea-shore, Tucker and his wife were living at that time with his widowed mother. The arrival of a stranger in martial costume, on a steed adorned with trappings of rank, and coming in "hot haste," created quite a sensation in the village, and men, women, and children gazed with wonder from windows, streets, and wharves at the messenger as he galloped along. They watched him till he rode up and dismounted in a yard where a man was chopping wood.

The officer, seeing a person dressed in rather ordinary apparel, — a tarpaulin hat slouching over his face, brown breeches, pea-jacket, red waistcoat, and a flaming bandanna waving dauntingly on his neck, — thought to himself that he must have mistaken the direction, and exclaimed roughly, —

"I say, fellow, I wish you would tell me if the Honorable Samuel Tucker lives hereabouts?"

"Honorable! honorable!" says Tucker, with a shrewd look at the stranger; "there is not any man of that name in Marblehead. He must be one of the family of Tuckers in Salem. I am the only Samuel Tucker there is here."

The express took his packet from his pocket, looked at the direction again and again — "Lives in a house two story — gable end — standing by itself on a hill — not far from the bay shore — piece of woods near it: surely this must be the place," and then eyed the young man from head to foot, and said, —

"Captain Glover told me he knew him, and he lived in Marblehead, and described his house; gable end, on the sea-side, none near it. Faith, this looks like the very place."

This parley, however, soon came to an end; for he saw in the gallant look and deportment of the young man, that he could not be mistaken; for Tucker, in early manhood, had a very striking appearance, and, from his rich curling locks and expressive features, is said to have been quite handsome. The officer handed him his commission, and after rest and refreshment returned to the camp at Cambridge.

Nor did the young captain, on whose fresh laurels the dews of the evening were glittering, delay a moment unnecessarily. At break of dawn he was on his way to the ship, which then lay at Beverly, and was soon scouring the ocean in pursuit of the enemy.

CHAPTER II.

THE CONDITION OF THE COUNTRY IN 1775.

IN the life of a distinguished individual about to enter the service of his country in the dark days of the Revolution, it may be well to ascend, as it were, one of the watch-towers of the country, and take a bird's-eye view of the state of things on land and sea.

The condition of the United Colonies at the commencement of the war with England was discouraging and sometimes desperate. Without finances, without maritime resources, they began to carry on vast military operations against the mother country, rich with the spoils of commerce, and gigantic in her strength and resources. She could boast of her glory in

"The stirring memory of a thousand years."

On the other hand, we had no regular, disciplined troops, and were unsupplied with the munitions of war. We were dependent on a militia suddenly mustered, and principally composed of yeomanry, who left their families and their farms, and were poorly equipped to contend with the veteran legions of England. There was then no Military Academy at West Point, to educate and

train a host of officers to take command and discipline
the troops. Indeed, at that time the whole country,
immeasurable in extent, was sparsely settled, and the
population of the thirteen United Colonies was less than
three millions. Moreover, England had an immense
navy; we had none. But we had Marblehead and
other ports ready to man our ships with as brave and
daring men as ever lived, the moment Washington had
created a marine defence.

When he arrived, in July, 1775, at the camp at Cambridge, according to the adjutant's report on the 29th of
that month, he found an army, ready to receive and
welcome their commander, composed of 17,355 rank and
file. According to Frothingham's Siege of Boston, —

Massachusetts furnished	11,688
Connecticut, ...	2,333
New Hampshire, ...	1,664
Rhode Island, ...	1,085
To which may be added Colonel Gridley's regiment of artillery, ...	489
And Major Crane's company of Rhode Island artillery, ...	96
Numbering, ...	17,355

These brave men, thus suddenly assembled, made in
numbers a formidable array. In all kinds of apparel, with
every variety of weapon, they were destitute of military
resources, especially of guns, tents, and powder, and
were unprovided for a long campaign. Yet in an in-

credibly short time they threw up a formidable line of intrenchments from their headquarters in Cambridge, to the River Mystic, and then along the heights of Roxbury and Dorchester, shutting up Boston on the land side by a complete circumvallation. Though suffering under numerous and nameless privations, they compelled the British general, with his disciplined troops and British ships at his control, to evacuate Boston after a possession of only eight months. This transpired on the 17th of March, 1776, when General Washington, at the head of his army, entered victoriously. It would seem as though Howe, before his retreat, looking to the armed heights, like the Carthaginian general of old, was ready to exclaim, " Did I not tell you, that cloud upon the mountains would soon come down upon us?"

At the commencement of the war, too, there was no navy. The enemy's frigates, privateers, and armed merchantmen infested all the seas, and threatened the bays, inlets, and shores of our unprotected coasts, preying upon our defenceless commerce, and endeavoring to sweep it from the ocean.

To protect the harbors, meet the severe exigency of the army, and obtain military supplies by spoiling the enemy, General Washington immediately, and without waiting the slow action of Congress, began to lay the foundation of a small but effective navy. The beginning, indeed, was very small but it was the infancy of Hercules in his cradle. He sent agents to Salem, Beverly, Marblehead, and Plymouth, to procure, or hire, or purchase, some merchant vessels constructed for swift sailing, and ordered them to be armed and equipped as soon as possible for cruising; and he sought out the best and bravest seamen he could find, who were qualified to take command of them. He found several such, and issued commissions to them himself, until Congress had organized a naval committee, and passed a resolve to build some ships of war.

The first person General Washington commissioned as commander of an armed vessel, "to take and seize all such vessels as are employed for the purpose of aiding and assisting the ministerial troops or navy," was Captain Broughton, of Marblehead, in the Hannah, of Beverly. This commission was signed by Washington, and bore date September 2, 1775. The second person was Captain John Manly, in the armed schooner Lee, which became afterwards so distinguished, and was the first that got to sea, sailing from Marblehead. His commission was dated October, 1775. The first legislation of Congress favoring a navy was on the 13th of October, 1775, ordering two vessels to be equipped, one of ten and one of fourteen guns, and on the 30th of same month two more as cruisers, one of twenty and one of thirty-six guns.

Some of the States, however, had already fitted out armed cruisers. Rhode Island, in June, 1775, voted in her General Assembly to procure and send out two armed schooners, one of ten guns, the other of less metal, fitted for cruising. The larger one, the Katy, Captain Whipple took charge of. The legislature of Connecticut also resolved to fit and send out two; and a law was passed in the General Court of Massachusetts authorizing the employment of armed vessels, and constituting a Court of Admiralty. This was on the motion of Elbridge Gerry, Esq. Other States also fitted out privateers; as the Lexington, of Delaware, commanded by Captain Barry, the Reprisal, Andrea Doria, Hornet, Alfred, and several others, which rose into note during the war. By the end of October, 1775, General Washington had commissioned Captains Broughton, Selman, Manly, Martindale, Coit, and Adams.

The result of these seasonable and well-equipped cruisers, got ready under the orders and authority of General Washington, was fortunate; especially when we consider not only the vast importance of these naval enterprises in aiding the supplies of our suffering army and checking the power of the enemy, but also the prophetic view of them which was held by the commander-in-chief; for it so happens that we can look back into the mind of this great man, and read his inmost thoughts of their value. In the letter of General Washington to John Hancock, president of Congress, dated at Cambridge, October 12, 1775, is this observation: " A fortunate capture of an ordnance ship would give new life to the camp and an immediate turn to the issue of the campaign."

The cruise of the little schooner Lee, under the brave Captain Manly, was highly successful. On the 29th of November, 1775, she captured an armed ordnance brig, the Nancy, from England, destined for Boston, and on the 8th of December three more prizes; but the cargo of the Nancy — just what Washington wished for in his letter

— was the precious boon, the Godsend to the American army; for she was laden with a variety of munitions of war, which they greatly needed: a thirteen inch brass mortar, several brass cannon, two thousand muskets, thirty thousand round shot of various sizes, one hundred thousand flints, and a large quantity of powder, with divers tools for mounding or mining were among her military supplies for the army in Boston. The prize was carried into Cape Ann harbor, and the cargo soon reached headquarters. A few months after, Boston having been just evacuated by the enemy, a remarkable instance of supplies occurred. Captain Mugford, in the small armed vessel Franklin, captured the Hope, from England, a transport with fifteen hundred barrels of powder and stores, which all went directly to the colonial army.

When the marine committee, appointed by Congress, were holding a secret session, a messenger in his joy burst in upon them with the schedule of the cargo of the Nancy; and Mr. Adams, the moment he saw it contained military stores so much needed by the troops, earnestly exclaimed, "We must succeed — Providence is with us — we must succeed." This anecdote is condensed from Cooper's Naval History; and the author of that work justly remarks, "The first important relief was obtained through the cruisers; and it is scarcely too much to add, that without the succors that were procured in this manner, during the years 1775 and 1776, the Revolution must have been checked in the outset."

Massachusetts had long been distinguished for her daring adventures and maritime prowess. In the French war of 1744, this colony, under Governor Shirley, gathered a large body of troops, which Colonel William Pepperrell, of Kittery, Maine, took command of; and she fitted out a squadron of twelve armed vessels, which Captain Edward Tyng, of Massachusetts, directed; and sent them to the attack of Louisburg, the key of the St. Lawrence. Commodore Warren, with his English fleet, joined them; and this celebrated fortress was invested by land, and the harbor blockaded by sea. In forty-seven days Louisburg was surrendered; but by the peace of Aix la Chapelle it was restored to the French, who fortified it anew. When another war broke out between England and France, this capital of Cape Breton, whose battlements frown over the south-east waters of that rich island, was again ardently coveted; and in 1757, a fleet of seventeen sail, and a force of eleven thousand troops, under Admiral Holbourn, invested the place, but with far different result. It was a failure. It is referred to here, because it was to Louisburg the Royal George was bound, in order to intercept a French cruiser, when Samuel Tucker, in that English frigate, first began his education in the navy; and because Massachusetts had long been a nursery of intrepid and able seamen.

The colonial armed vessels at this period of the Revolution were none of them large, being principally sloops and schooners, intended and fitted out for cruising, and better calculated for speed in taking prizes and storeships than for a conflict gun to gun with larger and heavy-armed ships of war. Those afterwards ordered to be built by Congress were from six hundred to a thousand tons. Their heaviest metal, of eighteen pounders, nines and twelves, with sixes and fours on the quarter-deck and forecastle, was generally adopted. Carronades, we are told by Cooper, had not then been invented, though they came into use before the termination of the war. "This gun obtains its name from the circumstance of its having been first used at the village of Carron, in Scotland, a place celebrated for its founderies, as the bayonet derives its appellation from Bayonne in France."

The flag, before Congress had ordained a national standard in 1777, some say, was a white bunting with a spreading green tree, the motto, " Appeal to Heaven ; " others describe the naval banner then used by the cruisers as having a device representing a pine tree with a rattle-snake under it, coiled at the root, with the motto, " Don't tread on me." Surely the first ensign evinced a purer and loftier taste. Congress, however, soon resolved on a national flag, bearing thirteen stripes, alternately red and white, united with thirteen stars, white, in a blue field, representing a constellation. This was established June 14, 1777, according to Felt's Annals of Salem, p. 272. Congress also, on the report of the marine committee, September 5, 1776, regulated the uniform of a captain in the navy, and required " blue cloth with red lapels, slash cuffs, stand-up collar, flat yellow buttons, blue breeches, and red waistcoat with narrow lace."

The necessity and importance of a navy, soon after the commencement of hostilities, arrested the attention of Congress ; and in October, 1775, they passed a resolve

to fit out two armed vessels, one of fourteen and one of
ten guns, and send them on a cruise. At the close of
the year they ordered several more to be built, to the
number of thirteen ships, at the navy yards in different
States. They were classed and named as follows: —

Washington, of 32 guns, to be built in Pennsylvania.
Raleigh,   " 32   "   "   " New Hampshire.
Hancock,*   " 32   "   "   " Massachusetts.
Randolph,   " 32   "   "   " Pennsylvania.
Warren,   " 32   "   "   " Rhode Island.
Virginia,   " 28   "   "   " Maryland.
Trumbull,   " 28   "   "   " Connecticut.
Effingham,   " 28   "   "   " Pennsylvania.
Congress,   " 28   "   "   " New York.
Providence,   " 28   "   "   " Rhode Island.
Boston,   " 24   "   "   " Massachusetts.
Delaware,   " 24   "   "   " Pennsylvania.
Montgomery,   " 24   "   "   " New York.

These ships of war were soon on the stocks. In the
Boston Gazette of Monday, May 4, 1778, is this paragraph: "Tuesday last, ship Hancock, thirty-six guns,
launched at Salisbury."

---

* It should be remarked that there were in the Revolution three
armed vessels of this name: 1. The schooner Hancock, of Massachusetts; 2. The privateer Hancock, of Philadelphia, commanded by Captain Wingate Newman, who captured the armed
brig Polly, and took many prizes; 3. The frigate Hancock,
above named.

Congress also purchased the Lexington, of fourteen, the Alfred, of twenty-four, the Columbus, of twenty, the Andrea Doria, of fourteen, the Providence, of twelve, guns, and some others, to the number of thirteen, making, when the frigates were completed, a respectable armament of twenty-six vessels in the American navy; but Cooper says, only six of the frigates ordered by Congress ever got to sea.

The first regular cruise, under the regulations of Congress in establishing a navy, is said to have been by the sloop of war Hornet, ten guns, and the Wasp, of eight, which sailed from Baltimore. They took many prizes, and were worthy of their names in bitterly annoying the enemy's merchantmen.

In the American Archives, Fourth Series, Vol. IV. p. 910, there is a statement of the officers of the armed vessels fitted out by order of General Washington, on the 1st of February, 1776.

HANCOCK.

John Manly, . . Captain and Com., 1st January, 1776.
Richard Stiles, . 1st Lieutenant, . 1st January, 1776.
Nicholas Ogilby, 2d Lieutenant,. . 1st January, 1776.

LEE.

Daniel Waters, . Captain, . . . 20th January, 1776.
William Kissick, . 1st Lieutenant, . 20th January, 1776.
John Gill, . . . 2d Lieutenant, . 20th January, 1776.
John Diamond, . Master, . . . 20th January, 1776.

FRANKLIN.

Samuel Tucker, . . Captain, . . 20th January, 1776.
Edmund Fettyplace, 1st Lieutenant, 20th January, 1776.
Francis Salter, . . 2d Lieutenant, 20th January, 1776.

HARRISON.

Charles Dyer, . . Captain, . . 20th January, 1776.
Tho. Dote, . . . 1st Lieutenant, 23d January, 1776.
John Wigglesworth, 2d Lieutenant, 20th January, 1776.

LYNCH.

John Ayres, . . . Captain, . . . 1st February, 1776.
John Rocke, . . . 1st Lieutenant, 1st February, 1776.
John Tiley, . . . 2d Lieutenant, 1st February, 1776.

WARREN.

William Burke, . . Captain, . . 1st February, 1776.

In this same work there is an interesting account of the
escape of Captain Manly, when he was pursued by an
armed brig from Boston ; and seeing he must be captured,
he ran his vessel ashore south of the river in Scituate. The
brig then anchored and fired upon him at least a hundred
times ; but fortunately no one was killed or wounded.
One ball passed into the cabin within a few inches of
the captain's body, who lay there sick. The next day

a hundred and fifty balls were picked up on the sea-shore, where the schooner lay. It was said, that after the brig ceased firing, she sent her boats to set the vessel on fire; but the enemy was driven off by the people who collected on the spot, and they were compelled to weigh anchor and leave her. She was soon got off and repaired.

Early among the thirteen frigates ordered to be built was the Randolph, the command of which was given to Captain Biddle, who sailed on his first cruise in her at the commencement of 1777. He captured several prizes and one armed vessel, and the True Briton, twenty guns. In an expedition in March, 1778, she was blown up in a contest with the British ship Yarmouth, off Barbadoes.

In May, 1777, Captain Manly took charge of the frigate Hancock, thirty-two guns, and Captain Hector McNiel, of the Boston, twenty-four. The Hancock took the Fox, twenty-eight guns. Afterwards sailing together, they encountered the double-decker British frigate the Rainbow, forty-four guns, and the Hancock, unsupported by the Boston, Captain McNiel, was obliged to strike. Captain McNiel was much blamed, and in consequence was removed from the service.

Esek Hopkins was the first and last commander-in-chief ever appointed, and with his squadron, the Alfred, twenty-four, Columbus, twenty, Doria, fourteen, Cabot, fourteen, Providence, twelve, Hornet, ten, Wasp, and Fly, was ordered to cruise to the southward. He sailed to New Providence, one of the Bahama Isles, which he invaded, destroyed two small forts, carried off several guns with some ammunition, and then retreated. He has been severely judged for this wanton invasion, and it was thought beneath the dignity of Congress to justify this act. But it was chiefly by his unskilful and injudicious attack on the Glasgow, an English ship of twenty guns, that he lost his credit, and by a vote of censure was dismissed from the service.

In reflecting upon Commodore Hopkins's invasion of New Providence, a candid mind would make some allowance on the score of retaliation for the outrageous and most unjustifiable attack upon Falmouth, in Maine, in the outset of the war. The peaceful and defenceless inhabitants of that flourishing seaport were invaded in a most wanton manner, and four hundred and fourteen houses and stores set on fire and destroyed, October 18, 1775, by Lieutenant Mowatt, of the royal navy, with a strong force under the orders of Admiral Greaves, then in Massachusetts Bay, with a large squadron. War itself in its mildest forms is terrible enough ; but such a savage sacrifice of life and property by fire and sword can never be justified by the plea of necessity, especially in a war conducted by Christian nations. It was said that some offence was given to a high officer by one of the inhabitants, and the admiral, to soothe his pride and mortification, took this mode of gratifying his inhuman vengeance. Again it was said that General Gage, on the 6th day of October, 1775, only gave orders, from his camp in Boston, to the admiral to take some armed vessels, and a detachment of troops, and then " to annoy and destroy all the ships belonging to the rebels in the harbors on the coasts," and that Lieutenant Mowatt exceeded his authority. Such was the defence set up by English writers to screen the ministry; but the stain has never been wiped away. (See History of Portland, by Willis.)

The rank of the officers of the navy was fixed by a resolution of Congress, October 10, 1776. Seniority in office, as captain, appears to have been their rule of estimation, and no one could ever be recognized as such until commissioned in due form. The rank of commodore was left in some uncertainty, as a commission to ·him *co nomine* was never issued. The title, therefore, did not originate by act of Congress.

The word *commodore* is derived from *comandatore*, Italian, or *comendador*, Spanish, for *commander*. In England it is applied to an officer in the navy who is a temporary rear-admiral. In our navy, before the recent regulation of Congress touching the title of the superior officers, that of the admiral was unknown. It is stated by Totten, that commodore is " a title given by courtesy to a senior captain, when two or more ships of war are cruising in company." The officer who commands a squadron of ships takes this title. It is a distinction of long standing in this country; for in March, 1745, Captain Tyng, who commanded the colonial fleet in the attack on Louisburg, was called " Commodore Tyng." On December 22, 1775, Esek Hopkins was appointed commander-in-chief in the navy. " His official appellation," according to Cooper, " appears to have been that of ' commodore.' " The colony of Pennsylvania gave

Captain Hazlewood that title in his commission. It was similar in Captain Barron's commission from Virginia, and in Captain James Nicholson's, from Maryland. In the letter of General Washington to Captain Manly, dated at Cambridge, January 28, 1776, the address is to " Commodore John Manly, of the Hancock, Armed Schooner," as may be seen in American Archives, Vol. IV. 1775 and 1776.

The rank of the captains then established by Congress is as follows : —

1.	James Nicholson.	13.	John B. Hopkins.
2.	John Manly.	14.	John Hodge.
3.	Hector McNiel.	15.	William Hallock.
4.	Dudley Saltonstall.	16.	Hoysted Hacker.
5.	Nicholas Biddle.	17.	Isaiah Robinson.
6.	Thomas Thompson.	18.	John Paul Jones.
7.	John Barry.	19.	James Josiah.
8.	Thomas Read.	20.	Elisha Hinman.
9.	Thomas Grennall.	21.	Joseph Olney.
10.	Charles Alexander.	22.	James Robinson.
11.	Lambert Wickes.	23.	John Young.
12.	Abraham Whipple.	24.	Elisha Warner.

It might be asked, Why is not the name of Samuel Tucker found in this catalogue of captains made October 10, 1776? Without disparagement to him, the question is easily answered. He returned from England in the fall of 1775, as already stated, was appointed captain January 20, 1776, and had begun to form a naval character. It was after this list of prominent commanders was made out, that he rose into public notice by his remarkable deserts. Having taken this general view of the country, we shall find him at his post doing his duty manfully.

CHAPTER III.

His first Cruise in the Franklin. — Transferred
to the Boston.

IMMEDIATELY on his arrival at Beverly, he began
to get the Franklin ready for sea ; and he must have
proceeded with great rapidity in making his cruises, for
in Dr. Sparks's Writings and Correspondence of Washington (Vol. III. p. 281) there is a letter from General
Washington to the president of Congress, dated February
9, 1776, in which he observes, " Captain Waters and
Captain Tucker, who commanded two of the armed
schooners, have taken, and sent into Gloucester, a large
brigantine . . . one of the transports in the ministerial
service."

There is a letter written to him by his friend Captain
John Glover, dated Marblehead, February 3, 1776, con-
gratulating him and Captain Waters on the success of
their last cruise, and informing him that a large transport
ship of sixteen guns, strongly manned, had recently left
Boston, and was 'last seen off' Cape Cod, chasing a
fishing vessel. He warns him to look out for her, and
not fall into her hands.

After the evacuation of Boston, March 17, he captured a transport, loaded with powder and stores, which was taken near the British fleet off Long Island, and almost under the protection of the enemy's guns. The prize was most fortunate and providential. The American army was then in a very destitute state for want of ammunition, and each soldier was reduced to only a few rounds of cartridges. For this timely exploit Captain Tucker received the thanks of General Washington and the gratitude of the army.

It was probably the same capture described to the writer of this life by a very aged surviving friend of the captain. The narrator remarked that he had often heard Tucker relate the particulars, before his decease. It is substantially as follows : —

A small schooner, of eighty tons, was fitted out in Marblehead, mounting four guns and six small swivels, for a short cruise ; and while his own vessel was undergoing some repairs, Captain Tucker was requested to take command of her. The colors which were hoisted were the handiwork of Mrs. Tucker. With a moderate breeze he got under way and sailed towards Cape Cod. Night came on, and a cannonading was heard from a distance, to which they directed their course ; and drawing nearer, it was perceived that the firing came from an English armed ship, attacked by two privateers, which she beat off until they left her, and she kept on her way to Boston harbor. Captain Tucker, sailing faster, followed her. It was now midnight; and discovering another sail at a distance, and the breeze being light, he sent his boat to reconnoitre the strange vessel, with a dark lantern, and gave orders, if she proved to be an English cruiser, the bargemen were to suspend the light near the water; if an American vessel, then to elevate it in the air. Seeing in a short time the light was raised on high, he sailed towards her, and found her to be a cruiser fitted out by Rhode Island. An agreement was made between the commanders to join forces and attack the English ship of war; and as Captain Tucker held a commission under the United Colonies, the command of both vessels devolved on him.

In the mean time the wind was dying away; and in pursuit of the English ship — which proved to be a transport with troops on board for Boston, and which probably had not heard of the evacuation of that place by the British — the two American cruisers entered the channel on each side of Long Island, Captain Tucker in the western channel, called Broad Sound, and the Rhode Island vessel in the eastern; and he soon overtook the transport, which had got aground. He fired a number of guns at her, and several shots were discharged in return; but they passed over the heads of his own crew, and endangered the Rhode Island cruiser, which lay on one side of the island, becalmed, and in the range of the enemy's guns, so that she had to move from her position, and could render him no assistance. The sails of Tucker's vessel were completely riddled, and his spars and rigging suffered from the heavy discharges of the enemy, while, in return, his own well-aimed shot were pouring destruction among the troops and crew of the enemy. This transport was from Scotland. Thirty-six of her men lay dead, and soon her brave commander was killed. Then she struck her flag; and the ammunition, clothing, and stores for the British army, became the spoil of Tucker. The troops on board of her were under the command of Captain Frazer. The dead were buried the next day on the island; and it was a heart-rending sight to see the women, who had accompanied these troops, weeping with loud lamentations, and to hear the funeral dirge on the bagpipes. They played an ancient air of the Highlanders; and the narrator observed, "Commodore Tucker, who had a musical soul, would often whistle the plaintive notes, as he wound up this story of one of his earliest battles."

Such is the narrative of Captain Daniel Weston, of Bremen, — a worthy and intelligent old gentleman, respected by all who knew him, — to the writer of this Sketch. He may have erred in the exact date, and have forgotten some particulars; but it must be remembered that aged persons who retain their mental powers have usually a better recollection of what was said or done in their early days, than of recent events. This capture is, without doubt, the same referred to by Dr. Sparks; and the copy of a letter of Samuel Tucker to Honorable John Holmes, of the House of Representatives, Congress, bearing date March 6, 1818, and which has recently been found, strengthens the account given by Captain Weston, though in some particulars varying. The copy is in Tucker's own handwriting: therein, among other things, he remarks, —

"I will give a sketch of our proceedings and doings at

the commencement of the Revolution. The first cruise I made was performed in January, 1776; and I had to purchase the small arms to encounter the enemy with money from my own pocket, or go without them; and the consort above mentioned [his wife in feeble health] made the banner I fought under; the field of which was white, and the union was green, made therein in the figure of a pine tree, made of cloth of her own purchasing and at her own expense. Those colors I wore in honor of the country — which has so nobly rewarded me for my past services [*ironical*] — and the love of their maker, until I fell in with Colonel Archibald Campbell, in the ship George, and brig Annabella, transports with about two hundred and eighty Highland troops on board, of General Frazer's corps. About ten P. M. a severe conflict ensued, which held about two hours and twenty minutes. I conquered them with great carnage on their side, it being in the night, and my small barque, about seventy tons burden, being very low in the water, I received no damage in loss of men, but lost a complete set of new sails by the passing of their balls; then the white field and pine tree union were riddled to atoms. I was then immediately supplied with a new suit of sails and a new suit of colors, made of canvas and bunting, of my own prize goods. I then went on duty again. I quit here, fearing any further detail would be too tedious, as I could fill a dozen sheets from memory."

What number of cruises he made, or prizes he captured, while in the command of the Franklin, we have no means

of ascertaining. That he was very successful there can
be no doubt. He did not continue long in the command
of that vessel; for in March or April of this year he was
transferred to the armed schooner Hancock. In the
American Archives (Vol. VI. p. 399, Fourth Series)
there is a letter from General Ward to General Washington, dated May 9, 1776, from which is the following
extract: "I have the pleasure to inform your Excellency, that on the 17th instant [the last month must have
been meant] Captain Samuel Tucker, commander of
the schooner Hancock, took two brigs in the bay within
sight of a man-of-war, and carried them to Lynn. One
of them from Cork, ninety tons burden, laden with beef,
pork, butter, and coal; the other from the Western
Islands, laden with wine and fruit, about one hundred
tons burden."

In the same work (Vol. I. p. 662, Fifth Series): "July
29, 1776. Yesterday, was carried into Marblehead, taken
by the privateers Hancock, Captain Tucker, and the
Franklin, Captain Skinner, the ship Peggy, commanded
by James Kennedy; mounts 6 three, and 2 two pounders:
bound from Halifax to New York." The same is also
mentioned in General Ward's letter to General Washington, July 29, 1776, as appears in the above work
(Vol. III. p. 68): "Captains Skinner and Tucker, — prize
brig; and yesterday a brigantine from Scotland, worth
£15,000 sterling."

And again this voluminous work, the Archives, is
referred to, where the capture of the brig Lively is
mentioned, and the grateful acknowledgments of her

captain and owner to Captain Tucker for his generous treatment. A copy of the letter or statement is here introduced, as these records of a huge mass of events and news, spreading over many large folio volumes, are not easy of access to readers in general who reside in the country.

Statement of Nicholas Martindale and George McCree.

In justice to Captain Samuel Tucker, of the Hancock, in return for his civilities, we hereby certify, that, on the 29th of October last, we were taken in the brig Lively, bound from Air to Newfoundland, by the Hancock, in the Continental service, and brought into this port on the 13th current; that Captain Samuel Tucker, commanding the Hancock, allowed us to remain on board the Lively till her arrival here, where we were treated with all manner of civility and good usage. Mr. Tucker, he not only gave liberty for Mr. McCree, the master, mate, and hands of the Lively, to take all their clothes and private adventures, &c., for their own particular account, but after some of the sailors had been robbed of some goods and clothes by the people, which were missing for some days, he was at the pains to search for the goods, &c., which he found and delivered, and such part as could not be found he generously paid the full price out of his own pocket. He has likewise been at all manner of pains, since we arrived, to introduce us to such gentlemen as could be of any service to us, and has done everything in his power to make matters as easy and agreeable to us as possible in our present situation.

Given under our hands, as witness our subscriptions, at Boston, this 30th day of November, 1776.

Commander of the Lively,

NICHOLAS MARTINDALE.

Owner of the Cargo,

GEORGE McCREE.

He captured, this year, in the Franklin and in the Hancock, a great number of ships, brigs, and smaller vessels, from thirty to forty, many of them with very valuable cargoes, and some of them armed vessels. In his lifetime he had a complete list, but it was lost with Dr. Shaw's papers, before referred to. The above number will not appear an extravagant statement, if the immense losses the British commerce sustained in that war with the American Colonies are considered. In the Naval History of the United States, by Thomas Clark, there is a list of English ships and vessels captured by American privateers during the year 1776, including the names, masters, where destined, and tonnage. Three hundred and forty-two vessels were taken, forty-four recaptured, eighteen released, and five burned. (See Vol. II. p. 168.)

It was not long after his appointment to the command of the Franklin, that, Commodore Manly having been confined at his home in Beverly, Tucker received a commission as commodore, signed by Samuel Adams, chairman of the naval committee, and others. This commission cannot be found among his papers. Colonel Hinds, his grandson, told the writer he was sure he had seen such a commission, and had repeatedly heard Captain Tucker speak of it; and from the title of " Commodore," by which, ever since the Revolution, he has been known and addressed, there is no doubt that it justly belonged to him at a future period of the war, if not so early as 1776. If, however, the command of more than one ship, when two or more, a fleet or squadron, are sent out, entitles the captain to that appellation, the following extract will be in point : —

" Jonathan Glover to the Massachusetts Council. April 9, 1776. May it please your Honors: The Committee of Correspondence have this day received from Captain Samuel Tucker, commanding the Continental armed vessels, twenty-two persons, who were in the brigantine lately taken by Captain John Manly, from Boston, bound to Halifax, among whom are four soldiers, with their wives."

In the background of the farm occupied by Deacon Gatchell, his father-in-law, overlooking the Gatchell Mills, there is a lofty hill, which commands a very extensive piece of scenery. Marblehead, with bays and inlets around it, and the distant ocean, are spread before the eye. There, one afternoon in the summer of 1776, Mrs. Tucker and her sister, hearing a report of cannon, and knowing the captain had recently left the port on a cruise, ascended this hill, and distinctly saw her husband capture two brigs, which he sent into Lynn harbor. They were probably the same vessels mentioned in General Ward's letter of May 9. This account was related to the author by a venerable lady, a connection of the family, who often heard her mother tell the particulars and speak of the clearness of the atmosphere at that time, and the distinctness with which they could see the vessels by the aid of a common spy-glass, as they anxiously watched the captain's movements. A few hours soon convinced them they had not been deceived in the vision. She mentioned many other interesting incidents.

It appears that Captain Tucker was indefatigable in his cruises this year; for even he is found upon his quarter-deck at sea in the cold and stormy month of December. On the 23d of that month General Ward wrote to the head of the Board of War, —

"Sir: Having been informed the army were in distress for want of clothing, and there being a quantity on board a prize lately brought into this port by Captains Skinner and Tucker, I have forwarded to the army at or near New York the several articles contained in the enclosed invoice."

In Clark's Naval History, the depredations on English commerce this year (1776) are stated to have been very great. He refers to an English work — the Remembrancer—for his authority; and, according to this work, which has been carefully examined, the English ships taken were three hundred and forty-two, as also stated in the American Archives. The United States navy, October, 1776, as represented by Cooper, in the Naval History, is as follows: —

Hancock,	32,	building in	Boston.
Randolph	32,	"	Philadelphia.
Raleigh,	32,	"	Portsmouth, N. H.
Washington,	32,	"	Philadelphia.
Warren,	32,	"	Rhode Island.
Trumbull,	28,	"	Connecticut.
Effingham,	28,	"	Philadelphia.
Congress,	28,	"	Poughkeepsie, N. Y.
Virginia,	28,	"	Maryland.
Providence,	28,	"	Rhode Island.
Boston,	24,	"	Boston.
Delaware,	24,	"	Philadelphia.
Montgomery,	24,	"	Poughkeepsie, N. Y.
Alfred,	24,	in service.	
Columbus,	20,	"	
Reprisal,	16,	"	
Cabot,	16,	"	
Hampden,	14,	"	
Lexington,	14,	"	
Andrea Doria,	14,	"	
Providence,	12,	"	
Sachem,	10,	"	
Independence,	10,	"	
Wasp,	8,	"	
Mosquito,	4,	"	
Fly,	—,	"	

Several of these vessels never got to sea.

March 15, 1777, Captain Tucker was appointed commander of the frigate Boston, directly from Congress, under the signature of " **John Hancock,** President," in conformity to resolutions **passed by them, which have** been already **referred** to in the Introduction. The **form of** the commission — concise **and yet comprehen-** sive — was reported by the Court of Admiralty, and adopted by Congress April 20, 1780. The following is a copy : —

In Congress.

The Delegates of the United States of New Hampshire, Massachusetts Bay, Rhode Island, Connecticut, New York, New Jersey, Pennsylvania, Delaware, Maryland, Virginia, North Carolina, South Carolina, and Georgia,

To Samuel Tucker, Esq.

We, reposing especial trust and confidence in your **patriotism, valor, and conduct,** constitute and appoint you **to** be Captain **of** the armed ship called **the Boston, in** the service of the United **States of North America, fitted** out for the defence of **American Liberty and for repelling every hostile invasion thereof.**

You are, therefore, **carefully and** diligently to discharge **the duty of** captain, by doing and performing all manner **of** things thereunto belonging. And we do strictly charge and require all officers, marines, and seamen, under your command, to be obedient to your orders as captain, and you are to observe and follow such orders **and** directions from time to time as you shall receive from **this or a** future Congress of the United States, **or committee of** **Congress** for that purpose **appointed, or** commander-in-chief for the time being of the navy of the United States, or any other your superior officer, according to the rules and discipline of war, the usage of the sea, and the instructions herewith given you, in pursuance of the trust reposed in you. This commission to continue in force until revoked by this or a future Congress.

Dated at Philadelphia, March 15 [or 14], 1777.

By order of Congress.

JOHN HANCOCK, *President.*

Attest.   CHARLES THOMSON, *Secretary.*

["A true copy of my commission."]

He captured a number of prizes in the Boston this year; but, whether on a temporary leave of absence, or part of the time transferred to some other ship, he did not command that frigate the whole time; for in May there was an eastern cruise of the Hancock, under Commodore Manly, and the Boston, under Captain Hector McNiel; and, coming up with the British frigate Fox, twenty-eight guns, a sharp engagement took place, and the Fox was taken by the Hancock. But soon after the 1st of June, they, with their prize, were pursued by Sir George Collier, from Halifax, in the Rainbow, forty-four, and two other ships of war. Commodore Manly was obliged to strike, and the Fox was retaken; and it was reported, that in the Boston Captain McNiel showed the white feather, escaped without rendering any assistance, and was afterwards cashiered for abandoning his consort.

There is one account of the capture of a British armed

vessel while he commanded the Boston, which is here given, as related to the author by a niece of Captain Tucker. The anecdote was told some time ago, but notes were taken at the time. She remarked that she recollected this more distinctly among many other descriptions which he gave of his battles to her because she was then on a visit to his house, and there were several of his neighbors sitting round a winter's fire, and eagerly listening and watching him, as he enchanted them with his stories of the war and the dangers he had passed.

Soon after getting out to sea, her uncle told her, he saw a distant sail, and steered directly for it. On approaching her, he discovered by her tier of guns she was an English frigate, larger than the Boston. Undismayed, he crowded sail, caused the drum to beat to quarters, and made quick preparation for battle. As the ships drew near, he told Lieutenant Magee that he should put the vessel alongside the frigate and board her. "And you," said Captain Tucker, " must head the marines." The lieutenant at first hesitated, as though he would rather decline the desperate office. "Then," said the captain, "take my place, and I will head the boarders ; for she must be taken." "No," replied the young officer, " I will go and do my best." He then handed the captain a ring and a watch, with the miniature of an only sister, to whom he was tenderly attached, with a request that, should he fall in the attempt, these bequests might be sent to her.

In a few moments, by a sudden and rapid change of the helm, — for in nautical manœuvring Captain Tucker

was unsurpassed by any officer in our infant navy, — he
laid **his ship** alongside the frigate, **gun to gun, and** before
a shot was fired or a piece **of** ordnance could **be brought**
to bear against him, he threw his **grappling-irons upon
the** gunwale **and began the boarding. But** the intrepid
Magee **fell in the onset : heading his band of** marines, he
leaped the bulwark ; and scarcely had his foot touched the
deck of the enemy, before this gallant, noble-hearted
young man **was assailed by numbers, and a sword pierced**
his heart. His death was not unavenged. **Tucker, like**
a lion, sprang into the midst of his foes, and his stalwart
arm cut down **all** before him. The frigate soon struck
her colors. Magee died gloriously. *Dulce et decorum
est pro patriâ mori* — **It is a sweet and beautiful** thing to
die for our country.

CHAPTER IV.

VOYAGE TO FRANCE WITH JOHN ADAMS, ENVOY.— CAPTURE OF THE MARTHA.

ON the 27th of December, 1777, Captain Tucker was again appointed commander of the frigate Boston, twenty-four, as will appear by his commission; and February 10, 1778, he received orders to carry the Honorable John Adams as envoy to France. He was authorized to fit her out for this purpose at his own discretion; consequently he supplied her with additional spars, canvas, and equipments. The canvas, it is said, was of a peculiar and original kind, having special reference to swift sailing, as the object of the mission to France was important, and so well known to the enemy, that a British seventy-four and two frigates, from Newport, had been waiting, and watching the motions and departure of the Boston. To escape a force so vigilant and formidable, and to avoid the numerous men-of-war, which infested the track across the Atlantic, required an officer of consummate skill and intrepidity, and Congress reposed full confidence in the ability of Tucker. So great was the trust that Mr. Adams put in him, that he committed not only himself, but his son, then about eleven years old, the future celebrated John Quincy Adams, to his charge.

The character of this embassy, in which a nation, in its infancy struggling for existence, was so deeply interested, will justify a publication of the following Instructions, copied from the original letter.

To Samuel Tucker, Esq., *Commander on Board the Ship Boston, at Boston, in Massachusetts.Bay.*

Sir : As soon as these Instructions get to hand, you are to get to sea as soon as possible. When there, you are to proceed on a voyage to some convenient port in. France, and at your arrival there, apply to the agent, if any, in or near said port, for such supplies as you may stand in need of. You are at the same time to give immediate notice by letters to the Honorable Benjamin Franklin, John Adams, and Arthur Lee, Esquires, or any of them, at Paris, of your arrival, requesting their instructions as to your future destination ; which instructions you are fully to obey, as it shall be in your power. If, however, in the course of your voyage, a favorable opportunity should offer of doing service to the States by taking or destroying any of the enemy's ships, you are not to omit taking advantage of it, but may go out of your course to effect so good a purpose. In this we trust to your zeal and discretion. You are to take particular notice, that whilst on the coast of France, or in a French port, you are, as much as you conveniently can, to keep your guns covered and concealed, and to make as little warlike appearance as possible.

On your arrival in France, send one of your officers with the letter you are to write to the commissioners, to prevent its falling into improper hands.

We are your humble servants,

WM. VERNON,
J. WARREN.

NAVY BOARD, EASTERN DEPARTMENT,
BOSTON, Feb. 10, 1778.

NAVY BOARD, EASTERN DEPARTMENT, }
BOSTON, Feb. 10, 1778. }

SIR: Notwithstanding the general instructions given you, you are now to consider the Honorable John Adams, Esq. (who takes passage in the Boston), as one of the commissioners, with the Honorable Benjamin Franklin and Arthur Lee, Esqs., and therefore any applications or orders received from him as valid as if received from either of the other two. You are to afford him on his passage every accommodation in your power, and to consult him on all occasions with respect to your passage and general conduct, and the port you shall endeavor to get into, and on all occasions have regard to the importance of his security and safe arrival.

We are your humble servants,

WM. VERNON,
JAS. WARREN.

To SAMUEL TUCKER, Esq.,
Commander of the Ship Boston.

On the 17th day of February, 1778, at seven o'clock P. M., Captain Tucker weighed anchor at Nantasket Roads, proceeded to sea, with the stripes and stars waving to a fine north-wester, and fired a salute of seven guns. His log-book having been preserved, the journal of his voyage supplied materials for an accurate narrative of every twenty-four hours until his safe arrival at Bordeaux, on the 31st of March, after a passage of forty-eight days. In the beginning of his journal are these words in his own handwriting: "Pray God conduct me safe to France, and send me a prosperous cruise." Is not this a sweet memorial of the care and influence of a pious mother, who more than thirty years before that time had offered him to the protection and guardianship of the Almighty in infant baptism at the altar?

On the 19th of February, at six P. M., he saw in the east three large ships belonging to the enemy, and hauled his wind to the southward, though he was not then pursued. On consultation with his officers, he wore ship, ran for an hour to the northward, and then discovered two of them under his lee, and with short sail. One of them was a ship of twenty guns, the other a vessel as large as his own, and the third was soon out of sight. But the man at the mast head immediately called out there was a ship on the weather quarter. Consulting with Mr. Adams and his officers, and not knowing how fast his own vessel would sail, the captain concluded to stand to the southward, and at ten A. M. he wore ship. The two sails under his lee then changed their course, and pursued him. At twelve at noon he lost sight of the small ship, while the other was about three leagues off, under his lee quarter. On the 20th the chase was kept up. Being poorly manned and actuated by prudential motives, Captain Tucker did not venture to attack her. At two P. M. he set fore and maintopmast steering sail, and soon found he was leaving her, and at six lost sight of her in the darkness of the night.

For seven or eight hours the Boston was running four points southerly, at the rate of seven knots an hour; and the other ship, it was supposed, pursued the same course. He conjectured that she was about eleven or twelve leagues off. The wind then heading them, he fell off and run at the rate of six knots for three hours, until he saw the same ship directly ahead, standing southward and westward about five leagues distant. He hove in stays and stood to the westward, as in his former track he could not weather her. After running three hours, he hove in stays again, and passed the frigate to the windward, about four miles off, under her lee quarter, and was then convinced she was the same vessel he had seen before. He then tacked ship, as she continued to chase him; but he found the Boston was gaining and distancing the enemy in pursuit.

On the 21st, the weather was cloudy, and a smart breeze sprang up, the frigate still being in chase of them. At ten P. M. a violent storm came on. Captain Tucker ordered the sails to be taken in, cleared the ship, and prepared for an attack. At twelve, midnight, the tempest became furious; the mainmast and topmast were struck with a flash of lightning, which wounded three men and knocked down several others. He remarked in his journal, "We were in great danger, the sea very cross and high." A heavy rain came on, and from the violence of the wind they were obliged to scud before it ; and they soon saw no more of the enemy. They were then in 38° 33′ north latitude, and in longitude 60° 30′ west.

The scene at this time on board the ship must have been terrific beyond imagination. In the noon of night, — in the "dead of darkness," to borrow the awful imagery of Prospero in the Tempest, — the rushing of the billows, the rage and foaming of the Atlantic, the rattling of the rigging, and creaking of timbers and spars, the dreadful roar of the angry winds, the glaring sheets of fire at times flashing over sky and sea, the sight of three wounded men, and the fall of others by a single stroke of lightning, the tall mast trembling beneath the blast, and in addition to all this the dismal echo from the pump of water in the hold, were enough to appall the oldest veteran that ever faced the cannon's mouth in the day of battle. Well might the captain, in his distress, alarmed for his distinguished charge and for his crew, and touched with such a mass of sea-sorrows, — behind him a heavy frigate ready to pounce upon him, before him and around him, a terrible storm of rain, thunder, and lightning, and the oceanquake threatening every moment to swallow up his ship, — well might he pour forth that short and simple prayer from the heart, which stands recorded in his journal of that day : " Pray God protect us and carry us through our various troubles." Gladly must every serious mind contemplate such a precious fragment of faith, left us by one of the noblest commanders in the navy of the Revolution. What must have been the sufferings of that man, at that dark hour, when he thought of home, of his family, of his bleeding country in a death struggle with the mightiest nation on the globe, and then beheld the grand object of his voyage to France in the most imminent peril! For it seemed as though the artillery of heaven was pointed against the mission. But it was not so. In the sailor's pretty fancy, there was a little cherub above that watched over them.

When, in our ideal conception, we summon up this awful storm at midnight, and look at a scene so terrific, through a vista of more than ninety years, as we sit in this happy land by our cheerful fireside, there arises a moral grandeur in the contemplation. Tucker stands before us in a sublime position. We see the dark outline of his stalwart form at the helm on the deck of his frigate, which at times was illuminated by the blaze of lightning, erect and commanding, and hear him issuing his orders with a voice of thunder rising above the tempest. He alone is calm and self-possessed — like Æneas of old,

"Curisque ingentibus æger,"

concealing his deep anxieties, peering into the black clouds after some ray of light, and cheering his brave companions with the hope of safety; while near him stands the sturdy patriot of Braintree, ready to cry aloud, "This is the HAND OF GOD, stretched out to shield us from the pursuit of the enemy." And there, too, was the young lad of so much promise, gazing with wonder more than fear at the war of the elements, for his father was with him.

February 22. The storm still raged with heavy gales and a dangerous sea. Something was continually giving way, and the ship leaked so badly it was necessary to keep the pumps constantly going. The foresail was split, and on examination below deck it was found that the mainmast had sprung, which had been already suspected by the captain, who was apprehensive of being dismasted. At two P. M. he kept away and ran before the wind under the foresail, having experienced the shock of a very heavy sea.

February 23. The hard gales continued, while they were running under foresail, which at two P. M. they hauled up and handed, and lay by under the mizzen. At three P. M. they sent down the top-gallant yards; and at four P. M. carried away the slings and chain of the mizzen-yard, furled the mizzen, and set the mizzen staysail. At four A. M. the storm began to moderate, and they made sail and commenced repairing the rigging, which had been much shattered by the tempest. At six they saw a sail to the north-east, running southward and westward. The captain then stood south-east about half an hour, when she crossed him about a league to the windward; and supposing her to be a French merchantman bound to America, he wore ship and crowded sail in pursuit of her. He came up with her very fast; but she made all the sail possible, and at eleven A. M.

there came on rain, and she was lost sight of for two or three hours.

February 24. The weather was close, with rain. He again got sight of the chase, came up with her fast, and within a mile and a half she hoisted American colors; and at the same time he took a squall from the west, which carried away the main-topmast overboard. "Thanks to God," he writes, "no man was lost or wounded."

The unknown sail now hoisted Normandy colors, and fired a gun to leeward, which Captain Tucker answered in return. The squall, however, compelled him to run before the wind. The other vessel, seeing his distress, bore up after him, running north-east half an hour; but not being able to come up, she kept her wind and stood to the northward. In the latter part of the day the gale became more moderate, with rain, and Captain Tucker made out to save his sails and rigging. He was then in latitude 37° 10′ north.

From February 25 to March 11, the weather was variable, but not violent, full of fresh breezes, then changing to light airs and pleasant skies, and again to clouds and sometimes disagreeable squalls. In the mean time they repaired the sails and rigging, got up a new main-topmast, and fished the mainmast, which was sprung, as before stated. During this period the marines were twice exercised with the guns and small arms, and the men kept constantly employed. After having been out twenty-two days, and thus far, by skilful manœu-vring, having escaped the prowling enemy and weathered a terrible storm without serious loss or injury, they reached latitude 44°, and longitude 16° west.

March 11, they were sailing with fresh breezes and flying clouds; when, at one P. M. Captain Tucker saw a distant ship to the south-east, standing west. In a short time he discovered that she was an armed vessel. He consulted with Mr. Adams and his officers with regard to attacking her; and as their opinion favored his own wishes, he shook out a reef in his topsails and gave chase.

"What should you do," said Mr. Adams, one day when the three ships were pursuing him, "if you could not escape, and they should attack you?" He replied, "As the first is far in advance of the others, I would carry her by boarding, and would myself head the boarders. I should take her; for no doubt a majority of her crew, being *pressed men*, would turn to and join me. Having taken her, I should be matched, and could fight the other two."

Such were the confidence and daring of this naval officer, who was no vain talker, but a doer in his profession. The trial, however, he escaped, and was rescued, probably by the storm, from this threefold danger and conflict at such fearful odds. At three o'clock he came up with the war ship, and his journal gives a modest, though very meagre, description of the rencounter and battle; for he only says, "I fired a gun, and they returned three, and down went the colors."

A gentleman, however, related to me the facts, as he heard them directly from Mr. Adams himself, a few months before the decease of that illustrious man. The

venerable patriot was at the time in his mansion at
Quincy, sitting by the fireside with his study-cap on
his head; and some remark, appertaining to the bravery
of Commodore Tucker, coming up in the conversation,
drew out from him several anecdotes of this naval hero.
He then described the voyage to France, the escape of
the Boston from three English frigates in pursuit, the
terrific storm, and the particulars of this capture. As
soon as they perceived she was an armed vessel, Captain
Tucker, after consultation, prepared for action, and boldly
sailed up to her. The drum beat to arms, and in the
mean time Mr. Adams seized a musket and joined the
marines, standing by a gun ready for battle. The captain stepped up to him, put his hand on his shoulder,
and with a voice of authority, said, "Mr. Adams, I
am commanded by the Continental Congress to deliver
you safe in France, and you must go down below, sir."
Mr. Adams smiled and went down to the cabin. Tucker
by this time had contrived to get his frigate in the position he wished. His guns were shotted, the marines
at their post, the match-stocks smoking; and yet he
hesitated to give the order to fire. At this delay his
men grew impatient, and seeing so fine a chance to
strike a fatal blow, they began to murmur and swear
bitterly; when he cried out aloud in these memorable
words: "Hold on, my men. *I wish to save that* egg
without breaking the shell." Nor were they compelled
to hold on long; for the enemy saw at once the ad-
vantageous position which Tucker had obtained, making
his own chance desperate, and he struck his colors.

6

Such is the account given by Mr. Adams of the capture of the Martha. In some particulars it may differ from some others. The narrator of this conversation with him did not say whether the Martha fired a gun or not. There is another statement, however, which avers that the enemy fired a broadside as the Boston approached, and shivered off a piece of the mizzen-yard, which, in falling, struck Captain Tucker on the head, and knocked him down; but he quickly recovered from the stunning blow, and resumed his command.

There is among his papers a copy, or minutes, of a letter which he wrote to the Eastern Department of the Navy, the next day after this capture; it is too imperfect to be fully transcribed. It was dated March 11, 1778, wherein he says that the enemy, on discovering that he hoisted his colors, "bore away, firing a broadside, which carried away my mizzen-yard, and did no other damage." And in another passage he says, the enemy "did not think himself able to get his colors down soon enough," for "he was horribly scared."

The prize-ship Martha, Captain M'Intosh, was bound from London to New York, with a very valuable cargo. After Captain Tucker had sent Mr. Barron and Mr. Reed, two of his officers, in a boat to take possession, and the prisoners were transferred to his frigate, he gave Mr. Welch the command, as prize-master, with a detachment of men; and a salute of seven guns having been fired, she sailed for Boston. The following is a copy of the orders to the prize-master: —

On Board the Boston Frigate,
March 11, 1778.

To Hezekiah Welch, *Gentleman.*

You are now appointed to the command of the ship Martha. I desire you would make the best of your way to Boston, running up your longitude in 37° 00′ north, as far as 68° 00′ west. Be careful to avoid all vessels you may see, keeping a man at the mast head from daybreak until dark, and if you should be so unfortunate as to be taken, destroy my letters with your signals. If you go safe, lodge my signals at the Navy Board, not showing them to your dearest friend. Be very certain of your lights, to show none in any respect. When you arrive, acquaint the Honorable Board of every instance that has happened in my passage; and I desire you would be as attentive to the ship in port as at sea. Keep regular orders, as you would at sea, and the men under the same subjection. Other orders are to yourself discretionary in defending the ship.

Your well-wisher,
Samuel Tucker.

It is said the Martha, on this voyage, was retaken by the enemy, and again recaptured by one of the Continental cruisers, and that she finally arrived in Boston. Of this second recapture I can find no satisfactory evidence.

The reader shall be spared in following day by day the monotonous detail of a log-book. Such fragments only shall be extracted from his journal and interwoven in this story of his life as may be interesting or necessary touching his voyage. Those who are curious in such matters will find a transcript of the log-book, with the courses and reckonings, in the Appendix.

After sending off his prize, he kept on his course to France, under a variety of weather and violent gales. There were but eleven pleasant days; the remainder of the voyage was very boisterous. On the 13th of March, he saw a suspicious looking ship at a distance, and got ready his guns for an engagement; spoke a Frenchman from St. Domingo, bound to Nantes. At eight P. M. discovered two sail to the windward standing west-south-west, and at eight A. M. saw two more on weather bow, standing northward and eastward. He supposed them to be cruising vessels. The one ahead had the poop-lantern out.

March 14. By the bursting of the second gun, Mr. Barron had his right leg broken, and two marines were wounded. The doctor and his mate found it necessary to amputate it, "which," says Tucker, "was done in a masterly manner." The doctor was the late Benjamin Brown, M. D., a skilful and accomplished physician, who, years after this event, settled in Waldoborough, Maine, was a member of the legislature of Massachusetts in 1809, 1811, and 1812, and in 1815 a member of Congress; he died in good old age, much beloved as a gentleman and a good man.

March 17. There appeared on his larboard quarter, at half past two P. M., two ships, laboring in a heavy gale and large sea; and at eight A. M., on the 20th, another vessel, which he made sail for, and came up with her at eleven. She proved to be a Dutch snow, bound to Demerara.

March 24. High land was visible at four P. M., about eight leagues off, bearing south-west to south-east, and at eleven St. Antony's Head — probably the insulated rock at the mouth of the harbor of Corunna — bore south-south-west, about five miles. The next day a pilot came off.

March 26. William Barron, his first lieutenant, whose leg had been amputated, died after extreme suffering. His remains were brought on deck; prayers were read; and "with all the ceremony," the captain remarks, "that possibly could be," all hands standing around on the quarter-deck, the body, with a heavy ball, was launched into the deep, there to rest on the bottom, in the ocean churchyard. There is something peculiarly solemn in a burial at sea — the great cemetery of the poor sailor, where no headstone, nor mark, nor monument tells the spot, nor records the name; age after age the wave passing over it, and the place where he lies forgotten forever! The heartfelt sorrow of the whole crew, and the eulogy of Captain Tucker, that "he was a worthy and respectful officer," are the best memorials of the humble virtue of William Barron.

They were now nearing their port. On the 25th, in sounding they found the depth fifty fathoms, with red sand and shells: after running thirty leagues more, they came to thirty-five fathoms, and coarse and black sand.

March 29. They spoke several Dutchmen ; at six A. M. they saw land, north-north-west, four leagues off, and fifteen to the westward of Bordeaux ; and next day a pilot came on board. The lofty lighthouse of Cordouan was visible, east by north, three leagues off.

March 31. They entered the River Garonne, on the west bank of which, fifty-five miles from the mouth and three hundred and seven south-west from Paris, lies Bordeaux, their port of destination. They came to anchor, and, April 1, went up within three miles of the city, saluting the little town of Larmoon, on the way, with thirteen guns, and the castle of Bordeaux with twenty-one, which returned the salute. Bordeaux — the ancient Burdigala, once a gorgeous and immense amphitheatre — is located on a semicircular bend of the river, and with its docks, quays, famous bridge of seventeen arches, splendid houses, lofty cathedral, and fine churches, situated on a crescent of the river, where it is a mile in width, must have been a magnificent sight to those voyagers long wearied and storm-driven on the ocean — more especially when they found themselves in this beautiful haven safe from an enemy so vigilant and terrible. On the 4th day of April, Mr. Adams took leave of the ship, and with his son and some passengers entered the pinnace and went up to town.

During the first four days in which the frigate lay moored in the stream, multitudes came down to see the ship. From morning to evening, parties of ladies and gentlemen were going on board. Crowds flocked round the vessel ; boats filled with visitors were successively alongside. The gentlemen looked pleased — the ladies spoke with admiration. No doubt the open, courteous manner — though a little roughened by the hardships of the sea — and the gallant figure and handsome features of the American captain increased the charm and novelty of their visit. He, however, wondered at the curiosity of a people so enlightened, and remarked in his journal, "One would think these strangers never saw a ship before." Perhaps he did not reflect that a noble frigate, recently sprung from the woods of a new continent, where a republic was just emerging like another star from the depths of the horizon, was an object of admiration to people of the old world amid the shadows of antiquity.

Captain Tucker remained at Bordeaux nearly two months, waiting the orders of the commissioners at Paris. The ship was his home — his castle; and there he was to be found at his post of duty. The seamen loved and honored a master who lived like them and with them. His fidelity to his country was a noble trait in the character of a deserving officer, too little known and remembered in the days of our national prosperity.

He devoted his time to repairs of his frigate, shattered in her spars, and sails, and rigging by a tempestuous voyage across the Atlantic. He shipped a new mainmast, put her in sailing condition, and procured a re-enforcement of his crew, weakened by the detachment sent home in his prize, the Martha. For on March 11, 1778, he wrote to the Navy Board, that he was "but poorly manned, to my sorrow, not even enough to attack a twenty gun ship." The truth is, that the frigate Boston was not half supplied with a marine corps for a voyage to Europe, exposed to the heavy-armed war ships of England. But the Navy Board was not in fault. Our country was then poor, its resources small, and the wonder is, that they accomplished so much with means so small and impoverished. The Navy Board, energetic and indefatigable, did all they could do ; while this brave officer silently and poignantly lamented his fate.

On the 17th of May he weighed anchor, saluted the castle of Bordeaux, which cordially responded, and proceeded down the Garonne, at the mouth of which he was delayed till June 6. On that day, in company with a fleet consisting of twenty ships, brigs, and smaller vessels, and also a French frigate and sloop of war, he put to sea. Captain Paul Jones — afterwards so celebrated — was there in a brig of ten guns, and joined the fleet. With a favorable breeze they passed the light-house, and were all winging their way to the great deep.

CHAPTER V.

RETURN OF THE BOSTON, WITH COMMODORE WHIPPLE AND OTHERS.

A FIRST-RATE man-of-war is said to be a world in miniature. She is a grand spectacle on the stocks, just ready to launch into the deep; she is a magnificent object at her moorings, with her lofty spars in the sky, and her broadsides frowning over the water like a cloud of hidden thunder; but it is when she spreads her sails and braves the boundless ocean, with the flag of her native land unfurled, that she appears sublime in her element.

> " How gloriously her gallant course she goes!
> Her white wings flying — never from her foes :
> She walks the waters like a thing of life."
>
> *The Corsair.*

Nor is the accomplished commander who guides her destiny less an object of admiration. Skilled in his profession, he is a master of nautical science. Familiar with engineering her dread artillery, he knows no fear, and only feels anxious, in the day of conflict, to serve his country and acquit himself with honor. At sea he is the sovereign of his own ship. He walks the quarter-deck in majesty. He superintends every movement of her complicated machinery; he regulates his course by the luminaries of heaven; and keeps his reckoning with geometrical accuracy. In his government over those committed to his care, he is a strict disciplinarian, ready to reward merit, merciful to the erring and ignorant, yet firm, but neither rash nor cruel to the transgressor. His *coup d'œil* embraces every cloud, and sail, and speck in the great circle of sky and water. His eye, accustomed to gazing at distant objects, becomes sharpened in vision, and the expression of his countenance has the appearance of looking afar off at sights not seen by men shut up in the narrow horizon of a city or a cell.

Such were some of the gallant captains of the Revolution — such as Manly, and Whipple, and Jones, and Tucker; such were Preble, and Bainbridge, and Decatur, and others that might be named, as our early navy from small beginnings rose into character and strength at the close of the last and beginning of this century.

The month of June is delightful in the Bay of Biscay, and each day had now a white mark in the calendar. Captain Tucker in his voyage to Brest passed many beautiful islands. As he sailed by the Isle de Dieu, he sent his pinnace to the brig of Captain Paul Jones with an invitation to dine with him. Between that island and the handsome town of L'Orient he saw a French frigate and snow at anchor; and, while sending his boat ashore for water, he discovered several sails in the distance, some of which he soon pursued.

On the 19th he captured a Scotch brig, — the John and

Rebecca, Captain Fenly, — and sent her with her cargo under a prize-master to Boston. For two days he crowded sail after a vessel, which, on nearing, he found to be the cruiser of his friend Jones, who returned the compliment by dining with him. The 23d of June he captured the brig Britannia, Captain William Baker, and the Elizabeth, Captain Anquetil, and sent them to L'Orient. The same day he pursued, and came up with, a Baltimore vessel, Captain Murray, who supplied him with American papers.

June 25. There was an eclipse of the sun at seven P. M. This fact is merely mentioned in his journal; but it must have been a solemn and magnificent sight at sea, to stand on the deck of a ship, isolated in a waste of waters, and to look up to the vast concave above, while the great luminary was shorn of his beams. It was a scene of surpassing grandeur, not very often occurring amidst the lights and shadows of a sea voyage. This eclipse was announced in the Boston Almanac of that year for the 24th of June, which, allowing for local distance and nautical calculation, agreed with the above.

He received a letter from the Hon. John Adams, who was residing in the vicinity of Paris, as follows : —

Passi. April 29, 1778.

Dear Sir: I this moment had the pleasure of your letter of the 22d instant. and am much obliged to you for your kind congratulations on my safe arrival and agreeable reception here.

The commissioners have recommended a lieutenant to

you, — Mr. Livingston, — a gentleman of good character, as the commissioners believe. But, although the honorable commissioners have recommended him as first lieutenant, I hope he will decline this, and be content to be made second lieutenant, as I have a great opinion of and esteem for Mr. Reed; I could wish him to be the first. However, this must be left to you. Mr. Livingston is said to be a man of a handsome fortune and good connections.

You will see by your orders, which Captain Palmes will deliver you, that your future cruise and voyage will be left to yourself. May God preserve and prosper you and the ship and her company.

I shall ever retain a pleasing remembrance of the civilities received from you, and the agreeable hours we spent together on board the Boston, notwithstanding all our bad weather and disagreeable chops.

I have written to Mr. Bendfield to put a few things on board your ship for my family. If you will take charge of them, I shall be much obliged to you. I had rather they should take their chance with you, how long soever you may cruise, than by any other vessel; because I have great confidence in your vigilance, prudence, and activity, of which I have written both to Congress and the Navy Board.

I am, with much affection and esteem,

Your friend and servant,

JOHN ADAMS.

CAPTAIN TUCKER.

A copy of his letter of " Instructions " is also inserted,

as it is a valuable state paper, and because it is complimentary to the skill and bravery of Captain Tucker, and testifies the confidence which those distinguished men, who then represented the United States at the French court, reposed in him. They left the plan of his cruise and the ports he should visit *entirely to his own discretion.*

Passi, Near Paris, April 13, 1778.

Sir : We duly received your letter, dated at Bordeaux, the 1st instant, and congratulate you on your safe arrival, as well as on your good fortune in taking the ship Martha, which we wish safe to port.

We approve of your zeal and industry in taking upon you to get the frigate as far in readiness as possible for the sea, during the absence of Captain Palmes.

As the number of your men has been reduced to so small a complement, we recommend to you to engage as many at Bordeaux by honorable means as possible, and proceed to sea.

If your ship was fully manned, in all respects fitted for such a cruise, we should recommend to you to take a voyage towards the entrance of the Baltic, or some other distant seas, where the ship's company might have an opportunity of making ample profits to themselves, as well as acquiring the honor of serving their country in her most essential interests by striking an important blow to her enemies. But we leave this entirely to your own discretion, as we do also an attempt to take or destroy any considerable part of the enemy's fishery at the Banks of Newfoundland, or any of the seas adjacent.

Having mentioned these things, we leave it entirely to your own judgment to plan your voyage homewards, and to touch at such ports as you shall think necessary in France, Spain, the West India Islands, or North America, recommending it to you to do everything in your power, to take as many prizes as possible, and to get into safe ports as many as you can man, and destroy all others. You are to be careful who are British subjects on board the vessels you may take, and transport them to America, that they may be exchanged for our brave but unfortunate brethren in the hands of the enemy. We recommend Mr. Livingston as your first lieutenant, if, upon examination, you find no objection to him; the other places you will fill up as you think best for the service.

You will take particular care that these orders may not, in case of misfortune,—which God forbid,—fall into the hands of the enemy. We wish you a prosperous voyage, and are

Your humble servants.

B. FRANKLIN,
ARTHUR LEE,
JOHN ADAMS.

SAMUEL TUCKER, ESQ.,
  Commander of the Frigate Boston.

PASSI, NEAR PARIS, April 15, 1778.

SIR: We this moment had the pleasure of your letter from Bordeaux, April 11, and approve of your activity in getting your ship ready for sea. We have despatched Captain Palmes your orders for your future government, and shall write this day to Mr. Bendfield to supply you with necessary provisions, and are your very humble servants,

B. FRANKLIN,
ARTHUR LEE,
JOHN ADAMS.

CAPTAIN TUCKER.

Mr. Livingston, his lieutenant, wrote him from Paris, July 8, 1778, " I have this day been with the commissioners, who are perfectly satisfied with all that you have done. . . . They think a great deal of our cruise; indeed, more than we do ourselves."

1778, July 3. He arrived at L'Orient, and anchored in the harbor of St. Louis. Here he found two of his prizes had preceded him; one of which was a Scotch brig, bound to St. Ubes, which he had captured on the 20th of June. On the 5th of July Mr. Schweighauser, Continental Agent at Paris, wrote to him about four prizes taken by the Boston frigate.

July 10. While they were making some repairs at this port, Mr. Latuche, one of his Most Christian Majesty's generals at L'Orient, came on board with a band of officers, and asked the French seamen and marines, in Captain Tucker's presence, being the persons who had enlisted for this cruise, if they wished to quit the service and go on shore. They answered they did, and alleged bitter things against Lieutenants Reed and Bates, besides complaining against the captain. Mr. Latuche released and sent away *forty-seven* of his men, and treated Captain Tucker with great harshness, utterly disregarding the respect due to character and naval rank.

These men enlisted voluntarily, and were well treated by the officers and men on board the Boston, and there was no sound reason for such an arbitrary and ungenerous interference. Captain Tucker threatened the French general, that he should write to the American commissioners at Paris, and make a representation of the injustice with which he had been treated. And he forthwith wrote to them, setting forth his grievances; but the commissioners replied fully and prudentially to the captain. In their answer, which has fortunately been saved from the wreck of his history, it is easy to see the delicate and ticklish circumstances in which they stood. This was the reply : —

Passi, July 22, 1778.

Sir: We have received your letters relative to the disputes between two of your officers and some of your men belonging to this nation; and we are of opinion that if the men are enlisted upon the ship's books, to go to Boston, they ought to return to the ship, and be received by you, and are entitled to their wages and prize-money. But, if they are not enlisted in writing to go to Boston, but only for a cruise, that cruise is completed by the ship's return to France; and they have a right to leave the ship if they choose it, and are entitled to their share of wages and prize-money, deducting therefrom, however, what has been advanced them by the captain and purser. You are strictly enjoined to take special care that all Frenchmen, who may be in the service under you, be at all times treated with justice and impartiality, and that suitable allowance be made for the difficulties they are under in not understanding our language and not being habituated to our customs.

We are your humble servants,

B. Franklin,
Arthur Lee,
John Adams.

P. S. If, however, the men insist on leaving the ship, although enlisted expressly to go to Boston, we advise you to agree to it; but, in that case, we think they are not entitled to wages or prize-money.

Such is the brief statement of a troublesome and provoking incident, which, in his journal — to use a sea phrase — is scudded over in only a few words, written in pale ink, and scarcely legible. We have become a great nation since that French officer, dressed in a little brief authority, caused no small anxiety and inconvenience to a faithful and honorable man, who showed him the enlistment papers and ship books, yet without avail. The passions, feelings, and persons of all concerned in that affair are now buried in the grave.

The resources of Captain Tucker were diminished, and discouraging. On mustering the ship's company the next day, he found that, with the officers, men, and boys, he could only enumerate a crew of *one hundred and forty-six persons* — much too small either to fight any large ship of the enemy, or send many prizes, with a detachment, to any safe port. The usual complement of a frigate, armed for a cruise in war time, is said by expe

7

rienced officers in the navy to consist at least of one hundred and eighty men.

August 1. Having sold his three prizes, he weighed anchor, warped his ship out of the harbor, and by noon, being clear of the rocks at the mouth of it, he hoisted in his boats and made sail for Nantes. Having passed Belle Isle, Groix, and Quimper Point, he came to anchor in the roads of Paimbœuf. Here Commodore Whipple came on board, and on the 7th, at 4 P. M., fired a gun and hoisted a signal at the top-gallant-mast head for the fleet to send their boats for orders. The next day, August 8, they sailed. There were eight ships in the fleet under convoy, besides other vessels bound to Brest, where the Ranger, Captain Simpson, was expected to join them. "Then," said Tucker, "there will be two frigates and a sloop of war belonging to the THIRTEEN STATES."

At 8 P. M. the tower of Le Croisic bore north-east half east, fifteen miles distant, and the whole fleet in sight. On the way they saw two ships, and set out in chase; but the wind failed them. The next day they saw seven sail in the distance, but could not discover whether French or English.

August 14. They arrived at Brest. Being in advance, he writes that he judged it proper to let Commodore Whipple precede him in entering the harbor. Such is the courteous demeanor of a true gentleman of the "old school" of chivalry. He who feels respect for the rank and merit of others will generally experience a return of it in those delightful delicacies of conduct which make life interesting.

Brest has a spacious bay, and lies beneath a steep declivity, with ramparts around the town, shaded with trees. An ancient castle, on a precipitous rock, protects the entrance. There are fine quays and a superb arsenal; and it is one of the greatest naval stations in France. The French fleet was lying there. Salutes were mutually fired, and a company of citizens paid them a visit at their anchorage. The French admiral, with Captains Simpson and Tucker, made a call on Commodore Whipple. The French fleet consisted of one three-decker, twenty two-deckers, eight frigates, three snows, and one lugger.

August 22. The Providence, Boston, and Ranger sailed with a fine breeze. It was reported that Admiral Keppel was in the vicinity, watching this fleet, and our little squadron was in immediate danger. In the Boston Gazette, published October 5, 1778, is the following extract from a letter dated at the mouth of Brest harbor, August 21, 1778. It describes the situation of our three ships of war at that time, and was written by some one who was on the spot.

"We are now in company with Commodore Whipple, in the Providence, and Captain Simpson, in the ship Ranger, formerly commanded by Captain Paul Jones. A fleet of French ships, under the command of Admiral and Duc Deenaso, consisting of twenty-nine sail of the line and eleven frigates; they are to be joined by eight more off Ushant. The fleet sailed on the 17th instant. Admiral Keppel has the same number of shipping at sea, waiting for the fleet. The French are in high spirits. We expect to see them in the channel. Captain Tucker is a brave man, and never will leave the Providence to be taken by the Rainbow."

August 24. The little squadron escaped. They gave chase, and took the brig Sally, Captain Ward.

September 1. The ships thus far had sailed in company, and interchanges of conviviality were often renewed between their commanders in the halcyon days of this season. Captain Tucker speaks with much interest of saving the life of a cabin boy who had fallen overboard; but being a good swimmer, he took off his coat in the water, and at last becoming exhausted, was just reached by the boat as he was going down the third time.

While the other two frigates were in sight, he gave chase to a brig called the Friends, Captain McFarling, and took it. On the 9th he captured the snow Adventure, Captain Symes.

September 26. They reached soundings, latitude 45° north, longitude 51° 23' west, on the Grand Bank, in eighty fathoms of water; the weather hazy and disagreeable.

September 29. It became so foggy that Captain Tucker fired guns, but heard no reply. Yet the frigates afterwards met again, and on the 15th of October all three arrived safely in Portsmouth.

Thus ends this interesting voyage of the frigate Boston to France. In his journal, or log-book, Captain Tucker records a few instances of corporal punishment. They were extreme cases, in which he deemed the terrors of the " cat " necessary to prevent gross and mutinous violations of duty, and to restrain others from like offending. In the perusal of this diary, it is pleasing to notice that

he seldom, and with reluctance, resorted to such ignomin-
ious measures; and whenever he felt obliged to punish
an offender, he tempered justice with mercy. In two or
three instances half the penalty was remitted to the peni-
tent culprits.

An extract is here inserted from the Independent
Ledger, published by Draper & Folsom, July 29, 1778.
" An officer in the Continental frigate Boston, in which
the Hon. John Adams, Esq., sailed from hence in February last for France, lately arrived from Halifax. He
was on board a rich prize taken by the Boston, and val-
ued at eighty thousand pounds sterling, which was afterwards retaken by a British frigate and carried into Halifax.
He reports that in her passage the Boston had a very
narrow escape, having been struck by lightning, which
shattered her mast and made its way almost to a magazine of powder, but, providentially, did not reach it; by
which the ship and all on board were preserved from
immediate destruction. We hear she took two other
prizes of considerable value, which were ordered to
Europe."

In the Life and Works of John Adams (Vol. X. pp.
26, 27) may be seen the copy of a letter from Ex-President
John Adams to J. B. Varnum, Esq., in which he relates
the very complimentary language of Captain McIntosh,
who was captured in the Martha, upon his examination
of the frigate Boston. The letter is dated Quincy, 5th
January, 1813.

" I said I would give you two anecdotes: I will add a
third. In 1778 I went to France in the Boston frigate.

We **took** a very rich **prize,** commanded by a captain who had served twenty years in **the British navy,** several of them as lieutenant. The **captain became** very curious **to** examine the ship. Captain **Tucker allowed** him to see **every part of her. As we** lived together in the cabin, we **became very intimate.** He frequently **expressed** to me **his astonishment. He** said he had never seen **a completer ship; that not a frigate** in the royal **navy was better built,** of better materials, **or** more perfectly equipped, furnished, or armed ; and ' **if you** send to sea such ships as this, you will be able to do **great** things.' "

A paragraph from the **eloquent** eulogy on Adams and Jefferson, by the **Hon.** Peleg·Sprague, July 26, 1826, will **close this chapter.**

" **Mr. Adams** was removed **from the Congress to other scenes of important** duty and usefulness. In August, **1778,** he **was sent to** Europe as commissioner **of** peace. The public **ship on** board which **he** embarked was com- manded by **the gallant Commodore Tucker, now living,** and a citizen **of** this State, **who took more guns from the** enemy during the Revolutionary war than **any other naval commander,** and who has been far less known **and rewarded than his** merits deserved. One occurrence on **their passage is worthy of relation, as** illustrating **the character of both. Discovering an enemy's ship, neither** could **resist the temptation to** engage, **although against** the dictates **of prudent duty. Tucker, however, stipu-** lated that Mr. Adams **should remain in the lower part of the** ship, as a place **of** safety. **But no sooner had the battle commenced than** he **was** seen **on deck with a**

musket in his hands, fighting as a common marine. The
commodore peremptorily ordered him below; but, called
instantly away, it was not until considerable time had
elapsed, that he discovered this public minister still at
his post, intently engaged in firing upon the enemy.
Advancing, he exclaimed, 'Why are you here, sir? I
am commanded by the Continental Congress to carry you
in safety to Europe; and I will do it;' and, seizing him
in his arms, forcibly carried him from the scene of
danger."

CHAPTER VI.

Cruises. — Capture of the Pole, Thorn, &c.

COMMODORE TUCKER in his life, it has been stated, — and there can be no doubt of the fact, — transmitted to a friend in Congress a list of all the prizes he captured during the war, with some account of his battles. Among his papers, since his decease, no such list could be found, and only imperfect fragments of his engagements with the enemy. A history of this kind in his own hand, or drawn up under his dictation, would have been a very interesting document; more especially as some of the principal battles he fought in his numerous cruises were attended with much loss of life and great peril and anxiety. He often narrated them in conversation with his intimate friends; but, unfortunately, a very few were preserved by the pen, and the rest are now beyond recall, for the generation has passed away, and there are not many living who knew him. Yet a few of such conversations have been preserved, though imperfect in a detail of names and dates.

Allusion to these battles, however, may be found in a few of the letters of his correspondence, and among the fragmentary papers which still exist. Among them is a letter from the late John Paine, Esq., of Thomaston, Maine, a gentleman well known and much respected in his day. He refers to a battle fought in the dead of night, when Captain Tucker captured an armed vessel, after a severe contest. The scene of the conflict was terrible. The dashing of the waves, the thunder of the artillery, and the uncertainty and horror of such a death struggle in darkness, or with only the gleam of the stars, was enough to appall the stoutest heart. The prize was taken, but her name and that of her captain now rest in oblivion. Some narratives, coming directly from persons who fought under his command, will appear in due season.

After his arrival in Boston, which was in the latter part of October, he spent a short time with his family in Marblehead, and then returned to duty. His country needed his services, and he was too loyal a man to waste his days in inglorious ease at home. In a few weeks the frigates were repaired, equipped, and manned, and ready for another cruise. They frequently left the port in company, were gone a short time, and made many captures. An arrangement like the following often occurred in our navy.

On Board the Continental Frigate Providence,
Banks of Newfoundland, September 27, 1778.

It is agreed that we cruise on the Banks of New-foundland till the 5th of October, and then pursue such methods as shall be judged best to make some port within the Thirteen United American States.

A. WHIPPLE.
S. TUCKER.
SIMPSON.

A true copy.
GEO. RICHARDS.

In the summer of 1779, the Deane, Captain Samuel Nicholson, and the Boston, Captain Tucker, made a cruise of this kind, and in August took several prizes. Though, in the Naval History, Mr. Cooper observed, " no action of moment occurred," yet he enumerates several, — " the Sandwich (a packet), and two privateers, the Glencairn, twenty, the Thorn, eighteen," among the captures, — and it is hardly to be supposed they were taken without a blow. The Deane and Boston returned safe into port, as observed in the Boston Gazette, September 13, 1779, " after a successful cruise."

It was some time during the year 1779, that the Boston, Tucker, and the Confederacy, thirty-two, commanded by Captain Harding, were ordered on a cruise to the West India seas, to convoy a fleet of merchantmen, sent from St. Eustatia, which belonged to the Dutch, with supplies of clothing for the American army. They had been purchased in Holland by our agent, and sent to this island for reconveyance on account of the British cruisers. War had not then been declared between England and Holland, nor until February 11, 1781. These supplies were greatly needed by the destitute and suffering troops, whose distressed situation was depicted in mournful colors in the letters of General Washington to Congress.

Some circumstances will tend to fix the date of this convoy of the two frigates. For the Confederacy, thirty-two guns, was built in Connecticut, and according to the Independent Chronicle, printed in Boston, November 19, 1778, she was launched on the 23d of that month. In June 16, 1779, there was a letter written from John Wharton, and James Reed, of the Navy Board, Philadelphia, to Captain Tucker, in which the Boston and Confederacy, are mentioned as in company; consequently their cruise was in the spring, or first of summer.

Commodore Tucker met the fleet of merchantmen on their way, pursued by two British frigates, hovering like eagles, ready to pounce upon their prey. At this critical juncture, he made a signal to the Confederacy to attack one, while he would engage the other. Seeing that the cautious enemy avoided them and sheered off, they convoyed the Eustatia fleet safe to their destined port in Philadelphia. It was reported that the commander of these British frigates was afterwards tried by a naval court martial in New York, and escaped disgrace by pleading that the men mutinied, and would not fight the Americans. Perhaps that was the fact; for British seamen were reluctant combatants against their own kith and kin, and besides, they knew too well that the Yankees fought desperately. The commodore used to relate, that this British officer, smarting under the imputation of cowardice, left New York expressly to redeem his character by seeking and finding the "rebel Tucker," as he called him, "and giving him a sound drubbing." He, therefore, had reënforced his ship, at New York, with a crew of picked men, and was determined to wipe off the stain on his reputation by a battle at the first opportunity.

Tucker soon discovered this same frigate under gallant sail on the high seas, for he knew her features well. Disguising his own ship with English colors, — a deception not then uncommon in our small and struggling navy, — he prepared for battle, and sailed up within pistol shot, under the quarters of the English frigate. Having got a commanding position, he immediately hoisted the stars and stripes, and ordered an instant surrender. The enemy, seeing resistance against a raking fire would be in vain, struck his flag, and gave up the ship. So true it is, that no warrior should boast until he put off his armor. Such is one of the accounts of this capture.

But a more particular description of the taking of this frigate was related to the author by a gentleman, to whom Tucker often described it.

His bravery and great success in taking prizes was a subject of daily talk among the British officers in New York, and they were resolved to stop the career of the "rebel Tucker." A frigate equal, if not superior, in metal to the Boston, was fitted out, and a hundred picked men were selected to board her. The news reached Tucker in some way. In a few days after he saw the English frigate coming along, and knew her well, from her *build*, as one he had formerly chased. He sailed towards her under English colors; and as soon as he came within speaking distance, the British captain hailed him : —

"What ship is that?"

"Captain Gordon's," said the commodore; for Captain Gordon commanded an English ship, modelled and built much like the Boston, and had taken a number of American prizes.

"Where are you from?"

"From New York," said Tucker.

"When did you leave?"

"About four days ago. I am after the Boston frigate, to take that rebel Tucker, and am bound to carry him dead or alive to New York."

"Have you seen him?"

Tucker rejoined, "Well, I have heard of him : they say he is a hard customer."

During all this conversation, the commodore was manœuvring to bring his ship into a raking position, so as to sweep the decks of the English frigate. He had every man at his post, the guns shotted, his gunners with lighted matches in their hands, and all waiting orders of the commander. There was a man in the maintop of the enemy's ship who had formerly known the commodore, and he cried out to the English captain, "That is surely Tucker : we shall have a h—ll-smell directly."

This was overheard by Tucker; and having got his ship in a raking position just as he wished, and seeing he was discovered, he gave the order to his men, —

"Down with the English flag, and hoist the American."

He then **said** to the British captain in a voice of thunder, " The time I proposed talking with you has ended. This is the Boston frigate — I am Samuel Tucker, but no rebel. Either fire or strike your flag." Observing that **his adversary** had all the advantage, and that a broadside **must be** fatal, the English captain struck his flag. **Not a gun was fired.**

The commodore, on taking possession of his prize, **was** astonished **at the** size of his prisoners: they were picked men, and so stout that the handcuffs had to be enlarged for them. The fact is, Tucker intended at first to have laid his ship alongside the English frigate, and after discharging a broadside, to have grappled and boarded her; **but when he** saw so many **of these** tall **fellows on** her **deck, he** suspected there was **a numerous and powerful body of** marines, and he changed his plan of attack. **When the** English captain came on board the Boston, **and** went **below** to the state-room, he shed tears to think he was captured **by a** vessel no larger than his own. It was afterwards reported that, on his return **to** England, he was tried and disgraced.

The reader may think that, after all, we **have** only Commodore Tucker's word for this brilliant achievement, **as no** notice has been taken of it in our naval histories; **but always** and everywhere truth will prevail: *Magna est veritas, et prævalebit.* Fortunately among the letters of the correspondence of Ex-President John Adams (Vol. IX. p. 483), is one dated Philadelphia, June 13, 1779; and therein is this paragraph : " Tucker has sent in a twenty-**four** gun ship **this** afternoon, which did not fire a shot at him before striking. It is at the Capes, with the Confederacy, one of the finest frigates in any service, as it is said by voyagers." It will be remembered the Boston only mounted twenty-four guns; and the vessel captured must have been the frigate Pole. In Tucker's letter to the Hon. Benjamin Brown, member of Congress, of whom we have already written, he mentions this capture, and says, " the taking of the Pole frigate, which was sent out of New York for the purpose of taking me." So there can be no doubt.

Tucker took a number of prizes and some other armed vessels. In some of the cruises he was in company with the Deane, as appears by a letter to him from William Whipple, Esq., of the Marine Committee, with instructions to proceed with her to the Capes of Delaware, and to Chesapeake Bay ; and on his arrival at Hampton, to obtain all the intelligence he could of the enemy's ships, or privateers, and, if none were in that quarter, to take such a cruise as he thought best. The subjoined copy of the original will best explain the purpose of the cruise : —

MARINE COMMITTEE,
PHILADELPHIA, June 25, 1799.

You are hereby directed immediately to proceed, in company with the frigate Deane, from the Capes of Delaware into Chesapeake Bay, and on your arrival there, at Hampton, or any other way, endeavor to obtain the best intelligence if any of the enemy's ships of war or privateers are in the bay ; and if you find them there, and of such force as you are able to encounter, you are to proceed up and attack them, and after taking or destroying as many of the said vessels as may be in your power; or, should there not be any British vessels in the bay then, without loss of time, you are to sail out of it, on a cruise, in which you are to choose such stations as you think will be best to accomplish the double purpose of intercepting the enemy's outward-bound transports for New York, from Great Britain and Ireland, and the homeward-bound West India ships. We are of opinion that between latitudes 36 and 41, and one hundred leagues eastward of the Island of Bermuda, will be your best cruising ground; but in this we do not mean to restrict you, leaving you to exercise your own judgment, which probably may be assisted by information which may be obtained in your cruise. All prizes which you make you are to send to the nearest and most convenient ports of these States, and addressed to the Continental agents.

You are to continue cruising, for the above purpose, until the middle of September next, or longer if your provisions and other circumstances will admit of it, and afterwards return to the port of Boston, where you must be governed by the orders of the Navy Board of the Eastern Department.

We have ordered the Continental frigates at the eastward to be sent out to cruise for the same purposes you are now going on, and we think it very probable that you will fall in with them. In that case, you, or they, or any of them are hereby directed to cruise in company, under the command of the senior officer; and should you be joined by any of those frigates, and find, by any intelligence you may receive of the situation of the enemy's sea force at Bermuda, that it will be advisable to make an attempt on their shipping, we recommend your undertaking it. By late accounts from that island, the Virginia frigate, and a privateer out of London, mounting twenty-nine pounders, were the only vessels of war then there.

We wish to draw your serious attention to the execution of the business before you. The great expense and difficulty that attend the fitting and manning our ships must make you and every commander in our service fully sensible how much they should exert themselves to employ them usefully while at sea. This consideration, we hope, will have due weight in your mind, and you will call forth such action and prudent behavior as will be of essential service to your country, and add to your own reputation, and honor to the flag.

We wish you health and success, and are, sir,

Your very humble servants.

By order, WM. WHIPPLE.

P. S. The Confederacy being for a particular service, we have ordered her up here. Messrs. Barrons, at Hampton, in Chesapeake Bay, will be proper persons for you to inquire respecting the enemy's shipping.

CAPTAIN SAMUEL TUCKER.

8

IN COUNCIL,
PHILADELPHIA. June 2, 1779.

SIR: I wrote you this morning, to which must now refer. This will be delivered you by Captain Tucker, commander of the Boston frigate, under whom you are directed to act for three weeks, any former orders notwithstanding. At the expiration of the three weeks, you are either to return within the Capes or keep the sea, as you may think best, and as your stores and necessaries will permit, on no account but in case of the most absolute necessity coming into port.

We shall forward to Lewistown necessary stores. It gives us great pleasure to hear the ship sails well; and as it will greatly redound to your honor and advantage, as well as of the States to make a stroke on the privateers of New York, we doubt not you and all on board will exert yourselves fully and effectually to this purpose.

Your obedient, humble servant,

JOS. REED,
President.

[Directed.]

ON THE PUBLIC SERVICE.

TO CAPTAIN JAMES MONTGOMERY,
    Commander of the State Sloop of Pennsylvania.

It was observed, in Chapter II. p. 53, that the origin of the title of commodore seemed to have arisen from the seniority of command of two or more ships of war sent on any expedition or cruise.* An instance of this kind occurred in 1779, when Commodore Manly was unable to leave home by reason of sickness, and Captain Tucker took his place. If this be correct, *à fortiori* Tucker would be entitled to the appellation of commodore, when he was ordered out as senior officer, in company with the commander of the Deane, July 25, 1779, and before that with Captain Montgomery, just quoted, under whom Montgomery was directed to act during their cruise. Tucker's title, however, as commodore, was never called in question; the object here is only to show its origin.

There is a copy of a letter from him to the Navy Board, dated July 18, 1779, written on board the Boston at sea, in which he speaks of his capturing, on the 15th of that month, the privateer Enterprise. This letter was

---

* It seems by the resolve of Congress, November 15, 1776, the rank of the naval officers was arranged as follows : —

Vice Admiral	as Lieutenant-General.
Rear Admiral	" Major-General.
Commodore	" Brigadier-General.
Captain of a ship of 40 guns and upwards .	" Colonel.
Captain of a ship of 20 to 40 guns	" Lieutenant-Colonel.
Captain of a ship of 10 to 20 guns	" Major.
Lieutenant in the navy	" Captain.

—General Navy Register and Laws, p. 224.

Commissions as admiral or commodore were never issued by Congress under this resolve.

sent to them by Mr. Bailey, prize-master in the sloop Mermaid, Captain Avery, of six guns, which he had taken. And on the 24th, same month, he writes again to the same Board, and mentions the arrival of the Deane and Boston at Hampton on the 19th instant, and of the above sloop Mermaid, which was a tender of the British frigate Vigilant. And in the same letter he refers to his capture of a privateer of seventeen guns and eighty men on the 13th of the same month, which was probably the Enterprise, named above. He then describes the state of his ship, which, having been ordered only on a cruise of three weeks, had become short of provisions, suffered from sour flour, and bad beef, and scarcity of water from leakage. The fact was, the resources of the Continental government were small and feeble, and they had to eke out the uttermost parings in their meagre supplies.

The prizes taken by the Boston alone, or in company with the Confederacy or Deane, as he cruised with each, were very many. In the Independent Ledger of May 21, 1799, printed in Boston, is the following piece of news: "By a schooner arrived here last Friday, we are informed that, a few days before, she spoke with a very large Jamaica-man taken by the Continental frigate Boston, Captain Tucker." Again, June 7, "Yesterday arrived safe in port a brigantine prize of the Boston, laden with sugar; and the Boston, we hear, has retaken from the enemy a ship with a valuable cargo, consisting chiefly of tobacco." In the same paper, August 16, " On Monday last was sent into Philadelphia, by the frigates Boston and Deane, the privateer schooner Tryall, of ten guns, of New York; by which we learn that the privateer Flying Fish is also taken by these frigates, and may be hourly expected. The Tryall and Flying Fish had taken several prizes, some of which had been retaken."

The Continental Journal of May 27, 1779, mentions a brigantine, laden with rum and sugar, prize to the frigate Boston, arriving at Newburyport, early in the week.

In the letter of June 16, from John Wharton and James Reed, Esqs., of the Navy Board, the very valuable prize frigate Pole is stated to have arrived at Philadelphia, and been sold, and that she brought one hundred and three thousand pounds. This was the prize of the frigate Boston. A copy of the original letter, fortunately saved, is here offered : —

NAVY BOARD, MIDDLE DISTRICT,
PHILADELPHIA, 25th June, 1779.

SIR : We embrace this opportunity to inform you that we have procured leave from the judge of the Admiralty to make sale of the prize-ship Pole, previous to her being condemned. And she was, in consequence thereof, sold yesterday for one hundred and three thousand pounds. We reserved the provisions, with the coal that was on board, for a separate sale, all which is not yet disposed of; therefore cannot say what the whole amount will be, but are in hopes it will come little short of one hundred and twenty thousand.

The measures we have pursued were such as we thought most likely to promote the interest of the captors, and we flatter ourselves we have not been mistaken. We made the conditions of sale for the ship that one half the purchase money be paid down, and security given for the payment of the other half in a month; these terms, we are confident, raised her price some thousand. A Court of Admiralty will be held the 8th July, for her condemnation, at which time we intend to claim the whole for the captors, but don't undertake to flatter you with any great prospects of our being able to succeed in it, as time alone will determine. We have had, and shall continue to keep, your interest in view through the whole of this business, and are confident the ship would not have sold for one half the sum in any other port of the continent.

The prize-masters have undertaken to apply several articles to their own private use, which they pretend to claim as perquisites, to the value of several hundred pounds which we know of, and we have some reason to think many things of less value have been applied in the same way. As a claim of perquisites by prize-masters is what we cannot see the propriety of, we shall charge them with the amount of every thing they have taken which has come to our knowledge. If the officers and men concerned in the capture think proper to admit the claim, we have no objection, though we confess we do not see the justice or the propriety of it. We would be glad to receive a few lines from you on the subject by the first opportunity that offers. We are, in the interim, sir,

Your very humble servants,

JOHN WHARTON,
JAMES REED.

SAMUEL TUCKER, ESQ.,
Commander of the Continental Frigate Boston.

The following extract from the Boston Gazette for September 13, 1779, will show the prosperous cruise which the Boston and Deane frigates had made: "Last Monday arrived safe into port the Continental ships Deane and Boston, commanded by Samuel Nicholson and Samuel Tucker, Esqs., from a successful cruise. They brought with them, and have landed, two hundred and fifty prisoners, among whom were Lieutenant-Colonel Duncan McPherson, of the seventy-third regiment; Major Gardiner, of the sixteenth; his wife and family; Captain David Ross, seventy-third; Captain James, of the navy; Mr. Robertson, purser of the Swift; Powell and Ashley, masters in the navy; passengers on board the Lord Sandwich packet, mounting sixteen guns, which sailed from New York 30th of June, 1779, for Falmouth; Captains Hill and Wardlow, of the navy, with several warrant and petty officers, who were taken in the Thorn, a British sloop of war, sixteen guns, copper-bottomed, only nine months old, from Portsmouth to New York, with despatches informing of a Spanish war; which ships they have brought into port. They have taken, during their cruise, the ship Earl of Glencairn, mounting twenty guns, with a cargo of dry goods, the invoice of which amounts to forty thousand pounds, besides four hundred barrels of provisions and fifty puncheons of rum; the brig Venture, from Madeira to New York, with one hundred and fifty pipes of Madeira wine, which is safely arrived; and four privateers from New York, which were ordered to Philadelphia."

Having weakened their ships by manning their prizes, and having so many prisoners on board, they found it necessary to return into port. From the Glencairn was thrown overboard a box containing a complete set of types and three reams of paper, with isinglass and silk mixed, for counterfeiting the Continental currency, which was afterwards taken up and brought in by Captain Nicholson. The printer, who was to counterfeit the same, was likewise taken in the above ship.

The same paper of the 6th says, " Friday last arrived at Sandy Bar, near Cape Ann, a prize brig taken, laden with one hundred and fifty pipes of wine, bound from Madeira to New York, taken by the Continental frigate Boston."

It should be remembered that in cruises where ships set out in company, they often got separated, and at such a distance from each other, that, when one of them gets into conflict with the enemy, the other can render no assistance. Indeed, more frequently each ship took its own prizes, however the division might finally be between them. The British sloop of war Thorn was thus taken alone by Tucker. A year afterwards he commanded her, and she became the " field of fame " to him in some of his most brilliant achievements.

In the Independent Chronicle of September 9, 1779, there is another confirmation of the success of this cruise. " Monday last, signals were made from the Castle, to apprise the town that a number of ships were off, approaching the harbor. They were found to be the frigate commanded by Captain Nicholson, and the Boston, Captain Tucker, with two prizes, one of the packet bound from New York to England, the other a new copper-bottom sloop of war, from England to New York, with despatches from the

British government to the officers in that place, upon the open rupture with Spain. The Deane and Boston cruised some time in company with another frigate of the United States — the Confederacy. They have taken a large number of prizes, *eight* of which have safely arrived. Some have been retaken; among which is a vessel from Scotland richly laden with dry goods. The Boston has made the capture of thirteen prizes this cruise. In the storm of war a privateer was taken."

There is a memorandum among the papers of Captain Tucker, wherein he enumerates seven prizes which he took in June, viz.: The Boyd, Pole, Patsey, Tryall, Flying Fish, Adventure, and Thorn. Of some of these the following particulars have been obtained: The Boyd was a brigantine, under license, and with a manifest of a cargo of sugar, coffee, and tobacco. The Pole frigate and Thorn have been already described. The Pole was two hundred tons' burden, Captain John Maddock master. Among her papers was found a receipt, dated October 8, 1778, for dues paid Register Office of Greenwich Hospital, in the port of Liverpool, viz.: twelve pounds, four shillings, three pence, on account of the crew of sixty-six men. The Dolphin was a letter of marque, July 8, 1778, Captain John Redmond, a brigantine of sixty tons, twelve-pounders and several smaller guns; and there was a commission dated May 4, 1799, from the King of England, to the schooner Patsey, of six four-pounders and four swivels. The Flying Fish and the Tryall, it will be recollected, were cruisers. So that six of these seven prizes were armed vessels.

CHAPTER VII.

NAVAL OPERATIONS AT THE SIEGE OF CHARLESTON, SOUTH CAROLINA.

ON the 11th of September, 1779, Captain Tucker was cited to attend a naval court martial, as a member, on board the Deane, lying in Boston harbor, George Richards, Esq., being judge advocate.

In a letter to the Navy Board, on the 21st of the same month, he remarked, that since he left Boston, in his last cruise, he had taken thirteen prizes, — the richest of which was retaken, — and also had captured the privateer Enterprise.

The Boston, and frigates in company, having been repaired and refitted by the middle of November, ready for another cruise, the officers and crews which belonged to them grew uneasy and restless; and notwithstanding the approach of winter and the inclemency of the weather, they were anxious to push out to sea. Consequently, on the 19th of that month, a petition to the Navy Board at Boston was drawn up and signed by Abraham Whipple, of the Providence, Samuel Tucker, of the Boston, John Peck Rathburne, of the Queen of France, and Thomas Simpson, of the Ranger, remonstrating against inaction and delay, and asking to be employed. This paper, from the patriotic feelings and energy which pervade it, bears the marks of Tucker's spirit and agency. It sets forth that the ships under their command were completely manned, victualled, and ready for sea, and prays the Board to grant them an immediate depart- ure. It states that the weather on shore was then inclem- ent, the men idle and discontented, sickness for want of employment was beginning to prevail, and that while they were in port, "there was neither health to our people, honor to ourselves, nor interest for our country to be obtained."

This application was not a dead letter. It touched the heart of the Navy Board, and they rose into action. The imperfect relics of an old journal of Commodore Tucker show that on the 30th of said November these four ships of war were cruising off the northern coast of Bermuda. In pursuance of a resolve from the Navy Board, of the 20th of November, they were ordered to proceed without delay directly to Charleston, South Carolina. They ar- rived at that port a few days before Christmas, as ap- pears from Tucker's letter to William R. Lee, Esq., of January 28, 1780, wherein he states that a brig of four- teen guns, from St. Augustine, which was taken on the route, had not reached any port, so far as he could ascertain.

The following may throw some light on the destination of Commodore Whipple's squadron : —

IN CONGRESS, September 20, 1779.

That the Marine Committee be directed to give orders to the commanding officer of the frigates or ships of war going to South Carolina, to confer and coöperate with Major-General Lincoln, or the commanding officer for the time being, until further orders of the Marine Committee.

Extract from the minutes.

CHA. THOMSON, *Secretary.*

MARINE BOARD,
PHILADELPHIA, September 22, 1779.

SIR: You are hereby ordered to pay the strictest observance to the indorsed Resolution of Congress. "The commanding officer for the time being" means the commanding officer of the State of South Carolina.

We are, sir, your most obedient servant,

WM. WHIPPLE, *Chairman.*

A true copy.

[Directed.]

To THE COMMANDING OFFICER OF THE FLEET DESTINED FOR SOUTH CAROLINA.

NAVY BOARD, EASTERN DEPARTMENT,
BOSTON, November 9, 1779.

You are hereby required to proceed immediately with your ship to Newbury, and, when off the bar, to hoist a jack at your fore-topmast head, and fire a gun as a signal, for the state ship, Captain Williams, to come out. You are to receive her under your convoy, and return with her to this port. You are to take due care that your ship be not exposed to any cruisers that may be on the coast, and be very vigilant to avoid any appearances of danger from British cruisers, and make as great despatch as possible.

We are, sir, your humble servants,

WM. VERNON,

J. VERNON.

To SAMUEL TUCKER, ESQ.,
Commander of Ship Boston.

To SAMUEL TUCKER, *Captain of the Navy of the United States of America, and Commander of the Continental Frigate Boston.*

SIR : Enclosed I transmit you a copy of the Resolution of Congress, September 20, 1779; also the copy of a letter from the Honorable Marine Board, Philadelphia, September 22, 1779, together with a copy of my orders from the Honorable Navy Board, Eastern Department, November 20; all which you are carefully to attend to, and in case of any misfortune the whole to be destroyed before any of the enemy's boats board you.

I am, with due respect, sir,

Your most obedient, very humble servant,

ABRAHAM WHIPPLE.

CONTINENTAL FRIGATE PROVIDENCE, ⎰
AT SEA, November 23, 1779. ⎱

The squadron was under the command of Commodore

Whipple. Tucker, in his letter to Mr. Lee, goes on to say, that the ships were detained at Charleston, where an invasion was expected from the British; and by a brig from New York to Savannah, which was " decoyed" into the harbor, it was reported, that eight thousand troops were being embarked from Georgia for this purpose. He then gives his own opinion, that, having examined the fortifications of the city, he was apprehensive they were not sufficient for its defence. We shall see that they proved so in the sequel.

After Count d'Estaing — who, on the 9th of October, 1779, with General Lincoln, made an unsuccessful effort to recover Savannah — had reëmbarked his troops and artillery, and retired from the coast with his fleet of twenty sail, to winter quarters, in the West Indies, Sir Henry Clinton seized upon this chance, in the absence of the French admiral, to besiege Charleston. To resist the British force, composed of a large fleet and body of veteran troops, General Lincoln, who commanded the Continental army of the South, could only rely upon fifteen hundred troops and a few armed vessels, together with such militia as were expected down from the country; the whole less than four thousand men.

Charleston lies on a neck of low land, or peninsula, formed by the junction of the Rivers Ashley and Cooper, whose confluence makes a harbor two miles in width and seven in length, south-east to the ocean. Ashley is twenty-one hundred yards, and Cooper fourteen hundred, wide, on the margin of the city, which, from shore to shore, is about three quarters of a mile, and extended in length, at

the time of the siege, a mile into the country. The Islands
of Sullivan and James bound the harbor on the sea side,
on the first of which was the celebrated Fort Moultrie,
on the last Fort Jackson, protecting the entrance.

To secure the conquest of this city, Sir Henry Clinton,
on the 11th of February, landed his troops about thirty
miles below Charleston, on John's Island, and, crossing
over, marched them up to Wappoo Creek, on James
Island, where he threw up an intrenchment, and deliberately prepared for the attack. In about a month, having
passed over the River Ashley to the neck, he there fortified
his camp, a mile from the American ramparts, and on
the 1st of April completed a parallel or line of batteries
within eleven hundred yards of the defence.

Nor was Charleston idle. The legislature, then in session, resolutely voted to resist the enemy ; and chose John
Rutledge, Esq., governor, — a man of distinguished talents
and energy. — who, with General Lincoln, **soon** put the
city in a defensive posture, so far as their **resources would
allow.** From the Ashley to **the Cooper, a line of redoubts**
was thrown up, with an *abatis*, **and a deep ditch in** front
of **the ramparts, with the intention of** sweeping, by their
artillery, **any force which should** be brought against it.
Every vulnerable point on the shores and around the city
was fortified by cannon and detachments of soldiers ; and
as a reënforcement was sent down from the adjacent
country and **uplands,** General Lincoln was soon **at the
head of nearly four thousand** troops — a number, however,
not sufficient to man the whole fortifications, and secure
every part exposed to the invasion of ten thousand veteran

soldiers. These fortifications are stated, in Marshall's Life of Washington, to have been three miles in extent. To defend them, therefore, against superior numbers, must have been a warfare exceedingly severe and hazardous, though it is said, that on the 10th of April they were strengthened by the arrival of seven hundred Continental troops, commanded by General Woodford, who had marched five hundred miles in twenty-eight days to the relief of Charleston.

While Sir Henry Clinton was conducting the land forces to Wappoo Creek, Vice Admiral Arbuthnot, with his fleet, viz., one ship of fifty guns, two of forty-four, four of thirty-two, and some transports and smaller vessels, lay at the mouth of the harbor, waiting the movement of Clinton, with the design of attacking the besieged by sea and land simultaneously. Fort Moultrie was then commanded by Colonel Pinckney, an intrepid officer, with a garrison of three hundred men.

It is not intended to enter into a detail of the siege, the particulars of which may be found in several histories. The writer only refers to what is connected with the naval operations.

In the mean time every effort possible was made to prevent the access of the British fleet to the city. A correspondence had taken place between General Lincoln and Commodore Whipple, as will appear by what follows.

To SAMUEL TUCKER, ESQ., *Commander of the Continental Frigate Boston.*

SIR : Having received orders from General Lincoln for two of the ships to proceed to sea for some days, and the others to remain in port till the return of the Providence and Ranger, unless the general should think proper to order you out, which would be very agreeable, — in the interim, shall desire that you will endeavor to keep peace and harmony among your officers and men, and obey the orders you may receive from time to time from the General or Captain Rathburne, as, on our return, it is more than probable you will be ordered out.

 Given under my hand, on board the Continental Frigate Providence, in the port of Charleston, South Carolina, this 20th day of January, 1780.

To SAMUEL TUCKER, ESQ., *Captain in the American Navy, and Commander of* **the Continental Frigate** *Boston.*

SIR : You are hereby ordered to unmoor your ship immediately (wind and weather permitting), and fall down into Rebellion Road, and there to anchor till further orders. It is expected that these orders will be complied with immediately.

 Given under my hand, on board the Frigate Providence, in the port of Charleston, this 29th day of January, 1780.

ABRAHAM WHIPPLE.

9

CHARLESTON, February 11, 1780.

SIR : You will please to send, this evening, a row-guard into the mouth of Wappoo Cut ; and on the approach of the enemy, you will fire three swivel guns at half minute's distance.

I am, dear sir, your most obedient servant,

B. LINCOLN.

CAPTAIN WHIPPLE.

SIR : The above is a copy of General Lincoln's letter, and you are hereby desired to send your boat immediately into the mouth of the Wappoo Cut, till the morning, when she may come away.   I have sent Mr. Swain, as a pilot, to show the officer, and on the morrow will station one of the galleys there.

I am, sir, your most humble servant,

ABRAHAM WHIPPLE.

CAPTAIN TUCKER.

Received this letter on the 13th inst. whilst }
   in bed, per hand of Mr. Baxter,   }

BOSTON FRIGATE, REBELLION ROAD, }
February 13, 1780.   }

DEAR SIR : I have to inform your honor of my arrival on board, and found no pilot for the purpose of your orders, and have sent on board the Queen of France, requesting her pilot; but he declines going ; therefore am obliged to trouble your honor for the assistance of a pilot. The bearer, Mr. Gardner, has his orders ; you will see them, if you please; make no doubt but he will answer the purpose designed.

I am your humble servant,

SAMUEL TUCKER.

[This copy had no direction, but it was probably to Commodore Whipple.]

To SAMUEL TUCKER *and* THOMAS SIMPSON, ESQS., *and Captains in the Navy of the United States.*

CHARLESTON, S. C., February, 13, 1780.

GENTLEMEN: In consequence of permission and orders from his Excellency John Rutledge, Esq., governor of this state, you are directed to immediately proceed, and without any loss of time destroy, level, and erase the beacon light-house, with all other ranges which may be of any use to the enemy in their attempts to enter this harbor. For your better information it will be necessary to take with you some experienced pilots of the harbor, who are well acquainted with all the ranges of this situation. As it will be proper to have this effected with as much secrecy as possible, I recommend and enjoin the same. The order from his Excellency, of which a copy is enclosed, permitting the destroying of all the ranges, it is left to your discretion the full completion and execution of so valuable a purpose. It admitting of no delay, I trust to your activity, and confiding in the same,

Am your very humble servant,

ABRAHAM WHIPPLE.

To SAMUEL TUCKER *and* THOMAS SIMPSON, ESQS., *Captains in the American Navy.*

CHARLESTON, February 15, 1780.

GENTLEMEN: In consequence of the orders from his Excellency Governor Rutledge, I have to direct that you immediately proceed, and by the most effectual ways and means possible, are to level, erase, and totally demolish the remains of Fort Johnson. As it may happen that a party of the enemy may attempt to surprise or attack you in the execution of these orders, you will communicate them to the commanding officers of marines on board the Providence, Boston, and Ranger, and give such directions as may be necessary for the landing of all their marines in good order, ready for immediate action, or to secure a retreat. The care of your men is an object of attention. You will reflect on the necessity of advanced guards to give timely notice, and use every caution consistent with a vigorous execution of this design.

ABRAHAM WHIPPLE.

HEADQUARTERS, }
CHARLESTON, February 26, 1780. }

SIR: I find, from some observations I made yesterday with respect to the frigates under your command anchoring near the bar, which from the representations made to me I did not expect. As the design of your being sent to this department was, if possible, to cover the bar of this harbor — a measure highly necessary — therefore an attempt to do it should be made, but on the fullest evidence of its practicability.

I have, therefore, to request that you will, as soon as may be, report to me the depth of water in the channel from the bar to what is called Five-fathom hole, and what distance that is from the bar; whether, in that distance, there is any place where your ships can anchor in a suitable depth of water. If any place, how far from the bar; whether there you can cover it, and whether at the station you can be annoyed by batteries from the shore; whether a battery can be thrown up by us so as to cover the ships and secure a retreat, if it should be necessary to bring off the garrison. If you cannot anchor so as to cover the bar, you will please give me your opinion where you can lie to secure this town from an attack by sea, and best answer the purposes of your being sent here, and the views of Congress, and the reasons for such an opinion. In this matter you will please to consult the captains of the several ships, and the pilots of the harbor. You will keep your present station, or one near thereto, until you report, unless an opportunity offer to act offensively against the enemy, or your own safety should make it necessary to remove; in either case you will judge.

I am, sir, your most obedient,

B. LINCOLN.

COMMODORE WHIPPLE.

ON BOARD THE BOSTON FRIGATE, }
FORT MOULTRIE, 27th February, 1780. }

DEAR SIR: Yours of yesterday we have received, and after having carefully considered and attended to the several requisitions therein contained, beg leave to return the following answer: —

'At low water there are eleven feet in the channel from the bar to Five-fathom hole. Five-fathom hole is three miles from the bar, where you'll have three fathoms at low water. Ships cannot be anchored until they are that distance from the bar. In the place where the ships can be anchored, the bar cannot be covered or annoyed; off the North Breaker Head, where the ships can be anchored to moor them, that they may swing in safety, they will lie within one mile and a half of the shore.

If any batteries are thrown up to act in conjunction with the ships, and the enemy's force should be so much superior as to cause a retreat to be necessary, it will be impossible for us to cover or take them off. Our opinion is, that the ships can do most effectual service for the defence and security of the town, to act in conjunction with Fort Moultrie, which, we think, will best answer the purpose of the ships being sent here, and consequently, if so, of the views of Congress.

Our reasons are, that the channel is so narrow between the fort and the middle ground, that they may be moored so as to rake the channel, and prevent the enemy's troops being landed to annoy the fort.

The enemy, we apprehend, may be prevented from sounding and buoying the bar by the brig General Lincoln, the state brig Notre Dame, and other small vessels that may be occasionally employed for that purpose.

We are, with respect,

    Your honor's most obedient, humble servants,

Signed by three captains and five pilots.

Here follows a copy of the pilot's certificate.

REBELLION ROAD, February, 1780.

SIR: Having considered General Lincoln's requisition to the 30th ult., viz., " Whether there is a possibility of the ships lying in such a manner as to command the passage of the bar of Charleston harbor, and leave their station, if it should become necessary."

After having sounded, tried, and made such observations as appear to us necessary, we do declare, upon due deliberation, that it is, in our opinion, impracticable. Our reasons are, that when an easterly wind is blowing, and the flood making in, — such an opportunity as the enemy must embrace for their purpose, — there will be so great a swell in Five-fathom hole as to render it impossible for a ship to ride, moored athwart, which will afford the enemy's ships, under full sail, the advantage of passing us ; should they effect that, the Continental ships cannot possibly get up to Fort Moultrie as soon as the enemy's.

COMMODORE WHIPPLE.

It will be perceived by this correspondence, that a question of great importance was submitted to Commodore Whipple by General Lincoln, " Whether there is a possibility of the ships lying in such a manner as to command the passage of Charleston harbor, and leave their station, if it should become necessary." Upon this matter a consultation was immediately held by the naval officers and pilots, and they gave their deliberate opinion, that it would be impracticable, especially at " Five-fathom hole," the place particularly designated, three miles below the bar, on account of the great swell in easterly winds, and because at low water it was too shallow for the ships to anchor there, and where they could anchor at a distance from that spot they could not annoy the enemy.

An essential service was rendered by Captain Tucker in the defence of the city. Governor Rutledge required of Commodore Whipple that the "Beacon Light-house," with the "Ranges," so called, should be immediately levelled and erased. His request was dated February 13. It was an undertaking of peril, to be executed with great secrecy and vigor, under the guns of the British fleet. Tucker was deputed to the task. With a chosen band he accomplished it, to the admiration of the governor, who thereupon wrote to General Lincoln the next day, —

DEAR SIR: I think Commodore Whipple's people, who were so dexterous in blowing up the light-house yesterday, would, by boats, very readily and effectually demolish the walls of Fort Johnson. If you think this a material service, I could wish you could be pleased to order it performed immediately; for, as Mr. Hutson told us, two loads of the enemy have landed on this island; a little delay might render this attempt impracticable. Give me leave to submit to your consideration the expediency of some artillery (if they can be spared), keeping the commanding ground near the fort, to prevent the enemy's doing so and annoying our navigation. A retreat might be secured. I am, dear sir, yours,

J. RUTLEDGE.

P. S. Mr. Lightwood just says that a man from

James Island confirms the account of the enemy's having sent over a party thither. Indeed, there is no doubt of it.

Commodore Whipple was requested to perform this hazardous work; and he issued his orders to Captain Tucker to select marines from the ships and execute it, which was done; and notwithstanding the difficulty and danger of the enterprise, Tucker accomplished the demolition of Fort Johnson.

The British ships, with favorable wind and flood tide, passed Fort Moultrie; but not without resistance, and the loss of two hundred and seventeen men, killed and wounded, Colonel Pinckney having kept up a brisk fire, damaging several vessels; at last, seeing he could not prevent their passage, he abandoned the fort. The fleet went up the bay, and anchored off the ruins of Fort Johnson. To prevent their ascending Cooper River, and enfilading the American lines, eleven vessels were sunk, and the Ranger and two galleys were stationed north of them. Mills, in his Statistics of South Carolina, observes that "Commodore Whipple considered it most prudent to transfer the crews and guns of all his vessels, except one, to the shore to reënforce the batteries." Colonel Pinckney also brought up his garrison to man the fortifications.

In the History of South Carolina, by William G. Simms, Esq., Chapter XV., there is a particular account of this siege, so disastrous to Charleston; and yet Commodore Whipple's name, and his squadron of four ships of war, are not even mentioned. I make no comment.

Mills, in his Statistics of South Carolina, speaks of the services of Commodore Whipple with respect; and his name is honorably mentioned in Marshall's Life of Washington, where he refers to the siege and loss of Charleston.

The besiegers were advancing in the outworks on the neck day by day. On the 20th of April they had completed a second parallel within three hundred yards of the American redoubts, and they summoned the city of Charleston to surrender. Distress and scarcity of food had now begun to prevail among the besieged population. Supplies from the country were cut off. All classes of citizens were put on allowance. Captain Tucker wrote home that six ounces of pork and a little rice were a soldier's daily ration. Several of the troops had been slain or wounded in sallies or skirmishes. The besieged were shut up by a vigilant enemy, and, in looking round, saw their soldiers daily lessening, while the force of the enemy was increased by two thousand regulars from New York. At last famine began to stare them in the face; there were not rations sufficient for another week. Yet they resisted the enemy and refused to surrender. One more struggle, one last battle, — the fiercest and most formidable during this invasion, — these brave defenders dared to attempt.

On the 12th of April a terrible cannonading of the British commenced along the lines of the American redoubts, which began to tremble; from twenty-one mortars numerous bombs were thrown into the city.

On the 11th of May the British troops were within twenty-five yards of the line of the besieged. For several days shells and hot shot had been thrown into the city, setting houses on fire in several quarters. At last a third parallel was finished, and again the city was summoned to surrender. For two or three days they had been exposed to a galling fire from the ships of war in the harbor, and from the batteries at Wappoo. Thirty houses had been burned to the ground; the intrenchments were shattered, the garrison weakened by losses, and the Carolina troops so exhausted and discouraged, that they retained hardly strength enough to make a firm stand against a general assault. Under these circumstances, on the said 11th of May General Lincoln capitulated on terms honorable and prudent.

The siege had lasted thirty days. The defenders were reduced to less than four thousand men, of which a large part was composed of raw troops; and they were opposed to an army of regulars of ten thousand soldiers, who were well supplied with artillery and the munitions of war, accompanied by skilful engineers, and backed up by a fleet to cannonade the fortifications. General Lincoln acquitted himself with honor.

It is worthy of remark that no small part of the heavy guns which bristled on the ramparts of the city was supplied from the squadron of Commodore Whipple, manned by his marines, and pointed under the eye of his officers; and on this Mr. Simms is silent, though these brave men would have been the last of the defenders to ask quarter.

The frigates Providence, Boston, Queen of France, and Ranger were never sunk in Cooper River to bar the entrance; they became part and parcel of the general spoil of the enemy. This will appear plainly from a copy of a petition found among Captain **Tucker's** papers, which bears date May 15, 1780, wherein Commodore Whipple and the other commanders of **these ships** pray his Excellency Mariot Árbuthnot, Vice-Admiral **of the** Blue, that they may be admitted to *parole*, " the Continental frigates in this department having been ceded by capitulation to the arms of his Britannic Majesty." These officers, who were prisoners of war on the surrender **of the city, were** therefore soon put on *parole*. It may be interesting **to** some readers, if not to all, to see the formula of a parole in the American Revolution. The following is a copy of the one Captain Tucker signed in Charleston, after the capitulation : —

I, the subscriber, **Samuel Tucker,** commander of the Continental ship of war Boston, do hereby acknowledge **myself** a prisoner **of war** to his majesty, **and** most solemnly and strictly bind myself **by all the full,** implicit, and extensive **faith** and meaning of a parole **of honor, which I** hereby **give his** Excellency Vice-Admiral Arbuthnot ; **and** I will **not, directly** or indirectly, either by word or deed, take **any further part in** the dispute **between** Great Britain **and** the British Colonies in North America until regularly exchanged for **an** officer of **equal rank** in **his** majesty's service.

SAMUEL TUCKER.

A true copy.

NICHOLAS BROWN.

May 20, 1780.

Amidst the horrors and sufferings of war, and more especially where the dread scenes of preparation, the confusion and alarm, and the pale and anxious visages of old men, women, and children, add gloomier shades to the picture of a besieged city, it is delightful to turn for a moment and contemplate deeds of generosity and kindness between any of the combatants. Many such instances bore witness to the humane and benevolent disposition which distinguished the life of this brave man. One occurred at an early stage of the invasion of Charleston.

There was a cartel ship lying in the stream, not far from his frigate, which was moored in " Rebellion Road," so called, below Fort Moultrie. In this vessel was a load of prisoners, some captives in battle ready for an exchange, and others refugees or tories who had been sentenced to exile, ladies and gentlemen, waiting a passage to England. While they were in this situation, an eastern storm arose ; and such was the violence of the wind and waves, that the ship was in great peril of foundering at her moorings, before the eyes of spectators on shore. Captain Tucker saw their dangerous situation, and exerted himself to relieve them ; but his efforts were vain ; he could give them no immediate help. In the following letter he expresses his sympathy, after their escape from destruction.

Boston Frigate,
February 24, 1780.

Ladies and Gentlemen : I received your melancholy manuscript by the hand of Mr. Devol, the gentleman who removed the flag, and am exceedingly sorry to hear of your situation, and could wish you, in your present distress, to be under my immediate command, where I should strive to convince the ladies and gentlemen of the principles of humanity, although we may be separated by the present contest. I think, with yourselves, that humane principles never ought to be eradicated. I assure you, both ladies and gentlemen, I sympathize with you. I have mentioned the matter to the commanding officer of the navy in this department. When I left the town on Tuesday last, had I known you had been just so situated, I should have come on board the Flag and relieved you, if possible. Gentlemen, I cannot describe my wishes toward you yesterday, when I beheld you in that distress, my boats having broke their mooring, all except the pinnace, which was on the booms, and the wind being so exceedingly high, I thought it impossible to send her to you in safety. I am exceedingly happy to send you some relief, while I remain, with sincerity,

Your friend, while it is in my power,

SAMUEL TUCKER.

To which the reply was this : —

ON BOARD THE CARTEL, }
24th of February, 1780. }

SIR : We received your favor by the hands of Mr. Devol. Your benevolent and generous attention calls forth our sincere acknowledgments. We acknowledge the receipt of other favors, can assure you that we shall ever have a grateful remembrance of them, and must

conclude with thanking you for your friendly assurance.
We remain, sir,

Your much obliged and very humble servants,

JOHN MORRIS,

For self and prisoners on board the cartel.

Perhaps the above incident, and the letters touching the
same, may seem of trifling import in the life of a naval
officer; for Mr. Morris and all the cartel prisoners have
long since passed away from the storms and sorrows of this
life, and are forgotten; but there is a world where the
deeds of the good Samaritan are remembered forever.

As the meritorious services of Commodore Whipple, in
some accounts of the siege of Charleston, have not been
appreciated, a recurrence to the foregoing facts may do
him justice, and prevent a misapprehension of the part
which he took in the defence.

In the Pictorial Field-Book of the Revolution, by
Benson J. Lossing, Esq., — a work written with much
ability, and generally with much candor, — are the following paragraphs (Vol. II. p. 764): "The little flotilla of
Commodore Whipple, then in the harbor, was ordered to
oppose the passage of the British fleet over the bar; but
his vessels were small and thinly manned, and little re-
liance could be placed upon them.

"Pinckney hoped that Whipple would retard the
British vessels, and allow him to batter them, as Moultrie
did four years before; but the commodore, with prudent
caution, retreated to the mouth of the Cooper River, and
sunk most of his own, and some merchant vessels, between

the town and Shute's Folly, and thus formed an effectual bar to the passage of the British vessels up to the channel to rake the American works upon the Neck."

In the first place, flotilla is defined to be a fleet of small vessels; and three of the ships under Commodore Whipple were frigates. The " little flotilla " mentioned in humiliating terms by this fascinating historian is very differently described by the enemy in March, 1780, who remarks, " The following rebel frigates blocked up in Charleston harbor, and must abide the fate of the garrison — Providence, thirty guns, Captain Whipple; Boston, thirty, Tucker; Queen of France, twenty, Rathburne; and Ranger, ten, Simpson."

Secondly. It has been stated, and proved already in the official correspondence, why the passage of the British fleet was not and could not be prevented by Commodore Whipple's squadron. A council of captains and pilots was summoned: they met in consultation, and made their report — that, from the shallowness of the channel, exposure to east winds and bad anchorage ground, the attempt would be impracticable. Governor Pinckney, if he made the remark, or " hoped that Whipple could retard the British fleet," among these treacherous sands, and exposed to the fury of the winds, must have forgotten that this spot was not Fort Moultrie, on a fast-anchored island. There is an inconsistency, too, in the statement; for if this squadron was indeed only " a little flotilla," the first broadside of a British seventy-four would have blown them all to pieces. Commodore Whipple was one of our first and bravest naval officers in the Revolution, one of the earliest commanders in **our** little intrepid navy, and, let me add, the one who fired the first gun on the water in defiance against haughty England. His reputation is dear to his country through all generations. He has left an imperishable character in her annals. If, on this occasion, " a prudent caution " prevailed in his measures, it was a noble, glorious caution — it was to prevent the heedless and wanton sacrifice of the brave men under his command.

A much more just and liberal view of this affair is exhibited in Marshall's Life of Washington (Vol. I. p. 332) : " On sounding within the bar, it was discovered that the water was too shallow for the frigates to act with any effect, and that in making the attempt they would be exposed to the fire of the battery, which the assailants had erected. Under these circumstances, the officers of the navy were unanimously of opinion that no successful opposition could be made at the bar, and that the fleet might move advantageously in concert with the fort **at Sullivan's** Island."

Again, Mr. Lossing is mistaken with regard to the fate of the four ships constituting the squadron commanded by Commodore **Whipple.** Not one of them was sunk in the **Cooper River ;** they fell, with the spoils of victory, into the hands of the British, as already stated. Commodore Whipple did all a patriot could do in defence of the city : when his ships were no longer useful, he sent ashore his guns to arm, and his marines to man, the redoubts.

If the animadversions of Pinckney were just, Captain Tucker must come in for his share of them. Yet at least his essential service in the demolition of the "Lighthouse," and "Fort Johnson," under the guns of the enemy, deserves some remembrance. He was the last to strike his flag, as the following anecdote will evince: When a special order from the admiral was sent to the commander of the frigate Boston, to strike his flag, Tucker replied, "I do not think much of striking my flag to your present force, for I have struck more of your flags than are now flying in this harbor."

CHAPTER VIII.

CRUISES AND CAPTURES IN THE THORN, UNTIL SHE WAS TAKEN BY THE HIND, AND TUCKER'S ESCAPE FROM ST. JOHN'S.

IMMEDIATELY after he had given his parole, he left Charleston, and hastened back to Boston, where he arrived on the 26th of June. Four of the best American frigates had been surrendered to the enemy in the capitulation; and even if he had been free, there was no armed ship then unemployed for him to command. He applied, however, for an exchange with Captain William Wardlow, whom he took prisoner when he captured his sloop of war, the Thorn, twelve months ago. This was effected, and, on being liberated, Captain Tucker obtained the command of that vessel. He was anxious to be in action, and again to cruise, as he remarked, against the enemies of his country. Whether this sloop of war was then fitted out by the Marine Board, or by individuals as a private armed ship, does not appear, although she went out next year in the latter capacity, as is manifest from the papers of the deceased.

Once more on the high seas, he was himself again, the starry flag waving over his head. The Thorn, a sloop of war, mounted sixteen, some said eighteen guns; her deck was to him a field of fame ; and with her he reaped a harvest of prizes, and fought several sanguinary battles, with equal and sometimes superior force. He often described them, in the most thrilling narratives, to his friends and neighbors, when he was dwelling in a cottage in the woods of Bremen, in the care of his glebe, his *pauca jugera*. Several of them have been perserved from oblivion ; one, in particular, comes from the reminiscences of an aged mariner, who died a few years since, who was with Captain Tucker, and took a part in the engagement he described. It was written down from his dictation, and may be relied upon as authentic, as the narrator was an industrious and religious citizen, much respected by his neighbors.

This aged marine, who enlisted under Tucker, in the Thorn, during her numerous cruises in 1780, and until she was captured in August, 1781, was Josiah Everett. Mr. Everett was in the army at Cambridge, and the regiment to which he belonged was stationed, by General Washington, on Dorchester Heights ; and after the evacuation of Boston, he was in the glorious battle of Saratoga, where General Burgoyne surrendered. At the close of the Revolutionary war, he emigrated to the District of Maine, and resided in Farmington, from which he finally removed to New Portland, where he cultivated a farm until his death — nearly twenty years ago. The author made inquiry about him, some time since, in a letter to the postmaster of New Portland, who gave him an excellent character as an industrious, upright man. The account he related of one of Tucker's cruises is as follows : —

He shipped, as a marine, on board the Thorn, in 1780. She was a new vessel, copper bottomed, and carried eighteen guns. Her crew was composed of eighty-one men and eighteen boys. She had been cruising about three weeks, when they fell in with the Lord Hyde, an English packet of twenty-two guns and one hundred men. Not long after she was discovered, the commodore called up his crew and said, " She means to fight us ; and if we go alongside like *men*, she is ours in thirty minutes ; but if we can't go as *men*, we have no business here." He then told them he wanted no cowards on deck, and requested those who were willing to fight to go down the starboard, and those who were unwilling, the larboard gangway. Every man and boy took the first, signifying his readiness to meet the enemy.

As Mr. Everett was passing by, the commodore asked him, —

" Are you willing to go alongside of her?"

" Yes, sir," was the reply.

In mentioning this conversation, however, Mr. Everett candidly confessed, " I did not tell him the truth, for I would rather have been in my father's cornfield."

After the commanders of these two vessels, as they drew near, had hailed each other in the customary way when ships meet at sea, the captain of the English packet cried out roughly, from the quarter deck, —

" Haul down your colors, or I'll sink you."

" Ay, ay, sir, directly," replied Tucker, calmly and complaisantly ; and he then ordered the helmsman to steer the Thorn right under the stern of the packet, luff up under her lee-quarters, and range alongside her. The order was promptly executed. The two vessels were laid side by side within pistol-shot of each other. While the Thorn was getting into position, the enemy fired a full broadside at her, which did but little damage. As soon as she was brought completely alongside her adversary, Tucker thundered out to his men to fire; and a tremendous discharge followed, and, as good aim had been taken, a dreadful carnage was seen in that ill-fated vessel. It was rapidly succeeded by a fresh volley of artillery, and in twenty-seven minutes a piercing cry was heard from the English vessel — " Quarters, for God's sake ! Our ship is sinking. Our men are dying of their wounds." To this heart-rending appeal Commodore Tucker exclaimed, " How can you expect quarters while that British flag is flying?" The sad answer came back, " Our halliards are shot away." " Then cut away your ensign-staff, or ye'll all be dead men." It was done immediately: down came the colors, the din of cannonading ceased, and only the groans of the wounded and dying were heard.

Fifteen men, with carpenters, surgeon, and their leader, were quickly on the deck of the prize. Thirty-four of her crew, with the captain, were either killed or wounded. Her decks were besmeared with blood, and in some places it stood in clotted masses to the tops of the sailors' slippers. The gloomy but needful work of amputating limbs and laying out the dead was commenced, and every effort was made to render the wounded prisoners as comfortable as possible.

The first question Commodore Tucker asked, as soon as his lieutenant had taken possession of the prize, was, " What damage is done in the action? " It was answered, " Thirty men were killed or wounded, and three shots hit between wind and water." He looked thoughtful, and being a man of very humane and tender feelings, he said to Mr. Everett and those around him, " Would to God I had never seen her! " Alas! how seldom do the benevolent feelings in warriors and men of blood rise above the pride of victory, and turn with disgust from the barbarous scenes of battle !

Such is the brief story of a bloody engagement. The particulars, if not the whole, would have been lost, if an intelligent listener had not committed to writing the relation by Mr. Everett. This is, perhaps, the battle referred to, in Felt's Annals of Salem, a work of much accuracy, written by an observer and preserver of facts. This is the paragraph : —

" 1781, June 7. S. Thorn, C. Samuel Tucker, occasionally mentioned as arriving in other ports, but more often as of Salem, had fought with a packet two gl. [two hours], and taken her. The prize had four killed, and fourteen wounded. Joseph Lynd, the lieutenant of the Thorn, died of wounds after he reached home." — Vol. II. p. 272.

There is no certainty, however, that this is the same prize described by Everett, as he mentions no date — a circumstance often noticed in men who keep no minutes : they are seldom precise in the time of any transaction.

Or it may have been the armed vessel referred to in

the Independent Ledger of April 16, 1781, wherein is this memorandum of news: " Yesterday, sevennight, arrived at Newbury the privateer ship Thorn, Captain Tucker, having captured a second prize, viz., a ship from Liverpool, bound to Charleston, mounting sixteen six-pounders; her cargo consists of wine, brandy, dry goods, &c."

The prize Lord Hyde, of which Mr. Everett gave an account, describing the engagement, arrived safe in port, he having been detailed as one of the detachment under the prize-master to take charge of her. He speaks of the prisoners as a " Christian crew," for they were steady and held prayer-meetings in the fore-steerage. What a comment is this humble, heart-touching incident on the horrors of war! In the mean time he remarked that the Thorn had captured another prize of sixteen guns, which was sent home. From the fruits of this cruise Mr. Everett observed that his share of the prize-money amounted to fifteen hundred dollars.

In the Pennsylvania Packet, a newspaper published in Philadelphia, 1776–1783, there is a notice of another armed vessel taken by Tucker: "March 27, 1781. Last Friday arrived at Searsport a packet from Jamaica, bound to London, captured by ship Thorn, Captain Tucker, who engaged her two glasses [hours], during which the packet had four men killed, and fourteen wounded. The Thorn had not a single man hurt." And same newspaper also notices the prize as a *second prize*, as stated in the Independent Ledger of April 16, 1781.

In the Boston Gazette of June 11, 1781, there is also a reference to captures made by the Thorn. " Since our last, the **Thorn**, Captain Tucker, has returned into Salem, after a cruise of ten days, to land his prisoners, having taken three prizes, viz., a sloop from St. Eustatia, bound to Halifax ; a letter of marque brig of fourteen guns, bound from Antigua for Quebec, laden with rum and molasses ; and has retaken a prize, being the snow taken by the Alliance above mentioned, with three hundred hogsheads of sugar, all which arrived in port."

The Thorn had been out of port on another cruise but a short time, when Commodore Tucker took a small prize, from which he ascertained that she was one of an English **fleet** under convoy, **bound to** Halifax. The convoy consisted of the Elizabeth, twenty guns, the brig Observer, sixteen, and the sloop of war Howe, of fourteen ; and there were two vessels under their protection with very valuable cargoes. With this information he determined, he said, to " make capital," and directly aimed to intercept them. He steered under full sail where he conjectured they were, and as they hove **in sight he** hoisted English colors, and boldly **sailed into the midst of** them. **Coming** up with the **heaviest armed ship, he** hailed her, **and inquired if** she were the Elizabeth from Antigua, bound **to** Halifax. **On** hearing **it** was so, he expressed his **joy.** He also hailed the Observer, and made friendly inquiries **of the** like kind ; and when questioned, he informed them **he was the** Thorn, taken from the rebels **a few weeks** ago, **now** from New York, and told them **the news, while** they were sailing on without suspicion, **trusting to his peaceable** appearance.

Stratagem in war has usually been **justified by historians,**

and has been resorted to in all ages. It certainly is more honorable than the low **cunning and intriguing** artifice too often the resort of aspiring politicians. **If it is right,** however, to deceive an **enemy in war, — which Jefferson defines as a state of society where each** nation tries to do **its adversary the most harm, —** then falsehood and decep-tion may seem a high accomplishment in a commanding officer — **but only in time of war.**

Having previously selected **thirty** of his **most reliable** men for boarding the Elizabeth, arranged his signals, **and** explained his plan of attack **to** them and the helmsman, Captain Tucker, by degrees and warily, placed the Thorn **in a narrow space** between **the** Elizabeth **and** the brig, **and then, as if by accident, run afoul of the Elizabeth's yards, and, pretending to find fault with the helmsman, ordered him to brace about, while he — who had his** les-**son —** only entangled the **vessels** more and **more, so that** they were now **in close contact.**

Seeing all was ready, **Tucker hauled down his English** colors, hoisted the American, **and then gave orders to** fire **a** broadside. Both vessels fired at **the same time. The** moment the terrible roar of artillery ceased, **the thirty picked men, of** whom Everett was one, followed **the lieutenant, and boarded her. In** this attempt **the** lieuten-**ant was shot, and Everett, who was next to him,** seeing him **fall, fired his boarding pistol at the assailant, and missing him, he threw his pistol at him. They soon got** possession **of the deck, drove the crew below, and hauled down the colors.**

The movements on board the brig **Observer indicated**

an immediate attack of the Thorn. But Tucker told them, in his thundering voice, he was ready if they were, and ordered his men to board her, when she sailed away.

The sloop of war Howe then ranged alongside the Thorn and fired, upon which Tucker exclaimed, "Captain Forson, if you fire another broadside I'll blow you out of the water." The captain of the sloop thought it prudent to be off. Mr. Everett remarked that the whole seemed the work of a moment. The Thorn had nine men killed and fourteen wounded, and it was said the enemy's loss was similar.

The Elizabeth and a large vessel laden with sugar, taken in a nine days' cruise, arrived safe in port. The prize-money amounted to about the same sum as the last cruise produced.

Such is the statement made by one of the marines concerning two battles on the sea in which he was present, in one case with an equal; in the other the vessel was superior in force to the Thorn.

The Independent Ledger of June 11, 1781, may have had reference to the last cruise, viz., "Thursday last arrived at Salem, from a cruise of about ten days, the ship Thorn, Captain Tucker, having captured four prizes, some of which arrived the preceding day; the others (Jamaica-men) he carried with him. One of the latter was a prize of the Alliance, which had been retaken by a British letter of marque ship of twenty guns, and then under convoy. Captain Tucker, by stratagem, boarded the ship, by which few lives were lost, and the prize recovered." This tends to confirm the narration of Mr. Everett.

A description of the engagement and capture of the Elizabeth was given by Captain Weston, an aged citizen of Bremen, to the author when he was on a visit there, which in some particulars varies from Mr. Everett's, and yet does not contradict it in any essential point. It may be compared to viewing an object from a different stand-point.

Captain Tucker, in the summer of 1781, went on board the Thorn, lying in Salem harbor, and wishing to remain at home the next cruise, proposed that Lieutenant Johnson should take the command, and go out in his place; but the crew were unwilling, and refused to sail in her unless Tucker went with them. He was obliged to consent, and they left Salem at dawn of day with a fair wind, and were not many days at sea before they retook an American vessel on her way to St. John's, which had been captured by Captain Glover, commander of an enemy's ship, the name forgotten by the narrator. From the crew of the vessel he was informed that the Elizabeth, of twenty guns and seventy-five men, with two smaller armed ships, were convoying the Jamaica fleet to Halifax. He shaped his course accordingly, pressed sail, and soon came up with her. Then he called his men together, told them his plan, — which was to get alongside and board her, — and put his brother William to the helm. Then he hoisted English colors, sailed up close to her, and hailed her. The English captain cried out, " You keep too close to me." The commodore then swore at his helmsman, and told him to luff—but meaning the contrary, as was understood. As soon as he got the Thorn in the position he wished, he hauled down the English and hoisted American colors, and each vessel fired a broadside. Tucker then grappled and boarded her. He headed his boarders, and sprung over the taffrail; and the English captain, Timothy Pine, aimed a blow at his head, which Tucker warded off, and broke his own sword in giving him a ghastly wound over his forehead. The crew were driven below, the halliards of the flag cut down, and the Elizabeth was taken. The English captain soon after died of his wound.

Some idea of his naval success, and of the value and variety of the exploits of Tucker during his frequent cruises in the Thorn may be got from the accounts current between him and his agents, William R. Lee & Co. In those of April and June, it appears he made five cruises — and it was so stated by Josiah Everett, above named — in this sloop of war, and each time was very successful. In one of the accounts credit is given for the sales of four prizes, viz., the Aurora, Success, Sincerity, and Biddy, and in another, those of the sloop Maria, the snow Fly, and the ship Elizabeth are specified. The number and names of a large part of his captures, the time when each prize was taken, and a description of the battles with armed vessels, were drawn up by the commodore himself, and had often been seen by Colonel Hinds, before the memorandum was lost. There was never a finer opportunity, if there be any truth or reality in the power of the *spirit rappers* to disclose the long-buried secrets of the past, —

for we live in an age of three millions, it is said, of believers in this supernatural power, — than the present to summon our naval hero before the tribunal of history, and get a plain, unvarnished statement of every particular. Let him who will dare make the experiment. We have no faith in such attempts.

The newspapers of that period in the Revolution have furnished numerous facts, and no small evidence, of his success and intrepidity ; but they give but a meagre account at the best, and we must rely, in some degree, on his conversations at sundry times with his friends, and on traditionary information. We learn from Captain Weston, — to whom reference has already been made,— that, in the sloop of war Thorn, of only eighteen guns, Commodore Tucker made, in all, *nine cruises;* that in the last one he took *nine prizes,* worth nine thousand dollars, and the last time was out at sea *nine days;* and that the sailors always called it the " *cruise of the nine.*" It is acknowledged in the " Remembrancer " of that year, that England lost an immense number of her merchantmen and armed vessels. This fact must have much weight in the scale of evidence.

After his return home from Charleston, it is probable that he spent some time with his family before an exchange was effected with Captain Wardlow, since the papers of that day do not speak of the arrival of his prizes before 1781. There is reason to suppose he got to sea towards the close of 1780, for in January following he obtained leave of absence, as these documents will show.

NAVY BOARD, EASTERN DEPARTMENT, }
BOSTON, January 20, 1781. }

Samuel Tucker, Esq., Captain in the American Navy, at his own request has leave of absence for six months to cruise against the enemy in private service.

WM. VERNON,
JNO. DISHON.

NAVY BOARD, EASTERN DEPARTMENT, }
BOSTON, May 23, 1781. }

Samuel Tucker, Esq., Commander in the Continental Navy, has leave of absence to go a cruise against the enemies of the United States.

WM. VERNON,
JNO. DISHON.

The Thorn was consequently engaged as a privateer, and fitted out on shares by a company ; for on the 19th of April, 1781, Elbridge Gerry, Esq., was interested in her, and wrote to Captain Tucker about disposing of some prizes — "as we have each of us *two thirtieths* of the Thorn." William R. Lee & Co., of Marblehead, were their general agents, as by his letter of January, 1781, will appear.

MARBLEHEAD, January 20, 1781.

CAPTAIN SAMUEL TUCKER.

SIR: The ship Thorn, under your command, being ready for sea, we desire you would embrace the present favorable wind and proceed upon your cruise. And we would recommend you to proceed to the southward and eastward of the Grand Bank, and cross the latitudes — where you will be in the train of vessels bound to and from Europe and the West Indies. But if you should not be so fortunate as to make any capture upon your excursion out, you will return by that route which promises most success, according as your own judgment or any vessels you may chance to speak may direct.

All the prizes which you may be so fortunate as to capture you will order to Newburyport, to the care of Captain Samuel Newhall ; and on your return from your cruise, you will proceed there with your ship, and deliver her to the said Captain Newhall.

You will give your prize-masters directions to hoist your signal off of Newburyport for a pilot, and will hoist it yourself for the same purpose when you arrive there with the Thorn.

All the letters, invoices, and public papers which you may find on board any prizes you may capture, pray forward by the prizes. You will strictly comply with all the orders contained in your commission. Relying on your experience, spirit, and discretion, we wish you the reward which those qualities deserve, and are,

Your friends and agents,

WILL. R. LEE & Co.

There is an ebb in the current of fortune, as well as in the deep. The neap tides often follow the highest flood of prosperity. Commodore Tucker set out on another cruise — reported to be his tenth — in his favorite Thorn, bringing to mind the old Roman adage of Ovid, —

Vastius insurgens decimæ ruit impetus undæ.

The tenth wave surged.

It was in the latter part of July that he sailed once more, and for the last time, with a propitious breeze, to the north-east, scouring the horizon with his spy-glass for some distant speck of a prize. Nor was it long before the British ship Hind, a heavy frigate, hove in sight; and the Thorn fell a sacrifice to her powerful foe. Whether there was a gun fired, or any resistance, there are now no means of knowing. She was captured near the mouth of the St. Lawrence, and the captain and crew, consisting of eighty-three men, among whom was Everett, were soon after landed at the Island of St. John's, now Prince Edward Island, to be conveyed to Halifax.

The Thorn, however, was recaptured afterwards by the French frigates Hermione and L'Astrea, as appears by a paragraph in the Independent Ledger of August 6, 1781. "Friday last arrived the privateer Thorn. . . . The Thorn lately sailed from this port, commanded by Captain Tucker, and had been captured by the British frigate Hind, five days previous to her falling in with the above frigates." The Boston Gazette of the same date also contains a similar notice, written evidently with some acerbity; for the editor remarks, that the Thorn was captured " by his *tyrannic* majesty's sloop of war," and then was recaptured " by his Most Christian majesty's frigates from Rhode Island."

After the prisoners were landed at the Island of ·St. John's, Commodore Tucker, with Dr. Ramsay and the officers of the Thorn, were furnished with an open boat for the purpose of being carried to Halifax. St. John's lies at the entrance of the St. Lawrence, the capital of which is Charlottestown. They left this place, and instead of coasting along the shore and steering directly for Halifax, to which they were sent, they laid their course across Massachusetts Bay, directly for Boston — a daring and adventurous experiment in an open boat; but Tucker knew that the sea is generally light and the weather serene in the month of August, and favored a safe return. They reached home safely ; and this bold enterprise is thus noticed in the Independent Ledger of August 17 : " Tuesday evening arrived in town Captain Samuel Tucker and Dr. Ramsay, late of the Thorn cruiser, having made their escape in an open boat from the Island of St. John's ; they profess to have been humanely used by Governor Patterson, of that island, and by Captain Young, of the British ship Hind, by whom they were captured, and acknowledged themselves under obligation to these gentlemen for their civilities."

A complimentary letter from Captain Young, which proved eventually of great service to Tucker, after his singular escapade in the boat, is here introduced.

To the **Commanders and Officers** *of his Majesty's Navy.*

HIND, CHARLOTTESTOWN, ST. JOHN'S, }
July 26, 1781. }

Captain Tucker, formerly commander of the Boston, American frigate, and commander of the Thorn, when she **was** taken by the Hind, having treated many prisoners of all ranks with such kindness and humanity as does him great honor, and entitles him to every good return that can **be shown him,** — I therefore recommend him **to** the attention and protection of every officer of the navy whom he may meet with, not doubting that they will be pleased to have an opportunity of returning to him that humanity and generosity which he has shown to many, and which he appears so well to deserve.

WILLIAM YOUNG,
Captain of the King's Ship Hind.

There is a mystery resting on his flight from St. John's; and it seems, from the correspondence **between him and** Sir Andrew Hammond, that there was something wrong. Among **his** papers is the **following,** labelled by Tucker himself, **thus:** " **My letter to Sir** Andrew Hammond, Halifax."

BOSTON, September 6, 1781.

SIR : Impressed **with a** proper sense of the very polite **and humane treatment** we experienced from Sir **William Young (commander of the** ship Hind), **and William Patterson, Esq., Governor, &c., of the Island of St.**

John's, and actuated by the strictest principles of honor, we beg leave to intrude upon your patience, while we clear up some matters that to you and many others may appear mysterious.

On July 7 we were unfortunately captured by the Hind, and carried into the above-named island ; and after having received every civility, we were indulged in the privilege of hiring a boat and proceeding to Halifax. Though nothing but a verbal promise was required from myself, I was, with the surgeon, determined to sail to Halifax. The boat we sailed in from St. John's proving leaky, and otherwise highly uncomfortable, we exchanged her at Chebucto, paying the promised price.

At Chebucto we hired another to prosecute our destined route, when, by superior strength of our first and second lieutenants, &c., we were forced to steer for Boston. Resistance was in vain, and remonstrance disregarded. We are happy in the assurance that this short narrative of facts will take from us the imputation of runaways, and that the very polite treatment which Mr. Cox, of the Hind, has experienced (and which his generosity will induce him to acknowledge), will convince mankind that we are capable of the warmest gratitude.

This was followed by a kind answer.

HALIFAX, 3d October, 1781.

SIR: I am directed by his Excellency Sir Andrew Hammond, Lieutenant-Governor of the Province, to acquaint you, that he is willing to think favorably of your not coming to Halifax from St. John's; but that he sees the conduct of your officers in a very different light. His Excellency, therefore, as well in consideration of Captain Young's testimony, as to your humane treatment of your prisoners, allows of your continuing at Boston on parole until exchanged for some officer of equal rank; but no person of that description has been sent in exchange, as you intimate in your letter. I am, sir,

Your most obedient, humble servant,

H. TRUMBULL,
Commissary for Naval Officers.

CAPTAIN TUCKER.

Thus ended this unpleasant affair. In due season he was exchanged, and his parole redeemed.

CHAPTER IX.

His Domestic Life in Boston and Marblehead. —
Misfortunes and Petition to Government for a
Command of one of the new Revenue Cutters.

HAVING been so successful in his cruises, and taken many valuable prizes, Tucker had become rich ; and he removed his family to Boston. The precise time when this occurred is uncertain; but from a letter he wrote to William R. Lee, dated at Charleston, S. C., January 20, 1780, it must have been in that year; for he remarks, "Be so kind as to assist Mrs. Tucker in removing, should she request it."

He occupied a house in Fleet Street, which his grandson, Colonel Hinds, said he purchased. It was a three-story brick building, with a cupola and front yard. In the Revolution, Fleet Street was the fashionable part of the town, and there was much commercial business carried on at the North End. Near the house, on the opposite side, was a large and spacious mansion, where several navy officers lodged. Not far from its western window stood Governor Hutchinson's handsome domicile, with a garden full of fruit trees. The late Captain John Pedrick, of Boston, knew the commodore well, and described his house with minuteness, and his style of living, which he deemed extravagant.

Colonel Hinds also informed the writer, that his mother resided at that time with her father in Fleet Street, and he often heard her relate, that, sitting at the western window of the parlor, she frequently listened to the preaching of the Rev. John Murray, in his church in Hanover Street, as there was no building at the corner to intercept the sound of his voice. Tucker's house has long since disappeared; new buildings have been erected where it stood, and Fleet Street widened.

As he was thought affluent, he associated with the first families in Boston; for riches then, as now, opened the doors of hospitality, and have always had a paramount influence in this place. He was genial, popular, and, indeed, too generous for his own good. His personal appearance was striking; he was in the mid-day of life, of more than average height, bright complexion, fine features, with deep blue eyes, which, when animated, seemed to grow dark. He wore the brilliant dress of a naval commander — a blue coat with lapels, scarlet vest, and dark-blue small clothes. Such was Commodore Tucker, almost ninety years ago, as he was described by his aged friend, Captain Pedrick, who has since followed the ocean warrior to the grave.

A similar account of him, when he resided in Boston, was given some years since by an intelligent old lady, who was born there, May 1, 1755, — Mrs. Elizabeth Perkins, a niece of the late eminent Samuel Adams. She was christened by the Rev. Dr. Byles, of such eccentric wit;

her first husband was the Rev. John Hunter, chaplain of
the frigate Queen of France, and her sister was married
to Benjamin Brown, M. D., surgeon in the frigate Boston,
when commanded by Tucker. This lady, of such honored
connections, was residing, when the writer saw her, in
East Boston, and was ninety-five years old. Her hearing
and her sight were remarkably good, and for sixty or
seventy years she had drank one cup of strong coffee, that
" *slow* poison," every morning. This fine, cheerful old
lady knew the commodore, and was enthusiastic in his
praise. He kept open doors, was hospitable, exceedingly
fond of company, ever in gladsome spirits, and ready to
make others happy. " He was a goodly man," she said,
" to look upon, so handsome, so animated. Often have I
danced with him in the minuet, which was a fashionable
accomplishment in those days, and he was so light of foot
on the floor! We girls were always after him for a
partner. But he lived too generously. Government owed
him a great deal of money, and treated him shamefully.
At last he lost his property, and after six years, moved
back to Marblehead. He was a noble-hearted man."

Such was the picture drawn by this venerable woman,
of one who filled no small space in her memory, when
she was in the bloom of girlhood. Mrs. Perkins was then
taking care of a sick daughter, and as our conversation
led to the spirit world, to which she has since gone, she
spoke so humbly, so meekly, and with such fervent faith,
resigning all her hopes in a Savior's love, that it left a
strong conviction that her cheerful frame of spirits, fondness for lively company, and that elegant and innocent

accomplishment, dancing, had made her old age serene and happy, and her powers of conversation a delight to all who knew her. She died at Boston, in 1853, aged 99. Funeral services were held at Christ Church, Salem Street.

Such are the gleanings of his domestic life in the fields of old reminiscences. It was like gathering leaves in the cave of Sibyl, — *rapidis ludibria ventis*, the sport of the winds of age, — or like drawing testimony touching some ancient landmark of an ancestral domain from the hoary witnesses of another generation.

After his return from captivity, in August, there is no evidence that he took the command of any armed vessel. It was his wish to resign his office, but he was not dismissed from service. His last public act was calling a court of inquiry in 1784, on the conduct of Seth Harding, Esq., for the loss of the Confederacy, and that duty was performed faithfully.

He lived in Boston about six years, in all the style and luxury of fortune; but he never knew the value of money, nor prudence in the use of it. He became reduced in circumstances, and found his resources, great as they had been, wasting away. It was not so much from extravagance, as from the careless way in which he lent sums of money to needy borrowers. How many instances of this kind occurred we have no means of knowing; but one stands out in bold relief, — a gross act of credulity on his part, — which was followed by years of suffering.

He had a friend, Major D. C., who had served in the army, afterwards entered into trade, became unfortunate, and finally was on the verge of bankruptcy.

To relieve this man Commodore **Tucker, contrary to the
remonstrance of his wife, and without consulting his
friends, lent him, on the** 23d **of November,** 1785, — **the
particulars are among his papers, — eighteen certificates of
United States scrip, of one thousand dollars each, and two
hundred dollars in cash, making eighteen thousand two
hundred dollars, though** Major **C. only asked a loan
of ·five thousand dollars. The debt was to have been
paid in a week, but the time of payment never came.
Mrs. Tucker warned him, and urged him to forbear, but,
said the generous commodore, "Can I not trust an old
soldier and a friend? What is this world coming to?"
Alas! the "old soldier" proved recreant; "the friend"
absconded, and years after years passed away before this
ungrateful man was discovered. But I will not anticipate;
we shall hear from him again at a future day.**

**Tucker applied to Congress for "arrears of pay on
account of services rendered his country," but without
success. His account had been adjusted by** Benjamin
Walker, Esq., **a commissioner and auditor for the** Marine
Committee, **up to August** 5, 1780, **before whom he attended in New York,** 1787. **The balance for about four years
was then left unsettled, and has never been paid, notwithstanding his urgent applications to government. At last
he was told, after many years had elapsed, that his claim
was not presented in season, and was barred by a resolve
in the nature of the statute of limitations. If such were
the fact, however salutary this law may be between citizen and citizen as a remedy against fraud, and that there
may be** *finis litium,* — **an end of suits, — yet no honest man**

ever took advantage of such a shield to ward off just debts, and no Congress nor parliamentary body, whose omnipotence is proverbial, should ever resort to such an infamous subterfuge to wrong a private citizen, and much more a faithful navy officer. Republics are said to be ungrateful, but they ought not to be dishonest. Even late as it is, — though more than ninety years have passed since the debt accrued, — yet if arrears are due to a public servant, beyond doubt, and uncontroverted, the voice of all mankind will echo this opinion, that Congress is bound in honor and good faith to do justice to his memory by providing for payment of the debt to his heirs. The petition he drew up contains a compendious summary of his naval pursuits and battles, and particularly refers to the vote of thanks passed by Congress, and presented to him by the committee in 1787.

The name of the member of Congress who presented the petition, and the session in which it was offered, do not appear in the copy. In it he speaks of his calling a court of inquiry upon the conduct of Seth Harding, Esq., on the recent loss of the frigate Confederacy, thirty-two, under his command. This ship of war was called "The Unlucky." She was launched in 1778; and, June 22, 1781, sent by government to Cape François. On her return was pursued by two English frigates, and one of them getting alongside of her while the other was very near, she struck her colors. The decision of the court is not stated in that paper.

The noble spirit of Tucker could not brook to run in debt, or live dependent on his friends. He saw no hope that the arrears of several thousands of dollars due him by government would be paid, at least for a long time, if ever. It appears that he resorted again to the sea, for in the Advertiser of Boston, published June 21, 1783, is the following notice: " Ship for London. The good ship Savanna, Samuel Tucker, Esq., commander; about three hundred and twenty tons, and in every respect accommodated for passengers, will sail in about twelve days." And in his letter to Mr. Adams, November 10, 1790, he refers in a note to seeing him in London.

In September, 1783, he commanded the merchant ship Sanana, from Portsmouth to London; and January, 1784, he had charge of the Caroline, between Baltimore and London; and July, 1784, he was master of the ship Cato. The last proved an unfortunate craft to him; for, in November of the same year, he sailed in her from the port of Aucaxes, Hispaniola, with a cargo of sugar, coffee, and molasses, bound to Virginia; and on the 25th of December it began to blow, and the gale increased in violence, until the 10th of January, when they lost their rudder from a heavy stroke of the sea. The ship became unmanageable, and leaked to such a degree, and took in so much water, that they could not work the pumps, and were fearful of foundering. On the 15th, they saw and hailed the ship Henrietta, Captain Wickes, from Maryland to Lisbon, who took them off in latitude 34° 37', longitude 62° 34', and conveyed them to Lisbon. The next morning the Cato had disappeared, having, in her waterlogged condition, probably sunk. Captain Tucker, on his return home, resolved to leave Boston.

This change, there is reason to believe, took place in 1786, for there is on record a deed of warranty from John Gardner, of ——, to Samuel Tucker, of Boston, Esq., dated August 28, 1786, wherein he conveys to him "two thirds of two grist-mills, and two thirds of a grainery, situated between Marblehead and Salem." He removed to Marblehead with his family, consisting of his wife, three children, and his mother. The children were Mary, Martha, and Samuel, the survivors of five; their first son Samuel having died September 5, 1776, and their daughter Betsey December 8, 1781. On this spot he resided six years. The contrast between the gay and joyous scenes in his handsome house in Boston, and this humble habitation in solitude, near a lonely mill and little mill-pond in Marblehead, must have been severe and trying in this day of his adversity.

His success in a grist-mill and granary, best known by the name of "Gatchell's Mills," could not have been very flattering. Tending a mill, whether in person or by proxy, was not a kind of business congenial to the taste of a naval hero. To doff the dazzling uniform of a commodore and don the white, ghost-like frock of a miller, to guide the water-power over the wheels instead of ploughing the great tides of the ocean, where he had so often gained victory and wealth, and to undergo the drudgery of keeping his hopper full, and filling sack after sack, ready for the horses and asses at his door, must have been humiliating beyond all common sorrow. It did not last long. The generous man gave away to the poor more than half the toll which all his grinding produced.

Perhaps, during his residence at the mills in Marblehead, he might have resorted to his old vocation of shipmaster, and left the grinding of corn to some sub-agent, while he reaped a better harvest in the ocean; but if so, there is no account of it transmitted among his papers. His circumstances, from loans and losses, had become straitened. When the Cato foundered at sea he was a great pecuniary sufferer. He was interested in the building of that ship at Portsmouth, and when he took command of her, he was owner of one half of her and her cargo. His loss was twenty thousand dollars.

Under these circumstances, he made an application for a command of one of the Federal cutters, ordered to be built for the service of the United States, as will be seen by the correspondence which follows — showing, in this world of change, that merit is not always rewarded, nor worth appreciated by men of power.

BOSTON, 1st of October, 1790.

SIR: Understanding there are to be built a number of Federal cutters, for the service of the United States, I humbly offer myself a candidate to serve in one, if your Excellency thinks me worthy. I served through the whole of the late war, without any kind of impeachment whatsoever, as captain. If you please, inquire my character, and afterwards, if your Excellency thinks me worthy to command, I shall be ever happy to serve. And I am, sir, with profound respect,

Your most obedient, very humble servant,

SAMUEL TUCKER.

TO THE PRESIDENT OF AMERICA.

BOSTON, 1st of October, 1790.

SIR : Understanding there are to be built a number of Federal cutters, I therefore humbly offer myself as a candidate for the command of one; and take the liberty of asking your influence with the President, not doubtful you will be pleased to favor me, if you think me deserving. I am, with sincerity,

Your most obedient, humble servant,

SAMUEL TUCKER.

To THE HONORABLE JOHN ADAMS,
Vice-President of America.

MARBLEHEAD, 4th October, 1790.

SIR : After your very favorable advice on the 1st instant, I wrote a few lines to the President, and likewise to the Vice-President, and gave them to your lady for your perusal, praying your goodness in directing them. Should there be any deficiency, be pleased to acquaint me by the bearer, and if necessary, of my seeing you before your return to York. I shall take care to be in Boston on your returning from your eastern journey. The President may have forgot, but the Vice-President cannot, by means of our passage to France. The commission I wore in the service of my country the last war bears date January 20, 1776, was received from the President in Cambridge, and another from Congress bearing date from the 15th of March, 1777; both of which I served under without the least impeachment whatsoever. In mentioning these,

with presenting the letters, shall be gratefully acknowledged, by, sir,

   Your Honor's most obedient, very humble servant,

SAMUEL TUCKER.

GENERAL KNOX, *Secretary of the*
   War Department of the United States.

MARBLEHEAD, 10th November, 1790.

SIR: On the 1st of October I happened in Boston, and
with pleasure was made acquainted with General Knox,
and with the general, had some conversation respecting
the building of those ten Federal cutters. He desired me
to write, and give him a line to the President. I immediately obeyed his desire, and also wrote a line to the
Vice-President, asking his influence with the President in
procuring me the command of one of those cutters, hoping
my request will not be deemed imprudence; as from an
early dawn of the American contest, until the close of the
Revolution, I served my country without any kind of impeachment, and since peace took place have been truly
unfortunate; and all this period such a command would
afford me a comfortable living in addition to the small
interest I possess. Your assistance in this request shall
be gratefully acknowledged by, sir,

   Your most obedient and very humble servant,

SAMUEL TUCKER.

N. B. The copy of the journal you mentioned to me,
when I had the pleasure of seeing you in London, was
prepared immediately on my arrival; but not knowing

whether **necessary or not to** forward them, the abstract
remains with me.

S. Tucker.

To the Honorable John Adams,
Vice-President of Congress.

Marblehead, 10th November, 1790.

Sir : I yesterday waited on the Honorable Elbridge
Gerry, who **gave me to** understand that you were the
gentleman appointed to nominate the officers for the
Federal cutters, and likewise desired me to transmit to
you a number of documents which he read, for your
perusal, or otherwise to come on to York. It not being
in my power, for various reasons, at present, I think proper
to enclose five, If you please, give yourself the trouble
to read them ; the originals, and a great number of
others to the same purpose, I have in possession.

At the dawn of the American contest, I received a commission from the President, in Cambridge, bearing date on
the 20th of January, 1776, as **a captain in** the marine
service, with which I served **until** the vessel was no longer
fit **for use ; and on** the **15th of** March, 1777, I received
another from **Congress in** Philadelphia, with which I
served on board the Boston **until** the reduction of Charleston, when **I was** made **a** prisoner to Vice-Admiral
Arbuthnot ; when liberated I came to Boston, and made
application for an exchange for Captain William Wardlow **of the** king's **ship** Thorn, which I **captured twelve**
months **before.** When my exchange **was completed,** and
no **other public** ship to serve **on board, I grew** uneasy,

12

being inactive. I applied to the Navy Board, told my
story, and asked leave of absence to cruise in a private
ship against the enemies of my country.

On my application, they refused me. But on my telling them the consequences, I obtained it, and went through
the remainder of the war, in that time of life with equal
success to that in a public ship, and always took care to
attend the Navy Board on my arriving and leaving them.
I would not wish to trouble you too much with a long letter,
but must say that my claim to any public service in the
marine department is before any man's in the State; and
if credentials would prove it, I could procure a letter from
every gentleman of character in our vicinity. I happened
in Boston the 1st of October, when I was informed of the
building of those cutters, the first day of my hearing anything of the matter. Also, I was informed by Major
Phelon, a land officer, that his Excellency the Governor
and General Lincoln had written in favor of Captain John
Foster Williams. I immediately attended the general in
his office, where I was very politely received, and after
addressing myself very cordially, asked the general why
he omitted me in the letter he wrote for candidates, my
being only at the distance of fourteen miles from Boston,
why he could have forgotten me? He told me there was
only one cutter for this State, and there were more than
one hundred applicants for her. I answered him, if there
were a thousand, mine was the only just claim, because I
served the public through the whole of the last war, without the least impeachment whatsoever, and should think
it very hard treatment for a private State officer to super-

sede me in any public command where honor was to be gained.

I wrote the President a few lines, and likewise the Vice-President, which General Knox did me the honor to be the bearer of, as I am informed no appointments are to be made until the next session of Congress, which will be in December 1st, ensuing. On the reception of these, if you please, inquire of my character of whom you may think proper, not omitting the Vice-President, Mr. Lee, or Mr. Gerry; and if you should be pleased to nominate me, pray let it be for this State, and your favor will be gratefully acknowledged, by, sir,

Your most obedient, very humble servant,

SAMUEL TUCKER.

N. B. Should you choose to give a line in answer, pray direct it to me at Marblehead.

ALEXANDER HAMILTON, ESQ.,
 Secretary of the Treasury of the United States.

TREASURY DEPARTMENT, December 4, 1790.

SIR: Your letter of the 10th ultimo has been received. The President of the United States having made the appointment of the commander of the cutter to be built in the State of Massachusetts, prior to your application, and your name not having been brought forward to him, either by your friends or yourself, it was too late for this vessel. Should any other boat be stationed on your coasts, and should your name be submitted to the President, he will duly compare your merits with those of any other candidates that shall be then **before him, and will decide, no** doubt, as justice and the public interest **shall require.**

   I am, sir, your most obedient **servant,**

      ALEXANDER HAMILTON.

CAPTAIN SAMUEL **TUCKER,** *Marblehead.*

     MARBLEHEAD, **30th December,** 1790.

 SIR: Yours of the 4th instant came safe **to** hand, whereby you inform me of the appointment being **made** by the President of the commander of the cutter built in Massachusetts State, prior to my application by General Knox of the 1st of October, **or** by those of the post. **I** was confident the former **would have been** presented the **President, and** likewise the **Vice-President, before any appointments** could have **been** made, because, from **the** information I had respecting the appointment of officers, they were to have taken place at this session, which is only thirty days past. Possibly **my letters which General** Knox did me the honor to be the **bearer of may have** been displaced before they reached **the seat of government;** if so, I am sorry, as my whole dependence **was in** that **early** opportunity.

 I do not understand by your letter to whom the command **has devolved,** but am sure the superior wisdom **of the** President **has made a just** decision. You **mention, should** my name be **submitted to** the President in season for **any** other maritime **command, that** he will compare my **merit** with that of other candidates **that shall** be laid before him. **I** must beg the favor **of your mentioning my name, and I**

shall also submit myself to the President by this post for the command of a cutter, and wish it may be obtained. My proceedings in every cruise in public service were duly committed to Congress on my arrival; which proceedings lay in the commissioner's office, and the originals or journals I have by me; and what is most, I have never received the least censure from the beginning of the contest until the end of the Revolution, and subscribe myself

Your most obedient, and very humble servant,

SAMUEL TUCKER.

ALEXANDER HAMILTON, ESQ.,
Secretary of the United States Treasury.

The request to be appointed commander of one of the Federal cutters was no more successful than his urgent appeal to Congress to discharge the arrears due him. Although he was one of the oldest surviving officers of the Continental navy, ever faithful and prompt to elevate the flag of his country, yet a more fortunate and less deserving aspirant for this humble office was patronized.

General Hamilton writes him, that there were prior applicants, and "*it was too late*"—words everywhere and at all times of fearful meaning: his name was not even brought forward. He replies with spirit and feeling to the Secretary, that he had a just claim for a berth of this kind on account of his long and faithful services in the war. But it is too plain he had no warm friend at court to whisper in the ear of power his merit and his misfortunes. The illustrious Secretary seems to have been an utter stranger to his services and exploits, and the office was in his gift. Could it be possible that the President of the United States could have forgotten him, when his petition for this small boon was made? No, never! General Washington never forgot a single brave officer in the navy which he originated, nor in the army which he led to victory. There must have been some mystery we know not of.

"*It was too late.*" Perhaps so. Yet it seems hard, and even a cruel circumstance, that an officer — is it too much to say, a naval hero? — who had served seven years in faithful duty, who had fought many battles on the ocean with extraordinary success, a pioneer who taught England what our navy would one day be, a man without reproach and without fear, a captain who had never been impeached by any court nor rebuked by any higher power, and who at the end of the war received the thanks of Congress for his valor and services, that such a man, when poor and needy, with a wife and children, should ask the gift of a small office, and be told "*it is too late,*" and then turned off with a needless and frozen promise that he should have the next vacancy if found worthy. When, in the last war with England, he took the armed sloop Crown, with a few raw volunteers, Commodore Tucker, old as he was, taught this great nation "*it is never too late*" to defend our country when attacked by the enemy!

On the 27th of March, 1794, six frigates were ordered by Congress to be built immediately. The Constitution, President, and United States, each of forty-four guns, and the Chesapeake, Constellation, and Congress, of thirty-eight, were soon added to our navy. In selecting commanders for these new ships when finished, regard, we are told, was had to the surviving naval captains of the Revolution, and especially those who had distinguished themselves. But what was the fact? John Barry, Samuel Nicholson, and Joshua Barney, were justly and deservedly commissioned. But what claim, under this rule, had Silas Talbot, a captain who never commanded a ship of war in the Revolution; or Richard Dale, only a lieutenant under Commodore Jones; or Thomas Truxton, merely the commander of a privateer, though all gallant and excellent men, to so exalted a rank, while Commodore Tucker, then not fifty years of age, a most skilful and successful officer through all the seven years' war, was omitted, passed by, and left to the cold chills of neglect?

There is among his papers the copy of a letter dated in December, 1806, which he wrote to the Honorable John Dawson, member of Congress from Virginia, on this subject, wherein he speaks of the Constitution, Constellation, and other new frigates ordered to be built, but in no one of which was any offer of command made to him. And he mournfully remarks, that " it was reported that Tucker was dead and buried five years ago. President Adams, at Quincy, told me he had heard the same report."

CHAPTER X.

Commodore Tucker's Removal to Bristol. — Its Early History. — Pemaquid Fort. — His Domestic Life on the Farm.

THE dark day of adversity was now coming upon this veteran naval officer. He found too sadly that the water-wheel of a mill was not the wheel of fortune. What could he do to support a family? Did he succumb to tears and murmurs against divine Providence, or complain against his country? No. He looked to the resources within him — the vigorous and independent efforts of his own mind. He bade adieu to the metropolis, to the seaport of his nativity, and to the fond associates of his better days, and plunged into the wilderness. There, with his own hands he cultivated the earth, and earned his bread by the sweat of his brow. Though lonely and forgotten by the magnates of the land, he never forgot his country.

He sold his interest in the Gatchell Mills, and August 4, 1792, purchased a farm in Bristol, Maine, of Daniel McCurdy. The deed specified two hundred acres, with a house and barn on the premises. The building was of one story, containing a kitchen, bed-room, and unfinished chamber in the garret. It was constructed of three-inch plank, tree-nailed into the frame, and finished in the cheapest manner — a sad contrast to the handsome mansion adorned with a cupola, which he once owned in Fleet Street. In this humble and incommodious habitation he resided with his wife, aged mother, and widowed daughter, Mrs. Hinds, and her son, until, in 1820, he was enabled, by his pension, to build another on the same spot, more convenient and suitable to his rank. It stood on a rise of ground in view of Muscongus Pond, and of two or three dwellings in the distance, and within a mile of Muscongus harbor beneath the hills.

The town of Bristol, where he selected his last residence, from its early history and the celebrity of the Pemaquid Fort before the Revolution, will justify a more than ordinary notice in a biographical sketch of this kind.

Bristol, one of the oldest settlements in Maine, was not incorporated till 1765. From Pemaquid Point it extended north about twenty miles, with an average width of five or six, and lies between Muscongus and Damariscotta Rivers. Blessed by nature with much fertile soil and several good harbors, it began to flourish at an early period, especially in the fisheries, and it became a favorite resort for men engaged in that occupation. The first inhabitants were a hardy and industrious race; but their ignorance and immorality for a long time hung like a dark cloud over the prospects of this place, until an emigration of Scotch-Irish, and some Germans, introduced agriculture, public schools, and a regard for religious instruction among them. Their descendants erected three churches; one in the Walpole district on the

Damariscotta River, one at Broad Cove, and the third at the head of Pemaquid harbor.

In 1773, Rev. Alexander M'Lean, a Scotch Presbyterian, was settled as their minister, and officiated alternately in one of these houses of worship each Sunday. He was a man of education, conversant with Greek and Hebrew, tall in stature, and stern in features; he had a loud and energetic voice, which, uttered in all the breadth of the broad Scotch brogue, gave to his doctrines a peculiarly dark and terrible import, as though he was armed with the thunders of Heaven. In repressing vice he was bold, though sometimes not very dainty in his denunciations. It is said that once, in rebuking a peculiar style of court- ship, somewhat prevalent in those days in Bristol, as well as at Cape Cod, he caused such a stir of handkerchiefs and blushes among his fair parishioners, that the female part of his audience rushed out of church. He was a good man, a self-denying and worthy Christian.

This town has now seven churches, and contains about three thousand inhabitants. Their first representative to the General Court of Massachusetts was William Jones, and one of the last, before the separation of Maine, was Commodore Tucker.

Bristol, however, is remarkable as the locality where one of the earliest permanent settlements in New England commenced in Pemaquid, its southern extremity. It is watered by four rivers; two interior, the Pemaquid and Johns Rivers, and two on the eastern and western sides, the Muscongus and Damariscotta; and has also five harbors, the Muscongus, Round Pond, New Harbor, Pemaquid, and Christmas Cove.

Pemaquid Point — from *Pemaquida*, the Indian for long point — and the Island of Monhegan, east of it, were first noticed by that bold adventurer, Bartholomew Gosnold, in 1602. Martin Ring followed him next year, and in 1605 Captain Weymouth coasted along the shores of Sagadahock, and visited the Kennebec, Sheepscot, and Damariscotta Rivers. His commercial report, in which he spoke of trade in fish, furs, and timber, was so favorable, that Chief Justice Popham, of England, in 1607, fitted out an expedition for a plantation at Pemaquid; but on arriving there, his brother Captain Popham found the natives shy and unfriendly, probably from some of them having been kidnapped and carried off by Weymouth; and he abandoned that project, and sailed along the coast of Sagadahock, until he came to the River Kennebec, at the mouth of which he selected a spot, now called Hunnewell's Point, lying on the western shore, for a settlement. This was in August, 1607. This Sagadahock colony erected a stockade fort, some houses, and a magazine for their stores, and spent the **winter** of 1607–8 there; during which they built a vessel, **called** the Virginia. In the mean **time Captain Popham** died, and also his brother the **Chief Justice** in **England.** They became discouraged, gave up the enterprise, and in the spring returned home.

In April, **1614,** the chivalric Captain John Smith **visited** these shores, and **has** left us a glowing description **of his** voyage along **the** coast. As he approached **the main, he landed** at the Island of Monhegan, **and remarks,** " Our plot was there to catch whales, . . . **and we found** the whale fishery a costly conclusion; we saw many, and spent much time in chasing them, but could not kill any." He then speaks of Pemaquid, Sagadahock, and Kennebec, thus: "I saw nothing but great high cliffs of barren rocks, overgrown with wood; but where the salvages dwell, there the ground is excellent, salt, and fertile." And of the sea-coast he observes, " Such high, craggy, clifty peaks, and stony isles, that I wonder such great trees could grow upon such hard foundations."

Adventurers resorted to Pemaquid not long after its discovery, and for several years it was a station for trade in fish and furs. The fishermen frequented its fine harbors, and spread their flakes on the shores; and in 1620 there were said to be several houses in that locality; but the most certain account is, that John Pierce, of London, in 1622–3, under a charter of the Plymouth Council, occupied it permanently. In the summer of 1625, John Brown, of New Harbor, purchased these premises with other adjacent lands of John Somerset or *Samoset*, Sachem of Pemaquid, by deed dated June 15, 1625, for fifty skins of beaver. There was also a patent granted by the Plymouth Company to Robert Aldsworth and Giles Elbridge, in 1631, of a tract which included Pemaquid; and afterwards, in 1664, Charles II. gave his brother James, Duke of York, the lands lying between Pemaquid River and St. Croix; but in 1753, Shem Drowne set up a claim to these premises, under Aldsworth's title. Thus a fruitful source of lawsuits for a coming generation was laid in this nest of litigation to disturb the public peace at a future day, as will appear in the next chapter.

In 1624, a small stockade fort, called Fort St. George,

was built; and the trade had become **so** prosperous, and **con**tinued to increase **so much from year to year, that in** 1631 there were **five hundred residents at this place and its vicinity.** But the next year, however, **they were** troubled by the pirates, Dixy Bull and his fifteen followers, who did them some mischief; but they killed one of them in a skirmish, and finally drove the rest away. For a long period they got along safely in the midst of suspicions and alarms from the Indian tribes, under the " excellent Abraham Shurte," .as. he was called, who resided there sixty years, and preserved peace. He must have been a man of extraordinary influence in such a community, for in 1665 royal commissioners were sent out from England to examine the condition of this plantation, and in their report observed, that " those people for the most part are fishermen, and never had any government among them." There was a custom-house there, and the place was named Jamestown, from the Duke of York.

In 1676, **the** Indians, instigated by King Philip, **attacked** and **burnt** several settlements in **Maine,** and among others **Woolwich,** Damariscove, **and New** Harbor. Pemaquid **was laid in ashes, and its inhabi**tants fled. The next **year, King Philip being dead,** and hostilities having ceased, **Sir Edmund** Andros, commissioned as Governor of New **Y**ork by the Duke of York, rebuilt the fort at Pemaquid, **and** called · it Fort Charles, garrisoned it with fifty sol**diers, and** furnished seven guns, with ammunition. This **place then began to revive.**

Again, in 1689, the Penobscot Indians, **having entered New Harbor, about two** miles east of **Pemaquid, in one**

hundred canoes, divided themselves into parties, and attacked the fort; the people were scattered at that time, the garrison contained only thirty men under Captain Weems, and resistance became hopeless. The savages laid the whole settlement in ashes, killed a number of persons, and carried off several women and children into captivity.

Among those who were slain was Thomas Giles, a peaceful and influential citizen, shot on his farm at Pemaquid Falls, three miles from the fort; his widow and four children — two of them daughters — were carried away as prisoners; and his eldest son escaped and fled to Boston. James, one of the captives, after three years escaped, was recaptured, and barbarously tortured and then burnt at the stake by these savages. In the "Giles Memorial" there is a most pathetic and graphic description of this massacre and destruction of the fort.

In 1692, Sir William Phips, Governor of Massachusetts, again fortified this place; he was son of James Phips, and born in Woolwich, Maine, in 1650, where his father resided after he left Pemaquid. Governor Phips erected a very strong fort; he was accompanied by the celebrated Captain Benjamin Church, the conqueror of Philip, with four hundred and fifty men, to subdue the Penobscot Indians.

This fortress was quadrangular, its height on the south side was twenty-two feet, west eighteen, north ten, east twelve feet, with a round tower; the walls to eight feet from the ground were six feet thick; with a gangway of twelve feet, and a tier of twenty-eight portholes; mounted from fourteen to eighteen guns, six of which were eighteen pounders; and was manned with sixty men. It enclosed a space of eight thousand feet around, and was called Fort William Henry, and cost a hundred thousand dollars. "In place of the flimsy stockade built by Andross, a fortress was erected in extent and strength superior to any English fort in America." Governor Phips soon after visited England, and died there in 1694.

Still the prosperity of Pemaquid seemed to have been short. July 14, 1696, it was again attacked and destroyed; for this formidable fort alarmed the French, and they resolved to reduce it. D'Iberville was sent by Frontenac, governor of Quebec, with two men of war and two companies of soldiers, which were reünforced at St. John by two hundred Indians, and at Penobscot they took on board the Baron de Castine, from whom Castine, in Maine, formerly called Bagaduce, derived its name. There was a garrison of ninety-five men at Pemaquid, and they were well provided with supplies for a long siege. Captain Pasco Chubb was the commander. When the enemy demanded a surrender on the 14th, the day when they landed their forces, he replied, "I will not give up the fort though the sea be covered with French vessels, and the land with wild Indians." The next day, however, on the discharge of five or six bombs into the fortification, Chubb, notwithstanding his mighty boast, immediately surrendered. The character of this man had previously suffered from perfidy and cruelty to the Indians, and in this surrender it was infamous. But cruelty and cowardice in most cases are closely allied. Having plundered their captives, and partly demolished the fort, the enemy set sail and left them. Yet the residents at Pemaquid in those days were always in jeopardy. There was but little respite from the treachery of the Indians. In the summer they could come down the rivers noiselessly in their birch canoes, in the winter on their snow-shoes glide over the deepest drifts, and suddenly their painted faces would peer out of the forest, and they would pounce upon flock or herd, or rush with tomahawk or firebrand on the homes of the defenceless.

Colonel David Dunbar, with the coöperation of Governor Philips of Nova Scotia, in 1729, repaired this fortification, called it Fort Frederic, after the Prince of Wales, and garrisoned it with thirty men. He took up his residence at Pemaquid. On the peninsula he laid out the plan of a city; houses were built, streets paved, and improvements made for the encouragement of emigrants. He caused the trees on that favorite spot, which was deeply wooded, to be cut down within a mile of the fort to prevent their being lurking-places for the Indians. Under such auspices Pemaquid began to flourish once more, and to such a degree that Massachusetts, in 1734, claimed jurisdiction over this territory. Colonel Dunbar, whose conduct met with disapprobation, was removed, and Pemaquid increased in population, wealth, and commerce, in her vessels and enterprise, until incorporated as Bristol, in 1765.

" After the breaking out of the Revolutionary war, the people of Bristol, fearing that the British might take possession of the fort, and from it annoy the neighboring territory, destroyed the fortifications." — *The Giles Memorial*, p. 547.

That part where the fort was built — for it must be recollected that Pemaquid extends some three or four miles into the ocean, where the light-house stands on a bleak point — is a level piece of land, two or three miles in circuit, forming a projection nearly surrounded with water. Southerly is a wide view of the sea, where sails are often seen passing beyond the headland, and westerly is Johns River, and several green islands. The scenery is very picturesque in every direction; woody hills, a long, oval-shaped harbor in the north, and a background of dark forest, where several farms seem to emerge from the woods sloping down to the shore, attract the eye. Farther up the bay, wild and craggy banks impend over the water. The entrance to Pemaquid harbor is a narrow passage, through which the tide rushes, and is apparently not more than five hundred feet in width, so that this deep basin, into which the Pemaquid River flows, seems like a small lake in the woods. The approach to it is near the ruins of Fort William Henry, well situated to protect the vessels within it in times of danger.

The whole peninsula is now a farm, where a goodly two-story house and barn on a gentle rise stands, near the ruins of the fortress. This homestead, like the Bleak House of Dickens, is the only thing of life which cheers the visitor where the city of Jamestown once stood. In the rear of the mansion were wide fields of grass and grain, and in the distance, by the northern shore, there is a small cemetery, very ancient, neatly enclosed, and overrun with bushes, in which are many gravestones, some the memorials of early settlers, and others of the recent dead. Most of these graves are very old ; one slate slab was said by some to bear date of 1635, though others could only decipher among the obliterations the year 1695. There was one inscription, which appeared to be 1665 ; but most of the epitaphs on these ancient mossy stones are too much corroded by time for any one but Old Mortality, with his chisel, to interpret. There are a few recent monuments of white marble among these ancient vestiges of the dwellings of the dead. Two graves thus commemorated are those of John M'Kown and wife, whose urbane hospitality was well known in a past generation. They were buried in sight of their ancestral farm, on the west side of the harbor.

The fortress, so celebrated in the annals of New England, was erected on a point near the water. It rested in one corner on an immense rock, some ten or fifteen feet in height, and fifty or sixty round, rising precipitously. On the sides of this rock is a thick growth of trees and bushes, except on the perpendicular margin near the steep shore. It overlooks land and sea, and with cannon would command the entrance to the harbor. From the top of this rock, on a summer evening, when the sun is going down, and reddening hills and waters, the view is magnificent. It was at such a time I gazed on a landscape not often surpassed on the sea-coast of Maine, which is so rich in scenery. It embraced, as I looked south, a glimpse of the ocean, the islands in the mouth of Johns River, the sails of many a fisherman approaching the land, and some

vessels at anchor near the shore; and in a northern direction, Pemaquid Bay, with its surroundings, was not less
enchanting. This peninsula, then so green, was once
covered with a deep forest; it is now a naked plain,
where only the voices of flocks or sea-gulls at a distance
are heard, or the murmuring of the waves touches the ear
mournfully in remembrance of its history long, long ago.
Near the northern side of the rock are two old cellars,
deep and full of briers and small bushes, and at the foot
of it the fragment of an old wall, part of the ancient
fortress, beyond which is the green mound of a rampart.
There is little more to remind one of Fort William Henry,
so formidable when it protected this embryo city, with
its stores and houses, gardens and paved streets, and
the numerous vessels which frequented those waters. Of
all this fortification and busy mart of commerce scarce a
vestige remains. It is said that some streets and pave-
ments have been discovered, but the grass or the crops
of grain must have hidden them from the view. The
hillocks and gravestones in the cemetery are the chief
memorials of what Jamestown once was.

Yet this beautiful spot is replete with many historic
memories — a place for pensive reflection — a cool retreat
on a summer's day to meditate on the blessings we enjoy
in happy New England. We are here taught, as we trace
the past, that whatever the song of the poet may tell, or
the pencil of the imaginative writer delineate, of the rural
bliss of the early settlers in our eastern country, even
though fascinating as the harp of Longfellow on Acadia,
yet the deep and awful shadows of Indian warfare rest on

the mind when we think of the poor emigrants butchered at their doors, or flying from their burning habitations. There is no sublimity in the tomahawk, no music in the warwhoop of the savage.

But it is time to return to the subject of this memoir, after so long a digression, which it is hoped may not be tedious to the reader. The history of Bristol * is a history of one of the first settlements in Maine, and Pemaquid stands prominent for its importance in the early commerce of New England.

A few years since I passed by Commodore Tucker's dwelling with his grandson, Colonel Hinds. It was a substantial, neat building, of two stories, painted white, and well suited for a farm-house; it is situated on a bleak rise, and though very retired from the great world, its cities and railroads, it stands on a pleasant spot, surrounded by hills and dales, and in view of the Camden Mountains. This location was once a part of Bristol, but is now in Bremen, which was taken from the northern end of that town and incorporated in 1828.

Here he followed the avocation of a farmer the remainder of his days. His habits were invariably industrious. He labored hard, rose early, and suiting the manner of his life to the color of his destiny, he soon learned to plough, sow, drive oxen, and do the work of a farmer; but

---

* With pleasure the author acknowledges, among his various authorities, his indebtedness for many facts in the above account of Pemaquid, to "Williamson's History of Maine," "The Giles Memorial," by the Rev. John Adams Vinton; and to "Ancient Pemaquid," by J. Wingate Thornton, Esq.

he said he could never mow. Probably that art, like elegant handwriting, is seldom, if ever, acquired in age. The cultivation of a garden was his peculiar delight; it was more congenial to his taste than agriculture. Whatever he did, he was active and cheerful, for nature had blessed him with a perennial fountain of animal spirits. In the winter season he taught navigation, and several able and efficient mariners owe to his instruction their accuracy and skill in keeping a log-book.

He was fond of reading, when not occupied on his farm. His social powers were great, and he delighted in pleasant company. At his fireside, when a circle of listeners gathered round him and touched a chord of his early reminiscences, he was in his glory. His voice rose, his eye kindled, his broad breast heaved with exultation as he narrated the stirring sea-fights and hair-breadth escapes in his numerous cruises during the war of the Revolution. To have heard him at such a time must have been like the charm of Mrs. Fanny Kemble's readings of Shakspeare, or that of Dickens in the life-pictured works of his own genius.

Sometimes he would mount his horse and ride over to Waldoboro', to see his old friend the late Benjamin Brown, M. D., an able physician and excellent man, who was his surgeon in the frigate Boston when he took out Mr. Adams to France; or he would extend his visit still farther, and call on his honored friend General Knox, who was then living in splendor at his elegant mansion on the banks of the St. George, in Thomaston. He was a fine horseman — an accomplishment very unusual in mariners. It is said that in the Revolution, when he was paying his respects to General Washington at Morristown, the general remarked of him, that "he was the best rider he had ever met with for a seaman;" and who could be a better judge than one whose magnificent figure on horseback was the charm of all observers?

His generosity to the poor and destitute where he lived was proverbial. Indeed, he was too ready to lend or give money whenever a piteous tale touched his heart. He could not endure to see any human being suffer, or even the dumb creation afflicted wantonly. All his aged acquaintances who have survived him — and I have seen many within ten years — spoke with enthusiasm of this trait in his character, and called him a generous person.

In a very interesting notice of Tucker, published in the New England Magazine, some years since (Vol. II. p. 138), written by the late Joseph T. Buckingham, he is described as a man of better manners and less severity than Commodore Jones; and he mentions a fact evincing his great power of endurance — that at one period he kept his place on deck during the chase of an enemy's ship seventy hours; and then his sleep was like the sleep of death — a forty-two pounder at his side would not have waked him.

His wife is reported to have been a very intelligent and superior woman, of a lively disposition and religious frame of mind. He was greatly attached to her. She was the daughter of a worthy and esteemed citizen of

Marblehead, Deacon Samuel Gatchell. With such a partner his domestic life was happy. She was the bride of his youth and the ornament of his gray hairs. She was spared to him a great length of time — sixty-three years. By her he had five children : Mary, who married Captain Benjamin Hinds, in December, 1789; Martha, who married John Tedder, and died October 21, 1805 ; Samuel, who died September 5, 1776; Betsey, who died December 8, 1781, and a son named after his deceased brother Samuel.

His daughter Mary's husband, Captain Hinds, was an able shipmaster ; and when, towards the end of the last century, a war was expected with France, he commanded the letter of marque Hercules, eighteen guns. She was lost in 1799. Captain Hinds and crew took to an open boat, where their sufferings for twenty-seven days were so intense and terrible, that on their arrival at Cork, in Ireland, all died except one and the captain ; and on the 12th of April, 1799, on his way home, Hinds fell a sacrifice to the exposure. His widow afterwards removed to her father's, in Bristol, and died a few years since. Their son, Colonel Samuel Tucker Hinds, is now the only representative of the family in the third generation.

The youngest son, Samuel, born March 2, 1778, followed the sea, and though not eighteen years of age, went out mate in a merchantman to the West Indies ; there he was cut off by the fever, December 23, 1795, to the great grief of his parents, who had reason to mourn the loss of a son of much promise.

The following letter, written, it is presumed, to a clergy-

man in Marblehead, who had condoled with the commodore in his affliction, is so fraught with feeling, and so
well expressed, that it reflects honor on the heart and
head of the veteran mourner. It is pleasing to see the
dreariness of grief united with such a submissive spirit, as
this touching and unaffected reply evinces.

BRISTOL, 4th March, 1796.

REVEREND SIR: The sudden change and late event in
my family being deeply impressed on my mind at this
sorrowful hour of tribulation, almost makes me forget to
acknowledge gratefully, what I shall ever esteem with
pleasing remembrance, your very great attention to me
and my distressed consort, bearing date of the 20th of
February past, which I must acknowledge was at such a
mournful period a great consolation on the death of our
only son. Distresses we are constantly liable to, and
with me, as well as many others, they have often been
repeated. But I desire to thank the great Disposer of
all human events, that my trouble is no greater: knowing it is the mighty arm of God, I therefore submissively
acknowledge the justice thereof. Although our bereave-
ment at present is great, almost too hard for nature to
bear, still we ought cheerfully to submit to the will of
our all-wise Creator in all his dispensations.

Sir, please to accept our sincere thanks for your attendance on our children, as well as the notice you have
taken of me and Mrs. Tucker, being secluded from
your vicinity, and without the least personal acquaintance
imaginable. And we shall be always glad in hearing

from you, when you may think it convenient; and we gratefully acknowledge the notice of all our friends; and with great fervency subscribe ourselves,

Yours, ever ready to serve,

SAMUEL AND MARY TUCKER.

REV. EBENEZER HUBBARD, *Marblehead.*

CHAPTER XI.

Squatter Troubles in Maine. — Insurrection. — The Great Trial of the Murderers of Paul Chadwick. — Adjustment of all Difficulties by the Legislature.

SEVERAL years of peace and quietness had passed away in the family of Tucker, when there arose a great flood of litigation and distress among the settlers on a large tract of land lying between the Kennebec and Penobscot Rivers. Several towns and plantations were embraced in this tract, and Bristol became deeply involved in questions of tenancy and title.

The claims set up by the proprietors were founded on various grants and conveyances. There were the Brown Right, derived from a purchase of July 15, 1625, already alluded to; the Grant of the Duke of York in 1664; the Patent of the Plymouth Company; the Drowne Right; the Tappan Right, and many latent titles emerging from the archives of speculators.

The history of these claims, and the numerous suits founded on them, would fill volumes of dry reading; but as Commodore Tucker was a landholder in Bristol, became a party concerned in this litigation, and took a

deep interest in the adjustment of the suits in which he
and his fellow-townsmen were entangled, some account
of the serious difficulties which threatened the peace of
the community will not be out of place in this work, for
1809 was a dark year in Maine. She was on the eve of
an agrarian war.

There had been much anxiety and heart-burning in
the minds of a large class of people, called " squatters ; "
men who, by purchase from pretended proprietors, or
from imperfect conveyances, or by improvement of lands
either with or without color of title, had entered on
lots purporting to be a hundred acres, cleared up a part
of the premises, built log huts or houses, and raised up
families. Numerous suits, ejectments, and bitter quarrels
were the result. In some cases the consequences to the
hard laboring yeoman, who had already paid for his land,
were peculiarly severe and oppressive. It was not long
before a whispering was heard in the woodlands about
the principle and application of the new discovery in
ethics, — the " Higher Law," — and very soon there followed combinations to take their rights into their own
hand.

To remedy these evils, the legislature of Massachusetts
in 1807, under the administration of Governor Sullivan,
passed an Act of Limitation, in which was embodied
a *quieting* provision, commonly called the Betterment
Law. Section third provides, " That where any action
has been, or may hereafter be, commenced against any
person for the recovery of any lands or tenements which
such person now holds by virtue of a possession and im-

provement, and which the tenant or person, under whom he claims, has had in actual possession for the term of six years, or more, before the commencement of such action, the jury which tries the same, if they find a verdict for the demandant, shall (if the tenant request the same) also inquire, and by their verdict ascertain the increased value of the premises, at the time of trial, by virtue of the buildings and improvements made by such tenant, or those under whom he may claim; and (if the demandant shall require it) what would have been the value of the demanded premises, had no buildings or improvements been made by such tenant, or those under whom he may claim." The demandant then could elect to abandon the premises to the tenant at the price set by the jury, and receive his money, or pay the tenant for his improvement, with interest, as in said statute provided. It is unnecessary here to refer to other provisions of this statute.

The operation of this law in Maine was often severe on the proprietor, because he usually lived at a distance from the disputed premises, and the tenant resided on them, and in the county where the lands lay, and in the *visne* of the jury. Consequently the value of the improvements was generally estimated at the highest rate, and the land, in a state of nature, at the lowest. On this account, and for other reasons, the constitutionality of the Betterment Act was called in question, but the courts sustained it. This statute, with some modifications, has become a permanent law; and whenever it has been applied, with due regard to the just rights of parties, it has been found salutary in its tendency and remedial in its operation.

The courts in Penobscot and Kennebec, session after session, resounded with the names of ancient proprietors, — Brown, Drowne, Tappan, Plymouth Company, Fifty Associates, and others. Old musty grants were spread out from the Waldo Patent and Pejepscot Purchase. Deeds and documents rose up before the jury, and lacerated plans and time-worn maps, with their ragged lines and boundaries, were cautiously unrolled to the jury. Grizzly-bearded surveyors swore to their copies, and aged witnesses, leaning on their staves, like apparitions from the grave, filled the ear with landmarks of every kind, chops in trees, curvatures and angles in brooks, boundaries of stakes and stones, and curious monuments in nature. A land trial of this kind was sure to empty the court-house of spectators, and even scatter for a while the gentlemen of the green bag.

The Ter-tenant generally found the ingenuity of the law too strong for him, and at last came to the conclusion — which some *wise* heads in modern times have pronounced the perfection of reason — to resist the statutes in such cases made and provided, because they deemed them unjust. The consequence was an agrarian insurrection. Companies were organized, armed and equipped in various sections of the country, particularly in Malta, east of Augusta, now called Windsor, in Palermo, Jefferson, Alna, Patricktown Plantation, — as unincorporated settlements were called, — and in Nobleborough, and Bristol. The insurgents lived principally between the Kennebec and Penobscot; the tract, where the disputes originated, was larger than a German principality, watered with fine streams and ponds, and in the vicinity of many beautiful towns and villages.

The alarm increased; savage threatenings were whispered about; suspicious persons in groups met at the grog-shops in villages; land agents, surveyors, and proprietors were denounced with a vengeance. Travellers on the lonely highway, or passing in paths through fields or woods, were eyed sharply, and often interrupted by strange questions. The danger grew formidable, for these insurgents were men of industrious habits and good character, the very bone and muscle of the country.

Such was the aspect of a rebellion in the heart of Maine, then a district, where thousands of landholders were leagued together to resist the officers of the law touching their homesteads; when Paul Chadwick, a chain-man, employed by a public surveyor, was coolly and deliberately shot while in the performance of his duty, at Malta. The crime was committed on the 8th of September, 1809, by Elijah Barton and six others, who were arrested, and at a session of the Supreme Court at the October term of that year, indicted for the murder.

To preserve the peace, and prevent the threatened rescue of the prisoners from the jail, a large body of militia was ordered to be in readiness; and several companies, detached and under arms, guarded Augusta from the time the prisoners were in custody until the trial was over. A cordon of troops surrounded the jail, and the greatest vigilance was maintained. Rumors were afloat that the insurgents would set the town on fire in the night, and on the eastern bank of the river, where the old block garrisons, called Fort Western, stood, there was great alarm in all the houses.

A full court was specially convened for an early trial of the prisoners. Chief Justice Sedgwick, with Justices Sewall, Thacher, and Parker, composed the bench. On the night of the first day of the term, when the grand jury was in session, the greatest fear of danger prevailed. A band of armed men, in the costume of Indians, supposed to be seventy, under the veil of darkness, came from the hills of Malta, through the woods, and was seen hovering on the outskirts of the dwellings, within half a mile of the Kennebec Bridge. One of them was captured by Major Weeks, who, with a small force, was stationed on the height of land near the junction of the county road; but the insurgents rushed down, rescued the captive, and took Major Weeks himself prisoner. After carrying him into a deep wood, they let him return unharmed. The news of this capture ran like wildfire. The court bell rang, the bells of Augusta, and Hallowell two miles below, responded as to a cry of fire, and the inhabitants of both settlements were roused from their slumbers.

> " Tempus erat, quo prima quies mortalibus ægris
> Incipit et dono divùm gratissima serpit." — *Virgil.*

It was at that hour of night when sleep, the gift of Heaven, begins to creep most sweetly into the bosoms of wearied mortals.

The night was dark, and each family started from their beds. They believed the tocsin was not without cause, and the threats of the squatters, and dreadful imaginings

of coming evil, added to the gloom of the midnight hour.
The artillery and light infantry companies of Hallowell,
and detachments from neighboring towns, were roused,
and soon marched in double-quick time to the relief of
Augusta. Within two or three hours a brigade was on
the spot, under the command of Major-General Henry
Sewall — a veteran soldier of the Revolution, and then at
the head of the eighth division. One who was under
arms that night describes the scene as filled with sublime
emotion. In ascending the hills between Hallowell and
Augusta, thousands of lights gleamed from the houses;
and the tramp of troops, and martial music, echoing at
midnight over the waters from cliff to cliff, must have
alarmed the insurgent mountaineers, and taught them that
it would be hopeless to contend with such a force.

Soldiers were stationed in dense ranks around the jail:
loaded artillery was pointed to sweep the two main streets;
and outguards were posted at the bridge, and on the hill
above it. But the night passed without attack or bloodshed. There were a few more alarms. In one case a
distant gun having been accidentally discharged, the out-
posts retreated to the bridge, reporting, " they were coming!" but they came not. All was soon quiet, daylight
dawned, and the terrors were dispelled.

Beyond doubt it was the intention of the insurgents to
rescue the prisoners, but not to commit any depredation,
or to set fire to the shire town; and they were compelled
to desist from any further attempt, when they found that
General Sewall had a large body of troops in defence, and
their spies saw a vacant plain in Augusta — now adorned

with handsome **houses,** streets, **and gardens** — converted into a tented field, from which the reveille and vesper drum could be heard on the distant hills where they were assembled.

The court was opened for trial; the bar was crowded, the press of spectators around was dense. The prisoners, each in manacles, were brought in from the cells of the jail by a strong posse of police officers, through a lane formed by double ranks of soldiers. They were **put to the bar, and the indictment for murder read by the late John Davis, Esq., the eloquent and accomplished clerk of that** county, **in a slow** and solemn voice. The tone in which he uttered, " Jurors, look upon the prisoners; prisoners, look upon the jury: " and then, " God give you a safe deliverance ! " seemed to impress the mind like the earthquake in the stillness of night.

The defendants were all tried together, and each one plead " **not guilty.**" They were seven young men, stout, muscular, and with hands and brows marked **by the** wrinkles of hard labor. Their **names were Elijah Bar-**ton, **David Lynn, Jabez Meigs,** Prince Cain, Ansel Meigs, **and Adam** Pitts. **Elijah** Barton, their ring-leader, was a young man, prepossessing in appearance —tall in stature, formed like an athlete, with an eye of command, goodly features, ruddy complexion, and curly hair. He might be called a handsome fellow : as to **the** rest, there was nothing remarkable in their looks; **rough.** but not savage. **The** look of Barton was sad, yet firm **and unchanged during the whole trial ; not a muscle in his face moved, nor did he betray any weakness.**

14

Two gentlemen of distinguished abilities, then at the head of the bar of Maine, were engaged in the defence, — Samuel S. Wilde, of Hallowell, and Prentiss Mellen. of Portland, — each of whom have since been eminently honored by promotion to the bench. Mr. Wilde was appointed Judge of the Supreme Court of Massachusetts in 1815, and Mr. Mellen, Chief Justice of the Supreme Court of the State of Maine in 1820. *Par nobile fratrum.* They died venerable in years, honored for their rank and erudition, and beloved for their goodness.

In behalf of the government was the elegant, and very able solicitor, Daniel Davis, Esq., whose winning address and flowing eloquence will always live in the memory of those who knew him. And he is gone from us ! — of whom that great jurist, Judge Story, was said in his lifetime to have remarked, " Daniel Davis was one of the most compact and eloquent speakers in the United States."

A detail of the testimony of the witnesses, and the arguments of the learned counsel, may be found in the elaborate report of this trial by John Merrick, Esq. Suffice it to say, the evidence was clear and plenary. Six of the criminals had voluntarily confessed their guilt, and the statement of the dying man confirmed their declaration. The trial lasted ten days: forty four witnesses were examined.

Judge Parker, — afterwards Chief Justice of Massachusetts, — being the youngest judge on the bench, first charged the jury, and when he had finished, Chief Justice Sedgwick observed, " that it was the intention of the whole court to give separate charges in this trial ; but our brother Parker has so fully taken a view of the evidence, so entirely corresponding with our opinions, that we shall forbear to make further observations, except to implore the Father of Lights to aid you in your deliberations on this solemn occasion."

On Saturday morning the jury came into court, and amidst the death-like silence and suppresed breathings of the spectators, the foreman pronounced the prisoners " not guilty ! "

Such is a summary of this great trial — the most important which ever transpired in Maine; the exponent of an insurrection, the most serious and alarming since Shays' rebellion. Its history is now among the things of the past. Upon the actors on that forensic stage of eloquence the curtain has long since dropped. Chief Justice Sedgwick, and his associates Sewall, Thacher, Parker, and Daniel Davis, and John Davis, and Colonel Arthur Lithgow, the hospitable high sheriff, brother of General Lithgow, distinguished in the Revolution, and the two great advocates Mellen and Wilde, have paid the debt of nature. And to these let me add spectators of distinction who were present, Judge Bridge, Judge Fuller, and Benjamin Whitwell, Esq., members of the profession, and the great philanthropist and scholar, Benjamin Vaughan, LL. D., with other magnates of that region, then listeners to the learning of the bench, or charmed with the eloquence of the counsel, all of whom have departed; but their portraits are preserved in the picture-gallery of memory. More than half a century has produced great changes, where this trial was held. The old wooden court-house has given way to a more splendid forum. Augusta has become a city and the seat of government, with a superb State House and various improvements; while squatter sovereignty has passed away with the dreams of the past.

The result of this homicide and trial, however, was, upon the whole, salutary. Proprietors became more cautious and prudent, tenants and occupiers of land less violent. Commodore Tucker saw and felt the disturbed state of the country, being, as a landholder in Bristol, personally interested. It was his advice to appeal to the legislature for redress. There is not a shadow of evidence, nor was it ever reported among his neighbors, that he was in favor of acts of violence. He perceived that there was a great wrong and injustice somewhere, and the course he pursued was honorable and worthy of a good citizen. He resorted to a respectful memorial to the legislature, and persuaded the other aggrieved parties to do the same. The town of Bristol chose a committee for this purpose, composed of six from among their oldest and best citizens, viz., Samuel Tucker, Robert Askins, William Rogers, William M'Clintock, Marius Howe, and Sullivan Hardy. The commodore, as chairman, drew up two petitions; one to the General Court, and one to Eldridge Gerry, Governor of Massachusetts, setting forth their grievances, "because men with different claims pretended, from ancient letters patent and Indian deeds, to hold the lands which they and their predecessors had purchased more than once with their blood and money;" and praying relief, "because threatened with immediate expulsion from lands held in possession forty, fifty, sixty, seventy, **and** eighty years, **for which** they paid taxes, defended them against the savages in 1756, and fought against the British in 1775 to 1783, when every fourth man in Bristol was drawn a soldier."

And to Governor Gerry, October 2, 1810, a similar petition was sent, praying, moreover, that his Excellency would " countermand the orders of the Honorable Judge Thacher for a survey, and calling out five hundred of the militia to **aid in running land in Bristol, settled from forty to eighty years," and furthermore praying " for the removal of J**udge Thacher, because he had violated the glorious constitution."

This petition, and others of the like purport from several towns, were not without effect. In the mean time, it was reported that Colonel Samuel Thacher was coming with James Malcolm, a noted surveyor, at the head of his regiment, **to p**rotect the officer in executing the mandate of the Supreme Court, to run out the lines in **the** disputed lands ; but Commodore Tucker either **sent a messenger or** a letter to him, stating that **the minds of t**he people of Bristol **were so highly excited that** there would be bloodshed **if he should attempt to execute** the order of the court, and it being known that petitions to the legislature for redress **were** pending, the proceedings were wisely suspended. Governor Gerry, in his message to the legislature, of January 25, 1811, informs them that alarming difficulties had arisen in Maine, and that Brigadier-General Payson, of Wiscasset, had been **required to call out five hundred militia to aid in** the **legal survey of certain** lands in Bristol; but Mr. Malcolm, the surveyor, saw "the imprudence of proceeding," and begged to decline the duty.

The legislature soon after took up the matter, and a committee was appointed, who made their return February 27, 1811, and having examined the subject fully, reported an order, from which the following extract is made: "Ordered, that his Excellency the Governor be, and he hereby is authorized and requested to appoint three commissioners to take into consideration his message to the two branches of the legislature, relative to the disturbances in the County of Lincoln, with the documents accompanying the same, and also to take into consideration the memorial from the inhabitants of the towns of Bristol, Edgecomb, Nobleboro', Newcastle, and Boothbay, and the memorial signed by Samuel Tucker and others, all which are now pending before the General Court." This alone was evidence enough to show the active and influential part which Tucker took in resorting to legal and peaceable measures in this agrarian insurrection.

The order was passed, and Perez Morton, Jonathan Smith, Junior, and Thomas B. Adams, were appointed commissioners. They met at Wiscasset, April 11, 1811, after due notice to the five towns aforesaid, and to Samuel Tucker, and having examined the deeds, vouchers, and documents, and after an investigation, as ordered, of the nature, causes, and state of the difficulties between the proprietors and tenants, among other matters reported, that "the Drowne Claim covered the town of Bristol," and "that the Tappan Right, and Brown Right, as claimed, each covers **most of** Bristol." Under **such** old, musty, clashing **claims, for the most part hunted up by** prowling **speculators, who** can **wonder that the poor,** hard-working husbandmen should have **risen,** peaceably if they could, forcibly if they must, against such cruel oppression?

The result was, that the legislature wisely enacted a remedial statute. Jeremiah Smith, of Exeter, N. H., William H. Woodward, of Hanover, N. H., and David Howell, **of Providence, R. I., men of eminence in legal science, were authorized in behalf of Massachusetts, to** buy **out the proprietors** by an equivalent in other lands of the Commonwealth — much like the British nation buying out the slave-owners in the emancipation of Jamaica. The commissioners performed their duty in a way and manner honorable and satisfactory to all concerned.

To end these controversies by an eternal quietus, the General Court, February 25, 1813, appointed two agents to give deeds of release to the settlers, on **each one paying** *five dollars* in cases where the **tenant or his assignee** had been **in** possession before **January 1, 1789,** and in all cases **after that time** thirty **cents per** acre, on a tract not exceeding **two hundred acres. The** Honorable Benjamin **Orr, of** Brunswick, and Jeremiah Bailey, of Wiscasset, were appointed agents to make the deeds — the first, a **very** distinguished **and** eloquent lawyer, the other, Judge **of Probate** for **the county of** Lincoln, a sound counsellor **and excellent man. These,** too, have passed **away ; teach-ing us, as we approach the shadows of the dark mountains, that the drama of life is but for a moment.**

This transaction occurred at the period of the last war between England and the United States. Commodore Tucker, though at home cultivating his farm, was no less anxious for the defence and honor of his country than for the private welfare of his fellow-citizens, as the following patriotic exploit will evince.

The capture of the English armed schooner Crown, in this war, has been represented and published in various ways. The following was put in writing, as the description was given to the author, in a conversation with Colonel Hinds, the grandson of the Commodore.

The English schooner Bream, of eight guns, and crew of one hundred men, which accompanied the seventy-four Rattler, on the sea-coast of Maine, in the summer of 1813, had harassed Bristol and the neighboring towns for some time; alarming, by their depredations, the peaceful inhabitants, carrying off cattle, burning fishermen and coasters, and keeping the people in jeopardy and watch-fulness lest their houses should be invaded. One vessel the enemy set on fire was towed into New Harbor, though too late to be saved from destruction.

Roused by these outrages, a number of seamen, young and middle-aged men, met together in a store at Muscon-gus harbor, one Sunday afternoon in April, to see what could be done. They concluded to send for Commodore Tucker, to consult with him, and get his advice. As soon as he came, he recommended that an agreement should be drawn up to procure a coaster, arm her, and go out into the bay to take the schooner Bream. Forty-five individuals signed this paper, and the commodore, then sixty-seven years old, was chosen the commander. The next day they procured a sloop, the Increase, of about one hundred tons burden, which was lying at the wharf, with her hold half full of wood. She was a good sailer, and the owners agreed to take one half of the prize for the risk of the vessel, which was under the charge of Captain Osier, one of the signers.

Their first step was to go to Waldoboro', and get the necessary papers from the collector, who at that time was Joseph Farley, Esq. This done, they armed themselves with muskets and a supply of ball cartridges, and each took sufficient rations for a short cruise. They got ready some poles, with bayonets fastened on the end, as a substitute for boarding-pikes; and thus equipped, they went down the river, and around Pemaquid Point to Townsend harbor in Boothbay, where Commodore Tucker came on board and took command. From this place they sent boats up to the fort at Wiscasset, which was under the charge of Captain John Binney, and from him they procured two small cannon, with a brass piece and ammunition. About thirty men from the intrenchment in Boothbay joined them in their enterprise.

Before sailing Tucker called together his little band of adventurers, and addressed them in these words: " Shipmates, the agreement which you have put your names to is voluntary, and not binding in law. If any one chooses, he has a right to withdraw his name. We wish no one to go with us — for there may be fighting — without his own free and full consent. Now is the time to make up your mind." Such is the substance of his speech. There was a solemn pause; one poor fellow saw in his mind's eye the horrors of a bloody fight, and he stepped out of the circle. Then he asked for his gun. "No," said his comrades, "that is pledged; you must leave it:" and he went away amidst the hisses of the crowd.

They hoisted sail and left the harbor. Rounding Pemaquid Point, they saw a sail and pursued it; but she proved to be a coasting vessel. They cruised two days east and west, and discovering no ship of the enemy, returned to Townsend harbor, — for the head of the detachment of thirty men, who had joined them from Boothbay, growing uneasy at so long an absence, thought it his duty to take his soldiers back to their post. The guns borrowed at the fort in Wiscasset were also returned. The fire-arms left them were only the muskets and a small swivel of their own.

Next day they sailed again on an eastern cruise, and passing Pemaquid Point, saw an armed schooner, which at first they supposed to be some coaster. They immediately steered east-north-east, as if heading for St. George's River. On the other hand, the schooner they saw changed her course, and steered south-west to intercept them. The commodore kept nearly all his men below out of sight. As the vessels neared each other, their own sloop, the Increase, kept working up towards the British cruiser. Captain Richard Jennings — as his name proved to be — said to his pilot, who was an American, "That vessel looks suspicious." The pilot replied, "that he thought he saw Commodore Tucker on deck, and believed it was he who commanded her, and there will be hot work."

Upon hearing this, the English captain fired, and cut through the sails of the Increase, and immediately her crew leaped on deck, hardly waiting the orders of the commodore, who found it difficult to restrain their impetuosity. He commanded them to form platoons — each platoon to take good aim, fire, and kneel, when ordered. The British schooner kept discharging her guns, and literally riddled the sails of the sloop beyond repair. The two vessels were drawing nearer and nearer, the Increase keeping the wind, and they were not far apart, when, in a voice of thunder, Tucker gave the word, "Fire!" and it was followed by such quick and sharp discharges of musketry, that the guns of the enemy were silenced, and the men rushed below. Their captain lay down on the deck and steered, which one of the sloop's crew observing, and seeing his head through a space in the quarter-boards, he fired at him, and the ball went through his hat, just grazing his head.

On board the Increase there was one volunteer remarkable for his height — six feet, six inches ; large in bulk, and of a swarthy complexion — a terrible looking champion in battle. This man Commodore Tucker ordered to take up a kedge anchor at the bow, and stand ready, when the word was given, to throw it as a grappling iron over the gunwale of the schooner. He lifted it up on his back, and stood ready, and seeing his chance from the near approach of the vessels, cried out, "Commodore, shall I heave?" The English captain saw him, heard his cry, and afterwards, describing the scene, exclaimed, "When I beheld a very tall, giant-looking fellow, more than seven feet high, standing at the bow, with a huge anchor on his back ready to throw on board of us through a space of fifteen or twenty feet, and heard the awful cry, ' Commodore, shall I heave?' I thought the devil was coming after my vessel."

The captain, seeing his men had run below, and that the sloop had taken the wind out of his sails, and the Yankees would soon grapple and board him, called out for quarters. "Then strike your colors," said Tucker. "The halliards are cut away," he replied. "Then cut down your flag-staff," he rejoined; which was done, and the schooner surrendered.

The prize was taken to Muscongus harbor, and the crew, consisting of twenty-five prisoners, were deposited in the jail at Wiscasset. It is a remarkable fact, that not one man was killed, or even wounded, in either vessel. The English schooner must have aimed badly, or fired exclusively at the sails, — for they were found full of holes, — and the muskets of the sloop must have fired over the heads of the English, who crouched or fled from a second volley. Thus without a death, or even a wound, in a wood-coaster, with a few resolute men, ignorant of naval tactics, Commodore Tucker gained a bloodless victory. Beyond all doubt he owed his success to his skill in manœuvring an armed vessel, and taking the wind out of his adversary's sails, thereby getting the advantage of a commanding position in an engagement. In this particular, and in cool, deliberate courage, no naval commander in America has excelled him.

Captain Jennings accompanied him home, and was

treated in a very kind and hospitable manner. He was afterwards carried to the county jail at Wiscasset, from which, it was said, he made his escape in woman's clothes. Such was the report, but the incident needs explanation. It seemed that England had claimed some of the American prisoners she had captured as British subjects, and intended to have them tried and shot. At this news certain English captains we had captured were held as hostages, to be tried and shot if England persisted in such intention. On this account Captain Jennings was kept in custody.

On his return to Halifax, he afterwards met some of the men who took the Crown, — as many of her crew were fishermen, — treated them very kindly, and told them he had no idea the American character combined so much hospitality and bravery, and remarked, " You will never catch me again in a privateer against you."

It should be observed that it was the schooner Bream, of eight guns, which Tucker, with his gallant band of volunteers, went out in a sloop to capture, when they fell in with the schooner Crown, of six guns, the captain of which had just arrived off Pemaquid from Halifax, with a full supply of provisions and ammunition for the seventy-four. Such was the scarcity of food that year in Bristol. from the interruption of coasters and fishing vessels by the British cruisers, and from suspension of trade, that the supplies taken in this capture were timely. They were gladly received and distributed among the suffering families on the sea-coast.

Tucker was not only anxious, but busy and active in

providing for the defence of Bristol **during the war. He wrote to Major-General William King,** at the **head of the** eleventh division, who resided in Bath, upon **this subject,** and his answer is among his papers. There is a copy **of** a letter of Tucker to the general, dated September 13, 1814, in **which he thanks him** for detaching Captain **Yeates's company of Bristol for their defence, "as their** own troops **were** best, on account **of their** knowledge of the creeks and inlets," to guard their shores; and then informs him that the Elba, a British sloop of war, was seen yesterday, and four barges were sent from her, and approached within three miles of New Harbor, but perceiving **there** would be resistance, they put back; for **"they generally retreat on** hearing alarm." In the same **letter he remarks, that " it is a common practice among seamen,** in nocturnal excursions, **to** case their hats **in white** canvas, that they may know each other in the dark."

There is an anecdote related of the commodore, which evinces that he never lost sight, in all his misfortunes, of the dignity which belonged to **one who had been** an officer in the navy. Not long after **the war of 1812** with England, **a** flotilla of gunboats was **got up in New York,** and **Comm**odore Tucker was written **to** with the offer of **commanding them.** He replied, with some asperity, that **" he would not accept** it: it **was below the rank** he had **sustained in the** Revolution." It is singular **that no** command **of a war ship was then** offered him: it **could** not have been **owing to old age, for his mental powers** were as bright **and vigorous as ever. That age does** not **necessarily impair the faculties, we have a striking**

instance in the Doge of Venice, Henry Dandolo, who
took Constantinople when he was ninety-seven years of
age, and even then was deprived of his sight.   Of him
Byron says, —

> " O, for an hour of blind old Dandolo !
>   Th' octogenarian chief, Byzantium's conquering foe."
>   *Childe Harold*, Canto III. Stanza 12.

CHAPTER XII.

Member of the General Court. — Petition to Congress. — Visit to Washington. — His Pension. — Anecdotes. — Close of Life.

COMMODORE TUCKER, though he had retired from a busy seaport to a farm on the Muscongus, sought not the seclusion of a hermitage in the woods. His mind, naturally active and lively, was ever ready to devote itself to the service of his fellow-citizens and the welfare of his country. His open, straightforward manner made him popular with his townsmen, and they appreciated his character. He was repeatedly elected one of the selectmen of Bristol, before that section of the town in which he lived was set off, and incorporated as Bremen: this was in 1828; and here too he was several times chosen into the same office. This honor, in a country municipality, is far from being a sinecure; and as for profit, the fathers of the town, as the selectmen are called, there received ten cents an hour, and it was thought a high remuneration for their magisterial labors.

He was chosen four times a member of the legislature of Massachusetts, to wit, in 1814, 1815, 1817, and 1818. In 1816, the town voted to choose no representative.

Each of the three last years he was put on the committee
of county estimates ; for wherever he was, his white locks
were not without honor.

Many old acquaintances called upon the veteran in
his official visits to Boston. His kind and illustrious
friend, Ex-President John Adams, received him at his
mansion in Quincy with much cordiality. The venerable
patriot, then in the evening of life, and with a mind un-
clouded to the last, took a warm interest in his welfare.
Among the number who remembered him well, and
showed him the kindest attentions, was Harrison Gray
Otis, Esq., the most graceful and eloquent orator in his
day, — for the star of Daniel Webster had hardly begun
to rise above the horizon, so soon after to culminate and
cast all other lights in the shade.

It was in one of these visits, as representative to the
General Court, that in a crowded room, where seats
were occupied, some juvenile buck, — perhaps " Young
America," — observing that he walked a little lame from
a rheumatic attack, stepped up to him, and said, as
strangers gathered round him, " Commodore, you have
been in three wars for your country, could you serve in
battle now, with your rheumatic limb?" " Sir," said the
veteran, fixing his eye upon him, and with that voice,
which often rose above the storm of the ocean, " wherever I had the honor to command — in my day — men of
war were furnished with chairs. I trust, sir, one might
be found even now."

He was energetic and influential in procuring the
separation of Maine from her parent State. He saw the

time had come ; and it was right, and it was expedient, that a large territory, rapidly growing in population and wealth, and whose representatives were obliged to travel to the General Court through an intervening State, should now become one of the stars in the flag of the Union. This event was brought about in a most harmonious manner. A convention met in Portland, October 12, 1819, to form a constitution, to which Commodore Tucker was a delegate from Bristol, and over which General William King, who was afterwards elected the first governor, presided.

He was twice chosen a member of the House of Representatives in Maine, for 1820 and 1821. The legislature then assembled at Portland.

The history of his repeated applications to Congress for payment of the arrears, due for services three years and ten months, or, if not granted, for some relief or pension, is singular and unprecedented. It evinces his character of perseverance on the land as on the sea. It was finally, in a degree, successful, though forty-eight years had passed before the slow hand of justice meted out any mark of gratitude to that gallant officer.

In 1784, he sent his memorial to the care of the Honorable Elbridge Gerry, member of Congress. His reply was as follows : —

ANNAPOLIS, June 5, 1784.

DEAR SIR : I should with pleasure have complied with the request contained in your letter of the 15th of May, had it arrived in time, but Congress had adjourned before

I received it. The Committee of the States cannot receive any matter that relates to a grant of money, for which reason I return the memorial, and remain,

Your very humble servant,

E. GERRY.

CAPTAIN TUCKER.

After his removal to Bristol, in 1793, and some time before 1800, he forwarded a memorial to Congress, and was informed that a resolve had been passed by them in 1794, which precluded and shut out all claims of Revolutionary officers not presented before a certain time, and thus he was cut off from the payment of his arrears.

In December, 1806, he forwarded a petition for relief to Congress, to the care of the Honorable Orchard Cook, member from Maine; and though the Honorable John Dawson, of Virginia, exerted himself to promote its success, it was ineffectual.

February 12, 1812, his application to Congress was renewed by the Honorable Peleg Tallman, of Maine, and the Honorable William Reed, of Massachusetts, got it referred to the Committee of Claims, where it slept in that oblivion, the waters of which are too often drank at the Capitol.

In 1816 he again applied, and there is a copy of a letter to the Honorable Benjamin Brown, of Maine, then a member of Congress, — and formerly, it will be recollected, his surgeon in the frigate Boston, — in which he sent on another petition. Honorable Albion K. Parris, of Maine, also a member, interested himself much for him, and sent him the following letter : —

WASHINGTON CITY, December 24, 1817.

DEAR SIR: I have the pleasure of informing you, that a bill has this moment passed the House of Representatives, providing relief for the officers, soldiers, mariners, and marines who served in the Revolutionary war. By this bill it is provided that all officers, both of the army and navy, should receive a pension for life of twenty dollars per month, and all the non-commissioned officers, privates, marines, and mariners, of eight dollars per month, during life, commencing on the 4th day of March last. This pension is, however, payable to those who are poor and in want. The bill has now gone to the Senate, where I sincerely wish it success. Let me hear from you, and believe me,

Your friend, sincerely,

ALBION K. PARRIS.

CAPTAIN SAMUEL TUCKER.

The next letter will show that under the general law he did apply, and received twenty dollars a month for three years, from January, 1817.

NAVY DEPARTMENT, 8th March, 1820.

MY DEAR SIR: In transmitting the pension, I cannot omit the occasion of writing you a few lines, and of expressing my opinion of the meanness and want of liberality in the House of Representatives, in reducing the sum fixed by the Senate, where the members were old enough to remember the Revolution and Revolutionary men; whereas, in the

House, one half of them were not born, or in their cradles, when you were fighting the battles of their country, and who at this day might have been hewers of wood and drawers of water, had not a few like you, and Washington, and Stark, and Greene, succeeded in obtaining our Independence of old mother Britain.

I have sent on this day, to the Branch Bank in Boston, the three years' pension due you on the 1st of January last, and you will receive six months' pension the 1st of July next; and so one hundred and twenty dollars every six months to come, which I pray God may be some comfort to your old age. I regret very sincerely that it is not fifty dollars instead of twenty per month.

Accept my best wishes for your health and happiness, and believe me to be, dear sir,

Your friend, and respectful humble servant,

BENJAMIN HOMANS.

COMMODORE SAMUEL TUCKER, *Bristol, Maine.*

This handsome letter from Mr. Homans must have been cheering to the hero of '76, when he found that men of noble spirits felt for his misfortunes.

While he was a member of the legislature of Massachusetts, his petition for arrears, or relief, was presented to Congress. It was read in the Senate March 18, 1816, called up next year, December 1, and referred to the Committee on Pensions and Revolutionary Claims; there it hung along for four years, as the claims of private citizens, however just and urgent, were too often deemed of trifling importance compared to some party measure

or flaming speech for home consumption peculiar to
petty politicians. The Honorable Mark L. Hill, representative from Maine, in 1819, exerted himself for the
petitioner, and his efforts were fortified by the following
powerful document, which is so honorable to the memory
of Tucker, that it is quoted in full.

QUINCY, January 18, 1816.

SIR: Samuel Tucker, Esq., a member of our Massachusetts legislature, has a petition to government for
justice, or customary favor to meritorious officers, which
will be explained before the proper judges. I cannot
refuse a request to certify what I know of his character
and history. My acquaintance with him commenced
early in the year 1776, when he was first appointed to a
command in the navy, in which he served with reputation
and without reproach to the end of the year 1783.

His biography would make a conspicuous figure, even
at this day, in the naval annals of the United States.
I can be particular only in one instance. In 1778
he was ordered to France in the Boston frigate. He
sailed in February, and soon fell in with three British
frigates, sent from Rhode Island expressly to intercept
him. Fighting of one against three was out of the question. In a chase of three days and three nights he baffled
all the inventions, and defeated all the manœuvres, of the
enemy, and was separated from him at last in the *Gulf
Stream* by a furious hurricane, which for three days more
threatened him with immediate destruction. Nor was it
his last danger from seas or from enemies. He had two

other storms, and **two other detachments of** British men
of war, to encounter; **one in the English Channel, and**
another **in the Bay of Biscay. He arrived at Bordeaux**
in April.

Nothing but vigilance, patience, and perseverance,
added to consummate nautical skill, could have preserved
that ship through so many dangers at that equinoctial
season, and with such a succession of irresistible enemies.

I heartily wish Captain Tucker success, and beg the
favor of **you, sir, to communicate to any committee who**
may be charged with the examination of his application,
this letter **from,**

Your friend, and humble servant,

JOHN ADAMS.

HON. MR. CROWNINSHIELD,
Secretary of the Navy of the United States.

The foregoing is a true copy of the original, now in my
possession.

MARK L. HILL.

The bill, however, passed **the** Senate, and it seems that
the pension **he had drawn of twenty** dollars a month was
not afterwards regarded **as** an estoppel, for in Niles's
Register (Vol. 19, p. 397) **is this** statement: "Much time
was spent on private claims and affairs — especially on a
bill reported by the Naval Committee to place the vener-
able Commodore Tucker, of the Revolutionary army, **on**
a pension list of fifty dollars per month. The merits of
that distinguished officer were fully **acknowledged, but the**
propriety of the procedure **was objected to on** general

principles. At last the bill was ordered to be engrossed for a third reading."

Honorable John Chandler, of the Senate, then wrote, —

WASHINGTON, 5th February, 1821.

MY DEAR COMMODORE: I have only time to say to you that the Senate has this moment passed your bill, granting you a pension of half captain's pay, by a majority of nearly two to one, notwithstanding a powerful opposition of Smith, Roberts, Macon, and others.

In haste, your humble servant,

JOHN CHANDLER.

COMMODORE TUCKER.

During the long period of time in which Commodore Tucker so often petitioned to Congress for relief, if not payment of the arrears due him, he wrote numerous letters, of which copies were preserved in his own handwriting. The publication of the whole would unnecessarily swell this volume; but a few extracts may be interesting to the reader.

At Boston, November 25, 1816, he wrote to the Hon. B. Homans, of the Navy Department, and in that letter remarks, "I have some papers in custody, which I wanted Mr. Parris to look over before he left Boston; they are no more than orders I received in 1779, when made a Commodore, having under my command Seth Harding, Esq., of the Confederacy, and Alexander Montgomery, Esq., of the General Greene."

Again, in a letter to the same, dated June 6. 1816, "I

have asked nothing more than my real due, — and it is a question whether I have asked that, — as it is President Adams's opinion I ought to be paid from 1780 to 1787, when I received the thanks of Congress for the services rendered my country during the Revolutionary war, and at the same time I was informed by that honorable committee that Congress still held me in the service of my country, being the senior maritime officer of the four New England States."

In his letter to the Honorable John Holmes, written at Bristol, December 23, 1817, he says, "Mr. Parris was in Congress when the report was made, and can give you every information concerning the affair; my venerable and worthy friend, President Adams, has taken an active part in my favor." And in a long letter to Mr. Holmes, March 6, 1818, he says, "The commission above alluded to is in manuscript, and signed by the Honorable Samuel Adams, deceased, late chief magistrate of this State we are citizens of, and I would to God he had been in the chair of magistracy the last war; then, my dear sir, our noble State had not lost her former glory. . . . Had I a moderate competency to subsist on for myself and my feeble consort, who has lived with me in a state of matrimony upwards of eight and forty years, I would have despised the idea of giving myself half the trouble I have already been at, although my aged friends, who perfectly recollect my former services, are still urging me to pursue it. . . . The first cruise I made was performed in January, 1776, and I had to purchase the small arms to encounter my enemy with money from my own pocket, or go without them'; and the **consort above mentioned made the** banner I fought under, the field **of which was white and** the union was green, made therein in the figure **of a pine** tree, made of cloth of her own purchasing, at her own expense. Those colors I wore in honor of my country, which has *so nobly* **rewarded me** for my past services, **and for the love of their maker, until I fell in with** Colonel Archibald Campbell, in the ship George, **and brig Ara-** bella, transports, with about two hundred and eighty Highland troops on board, of General Frazer's corps. About ten P. M. a severe conflict ensued, which held about two hours and twenty minutes. I conquered them, with great courage on their side. It being in the night, and my small **bark,** about seventy tons burden, being very low in **the water, I received** no damage in **the** loss of **men, but** lost a complete suit **of new sails** by the passing of their **balls. . . . I** was told **by** the Navy Commissioner, Benjamin Walker, Esq., that I was the only one who was not called on by a court martial, or court of inquiry, of the whole who had command of the thirteen frigates in public service ; and he then said, 'Since you have been in New York, you have been waited upon with the thanks of **Congress, for** the services rendered your country.' . . . Although my government's neglect is severe on me respecting **my former** services, it does not lessen the love of country **in me : I** positively declare in my own mind, aged **and disabled as I am, if** my dear country, United America, was invaded **by any power** whatever, and my advice **or** actions were called **for by the** public authority, **or private State, thinking as I do, I** would step forth with all the alacrity that my power could summon, or dispense with the last drop of blood that runs warm in my veins in its defence."

On the 20th of December, 1820, the electoral college of Maine unanimously appointed him a special messenger to carry the votes for President and Vice-President to Washington. Though nearly seventy-four years of age, he performed a journey exceeding six hundred miles in less than five days. It must be recollected that the facilities of steam travelling were then unknown, not having been introduced until several years after.

In his route to the capital, he passed through a large section of a country he had not visited for more than forty years, and then it was seen amidst the convulsions of war and distress in every direction. What astounding changes he must have noticed! — the splendid cities of New York, Philadelphia, and Baltimore, towering to the skies; flourishing towns, picturesque country seats, busy marts of commerce, cultivated fields, cosy farm-houses, and everywhere the United States exhibiting the prosperity of a great nation! Railroads, then in contemplation, were only wanting to give the magnificence of the present day to the picture. This naval veteran must have felt an electric thrill within his breast, when he looked round and thought that all these blessings of a free and happy people were purchased by the blood and valor of the patriots of '76. And was he not one of them?

Indeed, this beautiful panorama of peace and prosperity, such as no nation on earth had ever experienced in any age or country, must have been to him like the dream of an old man, when he sees visions of bliss, after long years of neglect, poverty, and affliction. Then, had Congress done their duty, and political jobbers, demagogues, and speech-makers laid aside their intrigues, and united with the more honorable and noble members in rewarding merit, and bestowing a liberal pension on this venerable patriot, it would have redounded to their glory, and the commodore would have returned a happier man to his humble home in Bristol. But it is the misfortune of the country that our republic has been too often represented in Congress by men who looked only to their own emoluments and self-interest.

When he first appeared in the House of Representatives, standing among a group of strangers outside the bar, his commanding figure and silvery locks excited much attention. It was soon whispered round that Commodore Tucker, one of the few surviving naval officers of the Revolution, was there, and all eyes were fixed upon him. Was it not, among the great men in that Witenagemote, a moment of sublime recollections of history, when he stood, as it were, revealed before them? As of old in the court of Carthage, —

" Restitit Æneas, claraque in luce refulsit."

There were many in that august assembly who had heard of the man, his bravery, his skill, his success on the ocean, while his daring deeds were yet fresh in the minds of the older members of Congress. It was quickly reported in the Capitol, over whose dome the stars and stripes were proudly waving, that there was one among them who had taken from the enemy sixty-two sail of vessels, more than six hundred pieces of cannon, and three thousand prisoners, in the Continental war.

Let not the reader suspect the author of this sketch of exaggeration in these numerical calculations; for such was the statement of his exploits in the National Intelligencer of December 16, 1820, when speaking of his mission from the electoral college of Maine. Forty-seven years have elapsed, and this generation is too ready to ignore or forget the past; but these are facts, which are clearly seen in the light of history.

The Honorable Mark L. Hill, of Maine, was about moving the House to admit the veteran on the floor, when, upon exemination, it was found that Congress, after the close of the Revolutionary war, had passed a unanimous vote of thanks to Commodore Tucker for the services he had rendered his country. Therefore, according to a standing rule of the House, no special vote was necessary, and he was admitted.

His visit to Washington probably awoke there a public sympathy and warm interest for his welfare: for, soon after his return home, his memorial was taken from the files of the Senate, and referred to the Committee on Naval Affairs. Their report was able, decisive, and honorary to the applicant. It was drawn up by the Honorable Freeman Walker, and a copy of it, from the American State Papers, entitled Claims, page 760, — a work edited by W. Lowrie and W. S. Franklin, — is here presented.

ARREARS OF PAY.

Communicated to the Senate, January 12, 1821.

Mr. Walker, of Georgia, from the Committee on Naval Affairs, to whom **was** referred the petition of Samuel Tucker, reported, —

That the petitioner was, as he states in his petition, a captain in the navy of the United States during the Revolutionary war; that he obtained his commission on the 20th January, 1776, and served his country with fidelity during the whole of our Revolutionary struggle; that, after encountering the hardships, privations, and dangers incident to his station, and having, by his successful exertions, contributed much to the advancement of the American cause, he was taken prisoner by the enemy, at Charleston, in the month of May, 1780, but was in the month of August, of the same year, exchanged, and again, as he states, entered the service of his country, in which he continued until the successful termination of our controversy, in 1783, having received the thanks of Congress for his meritorious services; that the petitioner has received no pecuniary remuneration for the services rendered his country from August, 1780, to the conclusion of the war; that although the petitioner does not appear to have been *actively* employed after his exchange, yet there is no evidence of his having been discharged; and as he was ready and liable to obey the call of his country at any moment, he could not profitably pursue any private avocation.

The committee are therefore of opinion, that the petitioner is entitled to some pecuniary remuneration, provision for which the committee the more cheerfully recommend to the Senate, from the consideration that the petitioner is a very aged person (being upwards of seventy-three years of age), that he is very poor, and from the infirmities incident to such advanced age is, as he himself states, incapable, by manual labor or individual exertion, of procuring a subsistence for himself and family. The committee are of opinion that both justice and gratitude unite in the call upon government to grant the prayer of the petitioner in the present case. They therefore report a bill for his relief. — *American State Papers, Claims.*

Mr. Hill wrote to him, February 15, that the bill, giving him **half pay as** captain in the navy during life, had passed the Senate. On the 20th of the same month, the House took it up. Niles's Register states, " **A bill for the** relief of Commodore Tucker **was rejected by a majority** of one **vote !"** Some members said that the statute of limitations had barred all claims for relief; others gave more pitiful reasons. Thus more than ten years elapsed before any liberal provision was made for " meritorious services," so clearly proved to, and acknowledged by, a committee of the Senate. At last, in June 4, 1832, a general act was passed, allowing full pay to all officers and privates of the Revolution who had served two years in the Continental army, and also in the navy.

In the Boston Weekly Messenger, of April 11, 1833,

containing an obituary notice of Commodore Tucker, is this paragraph touching his pension: "Although a former Secretary of War had reported the sum of twelve hundred dollars a year to be due by government, he remained without a cent from the government until a few years since, when he received twenty dollars per month; this last winter the stain of ingratitude was partially wiped away by an annuity of six hundred dollars per year settled on him by government."

The deep interest and sympathy manifested for him by members who presented or advocated his repeated memorials — the Honorable John Holmes and General John Chandler, of the Senate; Honorable Mark L. Hill, Benjamin Brown, William Reed, Albion K. Parris, and others, of the House; the generous report of the able Senator, Honorable Freeman Walker, which so much redounds to the exploits of the veteran; and the explicit and honorable testimony of his venerable friend, Ex-President Adams, it would seem, would have been enough to make the politicians of the hour withdraw all objections, and pass at least a silent vote in his behalf.

The following letter from his old friend John Barnes, was received at Washington: —

BRIDGE STREET, GEORGETOWN, COL.,
9th February, 1821.

DEAR SIR: Your late arrival at Washington brought to my recollection, that on your visit to New York, in 1785 or '86, to wait on the late Colonel Walker (to whom I was then an assistant clerk), you did me the honor to dine with me, in company with the late Commodore Whipple and Captain Manly, — now thirty-four years past; — and could you make it convenient, with your present business, before you leave Washington, I should be much gratified in your renewing the *favor*, so long delayed. My friend, Mr. Dunn, will inform you, if necessary, respecting my situation, &c.

Most respectfully, sir, your obedient servant,

JOHN BARNES.

CAPTAIN SAMUEL TUCKER, *Washington.*

When he was a representative in the General Court of Massachusetts, it will be recollected that Ex-President Adams took a deep interest in the welfare of his old friend. In confirmation of this fact, the copy of a letter from Mr. Adams to Matthew Carey, Esq., of Philadelphia, is here introduced. It was carefully transcribed from the original document, now in possession of Martin P. Kennard, Esq., of Boston, who has preserved it among his valuable collection of autographs. This gentleman has garnered up in his casket many precious jewels of other times, accompanied with some engraved portraits of our great men. Such relics are often of historic value.

QUINCY, June 1, 1813.

SIR: On Sunday last Samuel Tucker, Esquire, of Bristol in the District of Maine, very unexpectedly made me a visit. I was delighted to see once more, the Man, who in 1778 carried me safely to Bourdeaux, through the six and twenty misfortunes of Harlequin. He is sixty-five years of age. He has retired upon a Farm, and is a

16

Representative in our State House of Representatives; but is more anxious at present for his neighbors, *really* suffering for want of bread, than for the honors of his civil station, or for Naval Glory. He has lately stepped on board a sloop, loaded with wood, with a few Volunteers, only two of whom had ever seen a gun in anger; none were seamen; and by his address and intrepidity, took an English Privateer, which had long infested their coast and distressed the inhabitants. This fact deserves a place in your Naval History.

Capt. Tucker has promised me a list of the Prizes he took from the English, sixty or seventy I believe, in the revolutionary war, with the names of the Ships and their Commanders. When I receive it, I will immediately transmit it to you.

This Man was with his Boston frigate in the harbor of Charleston, when invaded by the British army and navy. His flag continued to fly. The British Admiral sent a special order to the Commander of the Boston to strike his Flag. Tucker's answer was, 'I do not think much of striking my flag to your present Force; but I have struck more of your Flags, than are now flying in this harbor.'

When I see, or hear, of or from, one of these old Men whether in civil, political, military or naval service, my heart feels.

I hope you will not think me officious; but believe me, a cordial Approver of your design and work and

Your obliged servant

JOHN ADAMS.

MATHEW CAREY ESQ. *Philadelphia.*

He was invited to attend the solemnities at Belfast, on account of the death of Adams and Jefferson, the commemoration of which the following correspondence will show : —

BELFAST, August 7, 1826.

SIR : We have set apart Thursday, the 10th instant, in this town, to call into recollection the patriotic and noble services of the deceased patriots, Adams and Jefferson, and have to beg the favor of your attendance on that occasion.

JOHN WILSON, *Per Order.*

COMMODORE TUCKER.

John Wilson, Esq., who wrote this letter, was a lawyer of high rank in that part of the country ; the invitation was complimentary, but the veteran had begun to find that the years were hanging heavy upon him, and he declined the invitation in a reply breathing the spirit of '76.

BRISTOL, August 9, A. D. 1826.

DEAR SIR : Through the medium of Mr. Benjamin Palmer, I received your polite invitation to attend at Belfast, on the 10th instant, to accompany my fellow-citizens in hearing a eulogy delivered on the occasion of the demise of two of the greatest statesmen and patriots of whom our country can boast, the illustrious Washington excepted ; and I think it highly meritorious in all our brother Republicans to hold it up, as it ought to be celebrated with some degree of solemnity. I was acquainted with both these gentlemen for many years, and with one of them much better than the other ; and firmly declare they were two of the greatest luminaries who brought us from thraldom into this glorious liberty, which all the children of men ought freely to enjoy throughout the universe. I doubt not in the least but they will be each crowned with a diadem in the celestial mansions, equally as honorable in their blest abode, as they merited amongst men here below.

Indisposition pleads the cause of my non-attendance, for which I was very sorry. Sir, please to accept of the best wishes of your servant, for yourself and for those for whom you wrote, and subscribe,

Your most obedient, &c.,

SAMUEL TUCKER.

JOHN WILSON, Esq.

He was a member of the Masonic Fraternity, and made a Mason at Boston in 1779. The author saw his diploma, and took the following extract : —

To SAMUEL TUCKER,

Then follows the Diploma, from " St. **John's** Lodge, **No. 1, Boston.**" It is dated 30th day of January, 1779.

(Countersigned.)	(Signed.)
NATHAN PATTEN, Master.	JOHN CUTLER, S. G. W.
WM. BURBACK, S. Warden.	JOB PRINCE, J. G. W.
RICHARD SALTER, J. Warden.	NATH. BARBER, JR., G. S.
ELIAS PARKMAN, *Secy.*	

He belonged to the Agricultural Society of Maine, as appears by a notice to him, dated January 1, 1819, when the late Judge Wilde was president. It was signed by John Merrick, Esq., who died at Hallowell, October 22, 1862, ninety-six years old.

The commodore and his wife, when they resided in Boston, attended the Episcopal Church, of which she was a communicant. Often in his family would he repeat parts and passages of what he called the beautiful Church Liturgy. His views were serious, and he always spoke with reverence of religion.

The following letter to the author, from Professor John Johnston, LL. D., of the Wesleyan University, Middletown, Connecticut, refers to an interesting incident illustrating that decision of character for which Commodore Tucker was so remarkable : —

I cheerfully comply with your request, to send in writing an anecdote of the late Commodore Tucker, to which allusion was made in our conversation a few days ago.

In the year 1832, being a member of the Senior Class of Bowdoin College, the late Professor Parker Cleaveland one day said to me, he noticed from the catalogue of the college that I was from the town of Bristol, and then proceeded to say, that he supposed he was indebted to a townsman of mine for the preservation of his life, *Commodore Tucker!* On my replying that he lived a few miles from my father's, but I knew him well, he proceeded to relate the circumstances of the case, which were substantially as follows : —

In the year 1816, being on his way from Brunswick to
Boston, he was obliged to cross a ferry, — it was either at
Portsmouth or Newburyport, — and the weather and tide
being unfavorable, the boat came near being wrecked, and
all on board lost. For some reason, soon after starting from
the shore, many of the passengers became much alarmed,
and no little confusion prevailed; but the boat kept on her
way. The alarm, however, rapidly increased, the captain
seemed to lose his presence of mind, the boat became quite
unmanageable, and all were in great danger; but just at
this time, the loud, sharp voice of one of the passengers
was heard above the noise and confusion, giving orders in
a very authoritative manner to those having charge of the
boat; and such was his wonderful self-possession in that
time of peril, and such the confidence he inspired in all
minds, in a little time perfect order was restored, all
yielded a cheerful obedience to the commands of their
new friend, and soon they were landed in safety. ·

Their preserver — for such he considered him — proved
to be *Commodore Tucker*, of Bristol, whom he had ever
since remembered with the sincerest gratitude.

The Portsmouth ferry must have been referred to, for
at that time there was no bridge between Portsmouth and
Kittery. A bridge was first opened for passengers September 10, 1822. This ferry, from the rapidity of the tide,
was dangerous in bad weather.

A nephew of the commodore, John T. Gleason, of New
York, who has since deceased, stated to the author that
the father of the late Commodore Barron was a lieutenant

on board of one of his uncle's ships of war, was fatally wounded in an action, and dying, left his son to Tucker's care, who put him to school in Boston. Mr. Gleason stated that this was told him by his uncle.

He was a man of tender heart, he felt deeply for the misfortunes of others, and such feelings extended even to individuals who had wronged and injured him. An interesting incident of this kind is related of him when he was a member of the legislature of Maine, which was sitting in Portland. It must have occurred in 1820 or 1821.

As he was walking in the street, he accidentally came across Major C., the gentleman to whom in November, 1785, he lent United States scrip, amounting to eighteen thousand two hundred dollars—referred to in Chapter IX., page 170 — to save him from bankruptcy and ruin. For this loan, which was to have been paid in a week, he never received one cent. More than thirty-five years had passed since that transaction, when Commodore Tucker immediately accosted him, and reminded him of the debt. Major C. did not know him, and denied the fact.

"Your words are useless," was the answer: "I should know that face among ten thousand."

The veteran returned to his lodgings, and despatched word to his family to send on immediately a small box of documents, containing the receipt which the borrower of the scrip had given him. On arrival of the papers, accompanied by one or two friends, the commodore called upon the major, whose son was in town, and whose presence there had been preconcerted. The lender and the borrower met face to face. Tucker held out the written receipt, and pointed significantly to the signature, —

"Did you ever see that writing before?"

"Never."

The major's son was now desired to examine the paper. He came forward, looked at it for a moment, then laid it down.

"Father," he exclaimed, in a broken voice, "this is worse than all! To stand here, before us all, and deny your own name, and the marks of your own pen — I cannot bear it."

The conscience-stricken soldier burst into a flood of tears. "O, my God!" he cried, "it is true. Take all I have! my pension — it is all I have left. Take it. I will go to the almshouse, and die a pauper!"

The moisture gushed from the old commodore's eyes. "No!" he said, "I cannot do it. The money your country gave you; it was coined out of your heart's blood. Not a dollar of it will I touch, not a dollar. Go in peace, my old friend. God forgive you, as I do." And he turned and left him.

The commodore was fond of telling humorous stories; and he told them well, for he was a man inclined to be jovial and of a ready wit. Some of his facetious sallies are related in the diary of Mr. Adams, in his passage to France, in the frigate Boston, which may be found in the Life and Works of John Adams, by his grandson, Honorable Charles Francis Adams.

A few anecdotes have been gathered for this biography, one of which was related to the author by the late Honorable Albert Smith, of Boston, who was at the convention he refers to, also a member of the legislature with Tucker, and afterwards marshal of Maine.

When the Representatives of Maine were preparing to organize their first legislature, they called a convention for the purpose. Commodore Tucker, member from Bristol, being the oldest person present, was requested to take the chair, and call the assembly to order, until a president was chosen; which he did. A secretary was then elected. Some member then rose, and by mistake began his motion by addressing the secretary, when the commodore, lifting up his voice, exclaimed, "Avast, there! I am not gone yet."

Another anecdote was handed me by a gentleman, who received it as a fact, but he did not vouch for its authenticity. *Valeat quantum valere potest.*

Commodore Tucker was about to sail from Camden, Maine, one evening after dark. Just before the hour of sailing a lady of genteel appearance, dressed in deep mourning, closely veiled, and apparently in great affliction, applied to him to take the body of her deceased husband on board, that she might bury it among her kindred in Massachusetts. Overcome by her solicitations he consented, though reluctantly; and then she informed him that the coffin had not yet arrived, and might be delayed two or three hours, and begged him to wait. To this also he assented, though with great inconvenience to himself. It was nearly eleven o'clock before the coffin arrived, which was then placed in the hold, and the mourning widow was accommodated with a state-room near the body of her husband.

As the commodore was pacing the deck at night, watching the movements of the vessel till it should get clear of land, the man at the helm, a shrewd old down-east seaman, says to him, " Commodore, may I have a word with you ? "

" Certainly," was the reply.

" Well, commodore, I tell ye, I don't like the looks of that ere widow very well."

" Why ? " says the commodore, " I am sure she is a very genteel person, and though closely veiled, apparently quite attractive."

" Yes," says the old sailor, " all that ; but she steps the deck too much like a naval officer to suit my notions of a woman. If I was you, commodore, I would just take a look at that coffin before I turned in to-night."

The commodore's suspicions were aroused, and furnishing his pockets with suitable instruments, and taking a lantern, he went into the hold, and first subjected the outside of the coffin to a close scrutiny. He noticed it was a very large one, and on further examination, discovered a slender black silk cord running from the inside of the lid, and passing through a crevice into the state-room of the widow. He gently raised the lid, and there was a stalwart form, quietly sleeping, dressed in the uniform of a British naval officer, and abundantly armed with sword, pike, pistols, &c. Before the man was fully awake, the commodore secured his wrists with handcuffs, and, peremptorily enjoining silence upon him, passed into the state-room of the widow. There he found the widow's weeds hanging upon the bulkhead, and a young, handsome, beardless British naval lieutenant sitting rather uneasily on the side of his berth. He was also instantly accommodated with handcuffs; and confronting the two, it was found, that by the aid of accomplices among the crew who lifted the coffin on board, they had formed a plot to seize the vessel, as soon as she should reach the open sea, and run her into Halifax, with the commodore, and his officers, and faithful crew, prisoners of war. But the handcuffs were already on their wrists.

The Rev. Professor Calvin E. Stowe, D. D., of Hartford, Connecticut, related this incident to the author: —

When he was a student at Bowdoin College, in a visit to Portland, he happened to be present at a session of the Maine legislature when Tucker was a member. A measure, which the commodore deemed impolitic and injurious to the public interest, had been embodied into a bill, and was on the point of being enacted, when he suddenly rose in his seat, and with his thundering voice exclaimed, "Mr. Speaker, you may force this law by a majority, but I warn you, look out for the undertow!" These few words opened the eyes of the majority, and killed the bill.

Congress at last passed a law, June 7, 1832, giving pensions to certain officers who had served in the Revolutionary war, in which class Commodore Tucker was included. The payment commenced March 4, 1831. Thus, after so many years of solicitude and deprivation, this veteran commander received an annuity of six hundred dollars for the remainder of his life ; but it came almost too late to cheer and comfort the prospects of futurity. The sun was already descending in the horizon of life. After the storms and trials of years, true it is, its setting beams shone beautifully ; but the shades of evening were near — he was soon to see it no more !

He lived to enjoy his pension as captain in the navy hardly beyond two years. He had become an old man. Though he possessed a strong and sound constitution, and, like many other pensioners, had a fair prospect of reaching even a hundred years, yet Providence otherwise ordained. He soon experienced bitter sorrow in his family. He was left alone. His beloved wife, who had shared with him, for sixty-three years, the weal and woe of fortune, was taken from him not many months before his own death. Such a handsome provision for their comfort and independence, at an earlier day, when both were younger, and struggling with want, would have been a real boon — a harbinger of happier hours. Then it would have relieved him from years of anxiety and suffering, as he looked around on his tough, rugged acres, and thought of his cattle, which needed to be housed more than six months of the year, and found the reality too real, that in Maine the life of a farmer was the pursuit of a livelihood under difficulties.

For nothing wears and tears the human constitution like penury in old age, when debts make the sufferer turn away his face from his creditor, and the wolf is at the door. Such a condition takes away hope, which is the sheet anchor of the soul, and chills the very life-blood of the heart. Surely the hands of the old ought to cease from hard labor, and age be exempted from all harrowing anxieties to procure food and raiment. The celebrated Junius, in his advice to Mr. Woodfall, makes this sage observation: " Let all your views in life be directed to a solid, however moderate, independence. Without it, no man can be happy, or even honest." One of the greatest sources of happiness to man is, in the words of Isaiah, that " *bread shall be given him, and his waters shall be sure.*"

But there is no certainty, no security, in the duration of human life. We know not what a day may bring forth. This hearty, robust, powerful man was assailed by disease. It came upon him suddenly: and it was reported, that from the imprudent management of his medical adviser, it soon assumed symptoms that were fatal. It is Homer, who said thousands of years ago, —

> " Fixed is the term of all the race of earth,
> And such the hard condition of our birth."

He died at his home in Bremen, after a short but sharp sickness. Under the watchful care of his daughter, and his grandson, Colonel Samuel Tucker Hinds, he expired March 10, 1833, aged eighty-five years and four months. He saw Death — the greatest of mysteries — coming towards him, like the dark angel, at whose approach almost all men tremble, and he looked him firmly in the face, as he had done on the ocean in the day of battle. A few hours before his departure, while the late General Denny M'Cobb, collector at Waldoboro', was standing at his bedside, he said, " Well, general, I am about to pass away to that world from which no traveller has returned. You are soon to follow me. I hope and trust we shall meet there, where no pain nor sorrow will disturb us, and be happy in the smiles and favor of Heaven. My trust is in CHRIST. Farewell." Gently and calmly he soon after breathed his last.

He retained to the last of a long life an unwavering loyalty to his country. Less than five months before his death, in one of the Maine newspapers appeared a circular signed Samuel Tucker, to the surviving officers and soldiers of the Revolution, denouncing the selection of General Andrew Jackson as a candidate for the presidency. He began it by reference to'himself, — " Fourscore and six years old, standing on the confines of another world." It is full of the ardor of youth, which, surviving still, like volcanic fires beneath a mountain top covered with snow, was hidden, but not extinguished, under his white locks of age. He gave his honest opinion. Perhaps, from a different standpoint, his view of that distinguished man would have been less harsh, for President Jackson certainly upheld the Union when Nullification first showed its hydra head.

There were many noble traits in the character of Commodore Tucker. As a son and a father, he was very affectionate. He sustained his aged mother to the last of her long and lingering life. His widowed daughter, Mrs. Mary Hinds, soon after the death of her husband, Captain Benjamin Hinds, found a home in his family while he lived, and survived him many years. That a good son seldom, if ever, fails to make a good husband, was verified in his conjugal and domestic life.

His personal appearance was striking, and always accompanied with dignity. He was a man five feet and nearly nine inches in height, very muscular, strongly built, and remarkably broad across the chest. At an earlier period of his life he must have wielded the broadsword with much skill and force, for he was said to have been an adroit swordsman. His weight was usually about two hundred and twenty-five pounds, and his erect and active figure, well proportioned and solid, seemed to move, in the street, as though walking the quarter-deck of a frigate, with the air of one having authority.

His features were well defined and marked; — an aquiline, or Roman nose, a mouth expressive of decision, a clear, broad forehead, dark eyebrows, and deep blue eyes, are well remembered; though when I last saw him, his locks, which were said in his youth to have been handsome and curly, were white as snow. His portrait, though not perfect, is a pretty good likeness. It was copied from an oil painting taken in England. His voice was unusually loud, even in common conversation: there was nothing soft or gentle in its intonations. It was like thunder, but it was without passion or excitement. He had spent much of his early and midday life at sea; and probably from habit of giving orders amidst the roar of winds and billows, he found it necessary to pitch his key to a sonorous, deep, and heavy note, and it became ever after a second nature. He retained his hearing, sight, and memory to the hour when the fatal disease of four days overpowered him.

Though often exposed during the war to great peril, and sometimes to the shot of the enemy, he escaped any permanent and serious injury. On board of the Boston, in her voyage to France, during a violent storm, he was knocked down and stunned by a piece of spar the lightning had splintered, yet he was not seriously hurt. Once a pistol shot, in a naval engagement, grazed one of his ribs, but it was only a flesh wound; and at another time a cannon ball struck one of the timbers near where he stood, and a fragment of it entered his leg, making a wound which occasionally was troublesome through life, but did not lame him.

The obsequies of this naval hero were performed in a manner honorable to his memory. Many came to his funeral from a great distance; but as the day was bleak, and the travelling bad at that inclement season, hundreds were deprived of paying their last respects to one so much beloved by his townsmen. His remains were laid in a grave in the Bremen cemetery. This burial-place lies on the declivity facing the east, where about an acre or two are enclosed by the side of the county road. It is full of the mementos of mortality, and among them are two neat marble monuments. The spot is picturesque: glimpses of the river are seen beyond the woods, and at a distance the blue Camden mountains loom up. For why should not the dead repose in the most beautiful parts of the earth, that we may think of heaven when we think of their last home?

The roadside is lined by a row of evergreens, the juniper, the fir, and the cedar; and this cemetery, compared to many burial-grounds in the country, is creditable to the town of Bremen. The stranger who visits this spot will observe one green mound, and at the head of it a slate slab, upright, with an urn beneath a willow foliage, and on it is inscribed, —

IN MEMORY OF

COM. SAMUEL TUCKER,

Who Died

March 10, 1833.

A PATRIOT OF THE REVOLUTION.

On one side is the grave of his wife, Mary, who died December 31, 1832, and on the other, that of his daughter, Mary Hinds, who died November 25, 1855. To their memory marble stones have been erected.

In the American Almanac, for 1835, there is a short obituary of him.

"March 10, 1833. At Bremen, Maine, in his eighty-sixth year, Commodore Samuel Tucker. He was born at Marblehead, in 1747; was apprenticed to the sea service at the age of eleven years; received a commission as Commodore in the early part of the Revolutionary war; and was distinguished as a brave, able, and successful commander. He is said to have been at the time of

17

his death, next to General **Lafayette**, the highest surviving officer of the Revolution."

Who can look upon the humble memorial of a man thus distinguished in the Revolution, — a PIONEER of the American navy, **so illustrious in the history of our country, — and feel no sorrow that a generous people had not** consecrated his grave by a **durable** monument fraught with their gratitude and worthy of his exploits?

He did his part, and did it nobly, when our navy was in an embryo state, and only consisted of a few armed sloops and schooners, and yet performed such essential **service in su**pplying the destitute army of Washington. **He was not alone.** Whipple, Manly, Jones, and **others, in such small** armaments, **also laid the foundation of their future fame.** Their daring little cruisers were **rudimental schools, in** which brave and experienced officers **and** marines were educated to man those frigates which **were** afterwards built by order **of** Congress.

" Tantum molis erat Romanam condere **gentem.**"

Through such a mass of difficulties was **the American navy** created, — a navy, which was glorious **in the Revo**lution, **gained so** many brilliant victories **in the last war** with **Great Britain,** and in the **late unhappy Rebellion,** under **gallant officers** and brave **men,** surpassed **all its** former achievements !

In this age of progress **and of wonders, in a nation of** more than thirty **millions of people, and with a territory** extending from the **Atlantic to the Pacific Ocean, is it** right, is it grateful, to ignore the merits, and neglect the exploits, of those who first led the way to victory and independence, and laid the foundation of our naval superiority? They have all gone to their rest! Fifty years ago they warmed the hearts of the patriot, and their names and deeds were fresh on every tongue. Now they are almost forgotten. And yet, do they not deserve a niche in the Temple of Fame — a place among the biographies of departed worth?

APPENDIX.

THE following Appendix contains a copy of the Journal or Log-Book of Captain Tucker, in the frigate **Boston**, when he took charge of the Hon. John Adams and son, to France. It is transcribed from the original, found among his papers. It commences on the 19th of February, 1778, and terminates October 2, 1778. The remainder of thirteen days, until Commodore Whipple's squadron arrived at Portsmouth, N. H., is wanting. Other documents, selected from a mass of manuscripts, may be of some interest, particularly the muster-roll of the frigate **Boston** on the next cruise, which comprises nearly three hundred names, of officers, marines, and seamen, among whom some of the living descendants may be enabled to trace their descent from ancestors who defended our country in the Revolution.

For this valuable document of a full muster-roll of the frigate Boston, in 1778 and 1779, the author, with pleasure, acknowledges his obligation to the Hon. James Gregory, of Marblehead, formerly collector of that port, and since a member of the Senate of Massachusetts. From that gentleman he received much useful information in preparing this life of Commodore Tucker.

I. COPY OF COMMODORE TUCKER'S LOG-BOOK.

A Journal of a Cruise, by God's permission, in the good Ship **called** *the Boston, appertaining to the United States of America.*

On the 11th of February, embarked on board a pilot boat at Boston, and went down to Nantasket Roads, on board said Boston frigate, the ship being ready for sea. The wind and weather prevented my going this day, the former being S. E., and latter very thick and full of rain.

Nothing more remarkable this day

Remarks on Thursday, February 12, 1778.

This morning, after overhauling my ship's stores, found several necessary articles omitted by being so much hurried, which I sent to town for immediately, by Mr. Barron, my first lieutenant, and Richard Palmer, Esq., captain of marines, who proceeded in the same boat that brought me down, but the wind being strong from the N. W. they could not reach the town until midnight, and I could not possibly unmoor ship.

Here ends these twenty-four hours.

Remarks on **Friday, February** 13, 1778.

This morning, still continues fresh gales from the N. W., which prevents me from unmooring; still I having some capital business at Braintree, sent my boat on shore to George's Island, and brought off a pilot to conduct me there. At 10 A. M. proceeded there, finished my business, and returned on board by 5 P. M., where I found my officers, to my satisfaction, returned from Boston, with all my necessaries I indented for, except it was pistols. I thought proper to send my ship's master, Mr. Bates, on board of a schooner for wood, which lay in the Road. Mr. Bates, not liking the wood, returned and acquainted me.

So ends this day. Still blowing from the N. W. hard gales.

Remarks on Saturday, February 14, 1778.

This morning, at 5 A. M., began to unmoor, still blowing fresh gales. At 2 P. M. got one anchor on board after a hard and heavy piece of work; at 3 do., put my pilot for Braintree on shore. Very clear weather, with fresh gales.

So ends this day. Nothing more material.

Remarks on Sunday, February 15, 1778.

This morning, at 6 A. M., began to heave ahead; at 8 do. got under way, and proceeded to Marblehead for some of my officers and men; at 2 P. M. came to anchor after firing several signal guns; at 4 P. M. sent my large boat on board a coaster, and furnished the ship with three cords of wood.

So ends this day.

Remarks on Monday, February 16, 1778.

This morning, the wind being N. E., and blowing quick, I weighed my anchor and dropped farther up the harbor. Very full of rain. I then seeing no probability of going to sea, gave two midshipmen, two mates, and my purser, liberty to go on shore. At 2 A. M. the wind got round to northward; I desired preparation to be made for getting under way, fired several guns to bring my officers off, but finally I was obliged to go and bring them on board, and after a great deal of trouble got them on board; the wind in the time had risen so high that I could not get under way until 7 A. M., on Tuesday, 17th; do., then weighed anchor, and came to sea, firing seven guns for a salute.

Remarks on Tuesday, February 17, 1778.

At 7 A. M., fresh gales of fair weather; the main gears broke, then I had the yard slung with a chain. The people employed as usual.

At 7 P. M., weighed anchor and came to sea with a pleasant gale from the N. W.; at 8 do., Cape Ann bore of us N. N. E., distance **about** three leagues, from which I take my departure. Pray God **conduct me safe to** France, and send me a prosperous cruise. Middle and latter parts of this twenty-four hours very clear, and pleasant gales.

Lat. of Cape Ann, 42° 46′ North.   Long. 69° 45′ West.

8
5

Lat. in 42° 38′   Long. in 69° 50′ West.
Lat. by obs. 41° 53′ N.

Course.	Dist.	X Lat.	Depart.	Lat. in.	X Long.	Long. in.	Mer. dist.
S. 69° E	127 m.	45′ S.	116 E.	45.53 N.	2.36 E.	67.14	116 E.

Remarks on Thursday, the 19th of February, 1778.

This twenty-four hours begins very pleasant, and a prosperous gale W. N. W. My people employed clearing ship and other necessary duty; at 6 A. M. saw three large ships bearing east; they standing to the northward, I mistrusted they were a cruising for me. I hauled my wind to the southward, found they did not pursue. I then consulted my officers; to stand to the northward after them. We agreed in opinions; wore ship, run one hour to the northward, then I discovered that one was a ship not less than ourselves, one out of sight to the northward, and the other appeared to me and officers to be a twenty-gun ship. The man at the mast-head called out a ship on the weather-quarter. At that time the other two under our lee, and under short sail. I then consulted the Honorable John Adams, Esq., and my officers, what was best to do; not knowing how my ship may sail, one and all consented to stand to the southward from them. At 10 A. M., I then wore ship to the southward, and stood from them. The two that were under my lee before I wore, immediately wore and stood after me. At 12 on meridian, lost sight of the small ship, and the other was about three leagues under my lee-quaster.

So ends this twenty-four hours.

Lat. by obs. 41° 28' N.

Course.	Dist.	X Lat.	Depart.	Lat. by Obs.	X Long.	Long. in.	Meridian.
S. 81 E.	156	25' S.	154 E.	41° 28' N	3° 24' E	63° 50'	270

Remarks on Friday, the 20th February, 1778.

This twenty-four hours begins very pleasant, the ship still in chase. I being poorly manned dare not attack her, and many other principal reasons. At 2 P. M. set fore and main top-mast steering sails, found I left the ship at 6 P. M.; it being dark, lost sight of the ship; in small sails, and hauled my wind, the cruiser supposing I bore away to steer the course I was going. When she saw me first, bore away and run E. S. E., while I for seven or eight hours had been running four points more southerly, at the rate of seven knots, brought her, in my opinion, to bear off me E. N. E., distance about eleven and half leagues. Then the wind headed me; I fell off to E. N. E.; then running at the rate of six knots for three hours, saw the same ship direct ahead, standing to southward and westward about five leagues distance; hove in stays, after making of her plain, and stood to the westward, because I could not weather her on the former tack. After running three hours to the westward the wind favored me. I then hove in stays, and came to windward of the frigate about four miles, and was entirely satisfied it was the same ship about four miles under my lee-quarter. They again tacked ship, and continued chasing that day, but I found I rather left my enemy.

Lat. by observation to-day, 40° 02' N.

Course.	Dist.	X Lat.	Depart.	Lat. per Obs.	X Long.	Long In.	M. Dist.
S. 43° E.	118 m.	86 S.	80 m. E.	40.02 N.	46 m. E.	64.04	350 E.

Remarks on Saturday, the 21st February, 1778.

This twenty-four hours begins with fresh gales and cloudy. Still chased by that ship at 4 P. M. Variable winds; at 6 do., calm; at 7 sprung up a breeze from the N. E., run until 10 P. M., S. S. E., attended with sharp lightning, and hard thunder; in small sails, cleared ship ready for an attack; at 12 midnight, the lightning struck the ship's mainmast and topmast, and wounded three men, struck several others down. Though we were in great danger, received but little damage. Latter part fresh gales and rain — saw no more of the ship. The sea being very cross and high, forced me to scud before the wind under my foresail, a very dangerous sea raging.

So ends this twenty-four hours, with hard gales, scudding.

Course.	Dist.	X. Lat.	Depart.	Lat. per Obs.	X Long.	Long. in.	M. Dis.
S. 37 E.	130 m.	89 S.	66 m. E.	38.33 N.	85 m. E	60.39	416m.E

Remarkable Observations on board the Boston Frigate, Sunday, 22d February, 1778.

This twenty-four hours begins with heavy gales, and a dangerous sea running; one thing or another continually giving away on board ship. Our ship made a great deal of water in several places, which caused the chain pumps continually to be kept at work. At 5 P. M. hove to under foresail, and lying very uneasy and dangerous. At 2 A. M. bore away and run before the wind to prevent any further damage if possible. At 2, the above-mentioned time, received a very heavy sea, but sustained little damage. At half past 3 A. M. discovered our foresail was split in the larboard leash, but could not prevent it at that time for the distress we were at that time in. I little expected but to be dismasted, as I was almost certain I heard the mainmast spring below the deck; afterwards discovered the truth of it. Still continues an extremity of weather.

So ends this day. Pray God protect us, and carry us through our various troubles.

Lat. obs. in 37° and 1′ North.

Course.	Dist.	X Lat.	Depart.	Lat. per Obs.	X Long.	Long. In.	M. Dis.
S. 29°E	106 m.	92 m. S	53 m. E	37°01′ N	1.08 E.	59.31 W	469 E.

Remarkable Observations on Monday, February 23, 1778.

This twenty-four hours begins with hard gales and close weather, running under foresail. At 2 P. M. I thought proper to haul the foresail up, hand it, lay by under mizzen. At 3 do. got down top-gallant yards. At 4 do. carried away the slings and chain of the mizzen yard, furled the mizzen, and set the mizzen staysail. Middle part continues fresh gales. At 4 A. M., something moderate, made sail and began to repair the rigging, it being much shattered in the gale. At 6 do. saw a sail to the N. E., running to the southward and westward. I stood on to the southward and eastward about half an hour. She crossed me about a league to windward. I supposed her to be a French merchantman bound to America. I then wore ship, made more sail, and pursued her, for fear she should not be one of them; I found I came up with chase very fast. I perceived she had set all the sail she possibly could. I then crowded sail. About 11 A. M. it came full of rain, and I lost sight of her for two or three hours.

Here ends this day.

No observation.

Course.	Dist.	X Lat.	Depart.	Lat.	X Long.	Long. in.	M. Dis.
S. 93 E.	56	55 m. S.	9 E.	36.06 N.	11 m. E	59.20	478m.E

Remarkable Observations on Tuesday, **February** 24. 1778.

This day begins with close weather **and rain.** At 2 P. M. got sight of our chase, which strove to cross me, ahead about one league, but as soon as they discovered me they kept by the wind. I then came up with **her very fast.** When I came up within a mile and a half, I hoisted American colors. I then took a squall from the west, very heavy, carried my M. T. mast overboard, lost nor wounded no man, thanks to God! She seeing **that,** hoisted Normandy colors, fired a gun to leeward. I answered **one, do.** I was obliged to go before the wind until the squall was over. The ship seeing my distress, bore after me, and run N. E. for about **half** an hour, but could not come up with me, though I was under short sail. She then kept the wind, and stood to the northward. I had the good fortune to save my sails and rigging, though very much **shattered. Middle and** latter **part** of these twenty-four hours my people employed clearing rigging. **Something moderate, with rain.**

Latitude observed in 37° 10′ North.

Course.	Dist.	X Lat.	Depart.	Lat. per Obs.	X Long.	Long. in.	M. Dist.
N. 40 E.	84 m.	64 m. N.	54 m. E.	37.10 N.	1.05 E.	58.15 W	532 m. E

Remarks **on** *Wednesday, February* 25, 1778, *on* **board** *the Boston Frigate.*

Moderate **gales with a** tumbling sea. Employed about getting a new **main-topmast to** hand, and fixing the rigging. At 2 P. M. reefed the **fore and mizzen** topsails **under** moderate sail.

Middle **and latter parts moderate gales and** cloudy.

Latitude **observed in 37° 48′** North.

Course.	Dist.	X Lat.	Depart.	Lat. by Obs.	X Long.	Long. in.	M. Dis.
N. 64 E.	88	38 m. N.	79 E.	37.48 N.	1.39 E.	56.36 W	611 m. E

Remarks on Thursday, February **26,** 1778, *continued on board thé* *Boston.*

This twenty-four hours begins with moderate gales and smooth sea; got a new main-topmast up, rigged it, and at 6 P. M. bent the M. T. sail.

Middle and latter parts moderate and cloudy.

Latitude observed in 38° 35′ North lat.

Course.	Dist.	X Lat.	Depart.	Lat. by Obs.	X Long.	Long. in.	M. Dis.
N.60°E	94 m.	47′ S.	81 m.E.	38.35 N.	1.42′ E.	54.54 W	692

Remarks on Friday, February 27, 1778, *on board the Boston* *Frigate.*

This twenty-four hours attended with light airs and calms. At 4 P. M. my people employed one hour exercising great **guns and** small arms.

Nothing more remarkable this day.

My people employed as usual about **necessary duty.**

Lat. in by observation 38° 18′ N.

Course.	Dist.	X Lat.	Depart.	Lat. by Obs.	X Long.	Long. in.	Mer.
S.36 E.	21 m.	17′ S.	12 m.E.	38.18 N.	15 m.E.	54.39 W	704 m. E

Remarks on Saturday, February 28, 1778, *on board the Boston.*

This twenty-four hours begins with moderate and pleasant breezes; my people employed mending my sails and getting my

T. G. yard up. Middle and latter parts very unsteady winds and disagreeable weather. Nothing very remarkable this day past.

Lat. by obs. in 39° 11′ North.

Course.	Dist.	X. Lat.	Depart.	Lat. by Obs.	X Long.	Long. in.	Mer. D.
N. 45 E.	75 m. N	53 m. N	53 m. E.	39.11 N.	1.8 m. E	53.31 W	757 E.

Remarkable Observations on board the Boston Frigate, **Sunday,** *March* 1, 1778.

The first part of this twenty-four hours moderate breezes. **At** 6 P. M. set M. G. S. The latter part cloudy with fresh breezes. Nothing very remarkable this day.

Lat. by obs. 40° 26′ North.

Mistook Course.	Mistook Dis.	X Lat.	Depart.	Lat. by Obs.	X Long.	Long. In.	M. D.
176	64 E.	75 m. N	159m. E	40.26 N.	3.22′ E. short 8′	50.09	916m. E

Remarks on Monday, March **2, 1778,** *on board the Boston.*

The first part of this twenty-four hours attended with fresh breezes and hazy weather. At 1 P. M. found our mainmast sprung; down M. T. G. yard; the carpenters employed in fixing the mainmast, The middle and latter part fresh breezes and cloudy weather. Nothing else remarkable this day.

My people employed as usual about necessary duty.

Lat. by obs. 41° 38′ No.

Course.	Dist.	X Lat.	Depart.	Lat. by Obs.	X Long.	Long. in.	M. Dis.
N. 62° E	156	72 N.	37 E.	41.38 N.	3.00 E.	47.09 W	1053 E.

Remarkable Observations **on** *Tuesday,* **March** 3, 1778.

The first part of this twenty-four hours attended with a fine breeze of wind. The middle and latter part, fresh breezes and cloudy weather.

My people employed as usual about necessary duty.

Nothing very remarkable this day.

Lat. per obs. 42° 48′ No.

Course.	Dist.	X Lat.	Depart.	Lat. by Obs.	X Long.	Long. in.	Mer. Dis.
N.70°E	200 m.	70 N.	188m.E	42.48 N.	4.24 E.	42.45 W	1241 E.

Remarkable Observations on Wednesday, March 4, 1778.

The first part of this twenty-four hours moderate gales and rain ; winds variable.

The middle and latter part fresh breezes and pleasant weather.

People employed as usual about necessary duty.

Nothing more remarkable this day.

Lat. per obs. 42° 15′ No.

Course.	**Dist.**	**X Lat.**	Depart.	Lat. in.	X Long.	Long. in.	**M. Dis.**
E.63½ S	**136 m.**	33 S.	132 E.	42.15 N.	2.58 E.	39.47 W	1373 **E.**

Remarkable Observations on Thursday, *March* 5, 1778.

This twenty-four hours **begins with** fresh and pleasant gales ; **all small sails** set, striving my **utmost** to gain a passage. Clear **and pleasant weather.**

Middle and latter parts continue the same.

Lat. in by obs. 43° 43′ North.

Course.	Dist.	X Lat.	Depart.	Lat. by Obs.	X Long.	Long. in.	Mer. D.
N.54°E	150 m.	88m. N.	121m.E	43.43 N.	2.46 E.	37.01 W	1494 E.

Continued on board the Boston Frigate, **March 6,** 1778.

Friday, this twenty-four hours begins and ends with pleasant weather and fresh gales from the S. S. W. Nothing more remarkable to my sorrow.

Lat. observed in 44° 08' North.

Course.	Dist.	X. Lat.	Depart.	Lat. In.	X Long.	Long. In.	M. Dis.
N. 83 E.	210	25 m. N	208m. E	44.08 N.	4.49mE	32.12W	1702 E.

Remarks on Saturday, March 7, 1778, on board the Boston.

Steady gales and pleasant weather. All small sails set. Some **part** of this day employed exercising great guns.

Nothing more remarkable.

Lat. **per obs. 44° 00' North.**

Course.	Dist.	X Lat.	Depart.	Lat. by Obs.	X Long.	Long In.	M. D.
S. ¼ E.	190 m.	8 m. S.	190m. E	44.00 N.	4.24 m.	27.48	1892

*Remarks Sunday, March 8, 1778, **on board the Boston.***

The first part of twenty-four hours attended with **steady gales** and pleasant weather.

The middle and latter part fresh gales attended with rain. **The** people **employed** as usual.

Nothing very remarkable this day.

Lat. **per obs.** 44° 00' No.

Course.	Dist.	X Lat.	Depart.	Lat. per Obs.	X Long.	Long. In.	M. D.
East.	185 m.	00	185 E.	44.00 N.	4.17 E.	23.35 W	2077 E.

Remarks on Monday, March 9, **1778, on board the Boston.**

The first part of this twenty-four hours attended with steady gales and cloudy weather, breezes and fair.

The middle and latter part steady weather.

The people employed as usual about necessary duty.

Nothing remarkable.

Lat. per obs. 44° 08′ No.

Course.	Dist.	X Lat.	Depart.	Lat. per Obs.	X Long.	Long. in.	M. D.
E. S.	180 m.	8 m. N.	180 E.	44.08 N.	4.10 E.	19.23	2257 E.

Remarks on Tuesday, March 10, 1778, *on board the Boston.*

The first part of this twenty-four hours attended with steady gales and pleasant weather.

The middle, fresh gales with squalls of rain. The latter part cloudy weather and squally; winds variable; got down T. G. yards.

The people employed as usual on necessary duty.

Nothing more remarkable.

Lat. per obs. 44° 5′ No.

Course.	Dist.	X Lat.	Dep.	Lat. by Obs.	X Long.	Long. in.	M. D.
East.	195	5′ S.	195 E.	44.5 N.	4.31 E.	19.50	2452 E.

Remarks on Wednesday, March 11, 1778, *on board the Ship Boston.*

The first part of these twenty-four hours attended with fresh breezes of wind and flying clouds. At 1 P. M. saw a ship to the S. E. standing to the west, out one reef of the topsails and then gave chase. At 3 P. M. came up with her. I fired a gun and they returned three, and then down colors. I ordered the boat hoisted out, and sent Mr. Barron and Mr. Reed on board, who sent on board us Capt. M'Intosh, of the prize ship, and some of the crew. The prize is called the Martha, and commanded by Peter M'Intosh; was bound from London to New York, with a valuable cargo of provisions, other stores, and merchandise of different sorts. Sent Mr. Tucker on board for the night. The latter part my people employed in bringing prisoners and their baggage from the ship.

The names of the prisoners taken in the Martha, viz. : —

1. Peter M'Intosh, ... Commander.
2. Robert Golch, ... Passenger.
3. John Wallace, ... "
4. Mr. Bennet, ... First Mate.
5. Andrew Munroe, ... Second Mate.
6. Hector M'Kenzie, ... Passenger.
7. Mordecai Isaac, ... "
8. Michael Levy, ... "
9. Joseph Staggs, ... Third Mate.
10. Alexander Webster, . . . Boatswain.
11. John Main, ... Cook.
12. John Williams, ... Captain's Steward.
13. (Not named) . . . . . . Carpenter.
14. John M'Kenzie, ... Mate.
15. Robert Hutchins.
16. Ralph Prescott.
17. John Pratt.
18. Andrew Berry.
19. Daniel Swords.
20. Thomas Woodnot.
21. Archibauld Frazier.
22. Peter Mitch.
23. David Morey.
24. Jeremiah Shaw.
25. James Bushell.
26. Benjamin Bushell.

27. John Cockran.
28. Peter Nowlan.
29. James Duncan.
30. Robert Wells.
31. Joseph Esther.
32. Richard Jones.
33. William Jordan.
34. J. P. Wevner, ... Doctor.

Lat. per obs. 43° 45'.

Course.	Dist.	X Lat.	Depart.	Lat. per Obs.	X Long.	Long. in.	Mer. Dis.
S. 80° E	55 m.	22 S.	54m. E.	43.45	1.15 E.	13.35	2506 E.

Remarks on Thursday, March 12, 1778, *on board Ship Boston.*

The first part of this twenty-four hours attended with moderate gales and fair weather. At 3 P. M. I dismissed Lieutenant Welsh, whom I had appointed prize-master of the Martha, and saluted him with seven guns. My orders were for him to proceed for Boston. At 5 P. M. the Martha bore W. N. W. Distance two leagues.

The latter part flattering winds and cloudy.

The people employed as usual.

Lat. per obs. 43° 29'.

Course.	Dist.	X Lat.	Depart.	Lat. per Obs.	X Long.	Long. in.	Mer. Dis.
S. 63 E.	35 m.	16m. S.	31m. E.	43.29 N.	43m. E.	12.52 W	2537 E.

Remarks on Friday, March 13, 1778, *on board Ship Boston.*

The first part of this twenty-four hours attended with light gales of wind. At 9 P. M. wore ship and stood to the southward. At

11 A. M. saw a sail bearing east from us, standing to the westward and north. Cleared ship ready for engagement.

Nothing more remarkable.

Lat. by obs. 43° 54'.

Course.	Dist.	X Lat.	Depart.	Lat. in.	X Long.	Long. in.	M. Dist.
North.	**25**	25m. N	oo	43.54	oo	12.52m.	2537 E.

Remarks on Saturday, March 14, 1778, on board Ship Boston.

The first part of this twenty-four hours attended with moderate winds and fair weather. At 2 P. M. tacked ship and stood to the southward and westward. A 4 spoke with a Frenchman from Bordeaux. Saw a sail just at this time to the eastward, standing to the eastward and northward. At 5 tacked and stood to the east. At 12 hauled the M. S. up in the brails, handed F. and M. T. G. sails. Mr. Barron, in discharging the second gun on the starboard bow, the gun burst in seven pieces, by which the worthy Mr. Barron had his right leg broke, and two men slightly wounded. The doctor and his mate consulted and thought it necessary to amputate the leg, which was performed in a masterly manner. At half past 3 spoke with a Frenchman from San Domingo, bound to Nantz.

Lat. per obs. 44° 47' No.

Course.	Dist.	X Long.	Depart.	Lat. by Obs.	X Long.	Long in.	M. D.
N. 40 E.	70 m.	53m. N.	45m. E.	44.47 N.	1.03 E.	11.49 W	2582 E.

Remarks on board of Ship Boston, Sunday, March 15, 1778.

The first part of this twenty-four hours attended with fresh breezes and fine weather. At 8 P. M. discovered two sails to windward of us standing to the W. S. W. Set M. and F. T. G. sails. Middle part moderate. At 8 A. M. saw two sail on our weather bow standing to the northward and eastward, suppose them to be cruising ships, the one ahead had a poop lantern out.

Lat. by obs. 46° 27′ N.

Course.	Dist.	X Lat.	Depart.	Lat. by Obs.	X Long.	Long. in.	M. Dis.
N. 43° E	113	8om. N.	8om. E.	46.27 N.	1.55 E.	09.54 W	2662 E.

Remarks on Monday, March 16, 1778, on board Ship Boston.

The first part of this twenty-four hours attended with fresh breezes and clear weather. At 7 P. M. reefed M. F. and mizzen T. sails, down jib and hauled up M. sail. At 12 reef M. T. sail and handed M. S. and F. T. S., and split the F. S.

The latter part, onbent the F. S. and bent another; onbent the old miz. and bent a new one.

Nothing more remarkable this day.

Lat. per obs. None this day.

Course.	Dist.	X Lat.	Depart.	Lat. per Obs.	X Long.	Long. In.	M. D.
S. 51 W	67 m.	42m. S.	52 W.	45.45 N.	1.15 W.	11.9 W.	2610 E.

Remarks on Tuesday, March 17, 1778, on board Boston.

The first part of this twenty-four hours attended with fresh gales and thick weather. At half past 2 P. M. saw two ships on our larboard-quarter. Set the M. S. and jib. The people employed in swaying up and slinging the fore yard. The middle part, a heavy gale and large sea; down miz. sail. At 6 A. M. saw two ships to leeward of us, standing to the westward. At 9 hauled up the M. S. and onbent the **mizzen T. S.** At **12 wore** ship, with her head to the eastward.

Lat. per obs. 45° 52' N.

Course.	Dist.	X. Lat.	Depart.	Lat. by Obs.	X Long.	Long. in.	M. Dis.
N.86 W	100 m.	7 N.	98 N W	45.52 W.	2.21 W.	13.30 W	2512 E.

Remarks on Wednesday, March 18, 1778, *on board* **Ship** *Boston.*

The first part of this twenty-four hours attended with **fresh** gales and squalls, with rain and a heavy sea from the S. S. W. At 1 P. M. onbent the miz. T. S. and bent a new one. At 2 onbent the F. T. S. and bent another. The latter part clear and moderate.

People employed as usual on duty.

Nothing more remarkable this day.

Lat. per obs. **45° 44'** N.

Course.	Dist.	X Lat.	Depart.	Lat. by Obs.	X Long.	Long. in.	M. Dis.
S. 73 W	27 m.	8 m. S.	26 W.	45.44	38m. W	14.08 W	2486

Remarks on Thursday, March 19, 1778, *on board Ship Boston.*

The first part of this twenty-four hours attended with fresh gales, squally, and a heavy sea from S. S. eastward.

The **middle** part squally, with heavy showers of rain; **shipping** considerable water on deck. The latter part more moderate and **clear.**

People **employed as usual.**

Nothing **more remarkable this day.**

Lat. by obs. 45° 34' N.

Course.	Dist.	X Lat.	Depart.	Lat. In.	X Long.	Long. in.	M. Dist.
S. 78 W	48 m.	10m. S.	47 W.	45.34 W.	1.8m W	15.16 W	2439 E.

Remarks on Friday, March 20, 1778, on board Ship Boston.

The first part of this twenty-four hours attended with a fresh breeze of wind and a large sea. At 8 A. M. saw a sail, which we made sail for, and came up with at 11. She proved to be a Dutch snow from Amsterdam, bound to Ise Capes and Demerara.

Lat. per obs. 45° 00′.

Course.	Dist.	X Lat.	Dep.	Lat.	X Long.	Long. in.	M. D.
S. 78 E.	170 m.	34m. S.	166m.E	45.00 N.	3.35 E.	11.21 W	2605 E.

Remarks on Saturday, March 21, 1778, on board Ship Boston.

The first part of this twenty-four hours attended with a fresh breeze and hazy weather. The middle and latter part, foggy and rain.

No observation this day.

Course.	Dist.	X Lat.	Depart.	Lat. per Obs.	X Long.	Long. in.	M. D.
S. 76 E.	170	40 S.	164 E.	44.20	3.50	7.31 W.	2769 E.

Remarks on Sunday, March 22, 1778, on board Ship Boston.

The first part of this twenty-four hours attended with a fine breeze of wind. Got the cables up and bent them. The middle and latter part, fresh gales and squally.

The people employed as usual.

Lat. per obs. 44° 55′ N.

Course.	Dist.	Dif. Lat.	Depart.	Lat. per Obs.	X Long.	Long. in.	M. Dis.
N. 77 E	160	35m. N.	156 E.	44.55	3.38m.	3.53 W.	2925 E.

Remarks on Monday, March 23, 1778, *on board Ship* **Boston**.

The first part of this twenty-four hours attended with a **very** fresh gale of wind and heavy sea. The middle part the same. The F. S. sheet broke, and split the sail in the after leash; got it down. Nothing more worth remarking.

Lat. per obs. 44° 32' No.

Remarks on board the Boston, Tuesday, March 24, **1778**.

The first part of this twenty-four hours fresh gales **and fair** weather. At 4 P. M. saw high land bearing from us S. W. to **S. E.,** distance about eight leagues. At 11 St. Anthony's head **bore** **S. S. W.,** distance five miles.

Lat. per obs. 43° 40' No.

Remarks on board the Boston, Wednesday, March 25, 1778.

The first part of this twenty-four hours moderate gales. **At 2** P. M. a pilot came on board from St. Anthony's; stood for the harbor close in with the land; tacked ship and stood to the north- ward to meet a brig standing eastward.

Lat. per obs. 44° 14' No.

Remarks *on board the Boston, Thursday, March* **26, 1778.**

The **first** part of this twenty-four hours attended **with fresh** gales **and clear** weather. At 7 P. M. my worthy lieutenant, **Wm.** Barron, **departed this** life, after enduring **the** greatest pain since his having **his leg cut** off. I sincerely **regret the** loss of **him, he** being **a worthy and** respectful officer. At 10 A. M. the **corpse of** the deceased **was brought on the** quarter-deck, and after **prayers** being read, was committed **to the deep, with all** the ceremony that possibly **could** be; all hands **being on the quarter-deck, all seemed** **to** lament **his** death.

Lat. per obs. 44° 31'.

*Remarks on board the **Boston**, Friday, March 27, 1778.*

This twenty-four hours with pleasant gales of wind and a smooth sea.

The people employed about necessary duty.

Lat. obs. 45° 26′ No.

Remarks on board the Boston, Saturday, March 28, 1778.

Light gales and fair weather. Saw a sail to the leeward. Sounded, and found we were in fifty fathom of water, red sand and shells. After running ten leagues had thirty fathoms of water, coarse black and red sand.

Nothing more remarkable.

Lat. per obs. 43° 03′ No.

Remarks on Sunday, March 29, 1778.

Light winds and fair weather; spoke with several Dutchmen from Bordeaux, bound to Amsterdam. At 6 A. M. saw the land bearing N. N. W., distance about four leagues, which we found to be fifteen leagues to the westward of Bordeaux.

Lat. by obs. 45° 52′.

Monday, March 30, 1778.

Light gales and fair weather; a pilot came on board. At 8 A. M. saw the light-house of Cordouan, bearing E. by N., distance three leagues.

No obs. this day.

Remarks Tuesday, March, 31, 1778.

Fine pleasant weather; came into the river of Bordeaux at 6

P. M.   Came to anchor at Poliask.   Another pilot came on board. The latter part dark and rainy.

Wednesday, April 1, 1778.

At 2 P. M. weighed anchor at Poliask, to go to town.   At 6 saluted a small town called Lavmon with 13 guns, and came to anchor.   At 5 A. M. weighed anchor, and went up within three miles of the town and landed the passengers.

Thursday, April 2, 1778.

This day squally without rain, wind S. W.   Plenty of company coming on board to see the frigate, who in general seem to be much pleased with her, particularly the ladies.

Friday, April 3, 1778.

Pleasant and moderate weather.   Employed the people in un-bending the small sails, &c.   Plenty of company coming on board.

Saturday, April 4.

Mr. Adams went to Paris.   This day people employed as usual. Great numbers of gentlemen and ladies came on board to see the ship.

Sunday, April 5.

All this day the ship has been crowded with company from morning to night; boats alongside.   One would think they never saw a ship before, but it is all on account of its being a Boston frigate.   Pleasant weather this day.   The wind to the northward.

Monday, April 6.

This day comes in and ends with pleasant weather.   The people employed as usual about their necessary duty.   Landed our sails.

Tuesday, April 7.

This day comes in with pleasant weather. A pilot came on board, and we dropped the ship down with the tide to *Lavmoon*. in order to clean her; but found the place was not fit to lay her on shore. The latter part of this day pleasant.

Wednesday, April 8.

This day fine pleasant weather dropped the ship with the tide up to Bordeaux, alongside of an old hulk, in order to heave her down, and clean her bottom.

Thursday, April 9.

This day drizzly and dirty weather. The people employed in getting the guns and other articles on board the hulk.

Friday, April 10.

This day the people employed in getting the ship clear. Very pleasant weather.

Saturday, April 11.

This day pleasant. People employed in clearing the hold, and casks, and wood; got down the topmasts.

Sunday, April 12.

This day pleasant weather; let a number of the men go on shore on liberty.

Monday, April 13,

This day pleasant weather. The carpenters from Lavmoon to work on board. The people employed in clearing the ship.

Tuesday, April 14.

This day very pleasant weather. The people employed in clearing out the ship.

Wednesday, April **15.**

This day pleasant weather. At 10 in the morning **began to** careen the ship. At 12 she was hove down; the **carpenters at work** on her bottom. At 8 P. M. righted ship.

Thursday, April 16.

This begins **with pleasant weather. The day being a** holiday, **the carpenters finished our starboard side, and at 12** o'clock went on shore.

Friday, April 17.

This day being a holiday, no work was done on board until 12 o'clock.

Saturday, April 18.

Fine pleasant weather. Careened the ship and finished her **bottom, and got** the shears **down.**

Sunday, **April** 19.

This day fine pleasant weather. Confined some of the people in irons for making disturbances.

Monday, April **20.**

It being a holiday on shore, we had very little **work** done on **board.** Let some of the people go ashore.

Tuesday, April 21.

This **day rainy** weather. The people employed in necessary duty. **Found the** mainmast sprung **so** badly that I shall be obliged **to get a new one. Began to** clear the rigging.

Wednesday, **April 22.**

This day rainy weather. Get two long spars for shears to hoist out the mainmast.

Thursday, April 23.

The fore part of the day cold, clear weather. The people getting ready to hoist the mast out. In the afternoon got it out, and found it to be gone in three different places.

Friday, April 24.

This day cold and cloudy weather. The people employed in getting the iron ballast out of the hulk on board. The carpenters on shore to work on the mast.

Saturday, April 25.

Received second lieutenant from Paris. Captain Palmer returned. This day pleasant weather. The people employed in getting the ballast on board. [(erased, but which reads) John Hileger received twelve lashes on his back with a cat for cutting a Frenchman with a scraper.]

Sunday, April 26.

This day very pleasant weather. The people employed on necessary duty.

Monday, April 27.

This day pleasant. People employed on necessary duty, and getting the guns on board.

Tuesday, April 28.

This day pleasant weather. People employed as usual. Some of the hands deserted.

Wednesday, April 29.

A very pleasant day. The people employed at necessary duty.

Thursday, April 30.

A pleasant day. The people employed as usual.

Friday, May 1, 1778.

A dark, cloudy day, attended with rain. Received some water on board. The people employed as usual.

Saturday, May 2.

This day cloudy. The people employed in getting the stores on board in order to drop down. The pilot came on board, and we dropped down opposite the Exchange.

Sunday, May 3, 1778.

A very pleasant day. Let some of the people go on shore.

Monday, May 4.

A pleasant day. The people employed in stowing the hold and overhauling the provisions.

Tuesday, May 5.

This morning Peter Cavey, a midshipman, got over the side to wear the boat astern, taking hold of a rope, which he thought was made fast but was not, fell overboard, and though all means were used to save him, was drowned. The people employed in necessary duty as usual.

Wednesday, May 6.

This day pleasant. Henry Payton deserted from the ship. At 3 in the afternoon got the mainmast in.

Thursday May 7.

This day pleasant weather. The people employed as usual.

Friday, May 8.

This day pleasant weather. Got the main top and main yard up in their places.

Saturday, May **9.**

Pleasant weather. People employed on necessary duty.

Sunday, *May* **10.**

A pleasant day. Let some of the people go on shore.

Monday, May 11.

A pleasant day. The people employed on necessary duty. The body of Mr. Cavey was found by the people on shore, and decently buried.

Tuesday, May 12.

Pleasant weather. **The people** employed as usual.

Wednesday, May 13.

Rainy weather. The people employed as usual.

Thursday, May 14.

Pleasant weather. **The** people employed as usual.

Friday, May 15.

Dirty weather. **The** people **employed in clearing the ship** for sea.

May 16, *Saturday.*

Pleasant weather. **The** people **employed** in bending the **sails.**

Sunday, May 17.

This day pleasant weather. The pilot came on board. Unmoored ship, and cleared the decks to go down the river. At 11 o'clock weighed anchor, and saluted the Castle of Bordeaux with twenty-one guns. They returned the salute. Fell down the river as far as *Boekelyan,* and moored ship.

Monday, May 18, 1778.

This day pleasant weather. Sunday stores came on **board from** Bordeaux. In the night two sailors left the ship.

Tuesday, May 19, 1778.

Dark, cloudy weather. The people employed in getting the **ship ready for the sea.**

Wednesday, May 20.

Dark, cloudy weather. The people employed about necessary duty.

Thursday, May 21.

This day fine pleasant weather. Unmoored ship and fell down **two miles** below Lavmoon, and there anchored. And 7 in the **morning** weighed anchor, and fell **down twelve miles** farther **and** anchored.

Friday, May 22, **1778.**

This day comes in with rain. Weighed anchor in the morning, and fell down within three miles of Blay. The pilot went on shore, and another came on board. At **3** P. M. weighed anchor, and fell down as far as the castle, and anchored; saluted the castle with seven cannon, which returned **the** compliment. A number of gentlemen and ladies came on board.

Saturday, May 23.

A **rainy day. The** people employed **about** necessary duty.

Sunday, May **24.**

This **day it** blows **very fresh, attended** with rain. The people employed **as** usual.

Monday, May **25.**

Fresh gales and rain. The people employed **as usual.**

Tuesday, May 26.

This day fresh gales and dirty weather.

Wednesday, May 27.

This day cloudy weather. In the afternoon weighed anchor, and came out in the channel, in order to go to Poliask in the morning.

Thursday, May 28.

This day fresh gales. Weighed anchor in the morning, and came down to Poliask; anchored there to fill the empty casks with water. The people employed this day in filling water.

Friday, May 29.

This day fresh gales of wind. The ship is now ready for sea, and I wait for nothing but Mr. Livingston, my second lieutenant, to come from Bordeaux.

Saturday, May 30.

This day flattering weather and winds.

Sunday, May 31.

This day dark and disagreeable weather. I should be glad to find Mr. Livingston come down this tide.

Monday, June 1, 1778.

This day cloudy and dark weather. No news from Mr. Livingston.

Tuesday, June 2.

This day cloudy and disagreeable weather. The people employed about necessary duty.

Wednesday, June 3.

This day pleasant weather. The people employed as usual.

19

At 12 o'clock Mr. Livingston returned from Bordeaux. Weighed anchor, and came down the river three leagues below Poliask.

Thursday, June 4.

This day begins with cloudy weather and rain; weighed anchor in the morning. At 7 P. M. came by a French frigate that was under sail, turning down the river. At 4 P. M. came to anchor below the commodore, and saluted with thirteen cannon; he returned the salute with seven, and I returned one.

Friday, June 5, 1778.

This day pleasant weather. The people employed as usual. Captain Jones, in a brig of ten guns, belonging to Maryland, came down from Bordeaux, and joined the fleet that lay here.

Saturday, June 6, 1778.

This twenty-four hours begins with pleasant weather. The people employed in clearing ship ready for sea. The middle part, moderate gales from the E. N. E. At 4 A. M. weighed anchor, and came to sail in company with twenty sail of ships, brigs, &c., a French frigate, and sloop of war. At 6 A. M., Cordean lighthouse bearing E. N. E., distance two leagues. All sails set at noon. I reckon the ship to be twelve leagues to the westward of the lighthouse. Variable winds and foggy weather.

Remarks on board the Boston, Sunday, June 7, 1778.

This day fresh breezes of wind from the westward. Captain Jones, in a brig from Virginia, and the French frigate, still in company. This twenty-four hours begin with fresh breezes.

Lat. by obs. 46° 08' No.

Remarks on board the Boston, Monday, June 8, 1778.

Steady gales of fair weather. At 4 P. M. the Island of Dieu bore N. E. At 6 do. the middle of the island E. by N., distance four leagues. Hoisted the **pinnace** out and **sent her on** board Captain Jones, desiring **himself, Captain Ward, and the doctor, to** come on **board the ship, who spent most of the day with me.**

Lat. by obs. 46° 44'.

Remarks on board the Boston, Tuesday, June 9, 1778.

Light breezes and clear weather. At 4 P. M. Captain Jones, in the Virginia brig, parted, and steered his course for Bordeaux. The Island Dieu bears S. E. by E., distance two and a half leagues. At 7 P. M. the island out of sight. At 10 tacked ship to the **southward, and half past one tacked ship and stood to the northward. At 4 A. M. calm, with rain. At 5 A. M. saw the island of** Bellisle, bearing N. N. **E., distance** 5 leagues.

Lat. per obs. 47° 11'.

Remarks on board the Boston, Wednesday, June 10, 1778.

This twenty-four hours moderate gales and pleasant weather. **In company with the** French frigate. Several vessels in sight. **The people employed** as usual on necessary duty.

Lat. per obs. 47° 07'.

Remarks **on** *board the Boston, Thursday,* **June** 11, 1778.

Light gales and pleasant weather; **several vessels in sight. At 7 P. M. Bellisle, distance 4 leagues. At 6** A. M. saw the **Island of Gron, bearing N. E. by E.,** distance five leagues. **At noon anchored between** Groa and **Loriant.**

(I find no observation.)

Remarks **on board** *the Boston, Friday, June* 12, **1778.**

Steady gales and pleasant weather. A French **snow and ship at anchor in company with us. Lieutenant Reed went on shore in the cutter to Loriant after water.**

The people employed as usual.

Remarks on board the Boston, Saturday, **June** 13, 1778.

Pleasant weather.   At 6 P. M. Mr. Reed returned in the cutter with eight casks of water.   At 10 A. M. weighed anchor and came to sail.   At noon the Island of Groa, bearing E. by S., distance 5 miles; from thence I take my departure.

The Isle Du Groa, Lat. 47° 40′.   Long. 3° 30′ West.

Lat. per obs. 47° 39′ No.

Remarks on board the Boston, Sunday, **June** 14, 1778.

The first part of these twenty-four hours attended with fresh gales. At 5 P. M. spoke with a Frenchman from Marseilles.   At 4 A. M. spoke with another from Nantz.   At 5 A. M. saw two vessels to the westward, standing to the northward.   At 9 A. M. saw a large ship and a brig to the northward, standing towards the S. W.; about 11 o'clock, they stood for us.   Supposing the ship to be a forty gun ship, wore and stood to the east; after that they tacked and stood to S. W.   We stood after them again; they set their small sails, and we set steering sails, and gave chase after them.   .

Course.	Dist.	X. Lat.	Depart.	Lat. by Obs.	X Long.	Long. in.	M. Dis.
S. W.	131	92 S.	92 W.	46.08	2.14	5.44	92 W.

Remarks on board the Boston, Monday, **June** 15, 1778,

The first of this twenty-four hours pleasant weather; still in chase of the ship and brig; saw several sails in sight.   At 8 A. M. the chase hauled up her courses.   I stood towards her, came up with, and found her to be a French frigate.   Wore ship and stood to the westward.

The latter part pleasant weather.

Lat. per obs. 45° 20′.

Course.	Dist.	X. Lat.	Depart.	Lat. per Obs.	X Long.	Long. in.	M. D.
S. 72 W	160	48 S.	152 W.	45.20	3.36	9.20	244 W.

Remarks **on board the Boston,** Tuesday, June 16, 1778.

This twenty-four hours attended with pleasant weather and steady winds. Saw seven large ships to leeward, gave chase to them; got the ship in readiness for engaging, but found them to be vessels of superior force; judged them to be an English fleet of men of war. At 7 P. M. saw another sail; gave chase and spoke with her; she proved to be a French brig from Bordeaux, bound to St. Domingo.

Lat. per obs. 43° 23'.

Course.	Dist.	X Lat.	Depart.	Lat. per Obs.	X Long.	Long. in.	M. D.
S. 54 W	202	115	165	43.25	3.51	13.11	109 W.

Remarks on board the Boston, Wednesday, June 17, 1778.

Fresh gales and pleasant weather. Spoke with a Portuguese snow from Oporto, bound to Cork. Consulted this day with my officers about our cruising. They all seemed to be for cruising on the banks of Newfoundland, to which I agreed.

Lat. per obs. 43° 49' N.

Course.	Dist.	X Lat.	Depart.	Lat. by Obs.	X Long.	Long. in.	M. Dif.
N. 80 W	138 m.	24m. N.	136 W.	43.49	3.10	16.21	545 W.

Remarks on board the Boston, Thursday, June 18, 1778.

This day attended with pleasant weather, and steady breezes. Spoke with a brig from Marseilles, bound to Middleburgh.

Lat. per obs. 43° 36'.

Course.	Dist.	X Lat.	Depart.	Lat. by Obs.	X Long.	Long. in.	M. Dif.
W. 4 N.	177	13 S.	177 W.	43.36	4.05	20.26	722 W.

*Remarks on **board the Boston**, Friday, June 19, 1778.*

Saw two sail to the northward, standing to the eastward. At 9 A. M. brought to a brig, George Fenly, commander, belonging to Scotland, bound from Venice to London, loaded with cream tartar and raisins; made a prize of her, and sent her for Boston, with Joshua Goss as prize-master, Jacob Tucker mate, Thomas Stevens, Thomas Brimblecome, James Harris (Tannique and Rousille, Frenchmen), as privates, and William Young as prisoner.

N. B.   The brig is called the John and Rebecca.

Lat. by obs. 43° 47′.

Course.	Dist.	X Lat.	Depart.	Lat. by Obs.	X Long.	Long. in.	M. Dif.
N. 83 W	88 m.	11 N.	87 W.	43.47	2.00	22.26	809 W.

***Remarks** on board the Boston, **June** 20, 1778, Saturday.*

This day moderate gales and pleasant weather. All the people on board well and in good spirits.

Saw a vessel to the northward and gave chase.

Lat. by obs. 44° 04′.

Course.	Dist.	X Lat.	Depart.	Lat. by Obs.	X Long.	Long. in.	M. Dist.
W. N W	45 m.	17 N.	41 W.	44.04	56 m.	23.22	850 W.

***Remarks** on board the Boston, Sunday, June 21, 1778.*

Moderate gales and pleasant weather. The sail in chase proved to be Captain Jones, that sailed in company with us from Bordeaux. He and his people are all well. Captain Jones came on board, and tarried a considerable time.

Lat. per obs. 44° 00′.

Course.	Dist.	X Lat.	Dep.	Lat. by Obs.	X Long.	Long in.	M. Dif.
West.	107 m.	4 S.	107	44.00	2.29	25.51	937 W.

Remarks **on board the Boston, Monday,** *June* **22,** 1778.

Steady gales and pleasant weather. At 4 P. M. Captain Jones parted with us, and saluted with nine guns. I returned four. Nothing remarkable.

Lat. per obs. 44° 40'.

Course.	Dist.	X. Lat.	Depart.	Lat. per Obs.	X Long.	Long. in.	M. Dis.
N. 65 W	95 m.	40 m. N.	86 W.	44.40	1.59 W.	27.50	1043 W.

Remarks on board the Boston, Tuesday, *June* 23, 1778.

The first part of this twenty-four hours light breezes and cloudy weather. Saw a sail to the northward, gave chase, and at noon came up with her. She proved to be the brig Britannia, William Baker, commander, from Newfoundland, bound to Oporto: took the master and crew out, and sent her for Loriant, with Giscard, prize-master, Wm. Alkins, mate (Alary, Arnaud, Battiste, Leger, Grassia, and Goodwin, all Frenchmen, as hands). She was loaded with about seventeen hundred quintals fish.

Lat. per obs. 44° 56'.

Course.	Dist.	X Lat.	Depart.	Lat. per Obs.	X Long.	Long. in.	M. Dis.
NE by N	18	16 N.	8 m. E.	44.56	12 E.	27.38 W	1035 W.

Remarks **on** *board the Boston,* *Wednesday,* *June* 24.

The first part of this twenty-four hours steady gales and pleasant. The boats employed in bringing the prisoners, chests, &c., from the Britannia. Despatched her, and she proceeded for Loriant. John Carter, one of the carpenters on board us, by accident fell

overboard. Had the pinnace hoisted out, and was just time enough
to save him from drowning.

Lat. per obs. 45° 01'.

Course.	Dist.	X. Lat.	Depart.	Lat. by Obs.	X Long.	Long. in.	M. Dis.
E. 8° N.	37 m.	5 m. N.	36m. E.	45.01	5.1 E.	26.47	999 E.

Remarks on board the Boston, Thursday, June 25.

Steady gales and pleasant. The sun this afternoon in the
eclipse. At 7 P. M. came up with the chase. The captain pretended
to be a Frenchman, from Newfoundland, bound to Oporto: he
afterwards proved a Jerseyman. Manned her, and sent her for
Loriant, with John Pickery, one of my mates, as prize-master,
John Elliot, Laour, Roussuelt, Donassusign, Daniville, and Bour-
gerinon, with him. The prize was a brig, commanded by Thomas
Anquetil, called the Elizabeth, and loaded with fish. In chase after
another brig, — gave her several shot.

Lat. per obs. 45° 35'.

Course.	Dist.	X Lat.	Depart.	Lat. per Obs.	X Long.	Long. in.	M. Dis.
N. 80° E	158	34m. N.	155	45.35	3.39 W.	23.08	844 W.

Remarks on board the Boston, June 26, 1778, *Friday.*

The first part of this twenty-four hours pleasant. Came up
with our chase, and spoke with the captain. She was a brig from
Baltimore, bound to Nantz, commanded by Alexander Murray,
out seventeen days — a fine sailing brig, pierced for sixteen car-
riage guns. At 10 A. M. saw a sail, and gave chase.

Lat. observed in 46° 14′ North.

Course.	Dist.	X Lat.	Depart.	Lat. per Obs.	X Long.	Long. in.	Mer. Dif.
N. 76 E.	126	30 N.	122 E.	46.05	2.56	20.12	722 W.

Remarks on board the Boston, Saturday, June 27, 1778.

The first part of this twenty-four hours light winds and clear weather. Saw a ship and gave chase. At 3 P. M. the wind took our ship aback: **got our starboard tacks on board, and set all sail by the wind. At 4 P. M. very moderate: the ship gained from us. Bore away,** and gave **over chase.** At 6 hove out the **pinnace,** and I went on board Captain Murray, with Mr. Reed, my first lieutenant. Captain Murray sent me some American papers to peruse, which I am obliged to him for.

Lat. observed in 46° 14′ North.

Course.	Dist.	X Lat.	Depart.	Lat. per Obs.	X Long.	Long. in.	Mer. Dif.
E. ½ N.	118	9 N.	116 E.	46.14	2.47	17.25	606 W.

Remarks on board the Boston, **Sunday,** *June* 28, 1778.

This twenty-four **hours pleasant weather.** Spoke with **Captain Murray, who told me that one of his** men fell from the **yard and hurt himself.** Hoisted out **the pinnace** and sent the **doctor on board him.** The man had put his shoulder out. At 10 A. M. saw a sail and gave chase. Nothing more remarkable.

Lat. observed in 46° 14′ North.

Course.	Dist.	X Lat.	Depart.	Lat. per Obs.	X Long.	Long. in.	M. Dist.
East.	180 m.	∞	180 m.	46.14	13.04	4.25	426 W.

Remarks on board the Boston, Monday, June **29.**

The first part of this twenty-four hours fresh gales **and heavy** weather. In chase of a schooner. At 5 P. M. gave over **chase.** At 7 P. M. saw two sail; gave chase, and came up with them; the one was a Scotch brig from Glasgow, bound for St. Ubes, the other a Swede. I took **the Scotch brig,** and sent her for Loriant. At 6 A. M. saw another sail; gave chase and came up to her. **She** proved to be a Frenchman.

Lat. obs. 46° 04′.

Course.	Dist.	X Lat.	Dep.	Lat. per Obs.	X Long.	Long. in.	**M. Dis.**
E ½ S.	111	10m. S.	110 E.	46.04	2.38	10.26 W	316 W.

Remarks on board the **Boston,** *Tuesday, June* **30.**

This twenty-four hours attended with moderate gales and pleasant weather for the most **part.**

Lat. per obs. 46° 11′.

Course.	Dist.	X Lat.	Depart.	Lat. per Obs.	X Long.	Long. in.	M. Dif.
N.86 E.	104	7 m. N.	104	46.11	2.30	7.56	212 W.

Remarks on board the Boston, July 1. **1778.**

The first part of this twenty-four hours steady gales and **hazy** weather. Saw a sloop and gave chase, but could not come **near** her. The middle part pleasant. Saw several Dutch vessels.

Lat. per obs. 47° 16′.

Course.	Dist.	X Lat.	Depart.	Lat. per Obs.	X Long.	**Long. in.**	M. Dist.
E.N.E.	174	65m. N.	161 E.	47.16	3.54	**4.02**	51 W.

After working **this** day's work, run upon E. N. E. **course** about fifty miles distance, and anchored **under the Isle du Groax.**

Remarks on board the Boston, Thursday, July 2, **1778.**

Steady gales and fair weather. We saw the land, bearing from N. N. W. to E. N. E., about three leagues distant. At 8 in the evening anchored between the Island du Groax and Port Lewis. Wind west.

July 3 1778.

This day foggy weather. **A** pilot came on board **from** Port Lewis. **At 4 in the evening weighed anchor, and went into the Harbor of Port Lewis, and came to the inner moorings.** The **wind S. W.**

Saturday, July 4, 1778.

This day fair and pleasant weather. The people employed about necessary duty. My second lieutenant, Mau. Lingstom, went off for Paris to the commissioners.

Remarks on board the Boston, Sunday, July 5, 1778.

This day pleasant weather. At 6 in the **evening two of my** prizes arrived **here,** one of them, Mr. Vickery, **prize-master, the** other, Mr. Snowdon. Nothing very **particular to remark to-day.**

Monday, July 6, **1778.**

This day pleasant weather. Got the main-topmast **down to get up new cross-trees.**

Tuesday, July 7, 1778.

This day pleasant weather. The people throughout **the ship employed on necessary duty.** Nothing more **worth remarking. William Roberts and Richard Smith received, each of them, twelve lashes on their naked back for trying to desert the third time, but were caught.**

Remarks on board the Boston, Wednesday, July 8, 1778.

This day comes in with pleasant weather. The steward delivering fresh beef to the people, two of the French marines, La Combe and Degout, denied to take their allowance, or to do any more duty on board; but their stomachs, and the others of the same sort, came to the next day.

Thursday, July 9, 1778.

This day pleasant and agreeable weather. Careened the ship and cleaned her bottom, then righted her again.

Remarks on board the Boston, Friday, July 10, 1778. .

This day very pleasant weather. Finished cleaning the ship's bottom. Mr. Latuche, one of his Christian Majesty's generals at Loriant, with a number of officers, came on board the ship, and asked the French sailors and marines, in my presence, whether they had rather tarry on board or go on shore. They answered, Go on shore. As they entered as volunteers, they signed the ship's book as seamen and marines; notwithstanding which, though I showed him the book, he took forty-seven out of the ship, and threatened to write to the commissioners at Paris about Lieutenants Reed and Bates treating the Frenchmen ill; — which was false, for they have been treated on board the ship better, if possible, than the Americans. The general did not behave to me on board my ship with all the politeness that could be expected from one of his rank. However, I shall write the commissioners the whole of the proceeding.

Remarks on board the Boston, Saturday, July 11, 1778.

This day pleasant weather. All hands employed as usual about necessary duty. Had the ship's crew mustered, and found that I have one hundred and forty-six men and boys on board.

Sunday, July 12, 1778.

This day pleasant weather. Let fifty of the men go on shore on liberty, they to return at night. Cuff Jennings received twelve lashes on his naked back with a cat, for being mutinous and making a noise on board the ship.

Monday, July 13, 1778.

This day pleasant weather. The people employed as usual on the ship's duty. Wrote to the agent at Nantz, and to Captain Whipple of the Providence **frigate.**

Remarks on board the *Boston, Tuesday, July* **14,** 1778.

This day pleasant weather. The people employed as usual. Bent our mizzen-topsail and top-gallant sail.

Wednesday, July 15.

This day pleasant weather. The brig Britannia, a prize I took the 2nd June, arrived here this evening; all well on board. I thought it was impossible but that she should have been re-captured, being out so long a time.

Thursday, July 16, **1778.**

This day pleasant weather. **At 10 A. M. I** ordered Wm. Atkins **on shore to** the broker, **to enter** the prize brig Britannia, he **being put on board of** second prize **on June** 23, 1778, as mate un**der a French** prize-master. After **doing his** business on shore, **he** coming on **board** the ship, was ordered by the first lieutenant, **Mr. Reed, to go on board the** prize, and behave himself in **his former station. He** went immediately on board, and deman**ded the charge of the prize, telling** the prize-master **he had orders from the lieutenant to take command** of the second **prize. The prize-master would not give up his** charge **until he had orders from one who gave it to him. They fell into a dispute,** whereby the honest prize-master received a wound by a knife, who complained to me immediately. After hearing the complaint, I sent **Mr. Reed on** board the prize to send all hands on board the frigate. I examined them to our satisfaction. I then inflicted twelve lashes on the bare back of Atkins, for assuming a false charge and suffering the prize-master to **be** wounded.

Friday, July 17, 1778.

This day pleasant weather. Sold **all** three of the **prizes to Mr.** Puchebergh, of Lorient, the half that belonged to **the crew to** receive and divide among them, the other to be paid **to Mr.** Schweighawser, com. agent at Nantz.

Remarks on board the Boston, Saturday, July 18, 1778.

This day pleasant weather. The people employed as usual.

Sunday, July 19.

A very pleasant day. Let the people have part of their prize-money. Nothing very remarkable.

Monday, July 20.

This day fresh gales, attended with heavy **rains. Had** the three **prizes** secured from the weather as far as possible.

Remarks on board the Boston, Tuesday, July 21, **1778.**

This **day fresh gales** and pleasant weather. The people **em-**ployed **as usual.** Paid the officers their shares of prize-money **for** the three prizes **sold at L'Orient.**

Wednesday, July 22, 1778.

This day **close** weather. **The people employed as usual. My-**self and Mr. Reed went to Loriant.

Thursday, July **23**, 1778.

This day rainy weather, and fresh gales of wind.

Remarks on board the *Boston, Friday, July* 24.

This day rainy weather and fresh gales.

Saturday, July 25, 1778.

This day cloudy weather and fresh gales.

Sunday, *July* **26**, 1778.

This day pleasant and moderate weather. **At 4 P. M.** Hans Persons, a seaman **on board,** departed this life after being four or five days sick, all which time he was distracted.

Remarks on board the Boston, Monday, July 27.

This day fair and moderate weather. I am now waiting for a fair **wind only to** go to sea. In the afternoon, the body of Hans was **sent on shore at** Port Lewis, and decently buried, — Mr. Reed, first **lieutenant, went on shore,** and Mr. Cooper read prayers **over his corpse.**

Tuesday, July 28, **1778.**

This **day** pleasant weather. **In the morning ordered Wm.** Granger to **be brought to the gangway, and** receive twelve **stripes on his naked back.** His **crime was talking** among the people, **and making them** believe that **the officers** on board had **embezzled** some part of the prizes, cargo, **and o**ther abuse.

Remarks on board *the Boston, Wednesday, July* 29.

This day I ordered twenty-three of the prisoners in irons on account of words they were heard to say, — as, if they were to go in the ship to Nantz, they would rise among them, &c. I am still waiting for a fair wind.

Remarks on Thursday, July **30.**

Fresh gales of thick weather, and I am waiting only **for a fair** wind to put to sea.

Remarks on board the Boston, July 31, 1778.

The first part of this **day fresh** gales and fair weather. The **latter part, moderate. The pilot came on board to carry us** out of **the harbor, but** the wind failing. the pilot went **on shore** again.

Saturday, August 1, 1778.

This day begins with a calm. Warped the ship out **of the** harbor. At noon got clear of all the rocks. Ordered the **boats** hoisted on board, then made sail for Nantz. At 5 P. M. passed through between the Isles of Houat and Quiberon Point, with **the three prize brigs under my convoy. At** 11 **P. M. spoke with Captain Giles, in a** schooner **belonging to New London, North America.**

Remarks on board the Boston, Sunday, August 2, 1778.

This day pleasant and moderate **weather.** At noon we **anchored,** it being calm, about five miles from **Point** Groziaet, **N. W.** At **3** P. M. weighed anchor, at 7 came past the **Point,** at 9 anchored.

Monday, August 3, 1778.

This **comes in with** pleasant weather. **At** 7 in the morning weighed **anchor. At** 9 a branch pilot **came** on board. At **noon** anchored. **Carried the** kedge anchor. **In** warping the ship, **the** bowline broke and **the anchor lost.** Made sail for the river. **At** 5 P. M. anchored opposite **the** lowermost lighthouse. **At** 7 weighed anchor again, **and at** 8 **anchored opposite a town called** St. Nazarie. Captain Whipple **came on board, and I returned** with him **on b**oard his **s**hip.

Remarks on board the Boston, **Tuesday,** *August* 4, **1778.**

This day pleasant weather. By my orders, left with Lieutenant Reed, he sent Mr. Jacobs in the cutter, with a guard of marines, to conduct the four prize-masters, with the men, to *Pienpreiaf,* and deliver them to Captain Whipple, for the Providence.

Wednesday, August 5, 1778.

This day pleasant weather. A frigate and several small vessels lying in company with me, they being bound to sea when the wind serves. My ship is only waiting for Captain Whipple.

Remarks on board the Boston, *Thursday, August* 6.

This day pleasant weather. The ship Providence, Captain Whipple, came down from *Pienpreiaf.* I saluted his ship with thirteen guns, and he returned the same compliment.

Friday, August 7, 1778.

This day foggy, the wind at N. E. The people employed in stowing provision in the hold. At 4 P. M. Commodore Whipple fired a gun and hoisted a flag at his maintop-gallant mast-head, as a signal for the fleet to send their boats on board him to receive orders. A pilot came on board; hoisted in the boats, and unmoored ship. Pleasant weather.

Remarks on board the Boston, Saturday, August 8, **1778.**

This morning, at 3 o'clock, weighed anchor at St. Nazarie, in company with Captain Whipple, of the Providence, and eight sails of ships, and other vessels under our convoy, we being bound to Brest, with the intention of joining Captain Simpson, in the Ranger [ship, and then, thank God, there will be two frigates and a sloop of war belonging to the thirteen United States together, and I hope Heaven will send us success in the cruise, and that we all may return to America, plentifully loaded with his divine goodness.]* At 8 A. M. the Tower of Crozia bears N. E ½ E., distance fifteen miles. The commodore and all the fleet in sight.

Lat. per obs. 46° 59' N.

Remarks on board the Boston, Sunday, August 9, 1778.

This day fresh **gales and fair wea**ther. Spoke with the commodore. **The fleet in sight.**

Lat. per **obs.** 46° 42'.

Remarks on board the Boston, Monday, August 10, **1778.**

Moderate gales and pleasant weather. All the fleet nigh together. Two brigs of the fleet, and the *Cashmeroy,* saluted the commodore with a number of guns. At 6 in the morning, the fleet consisting of eight vessels, left us and steered to the west.

Lat. per obs. 46° 41'.

Remarks on board the Boston, **Tuesday,** *August* 11, 1778.

This day moderate gales and pleasant weather. Captain Whipple came on board and dined with me. Light gales in the night. In the morning saw two ships **to** the westward of us. Spoke with Captain Whipple, and then **set** the small sails and gave **chase;** but the wind failing, could **not** come near **them. At** 11 took **in the** steering sails, and hauled the wind: there was eight **sail in sight.** Spoke **with** the commodore, who thought it best **to steer for the** land.

Remarks on board the Boston, Wednesday, August 12.

This **day pleasant** weather and light breezes of wind. Several sail in sight. **At** 1 A. M. sounded **in** seventy fathoms water. Spoke with the commod**ore, who had** the same depth. Saw two sail to the windward.

Lat. **per obs. 47° 47'.**

---

* **All** enclosed is partly **erased in the original, yet legible.**

Remarks on board the **Boston**, **August** 13, 1778, *Thursday.*

Moderate gales and pleasant weather. Saw seven ships to the northward of us, but could not discover whether they were English or French. At 8 A. M. wore ship, and laid by under the topsails. At 12 at night wore ship again, and stood to the northward and westward.

Friday, August 14, 1778.

Pleasant weather. Saw a schooner to the westward of us, and saw the land bearing E. by N., distant six leagues. At 1 A. M. wore ship to the northward, and stood to the southward. At 7 in the morning saw L'Orient bearing north of us. Stood in for Brest, and fired a number of signal guns for a pilot. Saw three sail of vessels coming out of Brest. Sent a boat on board a schooner, which returned with a pilot, who tarried on board the ship till 4 in the afternoon. I then sent him on board Captain Whipple, judging it most proper that Captain Whipple should be the foremost ship in going into the harbor. Anchored in the harbor of Brest at 4 o'clock in the morning.

Saturday, August 15, 1778.

A pleasant day. Was favored with a large company of gentlemen belonging to the French fleet. Captain Whipple, in the Providence, and myself, saluted the French admiral, whose fleet consisted of thirty-two ships of the line, with thirteen guns each; which was returned by the admiral, and also by the Ranger.

Sunday, August 16, 1778.

This day pleasant weather. I went on board Commodore Whipple with Captain Simpson. The French admiral came on board to pay a visit to the commodore. On his going from the ship he was saluted with thirteen guns, and passing by my ship, I saluted him with eleven. The admiral's ship returned the salute with eleven.

Remarks on board the Boston, Monday, August **17, 1778.**

This day pleasant weather, wind E. **N. E. The French fleet** sailed from Brest, consisting of one three-decker, **twenty-two two-** deckers, eight frigates, three snows, and one lugger.

Tuesday, *August* 18, 1778.

This day pleasant weather. The cutter went to town after bread and flour.

Remarks on board the Boston, Wednesday, August 19. **1778.**

A pleasant day, but little wind. Sailed to join the French **fleet,** six two-deckers, one frigate, the Lively of twenty guns, **and two** snows.

Thursday, August 20, 1778.

This **morning** pleasant. The **commodore gave his signal for** sailing. In purchasing our starboard bower the cable parted and we left the anchor. The **Ranger's** people, **some** being **on shore,** and **the** others not willing to go to sea this day, Captain Whipple sent his boat on board the Ranger with a number of hands, and **I** sent Mr. Tucker with sixteen men to help unmoor her. We all three sailed as far as Brest Water, **and** came to anchor **on** account of the Ranger having twenty-five **of her** men on **shore at** Brest. But **all** returned on board that night. **N**othing more **material this** twenty-**four** hours.

Remarks on board the Boston, Friday, August 21.

This morning, at 5 o'clock, came to sail with a little wind to **the** eastward. **At 9 anchored in a calm. At noon** little wind from the **N. W. This morning, Thomas Shaw,** a sweeper on board, received **a punishment of twelve lashes on** his naked back, with a cat **of nine** tails, for stealing **a shirt from one of** the negroes. I ordered **to** be given him twelve **more for stealing the same shirt** for rum, but forgave him, this being the first time. Likewise,

John Churchill received twelve lashes for getting drunk on duty, and twelve more for absenting himself from duty and concealing himself in the hold, so as not to be found. The said Churchill is a very bad fellow, and been often guilty of thieving.

Nothing more material this day.

Remarks on board the Boston, Saturday, August 22, 1778.

This day very pleasant weather. I went on board the Commodore. At 4 o'clock P. M. weighed anchor and bore away, the Commodore and the Ranger in company. At 7 o'clock Ushant bore N. by E., distance about six leagues, from which I take my departure in the Lat. in 48° 30′ N., Long. 5° 2′ W. from the meridian of London. The latter part of the day cloudy, and moderate weather. **Lat.** of Ushant 48° 30′ N. Long. 5° 2′ West.

Lat. per obs. 47° 36′ N.

Course.	Dist.	X. Lat.	Depart.	Lat. by Obs.	X Long.	Long. in.	M. Dis.
S. 46 W.	78 m.	54m. S.	56m. W	47.36 N.	1.24	6.26 W.	56m. W

Remarks on board the Boston, Sunday, **August** 23.

The first part of this twenty-four hours pleasant weather. At 6 P. M. hauled up the courses, and laid the after sails to the mast. The Ranger spoke with the chase; she proved a Spanish snow, bound to Havre de Grace. **Spoke with** the Commodore. At 4 P. M. set the fore-topsail and middle-staysail. A sail in sight; gave chase, and set the small sails.

Lat. per obs. 47° 00′ No.

Course.	Dist.	X Lat.	Depart.	Lat. per Obs.	X Long.	Long. in.	M. Dist.
S. 66 W	88 m.	36 m.	80 W.	47.00	1.58	8.24 W.	136 W.

Remarks on board the Boston, Monday, August **24, 1778.**

The first part of this twenty-four hours light winds **and** clear weather. Set the steering sails below and aloft. Still **in** chase. At half past 10 spoke with the Ranger. At 5 o'clock P. M. saw a sail; gave chase. The Ranger spoke with her; she proved to be the brig Sally, Captain **Ward,** from London, for Pensacola. Her cargo **consisting of the following** articles: **100 barrels** flour, 200 **bags bread, 139 tierces of beef, 300 barrels of pork, 70 firkins** butter.

60 doz. bottled porter,
  2 bbls. ale, } belonging to the captain.
  6 firkins of butter in cases,

The commodore sent Captain Proctor, from his ship, on **board** of her as prize-master. Am in chase of a sloop; passed **by a** Swedish brig.

Lat. per obs. 45° 54' N.

Course.	Dist.	X Lat.	Depart.	Lat by Obs.	X Long.	Long. in.	M. Dis.
S. 38 W.	123	66 m.	105 W.	45.54 N.	2.32	10.56	241 W.

Remarks on board the Boston, Tuesday, August 25, 1778.

The first part of this twenty-four hours pleasant weather. Spoke with the chase; she was from France, bound to America. Gave chase to a ship, and set all the small sails. Came up **with her, and** gave her a gun; she answered us, and hove **to.** Handed **the small** sails, hauled up the mainsail and foresail; all hands to **quarters.** She proved to be a ship from Bordeaux, bound to Cape **St.** Nicholas. Lay to for the Commodore to come up. At 7 P. **M.** bore away, the Commodore, Ranger, and the prize in sight.

Lat. obs. 45° 24' No.

Course.	Dist.	X. Lat.	Depart.	Lat. per Obs.	X Long.	Long. in.	M. Dis.
S. 78 W	148 m.	30 m. S.	144	45.24	3.24	14.20	385 W.

Remarks on board the Boston, Wednesday, August 26, 1778.

The first part of this twenty-four hours pleasant weather. Saw a sail, gave chase, and spoke with her; she proved to be a Dutchman. At 6 P. M. hove to. to wait for the prize. At 8 filled away again; clear and pleasant weather. I went on board the Commodore and dined. I sent from the prize a cask of bottled porter for my use.

Lat. obs. 45° 21′ No.

Course.	Dist.	X Lat.	Depart.	Lat. by Obs.	X Long.	Long.	M. Dis.
S.88W.	106	3m. S.	106 W.	45.21	2.31	16.51	491 W.

Remarks on board the Boston, Thursday, August 27, 1778.

The first part of this twenty-four hours light breezes and cloudy; the Providence and Ranger close to us. At 8 P. M. all the small sails handed. Spoke with Captain Proctor in the prize brig Polly.

Lat. per obs. 45° 25′ No.

Course.	Dist.	X Lat.	Depart.	Lat. per Obs.	X Long.	Long. in.	M. Dist.
N.87 W	77	4 N.	77 W.	45.25	1.49	18.40	568 W.

Remarks on board the Boston, Friday, August 28, 1778.

The first part of this twenty-four hours light breezes and clear weather. The Providence, Ranger, and the prize in sight. At 11 P. M. lost sight of the prize.

Lat. by obs. 45° 25′.

Course.	Dist.	X Lat.	Depart.	Lat. per Obs.	X Long.	Long. in.	M. Dist.
West.	89 m.	00	89	45.25	2.06	20.47	657 W.

Remarks on board the Boston, Saturday, August 29, 1778.

The first part of this twenty-four hours a fresh breeze of wind and clear weather. At 6 P. M. handed top-gallant sails and stay-sails; hauled up the mainsail. The latter part cloudy weather.

No observation this day.

Course.	Dist.	X Lat.	Dep.	Lat. per Obs.	X Long.	Long. in.	M. Dis.
W. ½ N.	161	16 N.	160 W.	45.41	3.49	24.56	857

Remarks on board the Boston, Sunday, August 30, 1778.

The first part of this twenty-four hours fresh breezes of wind and thick weather. The Providence and Ranger in company. The latter part cloudy weather. Commodore Whipple spoke with a Danish brig from St. Croix.

Lat. per obs. 46° 07′ No.

Course.	Dist.	X Lat.	Depart.	Lat. per Obs.	X Long.	Long. in.	M. Dist.
N.77 W	113	26 N.	110	46.07	2.39	27.15	927 W.

Remarks on board the Boston, Monday, August 31, 1778.

This twenty-four hours pleasant weather and light breezes of wind. The two ships in sight. Captain Simpson, of the Ranger, came on board. After tarrying some time on board, I went with him in his boat on board the Commodore, where we dined.

Lat. per obs. 46° 30′.

Course.	Dist.	X. Lat.	Dep.	Lat. per Obs.	X Long.	Long. in.	Me. Dist.
N.67 W	60	23 N.	55 W.	46.30	1.19	28.34	982 W.

Remarks on board the Boston Frigate, Tuesday, September 1, 1778.

The first part of this twenty-four hours light breezes and clear weather. At 12 saw a sail to the E. S. E. and gave chase. Began to blow hard, and heavy squalls with rain; close reefed the topsails and handed all the staysails. At half past 3 wore ship to the westward, the Commodore and Ranger in sight. Blowed hard; forked the topsails and mainsail, down top-gallant yards. At 6 P. M. saw a sail, to which gave chase. Set the mainsail, jib, and staysail, let two reefs out of each topsail, got up fore top-gallant yards; saw one sail more to windward. At 11 A. M. the Commodore hove out a signal, and I left off the chase. Tacked the ship to the eastward, and stood after the other sail. My cabin boy, Richard Jones, by accident fell overboard, and was in the water full half an hour; got the pinnace out, which got to him just as he was sinking the third time, and providentially saved him. He being a good swimmer, he had the presence of mind to pull his coat off after he was in the water.

No obs. this day.

Course.	Dist.	X Lat.	Depart.	Lat. per Obs.	X Long.	Long. in.	M. Dist.
NW½W	73	41 N.	60 W.	47.11	1.28	30.02	1042 W.

Remarks on board the Boston, Wednesday, September 2, 1778.

The first part of this twenty-four hours fresh gales and cloudy. The Ranger carried away her fore-topmast and maintop-gallant mast. Gave over chase and handed the top-gallant sails; lowered the topsail down on the cap, lay to up S. S. W. off S. E. At 6 A. M. wore ship to the westward. Squally weather with rain.

Lat. per obs. 47° 19′ N.

Course.	Dist.	X. Lat.	Dep.	Lat. per Obs.	X Long.	Long. in.	M. Dis.
E.16 N.	30	8 m. N.	29 m. E.	47.19	40 E.	29.22	1013 W.

Remarks on board the Boston, Thursday, September 3, 1778.

The first part of this twenty-four hours light breezes of wind and cloudy. The Commodore and Ranger close to us. At 6 P. M. double reefed the topsails; squally weather with showers of rain; handed the mizzen-topsail and all small sails. The middle part, heavy showers of rain. **The** latter part the same. The Providence and Ranger **close to us.**

Course.	Dist.	X Lat.	Dep.	Lat. by Obs.	X Long.	Long. in.	M. Dis.
West.	81 m.	oo	81 W.	47.19	2.00	31.22	1094 m.

Remarks on board the Boston, Friday, September 4, 1778.

Moderate breezes and cloudy weather; let out two reefs **of each** topsail. At 6 A. M. up T. G. yards. The latter part clear weather. The Commodore and Ranger close together.

Lat. per obs. 47^c 19' N.

Course.	Dist.	X Lat.	Dep.	Lat. per Obs.	X Long.	Long. in.	M. Dist.
West.	80	o	80 N.	47.19	1.58	33.20	1174 N.

Remarks on board the Boston, Saturday, September 5, 1778.

Light airs of wind and clear weather. Set main-topmast stay-sail, and all the small sails. At 5 P. M. spoke with the Commodore; handed top-gallant sails, and all the small sails. From 9 to 12 P. M. moderate breezes and cloudy weather. Double reefed the fore-topsails. At 1 A. M. a fresh breeze; set the main-sail, close reefed topsails. At 4 fresh gales, handed the topsails, and got top-gallant yards down. At 11 the Commodore made signal for chase. Set whole topsails, and up top-gallant yards;

set top-gallant sails, and steered **to the E. S. E.** Could not see our chase.

Lat. by obs. in 47° 36′ N. uncertain.

Course.	Dist.	X Lat.	Depart.	Lat. per Obs.	X Long.	Long. in.	M. Dis.
N. 76 W	75	17 N.	73	47.36	1.43	35.03	1247 W.

Sunday, September 6.

The first part of this twenty-four hours fresh gales; all sails set; the chase in sight. At 5 P. M. set the studding sails; pleasant weather; still in chase. At 11 the Ranger came up with the chase, which proved to be a French ship, from St. Peter's, bound to France. At 1 A. M. wore ship to the westward, took in the studding sails, and handed all the small sails. At 8 A. M. went on board the Commodore and dined.

Lat. per obs. 47° 25′.

Course.	Dist.	X. Lat.	Dep.	Lat. per Obs.	X Long.	Long. in.	M. Dis.
S. 72 E.	37	11 S.	35 E.	47.25	51	34.12	1196

Remarks on board the Boston, Monday, September 7, 1778.

The first part of this twenty-four hours pleasant weather. At 5 P. M. I returned from the Commodore on board my own ship. Calm weather and cloudy, attended with a very heavy swell. At 6 A. M. set the sail-maker to work to cut two new mizzen-stay-sails. At 9 light winds and heavy weather; bore down to the Commodore. At 12 the Commodore came on board to dine with me.

Lat. per obs. 47° 04′ No.

Course.	Dist.	X. Lat.	Dep.	Lat. by Obs.	X Long.	Long. in.	M. Dist.
S. 38 W	27 m.	21 m. S.	16 W.	47.04	24 m.	34.36	1212

Remarks on board the Boston, Tuesday, September 8, 1778.

The first part of this twenty-four hours light breezes and pleasant. The middle part the same. The Commodore and Ranger close to us.

Lat. per obs. 46° 34′.

Course.	Dist.	X Lat.	Dep.	Lat. per Obs.	X Long.	Long in.	M. Dis.
SW ½ W	60 m.	38 S.	46m. W	46.34	1.07	35.43	1258

Remarks on board the Boston, Wednesday, September 9, 1778.

The first part of these twenty-four hours light breezes of wind and clear weather. Bent a new foresail and mizzen-staysail; the Commodore and Ranger in sight. At 8 A. M. saw a sail, and gave chase. Set top-gallant sail and mainsail. At 10 came up with the chase, which proved to be a brig from the Granard's, bound to Glasgow; hove to and sent the boat on board. The brig is called the Friends, commanded by a Captain M'Farling, her cargo consisting of rum, and some bags of cotton. Captain M'Farling went on board the Commodore, and the following passengers and men came on board my ship, viz., William Kennedy, the supercargo, Wm. Hargart, and Thomas Marshall, passengers. John Torbit and Daniel Johnson, mates. Malcolm Maceset, Wm. Sharp, John Robertson, Daniel Ferguson, John Topson, and John Bogg, privates. I went went on board the Commodore.

Lat. per obs. 46° 31′ No.

Course.	Dist.	X Lat.	Dep.	Lat. per Obs.	X Long.	Long. in.	M. Dist.
West.	109	3 m. S.	109 N.	46.31	2.36	38.19	1367

Remarks on board the Boston, Thursday, September 10, 1778.

The first part of this twenty-four hours a hard gale of wind and

cloudy weather. At half past **12 I** returned from on board the
Commodore. At **2** P. M. I sent from the Boston on board the
prize one **new main-topsail, one new staysail, and one mizzen-**
staysail. The prize is manned by the Ranger. The wind fresh
under our foresail and mizzen-staysail. At 7 P. M. wore **ship** to
the **westward; the** Commodore, Ranger, and prize in **sight.** At
11 fresh gales and heavy rains. Still under foresail and mizzen-
staysail.

No observation to-day.

Course.	Dist.	X Lat.	Dep.	Lat. by Obs.	X Long.	Long. in.	M. Dis.
N. 36 E.	23	18 m. N	18m. E.	46.49	19 m.	38.00	1354 m.

Remarks on board the Boston, Friday, September 11, 1778.

Fresh gales of wind and cloudy weather, with rain. Handed the
foresail, and set the mainsail. At 9 A. M. light breezes and fine
weather: **the** Commodore close to us. Went on board the Commodore, and after **returning** sent away the following prisoners,
viz., Daniel **Johnson,** Malcolm Maccesset, William **Sharp, John**
Topsham, and John Bogg, on board the Ranger. **William Hagart**
and Thomas Marshall, passengers in the **prize, on board the**
Providence. Daniel Swords, one of **my men, on board the Com-**
modore, for being mutinous, and trying to make some **of the peo-**
ple so: likewise Anthony **Martin for the** same, both of them **being**
ordered on board by the **Commodore** in writing. Received **from**
the prize two hogsheads rum, **and** about forty gallons in **kegs.**
Mr. Vickory came on board from **the Commodore** in a **poor state**
of health.

Course.	Dist.	X Lat.	Depart.	Lat. per Obs.	X Long.	Long. In.	M. Dist.
N. E.	16 m.	11m. N.	11 N.	47.00	16 E.	37.44	1343 W.

Remarks on board the Boston, Saturday, September 12, 1778.

The first part of this twenty-four hours light breezes and clear weather. At 3 P. M. the yawl came on board; hoisted her in and made sail. The middle part, light winds. At 6 A. M. saw a sail, and gave chase. Set all the sails I could, but wind being small (almost a calm) could **not** come up with her. The Commodore, Ranger, and prize **nigh to us. Found a strong current from** the N. E. this twenty-four hours.

Lat. per obs. 46° 10′ No.

Course.	Dist.	X Lat.	Depart.	Lat. by Obs.	X Long.	Long. in.	M. Dist.
S. W.	71 m.	50 m. S.	50 m.	46.10	1.13	38.57	1395 W.

Remarks *on board the Boston, Sunday, September* 13, 1778.

Light breezes and clear weather, the chase still in sight. Hauled down all studding-sails, hoisted the yawl out and sent her on board the Commodore. At 4 P. M. the yawl returned. Wore ship to the S. westward; the ship in chase bore at 7 S. E. from us. The Commodore, Ranger, and prize in sight of us; handed top-gallant sails. At 4 A. M. wore ship and stood to **N.** eastward, the brig in sight. At 7 the Commodore spoke **to me, and ordered to** steer **N. E.** till 12 at noon. Lost sight of **the** chase.

Lat. per obs. 45° 54′ No.

Course.	Dist.	X. Lat.	Dep.	Lat. per Obs.	X Long.	Long. in.	M. Dist.
S. E.	23 m.	16 S.	16 m.	45.54	23 E.	38.34	1377 m.

*Remarks on board **the Boston, Monday,** September* 14, 1778.

Fresh breezes and clear weather the fore part of this twenty-four hours. At 6 double reefed our topsails; fresh breezes and cloudy. At 8 hauled up the mainsail and stowed the small sails. At 10 fresh gales and cloudy; took in the third reef in the topsails and furled the mainsail. At 2 A. M. the Commodore and Ranger in sight. At 6 A. M. saw a sail and gave chase; let one reef out of each topsail, down top-gallant yards, set the mainsail and all the small sails; came nigh the chase, which I found to be the prize Friends, already belonging to us. Half past 10 o'clock wore ship to the southward. The Commodore and Ranger close to us.

Lat. per obs. 46° 11′ No.

Course.	Dist.	X. Lat.	Dep.	Lat. per Obs.	X Long.	Long. in.	M. Dis.
W by N	77 m.	15 N.	75 m. W	46.11	1.48	40.22	1452

Remarks on board the Boston Tuesday, September 15, 1778.

The first part of this twenty-four hours light breezes of wind and cloudy weather. At 7 P. M. hove to for the Commodore and Ranger; hauled up the foresail. At 5 A. M. cloudy weather. Let the reefs out of the topsails and got up top-gallant yards. At 10 little wind and clear weather. Saw a sail; set the mainsail and all the small sails, and gave chase.

Lat. per obs. 45° 49′ No.

Course.	Dist.	X Lat.	Depart.	Lat. per Obs.	X Long.	Long. in.	M. Dis.
S. 60 W.	45	22 S.	39 W.	45.49	56 W.	41.18	1491 W.

Remarks on board the Boston, Wednesday, September 16, 1778.

The first part of this twenty-four hours light breezes of wind; still in chase. At P. M. hove to, the vessel in chase running down for us; hoisted out the yawl, and sent Mr. Bates on board. She proved to be the snow Adventure, Captain Symes, from Newfoundland, bound to Pont-a-Port, **loaded with fish. Mr. Bates** sent on board Captain Symes and **four of his men. At 7 P. M. I** went on board the Commodore with **Captain Symes. At 8 the** prize was manned by me with the following men : **Wm. Atkins,** prize-master, John Baneauf, his mate, A. Richardson, D. Orne, Joseph Cornish, *Imasurign,* John Allarey, Antonie Barazeir, and James Cummins. I left **Captain Symes on** board the Commodore, and have **four privates on board my ship, viz., Robert** Miller, **James Shea, Wm. Call, and Wm. Allen. Two sails in sight.**

Lat. per obs. 45° 47′ No.

Course.	Dist.	X Lat.	Dep.	Lat. per Obs.	X Long.	Long. in.	M. Dls.
W. ½ S.	21 m.	2 m. S.	21 W.	45.47	0.30	41.48	1512

Remarks on board the Boston, Thursday, September 17, 1778.

Light breezes and clear weather, still the chase **in sight.** At **half** past 5 hauled up the courses and spoke to the Commodore. At 8 P. M. wore ship to the westward; the two ships still in sight; fresh breezes and cloudy with **rain.** Half past 7 wore ship to the eastward. At 10 saw two ships **bearing S. E. from us; gave** chase; the weather being thick and rainy **lost sight of them.** Spoke to the Commodore, who ordered me to steer **E. by S.; the Ranger in sight. At 5 A. M. set the mainsail. At 7 heavy squalls of rain;** forked our topsails; spoke to the Commodore and Ranger. At 8 set single-reefed topsails and mainsail. At 11 saw a sail to **windward; gave chase; set** T. G. sails. Heavy showers **of rain; lost** sight **of the chase.**

Lat. per obs. 46° 16′.

Course.	Dist.	X Lat.	Depart.	Lat. per Obs.	X Long.	Long. in.	M. Dist.
N. 65 E.	69 m.	29 m. N.	62 m. E.	46.16	1.30 E.	40.18	1450 W.

Remarks on board the Boston, Friday, September **18,** 1778.

Squally weather and showers of rain. Handed all the topsails and mainsail; laid to under foresail and mizzen-staysail. At P. M. the weather the same; the Commodore and Ranger in sight. At 6 A. M. set all the three topsails; the wind more moderate. At 9 dirty weather, with showers of rain; forked the mizzen-topsail.

Lat. 46° 06' North.

Course.	Dist.	X Lat.	Dep.	Lat. by Obs.	X Long.	Long. In.	M. Dis.
S. 78 E.	47 m.	10 m.	46 m.	46.06	1.04	39.12	1404 W.

Remarks on board the Boston, Saturday, September 19, 1778.

The first part of this twenty-four hours fresh gales of wind and rain; under fore, mizzen, and mizzen-staysail. At 5 P. M. set the mainsail. At 7 took in fore and main-topsails. The middle part, fresh gales of wind and plenty of rain. At 7 A. M. set the topsails.

Lat. per obs. 44° 38' North.

Course.	Dist.	X Lat.	Dep.	Lat. per Obs.	X Long.	Long. in.	M. Dist.
S ½ W.	89	88 m.	8 W.	44.38	12m. W	39.24	1412 W.

Remarks on board the Boston, Sunday, September 20, 1778.

The first part of this twenty-four hours squally weather and rain. At 6 P. M. set the main-topsail. · The middle part, the weather much the same. At 2 A. M. clewed up the main-topsail. At 6 set the main-topsail. At 8 set the foresail and all the small

sails; all reefs out the topsails; light breezes of **wind and clear
weather.**

Lat. per obs. 43° 26' No.

Course.	Dist.	X Lat.	Depart.	Lat. per Obs.	X Long.	Long. in.	M. Dist.
S. 35 W.	88 m.	72 m. N.	50 m. W	**43.26**	1.10	40.34	1462 W.

Remarks on board the Boston, Monday, September **21, 1778.**

The first part of this twenty-four hours fresh breezes **and clear
weather.** Got up the top-gallant yards and set the sails. At 7
P. M. tacked ship, handed the top-gallant sails, and spoke to the
Commodore. At 10 fresh breezes and clear weather; hauled up
the mainsail and down with all small sail. At 1 A. M. double
reefed **the** topsails, handed the mizzen-topsail and mainsail.
Squally weather with rain. At **5 close** reefed our **topsails, down**
top-gallant yards, and took **in the fore-topsail. At 8 moderate
breezes and** cloudy, set the fore-topsail, **all** the staysails, and jib.

Lat. per obs. 43° 31'.

Course.	Dist.	X Lat.	Dep.	Lat. per Obs.	X Long.	Long. In.	M. Dis.
W. ¼ N.	59	5 m. N.	58	43.31	**1.20**	**41.54**	1520 m.

Remarks on board the Boston, Tuesday, September **22, 1778.**

The first part **of** this twenty-four hours moderate breezes **and**
clear weather. Hauled up the foresail, **and** bore away under the
Commodore's **stern, and** hove to. At **1** P. M. hoisted out **the**
pinnace and **sent her on board the** Commodore, for himself **and**
Captain Hinman to **come on board and** dine. After the boat
returned sent her on board **the Ranger, for Captain Simpson,**
who came **on** board. At 2 made **sail. At 5 took in the topsails**
and handed **the** mainsail; **fresh gales and rain. At 3 A. M. wore**

ship and stood **to the westward.** At 6 let the reefs **out** of the top-sails and set the **staysails. At 11 sent up main top-gallant** yards, and set **the T. G. sails.**

Lat. per obs. 44° 04'.

Course.	Dist.	X. Lat.	Dep.	Lat. per Obs.	X Long.	Long. in.	M. Dis.
N 58 W	62 m.	33 N.	52 W.	44.04	1.13	43.07	1572 m.

Remarks on board the Boston, Wednesday, September 23, 1778.

The first part of this twenty-four hours fresh gales **and** cloudy weather. At 3 P. M. **took** in top-gallant sails, took two reefs in the T. sails. At 7 took in M. T. sail. At half past 9 set the main-sail. At 1 A. M. hazy weather, with rain and sharp lightning. Half past 7 set the fore-topsail and mizzen-topsail. The latter part of the twenty-four hours fresh breezes and clear weather.

Lat. per obs. 44° 07' No.

Course.	Dist.	X Lat.	Depart.	Lat. by Obs.	X Long.	Long. in.	M. Dist.
West.	127 m.	3 N.	127	44.07	2.56	46.03	1699

Remarks on board the Boston, Thursday, September 24, 1778.

The first part of this twenty-**four** hours squally weather **and** rain. At 2 P. M. reefed the topsails, handed the mizzen T. **sail.** At 5 set the M. topmast staysail. At 8 I spoke with **the Com-modore, who** acquainted me he had sounded, but had **no ground.** At 10 out one reef T. sails; heavy weather with lightning. At 11 out all reefs. At 3 A. M. took two reefs in the M. and T. topsails; took one reef in the mizzen-topsail and forked it; fresh breezes and rain. At 7 out all reefs in topsails, set the staysails, unbent the fore-topsail and bent another. The **latter part of the twenty-** four hours light breezes and fair weather.

Lat. per obs. 44° 30′ No.

Course.	Dist.	X Lat.	Depart.	Lat. per Obs.	X Long.	Long. in.	M. Dis.
W. by N	94 m.	23 N.	91 m.	44.30	2.6	48.09	1790 W.

Remarks on board the Boston, Friday, September **25, 1778.**

The first part of this twenty-four hours fresh gales of wind and squally. At 3 P. M. took two reefs in the topsails, handed mizzen-**topsail.** At 4 set mizzen-topsail. At 6 fresh gales and **rain. Com**modore and Ranger in sight. At 10 close reefed T. sails, handed M. T. sail, hauled up the F. sail, and hove to for sounding **but got no** bottom. At 11 set M. **T. mast staysail and M. staysail. At 3 A. M.** down M. T. **M.** staysail; **fresh breezes and hazy. At 6 hove to and** tried for sounding, **but** had no ground. Set the miz-zen-topsail and M. T. M. staysail. At 10 set the M. sail. Sounded, but no bottom.

Lat. per **obs.** 44° 42′.

Course.	Dist.	X. Lat.	Dep.	Lat. per Obs.	X Long.	**Long. in.**	M. Dist.
N. 83 W	105	12 m. N.	104 W.	44.42	2.28	50.37	1894

Remarks on **board** *the Boston, Saturday, September* 26. 1778.

Light breeze **of wind** and foggy weather. **At 4 P.** M. hove to for sounding, but **got no ground.** Cleared up. Got up T. **G.** yards, out all reefs T. **sails; set the T. G.** sails; took two reefs in the M. T. sail; hauled up **the M. sail and handed it.** Thick weather. At midnight the Commodore **and Ranger in sight of us; hove to under mizzen and mizzen T. sails.** Clewed up the T. sails. At

12 made sail, and **bore down** to the Commodore. Latter part of this twenty-four hours light airs and **thick of fog.**

N. B. At 8 P. M. **spoke with Captain Simpson, who sounded** at 7, the hour before; got ground in eighty fathoms depth, **in the Grand Bank. In laying b**y caught several codfish.

Lat. per obs. 45° 00′ No.

Course.	Dist.	X Lat.	Depart.	Lat. per Obs.	X Long.	Long. In.	M. Dist.
N. 60 W	36	18 m. N.	31 m.	45.00	44	51.21	1925 W.

Remarks on board the Boston, Sunday, *September* 27, 1778.

Light breezes and foggy weather. At 2 P. M. out all reefs, topsails. Spoke with **the Co**mmodore. At 3 handed the topsails, and lay to under the mizzen and mizzen-staysail. Still foggy; reefed the topsails. At 6 A. M. saw a sail; out all reefs T. sails; set the topgallant sails fore and aft; set the driver. At 10 down steering **sails in T. G.** sails. At 11 A. M. came up and spoke with the brig **William, Captain Robert** Stonehouse, who sailed from Boston for Amsterdam the **10th day** of March, 1778, with a cargo **of twenty casks** tobacco, one hundred and ninety casks flax-seed, **fifty barrels** pot and pearl ash. Sailed from Amsterdam, **August 3, 1778; out** fifty days when spoke with. Registered **in Boston, before Nathaniel** Barber, naval officer.

Lat. per obs. 45° 24′ No.

Course.	Dist.	X. Lat.	Dep.	Lat. per Obs.	X Long.	Long. in.	M. Dis.
N. 27 E.	27	24. m N.	12 E.	45.24	17	31.04	1913

Remarks on board the Boston, Monday, September 28, 1778.

First part of this twenty-four hours fresh breezes and cloudy weather. At 1 P. M. hove the main-topsail to the mast. At 3 close reefed the topsails. At 6 P. M. I returned from on board the Ranger. The middle part foggy, disagreeable weather. At 9 A. M. hauled down the staysails, up foresail, out boats to scrub the ship's bottom, she being very foul. Nothing more material.

No observation this day. Coursing on the Banks.

Remarks on board the Boston, Tuesday, September 29, 1778.

The first part of this twenty-four hours light winds and foggy. At 1 A. M. fired several guns, but had no answer. I still continued cleaning ship. At 2 P. M. finished with my boats hogging and scraping. At 3 sprung up a breeze from the S. S. W. Made sail; fired a gun. The Providence answered. Run for the report. At 4 P. M. spoke with Captain Whipple. Middle and latter parts continuing thick and foggy.

Lat. per obs. 45° 16' No.

Remarks on board the Boston, Wednesday, September 30, 1778.

This twenty-four hours small breezes of wind; all hands employed in clearing the ship Boston. At 10 P. M. calm, ship's head to the westward. Continued hogging ship fore and aft. At 8 P. M. Captain Whipple and Captain Hinman came on board. At 5 returned on board the Providence. Middle and latter parts calm and foggy. Fired signal guns for company. At 10 A. M. clear. Captain Whipple hailed the Boston for me to come on board. I ordered the yawl out, and went on board to dine with him; quite clear and calm. Nothing more remarkable this twenty-four hours.

Remarks on board the Boston, Thursday, October 1, 1778.

This twenty-four hours first part clear and calm. At 3 P. M. I returned on board from the Providence. A light air from the E. N. E.; made sail to the westward.

Remarks **on board the Boston, Friday, October 2, 1778.**

This twenty-four hours begins with moderate breezes and cloudy weather. At 4 P. M. fresh gales; double reefed fore and M. T. sails; handed mizzen-topsail. At 6 do. sounded; had forty-five fathoms. Spoke with Captain Whipple, and bore away W. S. W. From this Bank I take a new departure, being about two degrees ahead of the ship, when getting ground, judging by the depth of water, in Lat. 43° 50′, Long. 51° 40′ W.

Course.	Dist.	X Lat.	Dep.	Lat. per Obs.	X Long.	Long in.	M. Dis.
SW½ W	132 m.	84 m.	102	42.26	2.20 W.	54.00	102 W.

II. GENERAL **SIGNALS TO** BE OBSERVED BY THE FLEET.

Signals to be Observed by Day.

To prepare for sailing, . . .	Fore-topsail loose **in top.**
To unmoor, ...	Three topsails loose.
To weigh, ...	Topsails sheeted home.
Weathermost and headmost ships to tack first, ...	Continental Jack, fore-topmast head.
Sternmost and leewardmost ships to tack first, ...	Continental Jack, main-topmast head.
All ship's to tack, ...	Striped flag, main-topmast head.
Bear up before the wind, . .	Pendant at mizzen peak and Jack at main-topmast head.
Discovering sails, ...	White Jack at main-topmast head; if to windward, fore-topmast head; if to leeward, hoist and lower it as often as you see sails.
Speak the Commodore, . . .	When any of the ships want to speak with the Providence, they must make the same signal which she makes them.
Discovering land, ...	Continental ensign at ensign staff, a flag main-topmast head.

Bring to on starboard **tack,** . | Continental Jack, mizzen-topmast head, **one gun.**

" " larboard tack, . . | White flag mizzen-topmast head, and two guns.

To make sail after lying by, . | Red ensign at mizzen **peak,** and three guns, if thick weather.

If in distress, ... | Haul up mizzen, and hoist three colors, one over the other at mizzen peak; if not discovered, fire **guns till answered.**

Losing company and meeting again, ... | The weathermost to hand the fore top-gallant sail, if set, and clew up fore topsails with yard aloft, and white flag at fore topmast head.

The leewardmost to answer by handing main top-gallant sail, if set, and clew up main-topsail with yard **aloft, and** white flag at **main top-gallant masthead.**

Providence **leads** ahead.

Signals to be Observed by Night.

Signals by **Night.**	Lights.	Signals by Night.
To unmoor, ...	2	One over the other in fore **shrouds.**
To weigh, ...	3	In same manner and place.
To anchor, ...	3	One at each M. head.
Cut or slip, ...	4	**One** at each **yard-arm.**
Head and weathermost ships to tack first, . .	2	Ensign staff.

Signals by Night.	Lights.	Signals by Night.
Sternmost and leeward-most ships to tack first,	3	Ensign staff.
Discovering sails, . . .	3	Mizzen shrouds placed triangular if to windward, if to leeward add an ensign staff.
To speak, ...	4	At mainpeak.
Discovering danger, . .	4	Of equal height fire three guns.

	Guns.	Lights.	False fire.	
To alter course, . . .	I	—	—	For each point of compass.
" " to starboard, .	—	—	I	
" " to port, . . .	—	—	2	
To bring to on starboard tack, ...	—	2	I	Ensign staff.
To bring to larboard tack	—	I	I	" "
To make sail after lying by, ...	2	—	—	Short time one after another.

Losing company and meeting again, . . .

The ship that hails first shall ask, " What ship's that?" then he that is hailed shall answer, " Carnes." Then he that hailed first shall answer, " Saratoga."

Signals to be Observed in a Fog.

To bring to on starboard tack, ...	2 guns.
" " " larboard tack, ...	3 "
" " " to tack, ...	4 "

To make sail after lying by, ... 5 guns.

Discovering land or danger, ... 6 "

Continuing same sail, ... —

Ringing bells, beating drums, &c., ... —

Losing company and meeting again, same as in the night.

Signals to Engage.

Striped Jack at main top-gallant masthead under the pendant, to engage.

To leave off Engaging.

The same color hauled down from them, and hoisted at fore top-gallant masthead.

If after signal is made to desist from engaging, it should be necessary for each vessel to use their utmost endeavors to escape from the enemy, I will hoist a French pendant under the striped flag, at fore top-gallant masthead.

Signals for the Boston.

Commodore to speak her, . .   Dutch Jack mizzen-peak.

Boston to chase, ...   Dutch ensign, ensign staff.

Station, ...   Starboard quarter Commodore.

Boston to quit chase, ...   Three guns.

Signals for the Ranger.

Ranger to chase, ...   White ensign at ensign staff.

To leave chase, ...   Two guns.

Commo. to speak the Ranger, .   Continental Jack mizzen-peak.

Station, ...   Larboard quarter.

Signals for the Queen.

Queen to chase, ...	Red ensign, **ensign staff.**
To leave off **chase**, ...	**One** gun.
Commodore **to speak Queen**, .	White Jack at mizzen peak.
Station, ...	**Queen** brings up the rear.

To form a Line of the Fleet ahead.

Whiff in the ensign.

Line abreast.

Dutch **Jack** mizzen-topmast head.

In case of any misfortune, which God forbid, these signals are to be destroyed.

Given under my hand, on board the Continental Frigate Providence, Nantasket Road, this 22d day of November, 1779.

By the Commodore commanding,

Abraham Whipple.

Joseph **West,** *Clerk.*

To Samuel Tucker, Esq., *Commander Boston.*

SIGNALS TO BE OBSERVED BY COMMANDERS IN THE CONTINENTAL NAVY.

By Day.

The ship to windward must hoist a French Jack at the fore top-gallant masthead, and lower the fore top-gallant sail or topsail.

If a sloop, a French Jack at the masthead, and lower the foresail.

If a schooner, a French Jack at the fore top-masthead, and lower the foresail.

The ships to leeward must hoist a Continental Jack at the main top-gallant masthead, and lower the main top-gallant sail, or main topsail. If a sloop, or schooner, they must hoist a Continental Jack at the maintop masthead, and lower the mainsail. Then each vessel to show her proper colors at the ensign staff. The windward vessel to fire one gun to leeward, and the leeward vessel one to windward.

By Night.

The ship to windward must show two lights abreast, and fire one gun. The ship to leeward, three lights, one above the other, and fire two guns.

N. B. All commanders are strictly ordered to destroy these signals before the enemy's boats board them.

YORK, January 14.

By order of the Honorable the Marine Committee.

JOHN BROWN, *Secretary.*

A true copy of the original.

Attest.　　WILLIAM STORY,
　　　　　　Clerk to Navy Board, Eastern Department.

To SAMUEL TUCKER, ESQ.,
　　　Commander of the Ship Boston.

SIGNALS FRENCH FLEET.

When his Majesty's fleet shall be to windward, the Britannia will hoist a flag at the fore top-gallant masthead, and will lower fore topsail, fire a gun to leeward.

When his Majesty's fleet shall be to leeward, the Britannia will hoist two white flags, one upon the other, at the main top-gallant masthead, and lower her main topsail, fire three guns to windward.

On board the Britannia, 17th August, 1778.

CAPTAIN SAMUEL TUCKER, *Boston.*

III. NOTES.

Page 19.

MARBLEHEAD, January 17, 1850.

This may certify that on examination of the Record belonging to the "First Church of Christ, in Marblehead, Lib. II., 1740," page 8, under the head **of Baptisms,** I find **recorded the name of**

"**SAMUEL** inf. $\left\{ \begin{array}{l} \text{ANDREW} \\ \text{MARY} \end{array} \right\}$ TUCKER,"

with the date, 1747, at head of the column, and November 8, opposite, on the left of his name.

RICHARD HOMAN, *Clerk of First Church.*

Page 19.

(A Copy from the Family Bible.)

RECORD OF MARRIAGES AND BIRTHS.

Samuel Tucker, son of Andrew and Mary **Tucker, of Marble**head, was married to Mary Gatchell, **daughter of Samuel and** Ann Gatchell, of Marblehead, **on the 21st day of December, in** the year 1768.

The time and births **of their children,** and their names, as follows : —

Samuel Tucker, ... November 1, 1747.
Mary, his wife, ... January 30, 1752.
Mary Tucker, ... 1st child, . . . May 21, 1770.
Martha Tucker, . . . 2d " . . . June 20, 1772.
Samuel Tucker, Jr., . . 3d " . . . April 5, 1775.
Betsey Tucker, ... 4th " . . . February 20, 1777.
Samuel Tucker, ... 5th " . . . March 2, 1778.

Mary Tucker was married to Benjamin Hinds, December,   1789.
Benjamin Hinds, ... March 19,   1791.
Benjamin Hinds, ... August 27,   1793.
Samuel Tucker Hinds, ... September 27, 1798.
Martha Tucker, married John Tedder, . . November 1, 1797.
Jane Talbot, ... born . . . August 21,   1798.
John Tedder, ... " . . . April 14,   1800.
Martha Elizabeth Tedder, . " . . . August 21,   1802.
Mary Tedder, ... " . . . September 28, 1804.
John Tedder, ... " . . . December 27, 1806.
Martha Elizabeth Tedder, . . " . . . November 14, 1808.

RECORD OF DEATHS.

Samuel Tucker, Jun., died September 5, 1776, at home.

Betsey Tucker, died December 8, 1781, at home.

Samuel Tucker, died December 23, 1795, in the West Indies.

Captain Benjamin **Hinds, son-in-law, died** April 12, 1799, at sea.

Benjamin Hinds, grandson, died January 19, 1792, at home.

John Tedder, my youngest daughter's son, died November, 1800, at home.

Martha Elizabeth Tedder, died **October 21, 1805.**

Mary Tucker, my mother, died March 6, 1808, aged 91 years and **6 months.**

Jane Tedder, granddaughter, died 1810, aged 15 years 6½ months.

Mrs. Mary Tucker, died December 30, 1831, aged 79 **years.**

Samuel Tucker, died March 10, 1833, aged 85 years **4 months.**

Page 49.

"Tempora mutantur, **et nos** mutamur cum illis," the **times** have changed, and we **change with them;** as the following **extract** will show from the Journals **of Congress,** October 16, 1778.

" *Whereas,* Frequenting playhouses, and theatrical entertainments has a fatal tendency to divert the minds of the people from a due attention to the means necessary for the defence of their country and the preservation of their liberties:

"*Resolved*, That any person, or officer under the United States, who shall act, promote, encourage, or attend such plays, shall be deemed unworthy to hold such office, and shall be accordingly dismissed." — Vol. IV., p. 602.

Page 56.

MARBLEHEAD, February 3, 1776.

SIR: This will acknowledge the receipt of your esteemed favor per Mr. Gould, and note contents. I heartily congratulate you, Captain Waters, and your officers, on the success of your last cruise, and I hope your next will prove as successful. I should have set off for Cape Ann with Mr. Gould, but the indisposition of my bodily health is such as will not permit of it to-day, but am in hopes by Monday shall be able to be at Cape Ann; if my disorder should not return, I will immediately attend. Captain Sargent, who is appointed agent for the Continent, will, you may depend, take all the care that man can do, as he will be accountable for any embezzlement. So that you have nothing to fear on that account. The sloop you mention you took within four leagues of the lighthouse, I hope the agent has taken the master and sent him forward to headquarters. If he has not, I would recommend to you that you send him immediately. I am informed that there is a large transport ship, that was fitted out at Boston, mounting sixteen guns. She yesterday got between the land and one of our fishing schooners, Skipper Dixey, and was chasing her off Cape Cod when seen last. I mention this, because I would have you keep a good look out for her, as I would have you avoid falling into her hands. You may depend on her being strong manned. I do not mean to direct you, only mention it, as I would be fond of giving you (and the gentlemen) that are concerned in the armed vessels all the intelligence I am able. I have this moment, since writing the above, been acquainted by Captain Joseph Hibbart, who is from Cape Ann, that the sloop you took came up from Cape Ann, run right to the man of war, who has taken her into his custody, and she is now gone by between the point of neck and Catt Island for Boston. By his account I fear the agent has let him go. I would hope still it is not the sloop.

Sir, I am informed that Captain Waters has not employed any person as agent for him and his officers; if that should be the case, shall esteem it a favor if you make mention of me to them; as I am agent for Captain Manly, Captain Burke, yourself, all the officers of them, I should be glad to serve them likewise, if not engaged, and it should be agreeable; on your mentioning the matter to Captain Waters and his officers, desire him to give me a line by way of desire that I would act as their agent, he and his officers sign it. Your interest in the matter will much oblige,

Your friend and humble servant,

JONATHAN GLOVER.

To Captain Samuel Tucker.

Page 71.

The following is a true copy of a paper forwarded on to Washington, in proof of the claim of Mrs. Sarah Reynolds, formerly the widow of Philip Follitt, to a pension under the law of July 4, 1836.

We the subscribers, officers, as well as seamen, belonging to the ship Boston, commanded by Samuel Tucker, Esq., have appointed Major Richard Reed to be our agent for us, for the intended voyage, to receive severally all *prizes*, vessels, goods, merchandises of any kind whatsoever that shall be taken by said ship during her voyage and sent into any port or ports in North America, to receive the shares severally belonging to us into *your* hands, for our account, and to receive of any agent or agents appointed by the United or Continental States of America, all sums of money, goods, &c., that he or they shall have in their hands, and you are ordered to give **receipts in our names,** and for our accounts, and receive **the same.   Dated, Marblehead, January 7, 1778.**

Benjamin **Reed.**
Philip Mohyes.
Joseph Proctor, for son.
Richard Horton, Midshipman.
Joshua Goss, Midshipman.
Thomas Brimblecom, Jr., boy.
Andrew Richardson.
(seems erased) Mate.
John **Fowler.**

Thomas Colley, X ^{his} mark.

John Main.
Benjamin Tucker, First Mate.
John Vickory, Mate.
Philip Follitt, Midshipman.
James Quilty, Ship's Cook.
John Goss, boy.
William Goss, Ship's Pilot.
William Goss, Jr., boy.

Jacob **Tucker, Jr.,** boy.
George Snowden, Mate.
Elias Bowden, Jr., Quartermaster.
Jacob Tucker, Quartermaster.
Philip Mohyes,   "   "
Richard Webber, boy.
Samuel Gatchell, boy.
John Davis, Boatswain's **Mate.**
John Fox,   "   "
Aaron (illegible), **Captain** taken.
Jeremiah Mahoney, Chief Boatswain's Mate.
William Robarts.
Henry Peyton, Mate.
Nathaniel Pearce, Purser.
Nathaniel Pearce, Jr., boy.
John Pearce, the 5th **boy.**
Thomas Brimblecom.
James Harris, boy of **Goss.**

ESSEX, ss.   November 11, 1867.

I **certify** that the above is **a true copy** of the original document which was forwarded to Washington by me, years ago, **in support of** the pension claim of the widow **of** Philip Follitt, **one of the officers** named in said document.

Attest,   **JAMES GREGORY,** *Justice of the Peace.*

Each Share of Prize Money.

		£	s.	d.
Benjamin Reed, . . . Lieutenant, ...		244	18	–
Benjamin Tucker, . . Master, ...		244	18	–
Joshua Goss, ... Midshipman, ...		84	16	–
Richard Horton, . . . "		84	16	–
John Vickory, ... "		84	16	–
Nathaniel Peirce, . . . Steward, ...		84	16	–
James Quilty, ... Cook, ...		84	16	–
George Snowden, ...				
Andrew Richardson, . Seaman, ...		18	10	3
Elias Bowden, . . . "		18	10	3
Philip Meheoy, . . . "		18	10	3
William Goss, ... Pilot, ...				
Jacob Tucker, Jr., . . Seaman, ...		18	10	3
John Davis, ... : "		18	10	3
John Peirce, ... "		18	10	3
Nathaniel Peirce, Jr., . "		18	10	3
Thomas Brimblecom, . "		18	10	3
Joseph Prockter, . . . "		18	10	3
Thomas Colley, . . . "		18	10	3
John Flower, ... "		18	10	3
John Rooseau, ... "		18	10	3
James Harris, ... "		18	10	3
John Main, ... "		18	10	3
Richard Webber, . . . "		18	10	3
Jacob Tucker, ... "		18	10	3
John Goss, ... "		18	10	3

By Sundry Goods Received.

	£	s.	d.
16 Barrels flour, £40 1s. 9d., ...	524	5	11
21 Bags of bread, £21 3s. 12d., ...	295	1	5
3 Firkins butter, 229 lbs. tare 45 lbs. = 184 lbs. at 6s.,	55	4	–
1 Hogshead of peas sold at auction, ...	17	0	–
7 Barrels of pork, at £25, ...	175	–	–
11 Half barrels pork, ...	137	16	–

Account of Men who **were Taken and Died during the Voyage** *Ship Boston,* 1778.

Benjamin Reed, Lieutenant.

Philip Mohyes, Quartermaster, died at Halifax jail.

Jacob Proctor, Jr., taken in ship Martha; carried to Halifax jail.

Richard Horton, Midshipman, taken; carried to Halifax jail.

Joshua Goss, Midshipman, taken; now in jail in Fortune prison.

Thomas Brimblecom, taken with Mr. Goss; never returned.

Andrew Richard, Seaman.

John Vickory, Ship's Mate.

Philip Follior, Midshipman, taken; put in Halifax jail; died of small-pox.

James Quilty.

William Goss, Ship's Pilot, taken, and entered on board man of war in Halifax.

John Goss, boy, taken.

William Goss, boy.

Jacob Tucker, boy, taken, and never returned.

George Snowden, paid by Mr. Johnott; owed £6.

Elias Bowden, Quartermaster, died at Rensford Island; came from Halifax jail.

Richard Webber, boy, taken in ship Martha; on board man of war.

Henry Peyton, runaway; left ship in France.

Nathaniel Peirce, Purser.

Nathaniel Peirce, Jr., boy.

John Peirce, 5th boy.

James Harris, boy.

John Roseau, boy, belonging to Lieutenant Reed; went on board in France.

Page 95.

To all Friends of the United States of America.

Whereas, We the subscribers, marines, belonging **to the ship** Boston, under the command of Samuel Tucker, Esq., have absented ourselves from said ship for some time past; we now declare to all the world, that it was not **on** any account we accused any officers on board, as **has been reported, injurious to their** characters, **particularly Mr.** Reed and **Mr. Bates.** And we declare that we have had while on board more indulgence than the Americans themselves, and that we are willing to continue on **board as** marines, and consent to be governed according to the regulations made and provided by the Honorable Continental Congress **for** the Naval Department, and promise to behave ourselves as faithful **subjects** to the American States; and to continue on board until **we arrive** at Boston, and there to be discharged.

In witness whereof we **sign our names,** on board **the Boston,** July 14, 1778.

N'ayant porté aucune plainte **au** Général Fayard.

Delhorn.
Brumont.
Canet.
Rateau.
Colomby.
Dazemar.

Page 120.

From a muster roll of officers, seamen, **and marines, belonging** to the Frigate Boston, Samuel Tucker, **commander. The wages** and **minutes on the same** are here **omitted.**

No.	Men's Names.	Stations.	Time of Entry.
1.	Samuel **Tucker,** .	Commander, . .	October 28, 1778.
2.	David Phips, . .	1st Lieutenant, . .	February 20, 1779.
3.	Hezekiah Welch, .	2d " . . .	October 28.
4.	Benjamin Bates, .	3d " . . .	October 28.
5.	William Pearson, .	Master, ...	December 3.

No.	Men's Names.	Stations.	Time of Entry.
6.	Seth Baxter,	Captain Marines,	February 17, 1779.
7.	Jeremiah Reed,	1st Lieut. "	December 3.
8.	William Cooper,	2d " "	March 28, 1779.
9.	Thomas Burns,	Surgeon,	December 10, 1778
10.	William Ash,	Purser,	October 28, 1779.
11.	Henry Newhall,	Carpenter,	December 26.
12.	Benjamin Balch,	Chaplain,	October 28, 1778.
13.	Joseph Lewis,	Boatswain,	October 28.
14.	Abel Wetherell,	Gunner,	October 28.
15.	Isaac Collins,	1st Mate,	December 3.
16.	Joshua Gifford,	2d "	December 27.
17.	Seth Pinkham,	3d "	December 8.
18.	Gideon Bailey,	Mate,	December 16, 1778
19.	Thomas Blinn,	Midshipman,	December 8.
20.	Thomas Le Moyne,	"	December 28.
21.	William Day,	"	January 16, 1779.
22.	Arthur Dunn,	"	January 1.
23.	Frederic Noodle,	"	December 16, 1778
24.	Hezh. Welch,	"	October 28.
25.	Edward Cades,	"	December 13.
26.	David Bell,	Captain's Clerk,	December 13.
27.	Isaac Bangs,	Doctor's Mate,	March 8, 1779.
28.	Edward Rice,	Ship Steward,	December 8, 1778.
29.	Isaac Collins,	Sailmaker,	March 3, 1779.
30.	Joseph Hooton,	Cooper,	December 4, 1778.

.Whole number was 287.

A MUSTER ROLL OF OFFICERS, SEAMEN, AND MARINES BELONGING TO THE FRIGATE BOSTON, SAMUEL TUCKER, COMMANDER.

No.	Men's Names.	Stations.	Time of Entry.	Wages per Month.		Prize Money Advanced.		Wages Advanced.		D. or R. D.	Sick, and where.
				£.	s.	£.	s.	£.	s.		
1.	Samuel Tucker,	Commander,	Oct. 28, 1778,	18							
2.	David Phips,	1st Lieutenant,	Feb'y 20, 1779,	9							
3.	Hezekiah Welch,	2d "	Oct. 28,	9							
4.	Benjamin Bates,	3d "	Oct. 28,	9		—		31	16		
5.	William Pearson,	Master,	Dec. 3,	9							
6.	Seth Baxter,	Capt. Marines,	Feb'y 17, 1779,	9							
7.	Jeremiah Reed,	1st Lft. "	Dec. 3,								
8.	William Cooper,	2d Lft. "	March 28, 1779,	—		—		—		In the Pole.	
9.	Thomas Burns,	Surgeon,	Dec. 10, 1778,	9							
10.	William Ash,	Purser,	Oct. 28, 1778,	9							
11.	Henry Newhall,	Carpenter,	Dec. 26,	90		—		—		Dis., April 6.	
12.	Benj. Balch,	Chaplain,	Oct. 28, 1778,	90							
13.	Joseph Lewis,	Boatswain,	Oct. 28,	90	12			24			
14.	Abel Wetherell,	Gunner,	Oct. 28,	90	6						
15.	Isaac Collins,	1st Mate,	Dec. 3,	90	12			—		In the Patsey.	
16.	Joshua Gifford,	"	Dec. 27,	90	12			—		In the Severn.	
17.	Seth Pinkham,	"	Dec. 8,	90	12			—		In the Pole.	
18.	Gideon Bailey,	"	Dec. 16, 1778,	90	12			—		In the Mermaid.	
19.	Thomas Blinn,	Midshipman,	Dec. 8,	72	12			—			
20.	Thos. Le Moyne,	"	Dec. 28,	72	12			3	12		
21.	William Day,	"	Jan'y 16, 1779,	72	12			—			
22.	Arthur Dunn,	"	Jan'y 7,	72	12			—		•	Hospital, Boston.
23.	Frederic Knodle,	"	Dec. 16, 1778,	72	12			—		In the Prize.	
24.	Hez. Welch,	"	Oct. 28,	72	12			—		In prize Severn.	

No.	Name	Rating	Date						Remarks
25.	Edward Eades,	Midshipman,	Dec. 13,	72	12				
26.	David Bell,	Capt's Clerk,	Dec. 13,	90	12		7 16		
27.	Isaac Bangs,	Doct's Mate,	March 8, 1779,	90	–				
28.	Edward Rice,	Ship's Steward	Dec. 8, 1778,	60	12				
29.	Thomas Collins,	Sailmaker,	March 3. 1779,	72	12				
30.	Joseph Hooton,	Cooper,	Dec. 4, 1778.	60	–				
31.	Ebenez. Ruddock,	Armorer,	Jan'y 16, 1779,	90	12				
32.	Jere. M'Carthy,	Boats'n Mate,	Dec. 30. 1778,	54	12				
33.	Francis Levidon,	" "	Feb'y 16, 1779,	54	12			–	Drowned 10th May.
34.	Richard Carswell,	Ship's Cook,	Jan'y 5, 1779,	90	12				
35.	Ths. Woodman,	Coxswain,	Dec. 13, 1778,	54	12				
36.	Benj. Newhall,	Sergt. Marines,	Dec. 31,	48	6				
37.	Daniel Mears,	" "	Jan'y 5,	48	12				
38.	Joseph Skinner,	Carp's Mate,	Dec. 26, 1778,	54	12				
39.	Thadeus Gale,	Gunn's Mate,	Dec. 25,	54	9				
40.	David Bell,	" Yeoman,	Jan'y 12,	48	12				
41.	John Smith,	Or. "	Jan'y 12,	48	6				
42.	John Chapman,	2d Master,	Feb'y 20,	48	–				
43.	Samuel Bell,	3d "	Jan'y 12,	48	12				
44.	James Brewer,	4th "	Jan'y 8,	48	12			–	Prize Wm.
45.	Wm. Baker,	Master Arms,	Dec. 30,	54	11	8			
46.	Hampshire Dean,	Seaman,	Dec. 7,	48	12				
47.	John Brailsford,	Joiner,	Dec. 7,	48	6				
48.	Noah Hobart,	Carp's Mate,	Dec. 11,	54	–			–	Discharged sick, Dec. 30.
49.	Jacob Whittemore,	Landsman,	Dec. 15,	40	6				
50.	John Lawrence,	"	Dec. 17,	40	–			–	Discharged, Dec. 30.
51.	Thomas Cooper,	Seaman,	Dec. 19,	48	12			–	Run, Dec. 19.
52.	Edward Thomas,	"	Dec. 18,	48	6			–	In the Pole.
53.	John Hogan,	Landsman,	Dec. 18,	40	2	8		–	Discharged, Jan'y 1.
54.	David Johnson,	2d Master,	Dec. 16,	48	12			–	Run, Feb'y 16.
55.	Willm. Hill,	Seaman,	Oct. 28,	48	6				

APPENDIX.

Muster Roll of Officers, **Seamen**, &c., Continued.

No.	Men's Names.	Stations.	Time of Entry.	Wages per Month.	1st 2d Money Advanced.	Wages Advanced.	D. or R. D.	Sick, and where.
				£. s.	£. s.	£. s.		
56.	Peter M'Kelley,	Landsman,	Oct. 28,	48	6			
57.	John Barns,	Seaman,	Dec. 14,	48	6	—	Run, Dec. 15.	
58.	Samuel Parsons,	"	Dec. 15,	48	6	—	Drowned 31st May.	
59.	Jack Breek,	"	Dec. 15,	48	6			
60.	Charles Devett,	"	Dec. 17,	48	12	—	Run, Dec. 18.	
61.	John Fyds,	Negro Seaman	Dec. 19,	48	—	—	Run. Dec. 26.	
62.	Francis Salmon,	Seaman,	Dec. 19,	48	12	—	In the Patsey.	
63.	Francis Hicks,	"	Dec. 17,	48	12			
64.	Jeremiah Shaw,	"	Dec. 21,	48	12			
65.	James Rogers,	"	Dec. 24,	48	12	—	{ On board the Alliance, Jan. 6, 1779.	
66.	Benj. Balch,	Landsman,	Dec. 1,	40	6			
67.	Warren Huntley,	Ship Corp'l,	Dec. 30,	48	12	—	On shore, sick, at Boston,	
68.	Thos. Bingman,	2d Master,	Dec. 30,	48	12			
69.	James Clark,	Landsman,	Jan'y 2,	40	—	—	Run, Feb'y 3.	
70.	Samuel Haley,	Boy,	Jan'y 4,	40	—	—	Run, Feb'y 3.	
71.	Wm. Kelley,	Boy,	Jan'y 4,	40	6			
72.	Charles Gould,	Negro,	Jan'y 5,	48	6			
73.	Chevier Cadozo,	Marine,	Jan'y 4,	40	—	—	Disch.,sick, Boston Feb. 16.	
74.	John Seasbrick,	Seaman,	Jan'y 1,	48	12	1 14		
75.	Joseph Bophal,	"	Jan'y 12,	48	12	—	Run, Feb'y 10.	
76.	John Smith,	"	Jan'y 12,	48	12			
77.	Lewis Cancadia,	"	Jan'y 13,	48	12	—	In the Pole.	
78.	John Barry,	"	Jan'y 14,	48	6	—	Run, Jan'y 21.	
79.	Samuel Hazelton,	Marine,	Jan'y 14,	40	—	—	Disch., March 1.	
80.	John Brown,	Corp. Marines,	Jan'y 16,	40	6	—	Run, Feb'y 9.	
81.	Thomas Warden,	Cooper's Mate,	Jan'y 16,	40	12	2 8	Run, March 2.	

No.	Name	Rating	Date					Remarks
82.	Thomas Yates,	Marine.	Jan'y 16,	40				
83.	Peter Meshall,	Seaman,	Jan'y 22,	48	12			
84.	Benj. Hutchings,	Boy,	Jan'y 24,	40	4	4		
85.	Joseph Colburd,	2d Gunner,	Jan'y 27,	48	6			
86.	John Crosley,	Landsman,	Feb'y 28,	40	6			
87.	Stephen Gatteau,	Seaman,	Feb'y 4,	48	–		–	Run, March 3.
88.	Jesse French,	"	Dec. 28,	48	12			
89.	Isaac Pain,	Boy,	Feb'y 14,	40	6			
90.	John Fossett,	Seaman,	Feb'y 15,	48	9		–	In the Severn.
91.	Doughty Randall,	"	Feb'y 15,	48	–		–	On board the Warren.
92.	Thomas Handy,	"	Feb'y 15,	48	6		–	Run, 6th of March.
93.	Russell Handy,	"	Feb'y 16,	48	6		–	Run, Feb. 17.
94.	Garrett Vanveen,	"	Feb'y 16,	48	12			
95.	Joseph Immassusan	"	Feb'y 16,	48	12			
96.	Wm. Hambelton,	"	Feb'y 19,	48	12			
97.	Peter Boreau,	Landsman,	Feb'y 20,	40	6			
98.	Robert Arderson,	Seaman,	Feb'y 16,	48	12			
99.	John Steward,	"	Feb'y 16,	48	–		–	On board the Tyrannicide.
100.	Alex. Smith,	"	Feb'y 16,	48	2	8	–	" "
101.	James Harrison,	Marine,	Feb'y 16,	40	–		–	" "
102.	Wm. Day,	"	Feb'y 22,	40	6			
103.	Lewis Chaplain,	Seaman,	Feb'y 22,	48	12		–	In the Mermaid.
104.	Wm. Harris,	Marine,	Jan'y 23,	40	6			
105.	Jacob Harvey,	"	Feb'y 23, 1778,	40	2	8	–	Run, 20th March.
106.	Joseph Espaniole,	Landsman,	Feb'y 23,	40	–		–	On board the Warren.
107.	James O'Neal,	Boy,	Feb'y 23,	40	–			
108.	James Ray,	Landsman,	Feb'y 23,	40	–		–	On board the Warren.
109.	Josiah Faxon,	Seaman,	Feb'y 23,	48	9			
110.	Garret Cannon,	2d Master,	Feb'y 15,	48	10	10	–	On board the Warren.
111.	John Moors,	Seaman,	Feb'y 23,	48	–			
112.	Thomas Cannaday,	Landsman,	Jan'y 16,	40	6		–	Died, July 24.

Muster Roll of Officers, Seamen, &c., Continued.

No.	Men's Names.	Stations.	Time of Entry.	Wages per Month. £. s.	Prize Money Advanced. £. s.	Wages Advanced. £. s.	D. or R. D.	Sick, and where.
113.	Charles Magnas,	Seaman,	Feb'y 22,	48	12			
114.	Simeon Poole,	Boy,	Feb'y 22,	40	–			
115.	Isaac Lufkin,	Seaman,	Feb'y 23,	48	12			
116.	John Robinson,	"	Feb'y 23,	48	12	–	Run, 10th March.	
117.	Michael Collins,	"	Feb'y 23,	48	12	–	On board the Warren.	
118.	James Kirkwood,	Landsman,	Feb'y 25,	40	10 4	–	" " "	
119.	Philip Orman,	Seaman,	Feb'y 24,	48	12	–	Run, March 18.	
120.	Christian Rodeker,	Marine,	Feb'y 25,	40	–			
121.	Thomas Gage,	Seaman,	Feb'y 25,	48	12			
122.	Philip Wild,	"	Feb'y 25,	48	12			
123.	Henry Pace,	Boy,	Feb'y 18,	40	–	–	Run, 29th March.	
124.	Isaac Young,	Landsman,	March 1,	40	6			
125.	James Dyer,	Seaman,	March 1,	48	3	–	Run, April 1.	
126.	Hermitage Gerrish,	"	March 2,	48	12			
127.	Moses Arnold,	Marine,	March 3,	40	6			
128.	Robert Hunt,	"	March 2,	40	6			
129.	Charles Dunn,	Seaman,	March 2,	48	6	–	On board of France,	
130.	George Davis,	"	March 3,	48	6	–	Mar. 6, " "	
131.	John Blight,	"	March 3,	48	6	–	Disch. " "	
132.	Thos. Larthrop,	"	March 3,	48	6			
133.	John M'Grow,	Boats'n Mate,	March 3,	48	12			
134.	John Handerfozin,	Marine,	Jan'y 3,	40	6			
135.	William Scott,	Landsman,	Oct. 28, 1778,	40	18	–	On b'd the Alliance, Feb. 6.	
136.	Francis Gipson,	Marine,	Oct. 28,	40	6	–	Drowned, April 12.	
137.	James Goodwright,	Seaman,	Dec. 24,	48	7 4			
138.	William Briant,	"	Jan'y 25,	48	12			

139.	John Wallice,	2d Corp.,	Feb'y 12,	40	6		
140.	Thomas Davis,	Seaman,	Feb'y 15,	48	12	—	Run, June 4.
141.	James Knight,	"	Feb'y 15,	48	12	—	Run, June 4.
142.	Peter Dezaux,	"	Feb'y 8,	48	12	—	In the prize Patsey.
143.	Samuel Edgecomb,	Landsman,	Feb'y 8,	40	6	—	On board the Warren.
144.	Stephen Stevenson,	"	Feb'y 16,	40	6		
145.	Richard M'Clure,	Seaman,	Feb'y 16,	48	12		
146.	Edward Antley,	"	Feb'y 18,	48	4 10		
147.	Benj. Lace,	Marine,	March 4,	40	6		
148.	Wm. Phillips,	Seaman,	March 4,	48	–		
149.	Sunday White,	"	March 5,	48	6		
150.	John Murray,	"	March 17,	48	12	—	In the Severn.
151.	Silas Johnson,	Marine,	Feb'y 17, 1778.	40	6	—	In the prize Boyd.
152.	James Cox,	Seaman,	Feb'y 17,	48	6	—	Run, 15th March.
153.	Edward Rawley,	"	March 11,	48	6		
154.	Jean Seaf,	"	March 11,	48	–	—	Run, 12th March.
155.	John Clarke,	"	March 11,	48	7 16	—	Run, 6th April.
156.	Benjamin Balten,	"	March 11,	48	6	—	Run, 12th March.
157.	John Cashaw,	Marine,	March 11,	40	–	—	Run, June 12.
158.	James Lemerick,	"	March 8,	40	–	—	On board the Warren.
159.	Francis Reiley,	"	March 8,	40	9		
160.	Alex. Bebe,	"	March 10,	40	6		
161.	James Whalan,	"	March 10,	40	6		
162.	Julian Andras,	Seaman,	March 11,	48	12	—	In the Severn.
163.	Nicholas Tyler,	"	March 14,	48	12	—	Run, 24th March.
164.	Oliver Jillson,	Marine,	Nov. 11,	40	6		
165.	Nathaniel Norton,	Seaman,	March 15,	48	12		
166.	Prince Gilbert,	"	March 16,	48	–		
167.	John Tileston,	Landsman,	March 16,	40	6		
168.	John Hambleton,	Seaman,	March 17,	48	12		
169.	Leml. Dillingham,	"	March 17,	48	4 10		

Muster Roll of Officers, Seamen, &c., Continued.

No.	Men's Names.	Stations.	Time of Entry.	Wages per Month.	Prize Money Advanced.	Wages Advanced.	D. or R. D.	Sick, and where.
				£. s.	£. s.	£. s.		
170.	Joshua Dillingham,	Seaman,	March 17,	48	4 10			
171.	Patrick Murphy,	"	March 18,	40	6			
172.	Jabest Post,	Marine,	March 19,	40	6			
173.	Benj. Kimball,	School Master,	March 19,	48	12			
174.	Wm. Kimball, Jr.,	Fifer,	March 19,	48	6			
175.	Josiah Higgins,	Marine,	March 19,	40	6			
176.	Oliver Drake,	"	March 19,	40	—			
177.	Elleanah Gage,	"	March 22,	40	6			
178.	Abner Kelley,	Seaman,	March 23,	48	6			
179.	Timothy Hicks,	Marine,	March 23,	40	6			
180.	James Cary,	Carp's Mate,	March 3,	54	12			
181.	John Blake,	Seaman,	March 23,	48	1 4			
182.	Daniel Learned,	Marine,	March 24,	40	6			
183.	Eliakim Swain,	Acting Mate,	March 27,	48	12	—	In the prize Boyd.	
184.	Robert Gorden,	Seaman,	March 25,	48	—	—	Run, April 4.	
185.	James Carey, Jr.,	Landsman,	March 25,	40	—	—	Run, April 2.	
186.	Gideon Nye,	Marine,	March 31,	40	6			
187.	Obadiah Nye,	"	March 31,	40	—	—	Discharged, April 2.	
188.	Thomas West,	"	March 31,	40	6	—	Sent on shore sick, to **Phila**.	
189.	Eliphalet Perrin,	"	March 31,	40	6	—	In the Mermaid.	
190.	Matthew Kellock,	Seaman,	Feb'y 17,	48	12			
191.	Thomas Gragg,	Landsman,	Feb'y 17,	40	3	—	In prize Boyd.	
192.	Francis Jarvis,	"	Feb'y 17,	48		.		
193.	Daniel Mears,	"	Feb'y 17,	40				
194.	Jean Fresneaux,	"	Feb'y 17,	48	—	—	Run, 1st March.	
195.	Hezekiah Breman,	Marine,	April 3,	40	—	—	Run, April 6.	

No.	Name		Rating		Date						Remarks
196.	John Langlarde,	.	Marine,	. .	March 2,	. .	40	—		—	In prize Boyd.
197.	John White, .	.	"	. . .	March 8,	. .	40				
198.	Pierre Feco, .	.	"	. . .	March 8,	. .	40	—			
199.	Peter Mifferer, .	.	Seaman,	. .	April 4, .	. .	48	—		—	Sent ashore sick.
200.	John Rush, . .	.	"	. . .	March 5,	. .	48	—		—	Run, 20th March.
201.	Philip Hennesy,	.	"	. . .	March 5,	. .	48	12		—	Died, 24th April.
202.	Peter Cartwright,	.	"	. . .	March 6,	. .	48	—		—	Run, 20th March.
203.	Abraham Temple,		Marine,	. .	March 6,	. .	40	—		—	Sick, at Philadelphia.
204.	Morris Wade, .	.	"	. . .	April 9, .	. .	40	6			
205.	James Gordon, .	.	"	. . .	April 9, .	. .	40	6			
206.	John Bacon, .	.	"	. . .	April 9, .	. .	40	—		—	Run, April 12.
207.	Patrick Welch, .	.	Seaman,	. .	April 9, .	. .	48	6			
208.	James Doughton,	.	Marine,	. .	April 9, .	. .	40	6			
209.	Wm. Mollineaux,	.	"	. . .	April 8, .	. .	40	6			
210.	William Wheeler,		"	. .	Feb'y 23,	. .	40	12		—	Died, 27th April.
211.	Joseph Chadduck,	.	Seaman,	. .	Feb'y 13,	. .	48	6		—	In the prize Severn.
212.	Samuel Thatcher,	.	Marine,	. .	Feb'y 18,	. .	40	6		—	Sent on shore sick, to Phila.
213.	John Martin,	. .	Seaman,	. .	March 12,	.	48				
214.	John Watkins, .	.	"	. .	Dec. 17, 1778,	.	48				
215.	William Game,	.	"	. .	Dec. 17, 1778,	.	48	6			
216.	Joseph Proctor,	.	Landsman,	.	Dec. 4, .	. .	40	6			
217.	Benj. Tucker, .	.	Volunteer,	.	March 1,	. .					
218.	Samuel Gatchell,	.	"	. .	March 1,	. .					
219.	James Otis, . .	.	"	. .	March 1,	. .	—	—		—	Died.
220.	Caleb Barber, .	.	"	. .	March 1,	. .	—	—		—	Died, June 10.
221.	Benj. Williams,	.	"	. .	March 31,	. .	—	—		—	Died, 15th May.
222.	Josiah Peirce, .	.	Drummer,	. .	Feb'y 18,	. .	40	5	14		
223.	Samuel Chapman,		Seaman,	. .	March 12,	. .	48	6			
224.	M. M'Namarrough,		Marine,	. .	March 12,	. .	40	12			
225.	Thomas Swindell,		"	. .	April 3,	. .	40	12			
226.	Peter Liscough,	.	"	. .	April 4,	. .	40	12		—	On shore sick, at Phila.

Muster Roll of Officers, Seamen, &c., Continued.

No.	Men's Names.	Stations.	Time of Entry.	Wages per Month.	Prize Money Advanced.	Wages Advanced.	D. or R. D.	Sick, and where.
				£. s.	£. s.	£. s.		
227.	John Bird,	Seaman,	April 4,	48				
228.	Alexander Munroe,	"	March 8,	48	12			
229.	John Bt's. Roubeau,	"	April 4,	48	12			
230.	Zephe'h Waistcoat,	"	March 12,	48	12			
231.	William Stevens,	"	Feb'y 17,	48	12			
232.	Richard Jones,	Landsman,	Oct. 28, 1778,	40	6			
233.	Jacob Lewis,	"	April 5, 1779,	40				
234.	Samuel Gragg,	Pilot,	Dec. 4, 1778,	90	12			
235.	Joseph Stacey,	Coop'rs Mate,	Feb'y 1, 1779,	48	60	—	Discharged, April 1.	
236.	Peter Osea,	Seaman,	Feb'y 17,	48	12			
237.	John Pearce,	Mast. Mate,	Dec. 12, 1778,	90	12	—	Sick at Marblehead, Mar.10	
238.	John Joseph,	Landsman,	Dec. 12,	40	12	—	Warren.	
239.	Thomas Shaw,	"	Dec. 12,	48	12	—	On the Providence, Feb. 12.	
240.	Peleg Pemberton,	"	April 20,	40	6	—	In the Severn.	
241.	Samuel Daily,	Marine,	April 24,	40	6			
242.	Antony Roteaux,	"	Feb'y 16,	40				
243.	Rainey Charloshea,	Volunteer,	Feb'y 16,	—	—	—	In the prize Boyd.	
244.	Peter Doreack,	Seaman,	May 10, 1779,	48	—	—	" " "	
245.	John Estavacho,	"	May 10,	48	—	—	" " "	
246.	Chaval Fahondo,	"	May 10,	48	—	—	" " "	
247.	Plavel Porter,	"	May 15,	48	—	—	In prize Flying-Fish.	
248.	James Broch,	"	May 15,	48	—	—	Drowned, June 5.	
249.	Puver Sentegray,	"	May 15,	48				
250.	Lewis Le Sevra,	"	May 15,	48				
251.	John Allen,	"	May 15,	48				
252.	John Hebo,	Marine,	Feb'y 6,	40	—	—	On b'd the Warren frigate.	

253.	Peter Lewis,	Seaman,	Feb'y 6,	48	—	—	On b'd the Warren frigate.
254.	Joseph Repeau,	"	Feb'y 6.	48	—	—	" " " "
255.	George Bird,	Marine,	Feb'y 6.	40	—	—	Run, April 1.
256.	Cato Franklin,	Landsman,	Feb'y 6,	40			
257.	Patrick Callahan,	Seaman,	Feb'y 10,	48			
258.	John Alary,	Landsman,	Feb'y 28,	40	—	—	In the Severn.
259.	Samuel Turpon,	"	May 10,	40	—	—	Sent to Philadelphia, sick.
260.	William Chub,	"	May 16,	40			
261.	James Webb,	"	June 4,	40	—	—	In the Pole.
262.	Ths. Shallingford,	Cr. Crew,	June 4,	48	—	—	In the Pole.
263.	Joseph Lay,	Landsman,	June 4,	40	—	—	In the Pole.
264.	Thomas Evens,	"	June 4,	40	—	—	In the Pole.
265.	Wm. Oram,	"	June 4,	40	—	—	In the Flying-Fish.
266.	John Conogea,	Seaman,	May 24,	48			
267.	Antony Brune,	"	May 24,	48	—	—	On board the Flying-Fish.
268.	Antony Rosell,	Landsman,	May 24,	40			
269.	Peter Lay,	Seaman,	June 11,	48			
270.	James Stevens,	"	June 11,	48			
271.	John Billings,	"	June 11,	48			
272.	James Gardner,	"	June 23,	48	—	—	In the Mermaid.
273.	John Cannon,	Landsman,	June 23,	40			
274.	Cato Hodge,	"	June 23,	40			
	Daniel Foster,	"	July 27,	48			
	John Lewis,	"	July 27,	48			
	Allen Wood,	"	July 27,	48			
	John Match,	"	July 30,	48			
	John Bapt'e Frank,	"	July 30,	48			
	Roven Gossham,	"	July 30,	48			
	James M'Million,	"	July 24,	48	—	—	Schooner Flying-Fish.
	Cody Austin,	Marine,	March 19,	40			

N. B. Under the last eight names is written " This list **from** Baltimore."

LIST OF MEN RECEIVED FROM ON BOARD THE BRIG RETALIATION, AND
BALTIMORE.

No.	Men's Names.	Stations.	Time of Entry.	Wages per Month. £. s.	Prize Money Advanced. £. s.	Wages Advanced. £. s.	D. or R. D.	Sick, and where.
272.	Thomas Cummins,	Mate,	June 26,	90				
273.	William Morris,	Midshipman,	June 26,	72	—	—	In the Enterprize.	
274.	George Reily,	Landsman,	June 26,	40	—	—	In the Mermaid.	
275.	Josiah Tolcot,	"	June 26,	40	—	—	Run, July 27.	
276.	Edward Griswal,	Seaman,	June 26,	48	—	—	In the Enterprize.	
277.	Michael Cremer,	Landsman,	June 26,	40			[Fish.	
278.	John Macumber,	Seaman,	June 26,	48	—	—	On board the prize Flying-	
279.	Walter Miller,	Landsman,	June 26,	40				
280.	Joseph Barteau,	Seaman,	June 26,	48	—	—	In the prize Mermaid.	
281.	John Lecause,	"	June 26,	48	—	—	" " "	
282.	John Newson,	Landsman,	June 26,	40	—	—	In the Enterprize.	
283.	(Erased).							
284.	Jonathan Brewer,	"	June 26,	40	—	—	In the Enterprize.	
285.	David Richards,	"	July 3,	40	—	—	In the Enterprize.	
286.	Benj. Pritteman,	"	July 3,	40	—	—	In the Enterprize.	
287.	William Barbor,	Midshipman,	July 3,	72	—	—	From on b'd Gen. Green.	
1.	Baptiste Boniface,	Seaman,	July 13,					
2.	Anthony Oselleau,	"	July 15,					
3.	Joseph Gyarbo,	"	July 15,					
4.	Michael Franco,	"	July 15,					
5.	Joseph Morgan,	"	July 15,					
6.	Gregory Ogago,	"						
7.	Manual M'Corry,	"	July 15,					

8.	Antony Trumbull,	Seaman,	July 15,
9.	Sebastian Surrett,	"	July 15,
10.	Francis Taveriss,	"	
11.	George Price,	A Mate,	July 30,
12.	Thomas Moore,	"	August 13,
13.	Jonas Fossbert,	Seaman,	July 5,
14.	Benj. Hall,		August 1,
15.	Hector Buskcarriek,	"	July 30,
16.	James Bush,	"	July 30,
17.	John Renkin,	"	July 30,
18.	Ezekiel Zelcutt,	"	July 30,
19.	James Cragg,	"	August 19,
20.	Robert Knight,	"	July 30,
21.	James Carr,	"	July 30,
22.	Philip Downey,	"	July 30,
23.	James M'Mellion,	"	
24.	Wm. Whitmarsh,	Volunteer,	

Page 106.

BOSTON, 21st Sept., 1779.

GENTLEMEN: This will be forwarded you by Mr. Wm. Ashe, my purser, who will acquaint you of my safe arrival. He has mine and Colonel Wm. Lee's orders to receive all the moneys that may or are due to my ship's company from the different prizes sent in your port. I doubt **not, gentlemen, of your exertion in** regard of a **speedy settlement, as** my ship's **company** is very impatient for the settlement. Gentlemen, I expect to receive one half part of all prizes captured in companies by the Deane and Con**federacy.** However, Mr. Ashe will settle everything relative thereto, as **well** as if I were personally present, agreeable to the orders given **him,** by **the** agents and myself.

I have taken thirteen prizes since I left Boston, but the richest **is** retaken, cargo dry goods, and provisions; likewise the privateer brig Enterprize. I expect to sail in **six weeks, and shall value all my prizes on** you, that may be sent **to the South. Colonel William Lee's** orders, I hope, will be duly **hon**ored, as he **is the** ship's company's sole agent, and this letter will indemnify you in compliance therewith.

I remain, gentlemen, your most obedient servant,

SAMUEL TUCKER.

HON. NAVY BOARD, PHILADELPHIA.

Page 115.

A law to establish and equalize the grade of officers **in** the navy was passed **by a** late Congress, and was approved by the President, July **16, 1862.** It creates nine grades of officers, namely, 1st. Rear Admiral**s. 2d.** Commodores. **3d.** Captains. 4th. Commanders. 5th. Lieutenant-**Commanders.** 6th. Lieutenants. 7th. Masters. 8th. Ensigns. .**9th. Midshipmen.** The first are to have equal **rank** with Major-General**s in the army, the second, with** Brigadier-Generals, the third, **with Colonels, the fourth, with** Lieutenant-**Colonels,** the fifth, **with Majors, the sixth, with**

Captains, the seventh, with First Lieutenants, and the eighth, with Second Lieutenants. **Under this law, the President commissioned, Wednesday, July 31, 1862, nine Captains of the navy to be Rear-Admirals, on the retired list, and four on the** active **list.**

The retired list contains, Charles Stewart, George C. Read, William **W.** Shubrick, Joseph Smith, George W. Storer, Francis D. Gregory, Silas H. Stringham, Hiram Paulding, Eli A. F. Lavallette. Several of whom have since deceased. Those on the active list, were David C. Farragut, L. M. Goldsborough, Samuel F. Du Pont, and Andrew D. Foote; the last died, June 26, 1863.

In the law of 1776, **among other** officers, **Congress fixed on** the grade **of Commodore as a Brigadier-General; but a commission as** Commodore was **not** issued.

See the N. E. Historical and Genealogical Register (Vol. XVII. p. 147) for year 1863, when it was edited by John W. Deane, Esq.

Since the above, a law was passed December 21, 1864, in which it **is** enacted, "That the President of the United States be, and he is hereby authorized and empowered, by and with the advice and consent **of the** Senate, to appoint one Vice-Admiral, who shall be **selected from the list of** active Rear-Admirals, and who shall be the **ranking officer in** the navy of the United States, **and whose** relative **rank** with officers of the army shall be that **of Lieutenant-**General **in the army."**

And July 25, 1865, another act was **passed by Congress, providing** that the **number allowed in each grade of line officers, on** the **active** list of the **navy, shall be one Admiral,** one Vice-Admiral, ten Rear-Admirals, twenty-five **Commodores,** fifty Captains, ninety Commanders, one hundred and **eighty** Lieutenant-Commanders, **one** hundred and sixty Masters, **one** hundred and sixty Ensigns, **and in** other grades the number **now** allowed by law. **Provided,** **&c. See Laws of the United States,** twenty-ninth **Congress.**

Page 146.

THE BOSTON. — There were three armed **ships of this name.**

1. The frigate commanded by Commodore Tucker, **of twenty-**four guns, and surrendered to the British, at the capitulation **of** Charleston, South Carolina.

2. The United States Frigate **Boston,** seven hundred tons, and thirty-two guns, built **in 1799, by a subscription of the patriotic merchants of** Boston, and **loaned to the government.** John Adams was then President, and war with France was apprehended in consequence of outrages on our commerce, commit**ted by** her cruisers, so well known as the *French Spoliations, previous to* 1800, and for which, though long since liquidated and settled by **treaty,** Congress has never seen fit to make any remuneration **to our** suffering claimants.

Soon after the Boston was built and ready for sea, President **Adams** appointed Captain George Little her commander. **July 24, 1799, she sailed on** her **cruise, and the** *Centinel* **pronounced her " one of the** handsomest model ships in the world." On the 12th of October, near Hispaniola, Captain Little encountered the French corvette *Le Berceau,* and after a sharp action, in which many persons were killed or wounded, captured her. But a treaty with France having been previously **signed,** she was given up to the French consul in Boston. The subscription am**ounted to $136,600,** and **the** cost of our frigate to $137,969. **She was burnt at** Wash-**ington, in** 1814, to prevent her falling into **the hands of the British,** with whom we were then at war.

3. The armed **ship** Boston, of seven hundred tons, and eigh**teen guns,** built in **1828.** She was lost under **the** command **of** George **F. Pearson, in a squall,** at night, on **the shore of** Eleuthera, W. I., November 15, 1846.

The particulars of the above may be found in the Army and Navy Journal, of January 19, 1867.

Page 157.

Dr.   SAMUEL **TUCKER**, ESQ., *to*

1780.		£.	s.	d.
Nov. 14.	To $\frac{1}{16}$ of the Thorn's outfits, 3d cruise, .	4,964	3	7¼
1781. Jan'y.	To $\frac{1}{16}$ of half the balance of charges on the Thorn's prizes, ...	1,179	2	5½
	To sund. per In. per the Aurora, . . .	92,922	3	9
	To " " per the Success, . . .	23,026	5	0
	To " " per the Sincerity, . . .	62,540	6	3
	To Hhd. corn per the Biddy, 3 £30 = 90 ⎫ To ½ " molasses " 47 gal. 12 = 564 ⎬ 654			
April 10.	To $\frac{1}{32}$ of the **Thorn's** outfits, 4th cruise, .	5,531	18	10
		£197,817	19	11¼
	Balance due to Samuel Tucker, Esq., . . .	414	16	8¼
		£198,232	16	7½

To WILLIAM R. LEE & Co., *Agents to the Thorn.*   **Cr.**

1780.		£.	s.	d.
June.	By balance per adjustment, ...	2,487	16	7¼
Nov. 14.	By sundry supplies per bill for the Thorn, 3d cruise, ...	3,870	–	–
	By $\frac{1}{16}$ the balance of damaged beef, &c., sold, and powder carried to 4th cruise,	220	10	7¼
1781, Jan.	By $\frac{1}{16}$ of the owners' part of sundry prizes, &c., sold at auction as per acct. Col. Ingersol's accts. of sales, ...	7,893	1	9
	By $\frac{1}{16}$ of half the amount of the Aurora's cargo, ...	98,890	1	5¼
	By $\frac{1}{16}$ of half the am't of the Success' carg.,	22,933	19	3½
	By $\frac{1}{16}$ of half am't of the Sincerity's carg.,	57,328	16	10¼
	By $\frac{1}{16}$ of half of the amount of the Biddy's cargo, ...	1,401	3	11
April.	By his acct. supplies, &c., for the Thorn,	3,207	6	–
		£198,232	16	7½

MARBLEHEAD, April 10, 1781.

Errors excepted,
WM. R. LEE, & Co.

Page 157.

Invoice of sundry goods delivered Samuel **Tucker, Esq.**, out of the sloop Maria, snow Fly, and ship Elizabeth, **captured by the** Thorn, 5th cruise, viz. : —

1781.		£.	s.	d.
June. 2 Cases gin per the Maria, at 48s., ...		4	16	–
1 " brandy per "		2	8	–
1 Cask white wine **24, 2 out Nt. 22 gall. at 2s.,** .		**2**	**4**	–
1 **Hhd. rum 110, 5** out Nt. **105 gall. at 5s.,** . .		26	05	–
3 Hhds. molasses, viz. :				

<pre>
            119 5
            121 6
            109 6
            ____
            349 17, 17 out is Nt. 332 gall. 2s. 4d.,   38 14 8
</pre>

4 Hhds of sugar, viz :

<pre>
            15 00
            15 3 7
            16   14
            15 0 4
            ____
            62 0 7
</pre>

	£.	s.	d.
Tare 12 pl. 6 2 17 cwt. 55 1 18 Nt. sugar 44s.	121	18	1
½ Cask Madeira wine, wth Mr. Gerry, 27½ Nt. 3s.	4	2	6
18 Bohea tea, 8s., ...	7	4	0
½ Cask rice, with Mr. **Gerry, 2 1 3** 24s.,. . .	2	14	7½
3 Cases gin per Elizabeth, 48s.,.	7	4	–
1 " brandy, ...	2	8	–
½ doz. hose 24s., . . . 0 12 0			
1 pr. " 3 0			

<pre>
                         ____
            slz.,   15
    Advance 3 for 1 is . . 25   3 0 –
</pre>

	£.	s.	d.
8 **Bags salt, yielding** 16 bushels, **5s.,**	7	04	–
20 **bushels salt to receive of Mr.** Lewis, 9s., . .	9	–	–

<pre>
                                           ____
            Specie, . . . £239 2 10
                                           ____
</pre>

Exchange 75 **is,** £17,935 15 7½

Carried **to his** Debit in acct. **current,**

Errors excepted,

WM. R. LEE & CO.

Page 166.

Among Commodore Tucker's papers is a copy of the following letter to him from some one, to whom, it would appear, he had done some generous deed : —

KIND SIR: After the unreserved friendship you have been pleased to honor me with, my mind elicits this only method of acknowledging therefor; and as I am convinced it flows from a free indulgence, notwithstanding my repeated demerits, permit me to assure the most interested friend, and I may justly say patron, that my ideas are too full to admit of expressing the sincere gratitude which overflows my soul; and as the kind indulgent proffer was free, and solely for my own happiness, my heart is too sensible of its influence, to decline an acceptance of it.

I am, therefore, your grateful servant, with filial respect, and through every reverse of capricious fortune, anxiously solicitous to corroborate so honorable an opinion, as nothing less than your real esteem could have extorted.

WILLIAM JENNISON.

MONDAY MORNING, January 17, 1780.

Mr. Jennison, probably, was the same person described in Bond's Genealogy and History of Watertown, page 802. "William, b. Aug. 4, 1757, grad. Harv. Coll. 1774, immediately afterwards commenced the study of law with Caleb Strong, and pursued it until the breaking out of the Revolutionary war. He, with his brother Samuel, then enlisted in the public service. . . . He served during the whole war, was at one time paymaster of the army, at another, a lieutenant of marines, and was United States pensioner for his services." He died in Boston, December 24, 1843, and his widow, Mary, died in Boston, April 11, 1853, aged 90.

Page 227.

Bristol, February **24, 1816.**

The Honorable Benjamin Brown, Esq.

Dear Sir: I take this opportunity of asking the favor of your attending the committee, who may have under consideration the application I now forward on to Congress, well supported by various gentlemen **of high respectability; which is for four** years' pay **and subsistence.** That I conceive **is** my **due for** Revolutionary services, that will be fully mentioned in the petition. By favoring me with your attendance on the committee, in my mind, **will** greatly contribute to my getting remuneration by only your saying what you have known of me in the Revolution and after-**wards.** I should have written my friend Parris, but he can **say nothing of** me, in those times. Be pleased to give him my most **respectful** compliments, if you please. You can mention our cruise **in 1799, on the coast** of Virginia and **Delaware,** when we **prevented the two British** frigates from **destroying the army's** clothing, **coming from** St. Eustatia, and bound to Philadelphia, under the **command of** Captain Barry, and the *taking of the Pool frigate, which was sent out of New York for the express purpose of taking me;* and note the French **ship** Severn, which we took; that cruise has never yet been settled for, **nor our crew** received the least compensation for that prize.

I am, with respect and esteem, yours, **&c.,**

Samuel **Tucker.**

Hon. B. Brown.

Page 240.

Washington, January 29, 1821.

My dear Commodore: **You do not** forget your friends, and your friends will not **forget you.**

Soon after you left here **I applied to the** War Department to know how **those** fared who were **in service at the** peace of '83, and **how many officers had** received **pensions.** This information I laid before the committee at another hearing I obtained. Soon after this, the committee of the Senate brought in a bill, which is to be taken up in a day or two, and we are waiting to see its fate, because we think a bill of this kind is more likely to pass the Senate than the House. This contemplates giving you half pay as a captain from 1818. Messrs. Holmes and Chandler are doing all they can for you, besides many others, as well as,

Your friend and humble servant,

MARK LANGDON HILL.

P. S. Commodore Tingey, Porter, and others called to see you after you left. They thought you were to stay some time in the city.

Page 246.

WASHINGTON, 19th June, 1820.

DEAR SIR: The prospect of doing anything for you this session is not great. The House is very mean and *parsimonious* at this time. Mr. Hill, however, and myself, will attend to your affair and do what we can.

Maine goes hard, as the Senate have loaded the Missouri on her. What will be the result I know not.

Yours, very affectionately,

J. HOLMES.

[N. B. Mr. Holmes was in the Senate.]

WASHINGTON, 22d July, 1821.

DEAR SIR: There has been a hard struggle in the House on your bill. They have amended it by reducing the pension to twenty dollars per month, and *passed it by a majority of* TWO only. As the pay commences in 1818, we shall concur in the amendment. I congratulate you even for this trifle.

Most affectionately,

J. HOLMES.

WASHINGTON, 23d February, 1821.

DEAR SIR: This day your relief came back from the House amended, reducing your pension to twenty dollars per month. It was carried in the House, even at this sum, with so much difficulty, and so small a majority, that we did not dare to send it back to them again. It, however, gives four or five hundred dollars to begin with. This is all we could do. In haste.

Your humble servant,

JOHN CHANDLER.

COMMODORE TUCKER.

Page 197.

NEW YORK, 9th June, 1787.

SIR: After your departure I received a letter written in this city, and exceedingly regretted that I had not the pleasure of forming an acquaintance with you.

The relation of whom you wrote has been unfortunate, but I am persuaded not guilty. Her conduct for three years has been more than irreproachable, it has been highly commendable. Mrs. Knox is strongly attached to her, and I shall feel a satisfaction in promoting her welfare.

If you should again come to this city, be pleased to inform me of it.

I am, sir, with esteem and respect,

Your most obedient, humble servant,

H. KNOX.

CAPTAIN SAMUEL TUCKER.

NEW YORK, 6th June, 1787.

SIR: It has been uppermost in my breast since I came to this city to have paid you my personal respects for the esteem I have for your private character, confirmed by your public patriotism and reputation; both which strongly combine, and point out the propriety of this attention; but when you reflect on a domestic misfortune, I am sure that your consideration will make every allowance for the omission.

With sincerity and gratitude to you and your good lady for your patronage and humanity to a relative of mine,

I am, sir, with sentiments of regard, your respectful,

Most obedient, and very humble servant,

SAMUEL TUCKER.

GENERAL H. KNOX.

Page 107.

MEMORANDUM AMONG COMMODORE TUCKER'S PAPERS.

Small piece of log book, where the crew of the Boston are enumerated, July 19, 1779, viz., number of men and boys 182.

Account of gunner's stores, &c., of the Boston, to wit. : —

1779, April 30,	1 **nine** pounder	to bring to	a Sloop.
" "	1 **six** "	"	a Schooner.
" May 1.	1 **six** "	"	a Brigantine.
" " 2.	1 **nine** and 1 **six** "	"	a Brig.
" " 6.	" "	"	a Brig.
" " 15.	" "	"	a Schooner.
" " 19.	2 nines, 2 fours,	"	**Ship and Schooner.**
" " 25.	1 " "	"	a Schooner.
" July 30.	" " "	"	Flying-Fish.
" August.	1 **nine** pounder	"	Ship **Thorn.**

There is also a letter of June 24, 1832, from Ebenezer Mayo to Captain Tucker, wherein he says, " William Stevens was with Tucker when he captured the ship Thorn."

There is also a broken account of supplies, stores, &c., on board of the Boston, Joseph Lewis, boatswain, and a list of men and boys, April 11, 1779, 168.

Page 222.

BATH, March 30, 1819.

DEAR SIR: Mr. Thompson, a political friend, will hand you this, and will leave with you some papers; have the goodness to distribute them, as will be most interesting to the election of our friend, Judge Hill, in particular. His election is considered of importance to the navigating interest. It is also desirable that a man who has been so uniformly opposed to the mercantile interest, as has been Mr. Orr, should have permission to remain at home. Contrary to my expectation, and every wish of mine, some votes were given me at the last election, in November. This I sincerely hope will not be repeated, but that Judge Hill, as he certainly ought, will have every vote in the district. The prospect is very favorable of the election of Crowninshield and Austin. Expecting a very good account of the present year from your town,

I remain, sir, you humble servant,

W. KING.

COMMODORE SAMUEL TUCKER, Bristol.

Page 247.

BRISTOL, March 12, 1816.

These may certify to whom it may concern, that Joseph Wilkinson, a native of Great Britain, and the bearer of this, was with me under my command on board the Boston frigate, in the year of 1778; and while in France, on the latter end of April, by accident fell from the lower deck into the hold and broke his thigh. This accident happened in righting the ship after being hove down. I sent him to a hospital in Bordeaux, wherein he continued with his wound for nearly two months, when he came on board the ship, and went to his duty as before, although he appeared to be much injured by the wound. He acted as ship's corporal the nine months he was under my command, and always behaved himself, in every respect, a faithful citizen and good soldier to the United States of America.

SAMUEL TUCKER.

This attested before a Justice of the Peace, March 13, 1816.

Page 247.

St. John, May 1, 1823.

Captain Samuel Tucker.

Sir: I, the writer of this, am a young man, a native of Greenock, in Scotland, who, having business that called me to St. John, N. B., and which may detain me here for two years to come, and hearing of your being of the same name and from the same part of the States, and a person perfectly able to give me correct information, I have been induced to trouble you with a few inquiries regarding my grandfather's relations. I am the grandson of Captain Joseph Tucker, who died about forty years ago at Greenock, but who was born in or near Boston, from about the years 1740 to 1750. He went home to Scotland, and fell heir to his uncle, Captain Richard Tucker, who died there possessed of considerable property. My grandfather left behind him in America two sisters, Sarah and Dorcas, and several brothers. He himself died when about forty years of age, leaving four daughters, Jane, and Sarah (who is my mother), and Dorcas, and Catharine, who were all alive at the time of their father's death, so very young that the correspondence that had existed betwixt their father and his relations ceased then; nor have ever since heard anything of them. Now, to trace out and recommence that correspondence betwixt the families is the *sole* motive for asking you for further information respecting them. If, therefore, you know anything of them, or can set me in the way to find them out before I return to Scotland, you will confer a lasting obligation on,

Your very obedient servant,

Joseph H. Ritchie.

P. S. Whether or not you can give me any information, please own receipt of this at your earliest convenience, to prevent my troubling you again. Please address,

Mr. J. H. Ritchie,
Care, Robert Rankin, Esq.,
St. John, N. B.

Captain Samuel Tucker.

Page 247.

A List of Nathaniel Appleton Notes loaned to D. C.

$.	No.	£. s.
1000	202	7 10
1000	201	7 10
1000	200	7 10
1000	204	7 10
1000	203	7 10
1000	209	7 10
1000	208	7 10
1000	207	7 10
1000	206	7 10
1000	205	7 10
200	11,421	1 10
1000	198	7 10
1000	199	7 10
1000	197	7 10
1000	196	7 10
1000	213	7 10
1000	212	7 10
1000	211	7 10
1000	210	7 10

£136 10

The above notes belong to Captain Samuel Tucker, Esq., lent to David Cook.

The interest paid up to '82.

$54½
$68½

$123

November 23, 1785, BOSTON.

Page 242.

A song was written by a citizen of Bristol, on the capture of the Crown by Tucker. The following is a copy, and is here introduced, more as a specimen of the spirit of the times, than of the beauty of the poetry, although it may compare, not very distantly, to some of the old English ballads.

I.

On the 26th of April, it plainly doth appear,
The brave boys of Bristol fitted out a privateer,
In command of *Captain Tucker* — a sloop both neat and trim,
And we set out to cruise the seas, all for to take the *Bream*.

CHORUS.

So cheer up, my lively lads, and never be it said,
That the brave boys of Bristol were ever yet afraid.

II.

We cruised the shores for several days, and nothing did appear;
At length our brave commander resolved to homeward steer;
It was on Friday morning, and clear was the sky,
And as we were returning a sail we did espy!

CHORUS.

So cheer up, my lively lads, &c.

III.

Then rose our bold commander, and to his men did say,
" My boys, be all stout-hearted, and do not fail to-day;
Our enemy 's before us, and after her we'll run,
For I'm resolved to take her before the setting sun ! "

CHORUS.

So cheer up, my lively lads, &c.

24

IV.

Then we bore away for her, and **up to her did come;**
We hauled down our foresail and gave her **a gun;**
'Twas broadside and broadside we showed her Yankee **play,**
'Till our enemy got frightened and tried to run away.

Chorus.

So cheer up, my brave lads, &c.

V.

Then they quit their quarters, and down below they run;
We shot away their halliards, and down their colors come.
Their captain he stepped forward, and waving his hand,
He cried, "I must surrender: this I can no longer stand!"

Chorus.

So cheer up, my lively lads, &c.

VI.

Then we hoisted out our boats, on board of her did go;
We **made them all** prisoners, and ordered them below;
We hoisted *Yankee* **colors**, and hauled the *British* down,
And when we did examine **her she** proved to be the " *Crown.*"

Chorus.

So cheer up, my lively lads, &c.

VII.

" Now," says **our** brave commander, "we'll bring our prize
    ashore,
For we're the bo**ys that fear no noise,** though cannons loudly roar;
And quickly we wi**ll clear the coast** of all these British boys,
For we will fight 'em **till we die, and** never mind their noise."

Chorus.

So cheer up, my lively lads, &c.

VIII.

Now we have fought this privateer 'till she is overcome;
And *God* bless Captain Tucker this day for what he's done,
Likewise his officers, and all his jovial crew, —
God grant that they may prosper in everthing they do.

CHORUS.

So cheer up, my lively lads, &c.

Page 249.

An anecdote is related of Commodore Tucker in the "Sketches of the History of the Town of Camden," Maine, by John L. Locke, 1859, page 45. It was recently pointed out to the author, and in substance is as follows : —

Captain Tucker, in one of his earliest cruises, was sailing near Blue Hill, in Maine, and came across an English East-Indiaman, with a rich cargo, bound from Halifax to Bagaduce, which he captured. The news reached Captain Mowatt, of such infamous notoriety for the burning of Falmouth, and he immediately went in pursuit of Tucker, who, seeing his approach, took on board, out of one of the fishing boats, a well known pilot, Robert Thorndike, of Camden. By his aid he was piloted along the shore, closely pursued by Mowatt, to New Meadows, now Harpswell; there, among the ledges and breakers he lay secure, until one dark, foggy night he weighed anchor, and by this skilful pilot was guided through the secret channels and numerous islands of Casco Bay, into the open sea, where, beyond the reach of the enemy, he escaped.

Pages 48 and 51.

The frigate Hancock, thirty-two guns, said to have been built in Boston, was captured about the 1st of June, 1777, by Sir George Collier, in the Rainbow, forty-four — according to the statements in Cooper's Naval History, and in the United States Navy, from 1775 to 1833, and other authorities. There seems to be a discrepancy between this account and the extract from the Boston Gazette, of May 4, 1778, in which it is said, "Tuesday last, ship Hancock, thirty-six guns, launched at Salisbury."

As there does not appear to have been another frigate of this name ordered to be built by Congress and equipped for sea, perhaps, if not an error of the press, the vessel launched in Salisbury might have been at first called the Hancock. and her name afterwards changed.

A few chronological dates, appertaining principally to the building of vessels for the merchant service, and for defence of the country at an early period of our history, may be interesting to the curious reader. They have been gleaned from various authentic sources.

1608. The first vessel built in New England, if not in the Colonial States, was the Virginia, said to be thirty tons, at Sagadahock, by the Popham colonists. They were conveyed home to England the same year in this vessel.

1614. Mr. Cooper states in his Naval History, that the first decked vessel built in the Colonial States was constructed by Adrian Block, on the banks of the Hudson, in 1614. She was called a *yacht*, thirty-eight feet keel, forty-four and a half feet on deck, and eleven feet beam. In this, Captain Block navigated Long Island Sound, passing through Hell Gate to Cape Cod, and discovered Block Island, named from him.

1632. A bark of thirty tons was built at Mystic (now Medford), called *The Blessing of the Bay:* afterwards converted into a cruiser against pirates on the coast. The ways on which she was constructed, it is said, are, or were recently, in existence.

1633. A small ship was built in Boston, said to be the first ship built in New England.

1641. Hugh Peters, of Salem, built a vessel of three hundred tons burden.

1642. The diving-bell was first used in this country at the

raising of the ship **May Rose, of** Bristol, sunk 1640, in Boston harbor.

1645. There was **the first regular naval engagement in America. The same year a ship was built in** Cambridge, Mass., **with an armament of fourteen guns** and thirty men.

1646. The colony of New Haven built a ship of one hundred and fifty tons in Rhode Island, and soon after a cruiser of ten guns; and the same year a ship of three hundred tons was built **in** Boston.

1671. Sir William Phips — knighted by King James II. on account of his raisin**g the immensely rich Spanish wreck near the** Bahamas, **from which he brought** home **to** England **£300,000 — built** a ship in Woolwich, Maine.

1678. De la **Salle** launched the first vessel ever built on the lakes, — a first **decked** boat of ten tons on Lake Ontario; and the **next** year a vessel of sixty tons was launched on Lake Erie.

1680. Connecticut had twenty-four vessels, making ten hundred and fifty tons of shipping.

1690. The whale fishery was established at Nantucket. This **year the Falkland, a** fourth rate, — seven hundred and seventy-six **tons, forty-eight guns,** — the first ship of the line ever **built in America, was launched** on the Piscataqua.

1696. **New York** had forty square-rigged **vessels, sixty-two** sloops, and sixty **boats** in employ.

1701. The Newfoundland **fishermen** belonging **to the colonies numbered one hundred and twenty-one.**

1713. The **first schooner ever seen** was built **at Glouscester,** Cape Ann. Mr. Babson, in his History of Gloucester, **informs us,** on the authority of Cotton Tufts, Esq., that Andrew **Robinson, of** that place, constructed a vessel which he masted and **rigged in the same manner as schooners are** at this day. On her **going off the stocks, and passing into the** water, a bystander **cried out, "** *O, how she scoons !* **"** Robinson instantly replied, **"A schooner let her be ! " And this kind of craft has ever since been in use.**

1714-1717. **Massachusetts numbered four hundred and ninety-two vessels in her navigation.**

1723. Mr. Drake, in his History of Boston, remarks, "There were built in New England above seven hundred sail of ships and other vessels, most of which were fitted out in Boston."

In 1800 there were a million tons of shipping owned in the United States, though before 1836 it is said few if any merchantmen much exceeded six hundred tons. Such was the beginning and progress of our commercial navigation, which is now so vast that it spreads a wing on every sea on the globe.

Page 258.

Vessels of war in the Revolution, compared to those since built, were small, and their guns of light calibre. The frigate Boston, built in 1776, was said to be less than five hundred tons, and the largest frigates constructed in 1778 did not exceed a thousand. They "rarely carried in their main-deck batteries, guns of a metal heavier than eighteen pounders." There was usually no spar-deck. Carronades had not been invented; light sixes, nines, and twelves were mostly used.

Larger ships were ordered to be built by Congress in 1798. The Constitution — in which Commodore Preble, with his squadron of six ships and a few gunboats gained, in 1804, such imperishable renown in his daring attack on Tripoli, and which forever put an end to Algerine tribute — was a forty-four gun ship, of fifteen hundred and seventy-six tons, and pierced for thirty twenty-four pounders on her gun-deck. The United States frigate was forty-four guns, and fifteen hundred and seventy-six tons, and the Constellation was thirty-six guns, and twelve hundred and sixty-five tons. It was in the battle and capture of the Insurgente, 1799, by the Constellation, that Commodore Truxton so much distinguished himself. His frigate first used carronades.

In the last war with England, though the number of war ships was somewhat increased, they were not built of greater burden, nor usually armed with heavier weight of metal. But they were remarkably successful, and gained many brilliant victories.

Since that distant period **an entire** change has taken place in naval armaments. **Sailing frigates have become mere store and hospital ships. Steam frigates have superseded them throughout the civilized world — some of which are** of immense tonnage, **such as the Niagara, of** twelve guns and forty-five hundred and eighty **tons.** Steam frigates have been multiplied; but the new invention of IRON WAR-CLADS, which did such terrible execution in the late Rebellion, has changed the aspect of naval warfare in all time to come.

Shells and cannon balls, or shot, were cast of great size, compared **to those formerly in use.** Shot were fired **weighing** four hundred and eighty pounds; **and in the experiments of the** engineers, one **was discharged from a twenty** inch gun which weighed ten hundred and nine pounds. **Shells of** seven hundred pounds were **thrown into** Charleston, **from a** fifteen inch gun, which required **forty pounds** of powder **for each** discharge.

It should be **remarked that** the largest **sailing** war ship in the world was the Pennsylvania, built in **1837,** of thirty-two hundred **and** forty-one tons, and one hundred **and** twenty guns; and also **that the first steam merchantmen, and** first steam frigates, as well **as the formidable iron-clads, originated in** this **country.**

INDEX.

A.

Adams, John, 15, 16; on a prize, 45, 71, 74, 80, 81, 91, 101, 102, 110, 172, 177, 183, 225, 231, 242, 248, 264.
Adams, Samuel, 63, 167.
Adams, Thos. B., 214.
Adventure, snow, 319.
Aldsworth, et al., 188.
Algerine corsairs, and escape, 24.
Alna, 205.
American archives, 49, 61.
Andros, Governor, 189.
Anecdotes, 27, 28, 37, 81, 245, 247, 249; the widow, 251, 271.
Arabella, brig, 60, 234.
Arbuthnot, Vice-Admiral, 128.
Armed ships in 1778, 48.
Army in Cambridge, 35.
Ashley River, 126.
Augusta, 207, 212.
Avary, Captain of Mermaid, 116.

B.

Bagaduce, 191.
Bailey, Jeremiah, 215.

Bainbridge, William, 90.
Barnes, John, 241.
Barron, William T., 84, 85, 276, 280.
Barry, John, 183.
Barton, Elijah, et al., 206.
Bay of Biscay, 90.
Belcher, Mary, 20.
Belle Isle, 291.
Betterment Act, 203.
Beverly, 39.
Biddle, Captain, 51.
Binney, Captain John, 217.
Birth of Tucker, and education, 19. 21.
Boothbay, 214, 217.
Bordeaux, 86. 88, 283.
Boston, 28; evacuated, 56.
Boston, frigate, 266; three war ships of this name, 358.
Boston Gazette, 48, 99, 106, 119, 152, 161. 172.
Boston Journal, 18.
Boston Weekly Messenger, 239.
Bream, schooner, 216, 221.
Bremen, 18, 196, 257.
Brest, 90, 98, 99, 307.
Bridge, James, Judge, 211.

Bristol, 185; history of, 192, 196, 202, 205, 212, 214, 221; scarcity, 224.

Britannia, Captain Baker, 91, 295.

Broughton, 43.

Brown, B., Dr., 84, 111, 168, **197, 227,** 240, 362.

Brown, John, 188, 202, 214.

Buckingham, J. T., New England Magazine, 198.

Bull, Dixy, 189.

Byles, Rev. Dr., 167.

C.

Camp **at** Cambridge, 41.

Campbell, Sir Archibald, 60, 234.

Captains, rank **in** navy, 54, 356.

Carey, **Matthew, 241.**

Caroline, **ship, 172.**

Cartel ship, **142.**

Castine, Baron de, 191.

C. D., Major, 169, 247, 368.

Census of troops, 41.

Chadwick, Paul, 206.

Chandler, John, 232, 364.

Charles II., 188.

Charleston, S. C., 126.

Christmas Cove, 186.

Chubb, Pasco, **Captain,** 191.

Church, Benjamin, **Captain,** 190.

Clark, **Thomas, 65.**

Cleaveland, Parker, **Professor,** 245.

Clinton, **Sir** Henry, 126.

Colonies, **condition** of, in 1775, **40.**

Commissions in Franklyn and Boston, 31, **67.**

Commodore, origin, &c., **53,** 115, **356.**

Confederacy, ship, 106, 107, 171.

Congress, 42, 49, 336, 374.

Connecticut vessels, 43.

Convention, Maine, 226.

Cook, Orchard, 227.

Cooper River, S. C., 126, **137.**

Cooper's Naval History, 15, **30,** 45, 65, 106, 372.

Cordouan, 86, 281.

Court martial, naval, 122.

Crew of Boston, 97, 342, 344, 355.

Crowninshield, B. W., 15, 230.

D.

Dale, Richard, 183.

Damariscotta, 185, 186, 189.

Davis, Daniel, 210.

Davis, John, 209.

Dawson, John, 183, 227.

Deane, **frigate,** 106; cruises **with** Boston, 111.

Decatur, 90.

Decnaso, Duc, 99.

D'Iberville, 191.

Dickens, **197.**

Distress in Charleston, S. C., **138.**

Diversions of officers forbid, 336.

Dolphin, frigate, 121.

Drowne, Shem, 188, **202, 205, 214.**

Duke of York, 202.

Dunbar, David, Colonel, 192.

E.

Earl of Glencairn, **ship, 106, 119.**
Eclipse of the sun, **91.**
Edgecomb, **214.**
Elba, ship of war, 222.
Elizabeth, brig, 153, 155, 296.
England and United States war, 216.
Enterprise, ship, 116.
Episcopal church, 245.
Everett, Josiah, description, 149.
Express to Tucker, **37.**

F.

Farley, Joseph, 217.
Father's death, **26.**
Felt's Annals of **Salem, 47,** 151.
Fifty Associates, **205.**
Flying-Fish **and** Tryall, 121.
Fort Charles, 189.
Fort Frederic, 192.
Fort Jackson, 127.
Fort Johnson, 137.
Fort Moultrie, 127, **137.**
Fort St. George, Maine, 188.
Fort William Henry, 191.
Forty-seven Frenchmen, **95.**
Franklin, Benjamin, **95.**
Franklyn, 31, 39.
Frazer, Captain, **59.**
French seamen's certificate, 342.
Frigate **Boston, 67, 121.**
Frontenac, 191.
Fuller, Judge, 211.

G.

Gage, General, **52.**
Gardner, John, **173.**

Garonne, 86, 88.
Gatchell, Mary, 25.
Gatchell Mills, 184,
George, ship, 234.
Gerry, Elbridge, 159, 212, 213, 226.
Glover, Captain, 56, 64, 156, 337.
Groa, 291.

H.

Halifax, 221.
Hallowell, 207,
Hamilton, Alexander, 179, 180.
Hammond, Sir Andrew, 163, 164.
Hancock (three of this name), 48, 61.
Harding, Seth, Captain, 106, 169, 171, 232.
Hidden, Joseph, Captain, 26.
Hill, Mark L., 230, 237, 239, 363.
Hind, ship, 161.
Hinds, Benjamin, **Captain, 199.**
Hinds, James, **Captain, death, 199.**
Hinds, Mrs. Mary, 254.
Hinds, Samuel, T., **17, 64, 165, 199;** his horsemanship, **family,** 198, 199.
Holmes, John, **233, 363.**
Homans, Benjamin, **229, 232.**
Hopkins, Esek, **Commander, 51,** 52.
Howell, **David, 215.**
Hubbard, John, Rev., 201.
Hunter, John, Rev., 168.
Hutchinson, Governer, 166.

380 INDEX.

I.

Incident in London, 28, 29.
Increase. schooner, **219.**
Independent Ledger, **101,** 116,
132, 155. **162.**
Instructions, 32, **93.**
Invoice of prizes, **360.**
Irving's Washington, **15.**
Isle de Dieu, 90, 291.

J.

Jackson, Andrew, 254.
James, Duke of York, 188.
James Island, S. C., 127.
Jamestown, 193.
Jefferson, 205.
Jennings, Richard, Captain, 218,
220, 221.
Jennison, William, 361.
John and Rebecca, 90, 294.
John's Island, S. C., 127.
John's River, **Maine, 186,** 194.
Jones, Paul, Captain, **16, 90, 99,**
258.
Jones, William, 186.
Johnson, Fort, destroyed, 137.
Johnson, John, Professor, 245.
Journals of Congress, 15.
Junius, 253.

K.

Kemble, Fanny, **197.**
Kennebec, 187, 202.
Keppel, Admiral, 99.
King Philip, 189.
King, William, Major-General,
222, 226, 366.
Knox, Henry, Gen., **176, 197, 364.**

L.

Latuche, 95, 300.
L'Croisie, 98.
Lee. Jeremiah, 27.
Lee, schooner, 28.
Lee, William R., **123, 157, 159,**
160. 166, 359, 360.
Lincoln, **Major-**General, 124,
130, 133.
Lind, Joseph, 151.
Lisbon, 25.
List of notes lent D. C., **368.**
Lithgow, Arthur, 211.
Livingston, 95, 289.
Log-book, 262–327.
London, 28.
L'Orient, 90, 95, 307.
Lossing. Benson, 143.
Lord Hyde. ship, 149, 152.
Lord Sandwich, ship, 119.
Louisburg, 22.

M.

Magee, Lieutenant, death, **69.**
Malcolm, James, 213, **214.**
Manly, John, Captain, **28, 35, 36,**
44. 63. 64, 68, 90, 115, **258.**
Marblehead, 19.
Marine committee, 16.
Marriage, 25.
Marshall's Washington. 15, 128,
138, **145.**
Martha, Captain of the. 82, 274.
Martindale and M'Cree, 63.
Masonic fraternity, 244.
M'Cobb, Denny, 253.
M'Curdy, Daniel, 184.

M'Farling, Captain, 100.
M'Intosh, Captain, 101.
M'Kown, John, 194.
M'Lean, Alexander, Rev., 186.
M'Niel, Hector, 68.
Mellen, Prentiss, 210.
Memorandum, 365.
Men taken or died, 341.
Mermaid, vessel, 116.
Merrick, John, 210, 245.
Mills, statistics, 137, 138.
Monhegan, 187.
Montgomery, Alexander, 232.
Morris, John, 143.
Morris, Robert, 30.
Morton, Perez, 214.
Mowatt, Lieutenant, 52.
Mugford, Captain, 45.
Murray, Captain, 91.
Murray, Rev. John, 167.
Muscongus Harbor, 185, 216, 220.
Muster-rolls of the Boston, 97, 342, 344–355.

N.

National flag, 47.
Nantes, 98, 292.
Nantucket Roads, 1778, 74.
Navy, 42; in 1776, 66.
Navy Board orders four ships to Charleston, S. C., 123, 356.
Newcastle, 214.
Newfoundland, Banks of, 327.
Newhall, Captain, 160.
New Harbor, 186, 188, 189, 216.
New York, 222.

Nicholson, Samuel, Captain, 106, 120, 183.
Nobleborough, 214.

O.

Orr, Benjamin, 215.
Osier, Captain, 217.

P.

Paine, John, 105.
Palermo, 205.
Palmer, Captain, 93, 94.
Parker, Judge, 207, 210.
Parole, form of, 140.
Parris, Albion K., 227, 228, 232.
Patricktown Plantation, 205.
Payson, David, General, 213.
Pedrick, John, Captain, 166.
Pemaquid, 185, 192.
Pennsylvania Packet, 15.
Penobscot, 202.
Pepperell, William, Colonel, 46.
Perkins, Elizabeth, 167, 168.
Petition to Navy Board, 122.
Phips, James, 190.
Phips, Sir William, 190.
Pierce, John, 188.
Pilot's certificate, 133.
Pinckney, Colonel, 128, 137.
Pine, Timothy, 157.
Plymouth Company, 188, 202, 205.
Pole, ship, 111, 117.
Popham, C. J., 187.
Popham, Captain, 187.
Portsmouth, 100
Preble, 90.

Prisoners' names, **274.**
Providence, ship, 99.

Q.

Quiberon Point, 304.

R.

Rainbow, frigate, 100.
Ramsay, Dr., 162.
Rank of officers, 115, 356.
Rathbone, Captain, 122.
Rattler, frigate, 216.
Reed, James, 107, 117.
Reed, Richard, 338.
Reed, William, 227.
Representatives, Maine, 226.
Representatives, Massachusetts, **224.**
Resolve **of Congress,** 16.
Ring, Martin, **187.**
Ritchie, J. H., 367.
Round Pond, 186.
Rutledge, 338.

S.

Sagadahock, 187, 188.
Sandwich, ship, 106.
Saves a ship of Morris, 30.
Schweighauser, **agent,** 95.
Sedgwick, C. J., **207.**
Selectmen **of Bristol and Bre-**men, 214,
Sewall, Henry, Major-General, 208.
Sewall, Samuel, Judge, **207.**
Shares **of prize money, 340.**

Shaw, Moses, 17.
Sheepscot River, 287.
Ships of war **in Revolution, &c.,** 372-374.
Shirley, Governor, 46.
Shurte, Abraham, 189.
Sibley, John L., 17.
Simms, William G., 137.
Simpson, Thomas, 99, 122, 307.
Skinner, Captain, 61.
Smith, Albert, 17, 249.
Smith, Jeremiah, 215.
Smith, John, Captain, 17, **18.**
Smith, Jonathan, Jr., 214.
Somerset, John, 188.
Song on taking the Crown, 369.
Sparks, Dr., 56.
Sprague, Peleg, Judge, eulogy, 17, 102.
St. Eustatia, 106.
St. John's or Prince Edward's Island, 191.
St. Louis, 95.
St. Ubes, 95.
Storm at sea, 75, 78, **266.**
Story, Judge, 210.
Stowe, Calvin E., Dr., **251.**
Style of Washington, 36.
Sullivan, Governor, 203.
Sullivan's Island, 127.

T.

Talbot, Silas, 183.
Tallman, Peleg, 227.
Tappan, Right, 202, 205, 214
Thacher, Judge, **207,** 213.
Thacher, Samuel, 213.

Thanks of Congress, 171, **233.**

The Friends, 316.

Thorn, ship, **106, 120, 147, 152;** her three prizes, **153, 161.**

Thornton, J. Wingate, 196.

Townsend Harbor, 217.

Triall, prize, 121.

Truxton, Thomas, 183.

Tucker, Andrew, 19.

Tucker, Mrs., 64.

Tucker's family Bible, 335, 336.

TUCKER, SAMUEL, birth, baptism, education, 19, 21, 335; on board Royal George, 22; second mate in vessel, 24; commission as Captain in Franklyn, 31; commission in Boston, 67; prizes off Long Island, Mass., 61; saves a boy's life, 100, 313; siege of Charleston, Chap. VII., 122; cruise in Providence, and Deane, 107; captures N. Y. cruiser, 110; captured by Frigate Hind, 161; returns from Edward's Island in open boat, 162; lends large sum to D. C., 169, and total loss, 368; life in Boston, 166; applies for one of the Federal cutters, 174; returns to Marblehead and becomes a miller, 173; removes to Bristol, 184; takes the armed cruiser **Crown, 216; representation, 236; death, 253; personal** appearance, **&c., 255;** obsequies, 257.

Tyng, Edward, **Captain, 46.**

U.

Ushant, **99, 309.**

V.

Varnum, J. B., 101.

Vaughan, Benjamin, LL. D., 211.

Venture, brig, 119.

Vernon, William, 73, 125, 159.

Vessels of war, size, 374, 375.

Vinton, John A., 196.

Voyage to France, 74, 262.

W.

Waldoboro', 197, 217.

Waldo Patent, 205.

Walker, Benjamin, 170, 234.

Walker, Freeman, 237.

Wappoo Cut, 127, 130.

Ward, Captain brig Sally, **100.**

Ward, General, 61, **65.**

Wardlow, William, **Captain, 147, 158.**

Warren, Commodore, in French War, 46.

Washington, **31, 35, 41,** 42; letter to Hancock, **44, 56, 182.**

Waters, Daniel, **15, 56.**

Webster, Daniel, **225.**

Weeks, Major, 207.

Weems, Captain, **190.**

Welch, **Hezekiah,** Lieutenant, **83, 275.**

Weston, Captain, **27,** 59, 158.

Weymouth, Captain, 187.

Whipple, Abraham, Commodore, 90, 98, 99, 122, 125, **329**, 130, 131, **132, 139,** 258, 206.

Whipple, William, **111.**

Whitwell, **Benjamin, 211.**

Wicks, Captain, **172.**

Wilde, Samuel S., **210, 211, 245.**

Wilson, John, **letter in reply, 243.**

Windsor, 205.

Wiscasset, 214, 217, 220, 22**1.**

Woodfall, 253.

Woodford, General, **128.**

Woolwich, 189.

Y.

Young, Captain, letter, 162.

Young Phœnix, **27.**

Yeates, **Captain, 222.**

www.ingramcontent.com/pod-product-compliance
Lightning Source LLC
Chambersburg PA
CBHW021537110726
47902CB00004B/915